DEC - - 2022

Praise for *Eight Perfect Hours*

"I read *Eight Perfect Hours* in one sitting, in four perfect hours, because I couldn't bear to put it down without knowing the ending."

—Jodi Picoult, #1 *New York Times* bestselling author

"Depending on your reading speed, *Eight Perfect Hours* also might describe the time you spend with this novel . . . a poignant rom-com about two strangers and the power of fate."

—*The Washington Post*, "Best feel-good books of 2021"

"Oh, what a joy this book is! Lia Louis is such a talent. It's a beautiful, intricately woven story, so romantic and so charming. I loved Noelle immediately, with her kindness and her patience and her rescued supermarket flowers."

—Beth O'Leary, internationally bestselling author of *The No-Show*

"Delightful. A gorgeous, romantic tale about fate and second chances."

—Sophie Cousens, *New York Times* bestselling author of *This Time Next Year*

"The sweetest, most romantic, most heartwarming book."

—Marian Keyes, internationally bestselling author of *Grown Ups*

"Eight perfect hours of escapist, romantic, life-affirming bliss."

—Gillian McAllister, internationally bestselling author of *How to Disappear*

"Louis (*Dear Emmie Blue*) fills this sweet romance with twists of fate and rich emotional considerations . . . Witty moments and a delightful supporting cast . . . Fans of clean contemporary romances will find plenty to enjoy."

—*Publishers Weekly*

A Best Winter Rom-Com Read.

—*USA Today*

Praise for *Dear Emmie Blue*

"A swoon-worthy British rom-com with big heart and a heroine worth rooting for."

—*The Washington Post*

"A sweet, poignant tale of love and friendship. I loved it."

—Beth O'Leary, internationally bestselling author of *The No-Show*

"This book is f**king perfect, buy it now."

—Julia Whelan, critically acclaimed author of *My Oxford Year*

"Lia is one of those rare writers who manage to break your heart and mend it all at once."

—Stacey Halls, author of *The Familiars*

"An absolute treasure of a book. A love story to cherish."

—Michelle Adams, author of *My Sister*

"*Dear Emmie Blue* is the new Eleanor Oliphant. Deftly crafted descriptions and characters who jump off the page and drag you into the story. I loved every moment of it."

—Bella Osborne, author of *The Promise of Summer*

"I will happily read every word Lia Louis ever writes, from novels to shopping lists, this is a very special book by a very special writer. *Dear Emmie Blue* is sweet, sparkling, and heartwarming, the perfect book to remind you dreams can come true."

—Lindsey Kelk, internationally bestselling author of
One in a Million

"Like *My Best Friend's Wedding* plus an unfairly gorgeous French-woman, mixtapes, and miles of inside jokes . . . *Dear Emmie Blue* will resonate long after readers turn the last page."

—*Booklist*

"There isn't anything we didn't love about this story! Every thread woven felt magical and beautiful, the way it played out was perfection! Perfection! The whole book from start to finish enthralled us and captivated us. One for the 2020 favorite list, that's for sure! Do not miss *Dear Emmie Blue!*"

—TotallyBooked

"Ebbing and flowing with the ups and downs of life, *Dear Emmie Blue* is a delightful read that fans of *Bridget Jones's Diary* and *Eleanor Oliphant Is Completely Fine* will enjoy."

—BookPage

Also by Lia Louis

Eight Perfect Hours

Dear Emmie Blue

The Key
to My
Heart

A Novel

Lia Louis

EMILY BESTLER BOOKS
—
ATRIA

New York   London   Toronto   Sydney   New Delhi

EMILY
BESTLER
BOOKS

ATRIA

An Imprint of Simon & Schuster, Inc.
1230 Avenue of the Americas
New York, NY 10020

This book is a work of fiction. Any references to historical events, real people, or real places are used fictitiously. Other names, characters, places, and events are products of the author's imagination, and any resemblance to actual events or places or persons, living or dead, is entirely coincidental.

Copyright © 2022 by Lia Louis

All rights reserved, including the right to reproduce this book or portions thereof in any form whatsoever. For information, address Atria Books Subsidiary Rights Department, 1230 Avenue of the Americas, New York, NY 10020.

First Emily Bestler Books/Atria Paperback edition December 2022

EMILY BESTLER BOOKS/ATRIA PAPERBACK and colophon are trademarks of Simon & Schuster, Inc.

For information about special discounts for bulk purchases, please contact Simon & Schuster Special Sales at 1-866-506-1949 or business@simonandschuster.com.

The Simon & Schuster Speakers Bureau can bring authors to your live event. For more information or to book an event, contact the Simon & Schuster Speakers Bureau at 1-866-248-3049 or visit our website at www.simonspeakers.com.

Interior design by Erika R. Genova

Manufactured in the United States of America

1   3   5   7   9   10   8   6   4   2

Library of Congress Cataloging-in-Publication Data has been applied for.

ISBN 978-1-6680-0126-4
ISBN 978-1-6680-0128-8 (ebook)

For you, Dad.
Because through it all, we've always had music.

The Key
to My
Heart

chapter one

I know exactly who Lucy's going to choose. I've known for the last half hour actually—could smell it a bloody mile away. Even before the third round of drinks had been brought wobblily back to the table, and even before Roxanne started waffling, as she always does around two cocktails and an appetizer in, about the different ways she'd assassinate her boss if it were only legal. Because my friends always choose me the same types. Dark haired, because all three of my exes were dark haired. Tall, because almost every crush I've ever had since the age of fourteen has been tall and with the height and shoulder combo that promises a decent house-fire rescue should you ever need it—Adam Driver, Vince Vaughn, that massive built-like-a-brick-shithouse bloke who dressed as Lurch at Roxanne's Halloween party in 2007. "Not facially," I remember slurring to his blank, prosthetic face, "but your frame, sir. *C'est parfait.* You're sturdy. You know. Like a ship. Like a . . . a *Megabus.*" And very much alive. That's the clincher actually. The man they choose must be alive, and with plans to be for many, many years to come (if possible).

"See that guy, Natalie," Lucy shouts over the music, setting a round, sticky tray down onto the table. Four cocktails on its surface wobble like drunks. "The one with the arms at the bar. Messy hair, white T-shirt . . ."

"Yep," I say, and I even throw a faux glance over my shoulder for effect. "Arms, hair, clothes, yep, I see him."

"Name's Tom. *Single*. And has been for eight months."

Beside me, Roxanne makes a noise in her throat—a "Well, there we are then I suppose," in a single "hm," and over a pile of guacamole, Priya adds, "Oh, I *would*. Well, I would if, you know, I hadn't just signed my life away to matrimonial monogs."

"And pregnancy," adds Roxanne.

"Oh shit, yeah, that too," says Priya as Lucy slides into the booth beside her and beams over at me. "You should go over there, Natalie," she says. "He was *so* chatty and lovely. Nice teeth too. I said I'd send you over!"

And it's always around this time of the night that I have to squash down the urge to do what I really want to when I find myself on nights out like these with my friends—sprint. *Bolt.* Stick a rocket up my arse, propel upward, burst through the ceiling. Or at least, grab Lucy by the lapels, drag her across the table, and say, "When are you going to stop this? When are you going to stop looking at me with the eyes of a slimy car salesman who's sure they're finally about to flog that van with half a bumper and a dead body in the trunk, and let me fester? I'm not interested in dating. I will *never* be interested." And the urge is even stronger tonight. I knew it would be, the second I woke up this morning thinking only about Russ. It was the sheet music from yesterday that did it—that singular, oddly glossy page of comforting symbols and notations, left anonymously, at the piano. For me. Or for someone else. Or of course, for absolutely nobody and for no reason at all. That's why I haven't mentioned it. It could be nothing—probably *is* nothing altogether. Plus, I'm sure if I did mention it, drop a casual "So, someone left me some music at the public piano I secretly play at, and I think it might be from my husband. Yes, that's right! Russ! The dead one," over cocktails and tortillas, Lucy would send up an instant smoke signal to alert my parents I was finally full-blown mad. Roxanne would probably start recommending that bereavement therapist again too—the one with the bongo drums.

"Did I tell you I had an orgasm?" asks Priya over the music. "In my sleep again." Thank God (and Priya) for the clapper-board cut of a subject change. "It must be the hormones. I was dreaming about the scaffolder."

"Again?" I laugh.

"Yup. The one next door. *Clive.* And I wouldn't mind but he isn't even hot. He has really spiteful features actually, poor soul. I mean, it can't be helped, can it? The features you're dealt. Anyway, in this dream, gosh, you should've seen him. He was *so—*"

"Natalie, are you going?" barges in Lucy.

"Am I . . . ?"

"*Going.* Are you going over there, to the bar?"

"To Tom," adds Roxanne.

"Oh. Right. Um . . ."

They stare at me, my friends. Six eyes, round and hopeful. And I throw them a smile. A bone to three hungry dogs. A big, bright, wholly convincing, "what a great idea" smile. "Well, I suppose I could just go over and order another drink . . ."

"*Yes,*" says Lucy.

"Say hi, suss him out . . ."

"*Totally.*"

And in one go, I stand and down my cocktail, my friends looking up at me proudly, like I just got called up onstage to accept a Brit Award. International Breakthrough Act. Best British Single.

"Bloody hell, he's looking over." Priya giggles as I slide out of the booth, stumble a little. The downed margarita is already tasering my brain cells.

"Oh my god, *look at him*. He actually is," cheeps Lucy, and I flash them yet another smile that drops off my face and hits the floor the second I turn my back to them.

I don't want to go over there. I really don't want to go over to that sticky, busy bar and talk to some tall bloke called bloody *Tom* who probably opens dating app comms at two a.m. with "hi babe, got any kinks lol." I can think of nothing worse. Well, I can actually. *Lots of things*. Some I'm on first-name terms with these days. But the thing is, the alternative is worse—*so* much worse. Because if I don't go over to this earmarked guy with the hair and the arms and the steady pulse, they'll give me that look again. That look they give me sometimes, my friends, like I'm a new gazebo that just keeps slowly and sadly sagging at a garden party and leaking rain all over the cheese scones. That "Oh, Natalie. What are we going to do with you?" look. The one that is wordless but so obviously "We all loved Russ, we really did, but it's been over two years. He's gone. And we're worried about you. We're all very worried." And that look—that look is something I hate far more than listening to single pervs waffle at me at the sticky, busy bars of tacky Mexican restaurants. And so, tonight, I choose the lesser of two evils. I choose Tom.

I make my way through too-close-together tables, through flustered waitstaff, and gaggles of diners, perfume-skinned and garlic-breathed, my head swirling a bit now. That'll be the three margaritas, definitely, without a doubt. But it's also too hot, and far too jubilant, if you ask me, for somewhere that charges fifteen quid for a bowl of guacamole served in the ceramic stomach cavity of a smiling cartoon avocado. Ugh. I shouldn't have come tonight. I should have canceled instead—made up some disgusting sounding stomach flu. (Or licked a few shoe soles and purposely contracted one.)

"Sorry." A waiter steps aside, makes way for me, and I nod a thank-you and pass him, and the huge platter that balances on his open palm. A single, mutilated, eaten chicken carcass sits on it. I feel you, knackered, little pecked-at carcass. I feel exactly the same.

"Why is it you bother going out with them if you dislike it so much?" my sister Jodie asked a few weeks ago, and I'd brushed it off, said, "Oh, don't listen to *me*, Jode, I do enjoy it sometimes." But the true answer to that question is the same as why I'm approaching this stranger at the bar. The alternative is worse. The alternative is those looks of pity I avoid like cracks in the pavement and crisps made of anything that isn't a potato. The alternative is sitting at home with the cat, drinking frozen cocktails to numb the repetitive doom of "I am alone" that churns over and over in my tummy. It's wasting entire evenings watching re-runs of TV shows I've already seen so I don't have to concentrate, and wondering whether the cat would miss me if I suddenly just vaporized from beneath his chubby, furry body.

A gap parts in the crowd at the bar, and I slide in, right next to Tom with the hair and the arms and T-shirt, and like an actor on cue, he looks at me and smiles.

"Hi," he says, stooping a little as the music volume increases. Lucy's right, although annoyingly, she mostly always is. He *is* good-looking, this poor targeted man chosen to heal my squashed, run-over crab apple of a heart. And the teeth—Colgate-ad levels of nice. Lucky him. "Natalie, right?"

"That's right."

"Cool." He extends a large hand, and I take it. Strong, smooth, not dirty, not sweaty like a bag of damp turnips. That's something at least. "I'm Tom."

"Tom."

He dips his head in a nod.

"So, er, your friend said you're here because your mate got married?"

"Yep," I say, as someone squeezes past, jamming my ribs into the side of the wooden bar. "Yep, that's—that's right. Priya. She got married a couple of months ago, then buggered off on the longest honeymoon on earth. It was a Christmas wedding. All the bells and whistles."

"Interesting." Tom gives a twitch of a smile. "Any snow?"

"Faux snow. Loads of it."

"Blimey." He blows out a breath between his lips. "I was expecting a no, but—faux snow. They meant business then, these friends."

"Yeah," I say. "They definitely did. Even made a honeymoon baby."

"Productive."

A woman behind the bar leans across the counter, tips her chin at me. Two giant acrylic pineapples for earrings swing like pendulums at the side of her head. "Margarita, please," I order loudly, and she nods, as another ridiculous out-of-place dance song strikes up to actual diners' *cheers*—weirdly out of place for a restaurant with a crayon station and a sunbathing spatchcocked chicken embellishment on the window. "I don't understand this place," I'd said to Lucy when we arrived, and she'd replied, "Well, why do restaurants even need to be understood, Natalie?"

I turn to Tom with the teeth. "So, who are you here with?"

"Couple of mates," he says, swirling the drink in his glass. His eyes are blue, and his dark lashes are curly in the way they only are for people who don't care for them. Teeth. Lashes. *Lucky him times two.* "One of them, Si, he's back from traveling. Got divorced and went all *Eat Pray Love* on us. Hadn't seen him in—maybe two years, until tonight?"

"Oh. That's nice."

"*Sort of,*" he says with a wince.

"Sort of?"

"Yeah, well, he's come back a bit Russell Brand. You know? Full of wisdom. Grown a beard. Rocked up wearing a carpet."

I laugh. Well, at least he's funny. The last time I found myself at a bar like this, the guy produced a piece of paper from his wallet that listed a treatment plan for his ingrowing toenail. "Ah, well, it happens to us all, I'm afraid, Tom. I lost my mate Lucy for a while—to wisdom and carpets."

"Oh yeah?"

"Yep. She went traveling for six months. Came back *obsessed* with essential oils and enemas. Kept meditating. Hollowed out an alarming amount of roasted sweet potatoes."

Tom laughs, and it's a laugh I know Priya would say made her vagina explode, if she were sitting here instead of me. It's deep, warm, a slight rasp. He smells nice too. Fresh, like showers, warm, lemony aftershave.

"Six ninety-nine." The bartender with the earrings places a drink down on the bar, on top of a tiny, black napkin. She holds out a card reader, unsmiling.

"Thanks."

"Ah, shit, let me—" Tom dives a hand into his back pocket, and I scan my debit card on the luminous screen before he can grab the bill.

"It's fine," I say, taking a huge mouthful, then another, and he looks at me like he's witnessing someone go to town on a whole Peking duck with their bare hands beside him. "I've got it."

"O-*kay*, but I was actually going to—"

"Look. Tom." I duck now, as if to level with this poor soul lumbered with me. "I'm sorry—and *thanks*. But I don't want you to buy me a drink. Honestly. It's very sweet. But no."

Tom the Target stares at me.

"But I'd really appreciate it if you could just—you know, carry on doing this? Talk to me for ten minutes, laugh a bit, and then I don't know, you can say you got bored or something—"

Tom laughs then, a surprised flick of a raised eyebrow, and pulls his phone out of his back pocket, holding it in front of me, like a sommelier presenting a bottle of wine. "My uh—my phone was ringing." He grimaces. "I wasn't . . . buying you a drink."

"Ah. Well. Right. I see." *Fuck.*

"But look, I'll happily talk to you for a bit." He ruffles a hand through his dark hair, shrugs. "Laugh a bit. I can be your . . . I don't know. What would you call it? Puppet? Pawn? Stand-in?"

"Sorry," I say, and I can't figure out whether it's shame or alcohol turning my cheeks to hot, sizzling lamb chops. "I'm sorry—for jumping in there like that. I'm just—"

"Ah." Tom waves me away and says, "Seriously, no worries, forget about it," and I don't finish my sentence. I drink instead. Mostly because I don't really know how to finish it. I'm just—*what*? What am I? Jaded at thirty-two? A mess? Not in the game anymore for meeting people? New people. *Old.* For falling in like, or in lust, let alone actual love, again? And sad enough to be preoccupied by a piece of mystery sheet music left at a train station piano, like those people who hunt aliens when they find a bit of flattened wheat in a field off the A12? I don't know. That's the thing. Since Russ died, I don't know anything. How I feel, who I am, what's fun anymore, what I *want*. My life is nothing but a tangle of unfinished sentences. *I* am a tangle of unfinished sentences.

"And would you mind?" I say instead. "Being my . . . shall we say, stand-in? Just for a minute."

Tom smirks, gives another shrug, and lifts the short whiskey glass to his lips. "Works for me." He swallows. "Plus, Si's pulled some weird, stare-y stranger, and Phan—he's on the phone to his wife outside. She doesn't trust him an iota."

"Should she?"

"Fuck, no. I don't." He swigs back another mouthful and grins at me. "So, I'm all yours. Come on. What's my first job? As Natalie's stand-in."

I laugh—and *thank God.* Thank God Tom the Target seems normal and laid-back and very much without that look in his eyes where he thinks I'm nothing but a tough nut to crack. I'm used to that look. That "ha-ha, she *says* she's not interested, but a few drinks, a few silly little compliments, and she'll soon change her mind and be putty, mate" look.

"Just stand there really," I answer, "and as I said, just laugh a bit, chat a bit . . ."

"Easy enough."

". . . nod here and there."

"All right. And you'll . . ."

"Oh, I'll pretend I'm having a nice time. As payment."

"Make that a *really* nice time," Tom adds. "You never know who's watching."

"Deal. And I'll give off the air that I'm really glad we met, if you like? That every hour feels like a minute because it's just so *easy to talk to you*—"

"*Obviously.*"

"So much chemistry—"

"Loads."

"And I'll pretend I really, really, *really* beyond-belief fan—" I freeze then, lips parted, like a haunted portrait. The fourth margarita has already done its thing—pushed me that teensy bit too far. My guard and my filter a little pile of rubble at our feet. I don't fancy him. Because I don't fancy *anyone* anymore, apparently, but saying "I'll have to pretend to fancy you" to a cool and kind stranger at a bar is not exactly something that would be endorsed by the Good Samaritan, is it?

Tom arches a dark eyebrow. "That you . . . ?"

"Nothing."

"Nothing," he says, amused, with a smile that's almost a burst of laughter, and this time, it's Tom who ducks. "If I'm going to be nothing but a puppet—sorry, a *stand-in*—I reckon it's only fair you finish that sentence."

I grimace behind my glass. "Ugh. Fine. I—I was going to say . . . *fancy you*," I admit, shamefully, then I rush out with barely a space between each word, "but what I mean is, I don't fancy anyone these days. Seriously, I don't. And you could be—you could be like, Adam Driver, or Vince Vaughn, or—" I stop myself when I find the words "that Lurch guy with the shoulders at Roxanne's party" gathering in my throat. "I just . . . it's just something I don't really do. Not anymore. That ship—sailed. Bombed. Shipwrecked at the bottom of the sea. Covered in . . . *moss*."

For a moment Tom looks at me, then a smile breaks out on his handsome face. "Well, that's—that's good." Then he leans in and says, "Because I don't really fancy you either."

"Good!"

"Bit mossy myself, actually . . ."

"*Perfect.*"

Tom laughs, throwing a glance over his shoulder. "OK, so—what's the first subject? Your friends are looking over, by the way."

"Of course they are," I say, and I feel a weird bloom of affection toward Tom the Target for being a good sport, for aiding and abetting me, for being on my side. "And I dunno. How about . . . ramble about your job? For say, ten minutes. That should do it."

"OK, that's easy. Photographer."

"Interesting."

"*Interesting*." Tom groans, pulls his mouth into a grimace. "Jesus, Natalie, go easy on me—"

"I mean it!" I laugh. "It *is* interesting. Seriously."

"Oh, shit, you were being sincere."

"*Yes.*"

Tom laughs, moves in closer, a warm, taut, shirted arm touching

mine, and I know the girls will be watching from afar, feeling victorious, nudging one other, hopeful that *this is it*, and the thought
makes me want to dive over the bar and drown myself in a keg, to be
found months later, like an oversize tequila worm. "Shall I start with
photography equipment? Or shall I go for tricky and cool celebrity
encounters or—"

"Oh, definitely cool celebs."

"I've got an Adam Driver story actually."

"*Do you*?"

Tom grins. "They chose wisely with me, your mates, eh?"

chapter two

"Three Sycamore, was it?"

"Please. Off Dark Lane."

The taxi driver nods from the dim, fuzzy darkness of the front seat, and the car rumbles away, the golden strip of lit-up pubs and bars blurring in the distance through the window like distant searchlights. Thank God it's over. Another night out—done. Big tick in the box. And this one was successful enough that it should keep them at bay for a few weeks at least. Six, maybe even into the two-month zone. *God.* How bloody depressing am I? I used to love these nights with my friends. I used to love how our lives were all so busy that our nights out used to feel more like a challenge as to how many words and pieces of news we could cram into a four-hour slot. I used to love listening. I used to love laughing. I used to love planning the next one at the end of the night, our phones under our noses, all of us with our calendar apps open, the jolt of joy when a date worked for us all. Now I just spend them planning my escape, like a margarita-fueled hostage.

♪   ♪   ♪
♪   ♪   ♪

They bought it of course. Lucy, Roxanne, and Priya had bought
the whole Tom thing, hook, line and sinker, and I think even *I*
might've bought it too, if I wasn't the one sitting at the bar. We'd
made quite the team in the end—Best British Single and Tom the
Target with the Teeth. We were the perfect duet. We'd talked nonstop, and for longer than the agreed few minutes, and he'd actually made me laugh. And *really laugh*—not one of those fake,
hoggy snorts I usually have to tiresomely force through my nostrils
whenever Lucy decides to put on her ridiculous matchmaker's hat.
Then his phone had lit up in his hand, his eyes flicking down to it,
and I'd felt a pang of relief. Finally, I could go home; leave Avocado
Clash and its chicken carcasses and overpriced guacamole behind.

"Ah. I've got to go and get drunken Si on a bus home," he said,
finishing his drink. "He left with that stare-y woman and now he's
somehow . . . chundering outside that Burger King on the corner? But
listen, I can come back. Or I'm happy to not, for you to blame me. Say
I . . . ducked out or something?"

"Went to the loo—" I added.

"Never came back."

"*Yes.* A perfect arsehole. Tom the Perfect Arsehole."

"That's me." He'd laughed, a glimpse of those lovely straight teeth.
"So, I'll see you then, Natalie?"

I nodded once, in a grateful bow.

"I'd better go and er . . . get to standing you up."

Then he'd hesitated, touched my arm, just a gentle brush of fingers, and disappeared into the bustling, garlicky fug of the restaurant.
I sat at the bar for a little while longer after, fraying the edges of a
damp napkin, swallowing down the tears that were globbing together,
desperate to break free, turn my face into a snotty, blotchy mess a little
too ahead of schedule. Of course, when I turned back to my friends,
they were already angled toward me. Three settled women out for

the night away from their busy, full lives, watching a tragic play, starring: me.

"Stood me up," I'd mouthed over to them with a theatrical shrug, then I'd finished my cocktail, feigned exhaustion, and excused myself to the rainy street to meet my Uber. And I'm glad I talked Priya into staying inside with the others, because I was crying before I'd even got out onto the pavement, and now they're streaming. Hot, plump tears. Buckets of them, running down my face, endlessly, like the rain from the broken guttering outside our bedroom at home. Tom the perfect arsehole, me the perfect cliché—drunk and crying on a Friday night in a trying-to-happen commuter town. And it was the margarita effect, sure, but of course, *not*, all at once. It was the bar, full of happy people. It was Priya, newly married, newly pregnant, Roxanne texting Ian about what time she'd be home, a tiny curl of a contented smile on her face. It was seeing Russ's favorite meal on the specials menu. It was knowing this empty taxi ride awaited. It was Tom. Lovely, kind, normal, handsome, funny Tom—and how I'd felt nothing. And it was the music—that single song I found at the piano yesterday, at the train station. A song I played countless times for Russ over the years. At the keyboard in my tiny student digs, as he sat propped up watching me from my bed, messy hair, sleepy grin. At home. At a hotel piano in Crete as we waited for our taxi to the airport. At the hospital, before he died.

And I know that it probably means nothing. But then, why was it there? *Was* it meant for me? In all the time I've been playing there, it's never happened before. . .

♪   ♪   ♪
♪   ♪   ♪

Traffic radio bumbles on and on in the taxi—delays on the M25, a road closure, a diversion—and the car seems to take too many corners as it leaves the bustling town behind us for the dark, leafy outskirts.

My head shudders against the damp, cold window, raindrops trailing the glass like rivers on a map. I've lost count of the number of taxi rides we took together, Russ and I, squashed together on the back seat, him brushing the hair from my face, the smell of our fabric softener, exactly the same—evidence of our shared lives. Russ's work shirts and my tops and our pajamas, going around and around together in the machine, a tangle. And I wish so much I could tangle myself up in him now. I wish I was going home to him. I wish I was a few miles away from stumbling through the front door to find him on the sofa, asleep, an anime on Netflix left playing to nobody, our cat Toast curled up on his chest.

"Is it too hot for you back there?" asks the taxi driver, his fingers poised over a glowing, fire-orange button on the dashboard.

"No. It's fine," I say thickly.

"Right-o." At that, a gust of warm air encircles my feet.

It was two and a half years, last month, that Russ died. Thirty whole months. Well, thirty-one now. And my friends never say the words, but I know they think it. *Why isn't she over it yet? Why does she not want to move on? It's been over two years. Two!* And I know how they feel, because I feel the frustration too. I read a post on a forum once that it was after two years that someone—and she was my age— suddenly noticed she wasn't waking and instantly thinking about her husband anymore. And seeing our matching ages as evidence it would happen for me too, I waited for the same. I waited the way some- one waits for a break, for a holiday, for a notice period to end at a shitty, toxic job. But the two-year milestone came and went, passed like a season, and the thoughts are still the same. Watered down a bit, but the same. Sometimes I even think they're worse, which I dare not say out loud for fear of Mum carting me off to some sort of insti- tution while squawking, "She can't move on! We've tried everything! She simply isn't *doing* it properly, Doctor." I think it's the worrying I'll forget that's worse. Russ's smell, the groove of the scar on his gorgeous hands, the deep, gentle voice, the shy chuckle and blush on his cheeks when I'd say something too loudly or kiss him in front of too many people. I test myself sometimes, and I'm always relieved when I can still recall everything—like getting all the answers right at some sort of dark, messed-up pub quiz.

The driver clears his throat. "Three Sycamore, yeah?" he says again, and when I answer, "Yes, please," I realize just how much I've been crying. I sound like Vin Diesel. But huskier somehow. Vin Diesel with a cold. Vin Diesel post–tonsil removal (with perhaps an unfortunate post-op infection thrown in for good measure).

The car turns into the familiar and true-to-its-name *dark* Dark Lane, and I watch the landscape pass in a blur through my window. Trees, trees, trees, thatched chocolate-box set-back cottage, field, field, trees, another picture-perfect chocolate-box cottage. I still find it hard to believe we ever managed it: buying a house here, in beautiful little Bournebridge, with its actual *ford* and farm, and ivy-blanketed houses with honesty boxes and gardens shown on BBC2. And it never matters how tired and deflated my heart feels, that fact never fails to make it beat that little bit prouder, even on the worst days. *We bought a house.* Russ and I bought a house. In an actual village, like real grown-ups. With a fireplace that needs actual wood. With a compost bin, and flower beds, and roads lined with more horse poo than cars.

"Just here," I say pointlessly, because Sycamore is a tiny little arc of three set-back cottages on a country lane, and he couldn't really pull in anywhere except in front of them, or the deep, dark bloody forest. But I say it anyway, because not to is to disobey an unwritten taxi law.

We pull up in front of the house—our little number three. A warm, yellow light beams through the diamonds of the ever so slightly wonky lead window. Relief. Dread. All at once.

I pay the driver, tip more than I usually would. Mostly for crying in his car, and for him not asking why, or if I'm OK.

"Thanks, love," he sighs. "You take care." And he drives off as soon as I shut the car door behind me, tires crackling on the wet tarmac until he disappears. In a blink, it's just me and the cold, pitch darkness. That's something you don't realize about the countryside—and I think we'd be allowed to call this little village away from the town and all its bustle, countryside—until you move into it. Just how bloody dark it is. So dark, your eyes play tricks, create figures, imagine movement where there isn't any. It's why I leave a light on at all times. That, and so if I ever feel weird about being in a car with a taxi driver who freaks me out a bit, I can tell them my husband is home, and the light already on makes my story all the more realistic. And sometimes I just like to hear the words come out of my mouth. *My husband's home.* Present tense.

I reach into my bag for my door keys, my shoes squeaking on the tiled garden path—the ancient terra-cotta-colored diamonds Russ had been quietly enamored with when we viewed the cottage four years ago, photographing them discreetly on his phone like a paparazzo with one mission: to get a single perfect shot of original period features.

"We can't just buy a whole cottage based on the garden path," I'd whispered as the estate agent showed us around.

"Yeah, but it's not just the *path*, is it, Nat? It's the beams, and the windows and—shit, look. Look at that little storybook old man out the window—the neighbor. He's planting something."

"He's *not*, is he?"

Russ had grinned. "That's what they do in the country, Nat. Live off the land. Like that bloke your sister fancies. Hugh Fearnley-Thingy-bob. They make chutney and soup and pies and stuff, from their own carrots. That could be us. We could get our own greenhouse. I know suppliers from work, we could get a proper awesome one—"

"Russ. I kill cactuses," I'd said, joining him at the window. "I buy soup, and then throw it away after a mouthful because I remember I hate soup and just wish I was a person who liked soup. I do not have it in me to grow a vegetable." Then as our estate agent left the room, Russ whispered with a smile, "I mean, to be fair, how do we know it's vegetables. How do we know he's not just buried a body? All that money, and we get Patrick Bateman for a neighbor . . ." And I knew then, from his smile, from the way he talked about greenhouses and chutney, the way he said *neighbor*, like it was already ours, that we'd do it. That we'd buy this wonky, ramshackle little cottage with the tiles and beams and damp and crumbling plaster, next to the cute old man in the jumper. (Roy, his name is. And it was leeks, we later found out. Not a single corpse. Although he's so embittered, I often think serving up a good, fresh corpse or two might cheer him up.)

The front door gives a sad, pained wail as it opens, as it always does when it rains and the wood swells in the frame, and it does it again when I close it, lock it behind me. I pee, don't bother removing my makeup, put on a pair of fleece pajamas that I've worn for too many nights in a row, and thanks to too many margaritas and too many tears, I fall asleep quickly, as I always do, since Russ died, on his side of the bed.

chapter three

Shauna arrives through the door behind Goode's shop counter like an actor from the wings for her turn onstage—shoulders back, hands on her round hips, lips parted ready to deliver the first line of the scene. But at the sight of Jason, her face scrunches up, like a walnut.

"What are you doing just standing there? Waiting for her to do a bloody dance? At least get her coffee on. Sorry, Natalie."

"Can't, Shauna," says Jason. "We're mid–guessing game."

"Oh, Christ, not this again."

"Yup." Jason shoves his hands into his barista's apron, squaring his shoulders like he's preparing for a scuffle in a pub. "Natalie has to guess which band I went to see this weekend, and *I* have to guess which song she played downstairs just now. The last one."

"What, and then she gets served?" asks Shauna.

I nod over at her. "Yep. And *he* gets a brownie. That's the deal."

"Give me strength." Shauna lifts her round eyes to the ceiling, but there's a small tug of a smile at the corner of her pink mouth, like a mother who wants to throttle her misbehaving children and ruffle their hair all at once. "Just so you know, he gets enough brownies,

Natalie," she says. "Eats all the wonky ones for me. The ones I can't sell to the customers. He doesn't need any more. Do you? Bloody shirker."

It's Tuesday, four days since dinner and margaritas at Avocado Clash, and as often is the case, Shauna and Jason are the first people I've spoken to face-to-face since. I first came here, to Goode's, a tiny little sliver of a coffee shop in St. Pancras train station, eighteen months ago, a few months after I lost Russ. Like today, it was a bitterly cold London day, the station one big fridge, and I'd fled a painful lunch meetup with Lucy and some old uni friends after about an hour. It was a vest that set me off, of all things. A bloody *sleeveless* jacket on a man at the next table, and the beat of hesitancy that followed as I'd considered whether it was worth getting one for Russ for his birthday. He liked wearing them for work—gardening. Grounds maintenance mostly, for huge houses with even huger gardens—because the man was a walking, talking kiln. Always hot, never in a coat, but in the depths of winter, he'd wear a padded vest until it fell apart. I don't remember much about that day, just that I made my excuses and cried on the tube next to a man dressed as Charlie Chaplin (complete with tiny drawn-on kohl mustache) who offered me a piece of kitchen towel from his pocket to blow my nose on. And it was when I was waiting for my train home, at St. Pancras, my heart in my shoes, that I saw the piano. I knew it was there. I'd passed it so many times when I worked in the city with my friend Edie, when we taught at a small music school, but that day, I saw it like it was the first time. Empty and still and comfortingly silent in the bustling chaos of the station and my own noisy, desperately wailing brain. I'd sat on the stool, edged it closer to the cold, shiny keys. I'd been scared to play, before that moment. Playing reminded me of hope and happiness and success. Playing reminded me of Russ, and the plans we had in a world in which he was *here*. And the idea of playing again always felt painful—like peeping behind a curtain to a world I could never, ever enter again, even if I desperately wanted to. But I'd pressed the first key, then the second—and I'd played. It didn't feel painful—not at all. It was anonymous. Nobody knew me at the station, nobody was taking notice of me. It meant nothing. It was just me, and the music, and a lightness I've only ever found in playing.

I played for twenty minutes that day. It felt like healing. It felt like home. It was after that I'd grabbed a coffee plus a slice of carrot cake from Goode's to eat on the train home. And like all habits, I could have never seen it coming. Playing piano at the station and grabbing coffee here, at Goode's, just sort of happened on its own, taking root Tuesday and Thursday mornings, two of my days off work.

"Ummmm . . ."

"Not being funny, Jason," I say, "but I feel like I'm getting whatever hangry is, but for caffeine. Caffiending? *Caffuriated*?"

"OK, OK, I'm going with—it's an Elton John song, right?" Jason bites his lip and points at me like a market stall trader striking a deal. Jason is the likable naughty boy we all knew in secondary school, but all grown-up at twenty-three years old. Always dodging his lectures at art college, always looking like he's just finished laughing at the best joke he ever heard.

"Mm, but which song?"

He groans, drags a hand through his long, tawny hair. "Ah, shit, I don't know, I now can't think of a single one. The one with the . . . piano?"

"*Wow*. An Elton song. With a piano. Narrows it down."

"I give up, Nat."

"Well, I don't," I say. "I know which band you went to see."

"Nah, you don't, but go on."

"Hyyts?"

Jason gawps at me and stretches his arms up and behind his head, like someone witnessing a football hitting the crossbar. "Holy shit. It *was*. How the hell did you know that?"

"You told me," I admit. "Last week. I remember because I looked them up afterward. Followed them on Spotify and thought OK, maybe he isn't totally devoid of taste."

Jason laughs and gives a heavy shrug. "Fine, Marple. You win. You get your coffee."

"Which I have to pay for, though, which is not really a prize at all, is it? Not even a shitty one."

Shauna chuckles as Jason hits a few buttons on the till.

"And we get a brownie," she says. "That's the deal. Eh, Natalie? And put this one through as a wonky one, Jason. This shop gets enough out of me to warrant the odd dodgy backhander."

I head for the little round table at the front of the shop, on the station's vast, shiny mezzanine floor. It's nothing really. A tiny round silver table with a leg that makes the surface rock. But it's my favorite. It's the one that's in perfect view of the trains leaving to travel up north—from London to Nottingham, in the time it takes to eat a whole overpriced buffet cart sandwich and make up half a story about the weird couple three seats over. It's also nowhere near the electronic billboard showing theater posters. Or at least, *Edie's* poster, of the musical she's in at the moment, which I'm happy to never see again. The only ad I can see right now is for denture glue, and that suits me just fine.

"Here we are. Gonna take my break, have a sandwich." Shauna places down the brownie in front of me, and a cup of tea the color of rosé in front of her, and with the zip of a fleece jacket and the scrape of a chair, she joins me. "The bloody temperature today . . ."

"Bitter."

"I'm surprised we can't see our breath out here."

"I know." I leave out the bit about how she definitely *would have* a few hours ago, when I first got here—and mega early—just to see if there was any more sheet music left for me. There wasn't. And I'd be lying if I said my disappointed heart didn't fall like a rock.

"Your fingers freeze over on that piano this morning?" she asks with a warm chuckle.

"Almost. But I planned ahead. Packed my trusty burglary gloves." I wriggle my hands at her, my fingers poking out the top of beige fingerless gloves, and Shauna smiles over at me.

"She has brains, this girl."

"Debatable, that."

Shauna is the manager of Goode's—one of eight chain coffee shops in London—and she is all the dinner ladies I was drawn to in primary school rolled into one sixty-four-year-old Irish woman. I loved her the moment we had our first conversation. Shauna is strong and doesn't suffer fools, but she's also the first person to scoop you up in a cuddle when you need it most, even when you don't think you do. She has that sort of wise intuition—the sort you take to be the truth, without question. She also loves swing dancing and Dwayne Johnson, but not as much as her sons. She has bloody loads (five, I think), and she talks about them all as if they're patron saints, but with added muscles and DIY skills. I never expected to like her as much as the coffee and its perfect, little table—that was a just a bonus, really.

"How's the house?" asks Shauna, sipping at her tea, then straightening it back on the saucer. "Any frisky foxes wake you up?"

The question makes me smile. Shauna probably knows more about me than most people these days. Even when she's busy, we always manage a little chat, out here.

"None today. They were probably off shagging the night away somewhere . . ."

"And your pipes?"

"Ugh, frozen again this morning. Got up, couldn't run the tap for the coffee machine and—well. Hair dryer came out again. And all be-fore six a.m., which was obviously fantastic. Old country cottages are nothing but problems . . .".

"Oh, gosh, Natalie, you're joking. *I told you.* Let me send one of my boys round. Five of them to choose from. *Five.*" Five. Knew it. One point to me.

"I mean it," she says, then she looks past me and smiles as one of Goode's newest regulars lopes inside—Notebook Man, as I call him (because, surprising nobody, he sits silently in the corner bent over a, wait for it, *notebook*.) I like seeing Goode's regulars turn up at the same time every week. It brings a sense of comfort somehow. Some-thing to depend on, maybe. Like soap operas airing on certain days, like roast dinners served at the same time every Sunday, the table set just so. And perhaps, because it's a reminder that it might not just be me, Natalie Fincher, living in a monotonous routine cycle while the world propels on having lots of hoo-ha-hooray fun.

"I'll get a plumber, Shauna," I say. "I keep meaning to, I just—"

"If you're wanting to sell up, you're going to want to save as much money as you can—"

"I still don't know about selling the house." And sometimes I think I do—sometimes I go to bed feeling like I've made the decision—that Three Sycamore was more Russ's dream than mine, and it was excit-ing only because we were going to renovate together. Live there to-gether, grow there together, start a family there together. Most of the time, it feels like living in a shell. A television set or something, years after the final episode aired.

"Well, regardless," says Shauna. "Plumbers from the internet will rip you off."

"And your boys won't." I smile.

"My boys are *angels.*"

Jason appears then, stocky and cocky, and sets down a toasted sandwich in front of Shauna. "Of course they are," he says, and he shoots me a schoolboy smile.

"I don't lie," says Shauna.

I sometimes wish Shauna was my mum, and I know *my* mum would be gutted if she knew I'd even had that thought. She'd grab her chest in that way she does when she's upset and wants to convey just how much. (Think: a below-average amateur dramatics group's portrayal of a heart attack.) And it's not that my mother isn't a good mother—of course she is. But she knows too much. She knows me too well. And that means I can't hide anything from her, how I'm coping, how I'm *not*, even if I tuck it deep, deep within. She sees it—eyes like an airport baggage scanner. Whereas Shauna—Shauna doesn't press like Mum. Nothing I ever say seems to shock her. If I was to announce I couldn't be arsed with life anymore and was off to be cryogenically frozen, she'd likely nod, say, "I understand, but shall we just sit and have a tea and a little chat first? Before we go and pack your holdall for the final deep freeze."

"So, how was the wedding?" I ask. A pigeon lands on the ground beside us, bobs along the tiles, pecks at what looks like a dried-up McDonald's chip.

"Oh well—" Shauna shrugs. "It was OK. We left not long after the dessert. Don isn't keen on these things, wanted to get back for the rugby, you know."

"Tell me you at least got to dance, though? To show off your new swing team *moves*?" Shauna has recently started swing dancing classes with a woman who works downstairs in the bookshop, and it's all she talked about after her first lesson. She glowed with it—with the stories of the bad dancers and tripping over and the man who turned up purely to pick up women who was thrown out by a woman dressed head to toe in polka dots who announced to the room she was tae kwon do trained. And mostly how the teacher called her a natural. "*Me.*" She'd beamed. "*Would you believe it?*"

"Don wasn't so keen," says Shauna now. She runs a finger under the tight, blush-pink leather strap of her watch, her eyes fixed on it. "But ah, well, I don't mind. I can dance when I like, right? I have my classes twice a week—"

"But why didn't Don want you to dance?"

Shauna shrugs again, the lilac fleece of her jacket gathering at the shoulders. "My husband's not really a dancer. Not really into all that himself and—well, I'd have felt like a right idiot going it alone so . . . *anyway.*" She clears her throat, clasps her hands together, and although I always want to press when it comes to Don, Shauna's husband, I know this is Shauna Madden for "That's enough of that, then." "So the dinner," she deflects. "With the girls. Was it just like you dreaded? I bet it wasn't, these things never are . . ."

"Erm."

"Oh, *no.* A nightmare, was it?"

"No, no, it was OK, but they—"

"They tried to set you up again."

I groan into my mug. "Lucy did. And he was lovely, actually—really hot, super tall too. Smelled really nice."

"Well, that's something."

"I know. But . . . it might as well have been Mr. Bean. A waxwork. A man sculpted out of old cake. I'm just not ready."

"To meet someone you mean?"

"Or to be—to be what everyone thinks I should be by now? Or something. God, I don't even know . . ."

Shauna nods gently, the twisted gold hoops piercing her ears swaying. Two women stroll past us, the wheels of their matching, hot-pink suitcases squeaking behind them, as if excited for the imminent train ride.

"It's fine that you're not ready, Natalie," says Shauna. "And listen, you don't have to be anything. You know? You can just be *this* person for a while. This Natalie, in front of me, here. What's wrong with that?"

I grimace.

"Well, *I* like her," she says, taking a glug of tea.

"But this Natalie is no fun," I reply. "This Natalie's grumpy and doesn't like having dinner with her friends and doesn't fancy tall and handsome strangers who have amazing teeth. I can't even *imagine* what it'd be like to feel like that. And that's who they want."

"They being your friends?"

"They being pretty much everyone I know. My friends don't say it, of course they don't. But I think they all want me to be who I used to be. Single Natalie Fincher from university. Single Natalie Fincher who had one-night stands and chatted guys up at house parties and snogged them in the understairs toilet." Lurch had been a good kisser to be fair. Tender, passionate.

"But . . . you're bereaved, my love. Surely they must understand that."

And I swallow at that. *Bereaved*. Me. It still seems completely incomprehensible that I would be bereaved. A widow. A widow at thirty-two. Widows wear black and wail at gravesides. Widows crochet the days away and wait for their grown-up daughters to call. Widows fall out of lofts getting their Christmas lights down because their grown-up sons are too busy in business meetings to pop in. I'd said that to Lucy once, who dropped her voice low, as if we were surrounded, and said, "That is *so* stereotypical, Natalie. And not to mention bleak. Besides, crochet is very trendy now. I follow someone on Insta who crocheted themselves a sofa."

Shauna gulps down her tea again, as if it isn't steaming like a jacuzzi bath. "The thing is," she says, "regardless of what they might want, Natalie, nobody can turn back the clock, be who they used to be. And believe me, I'd love to. I miss my *waist*. I miss having so much energy I'd skip a night's sleep. Karaoke. Watching the wrestling at our old civic hall. Going to work on an empty tank but getting through it with a coffee and a cigarette. Gosh." She smiles as if she can see it in moving pictures on a private screen. "But you just—you can't. Things change, and so people change. We have to just keep waking up and moving forward. Right?"

I nod. "Right," I say. I don't add that I don't feel like I've moved forward a single pace in two and a half years. Longer, if you count the months Russ was in hospital after his accident. Life stopped then, for me. And that I have no desire really, to take another step. Stagnant. That's what I am, I guess. The opposite of what I used to be, not so long ago.

"Like this sandwich, for example." She lifts a slice of the bread in front of her as if it's a snotty tissue. "If I could turn back the clock, I'd tell Jason to take his bloody eyes off the girl with all those piercings and listen to me when I say cheese *and* tomato. I swear to God. Brains are in his knackers."

Shauna slides out her chair, pats my shoulder with a chubby hand. "Better go back in, sort my sandwich, get back to work." And she disappears back into the coffee shop, the toastie in her hand.

I stay for an hour and grab some milk, wine, and cereal from the little M&S, and it's when an icy blast of wind ruffles my hair that I realize I'm not wearing my bobble hat. I definitely arrived with it. And I definitely had it at the piano. I left it in the lid of the beaten-up stool—where I hope it still is. See, this is what happens when you start the day thawing out pipes in your dressing gown and odd socks and catapult yourself out of the house far too early, far too tired, in the far-too cold. By midmorning, your brain turns to a giant useless joint of ham.

"*Fuck,*" I say to nobody but my bag of Coco Pops and bottle of red, and I whisk down the escalator. Panic rises in my chest. Actual panic. I've been late for flights. I've played to crowds of five hundred people. I posed topless with nothing but antlers covering my crotch for a charity project Roxanne ran in uni fighting for Greenpeace. Didn't break a droplet of sweat. But a *hat*. A hat is what makes me panic these days. A hat that had cost fifteen euros ninety-nine as part of a set. A hat that makes my hair stand on end like I have my hands on some sort of device in the Science Museum. But Russ chose them. He picked them off the rack, he'd wrapped the scarf around my neck, pulled me toward him holding each end, and kissed my forehead. We were in Barcelona, a year before his accident, and it had *snowed*. The Beast from the East, as the media had called it, and I had a suitcase full of nothing but jeans and T-shirts and after-sun lotion. He'd walked for blocks as I waited in a café, found a shop that sold hats and scarfs and climbing gear, and as sleet fell and fell outside, and I'd sulked, he'd returned, a purple set for me, and charcoal gray for himself. I can still remember him appearing at the glass door of the café, laughing at me shivering through the window, the edges steamed up, holding the scarf high like a trophy. And I can't lose it. He traipsed across snow to get it for me. He chose it for me.

The piano is empty when I get there, nobody playing, no tourists holding fingers down on bum notes trying to remember the tunes they learned in school, nobody posing for photos. And I'm relieved to find that my hat is right there, in the shabby donated stool that most people don't realize opens. But—there's a piece of music there too, resting on top of it. *Another* one. A piece of glossy paper, the same squeaky shininess as the last, with sheet music printed on either side—a piece of music that wasn't here when I started playing this morning.

I pull it out, flip it over to the headed title page, heart drumming in my ears.

And then it stills. The music in my hands—it's Russ's favorite song.

chapter four

"Will you just hold her hands, Natalie?"

"Huh?"

"It's just, I'm trying to tie this thing on the jumper, and every time I do, her head falls off, and you're just sort of . . . standing there."

The mannequin between Priya and me wobbles, its dead eyes fixed on me, judging.

"Sorry, Priya. Sorry, I'm just—"

"You're daydreaming, I know," she says. "Physically *at* work, but not actually mentally *here*. And meanwhile I'm—I'm—" Priya grits her teeth, ties a ribbon at the back of the mannequin's hard, shiny neck, and its big, plasticky head shudders. "Seconds from tying this ribbon around my own neck. I know she's your sister and I know she says they're in demand, but fuck—*ribbons*. When will it end? When?"

It's Friday today, and because it's the last one of the month, it's also what my sister Jodie has termed Freshen Up Friday. (She was proud of that. Announced it like she'd discovered penicillin on an old moldy coat out the back.) Freshen Up Friday is the day of the month we re-dress the mannequins with something new. And my sister Jodie is all about ribbons at the moment, so her little clothes shop in Camden

Town is packed with them. Everything for sale has a ribbon on it. Jumpers with bare backs and crisscross ribbons, bags with ribbons as tassels, ribbons as shoelaces like we're selling footwear to Noddy and nobody else. And Priya and I, as mere employees, have no choice but to love ribbons. Worship ribbons. *Become* ribbons. And I daren't question Jodie's fashion know-how of course. Last time I did, she froze, like I'd casually informed her that I'd just discovered her new mannequins were a collection of freshly embalmed corpses.

"But I've researched," she'd said, her eyes wide. "Florals are very *specifically* in, Natalie. So are the seventies. Flares, blouses—*beards*."

She'd brought a copy of *Vogue* in with her the next day. "See," she'd said, slapping a magazine down in front of me on the counter. "*Florals.* Stick that up your arse."

Tina is Mum and Dad's shop—they have three of them. Clothing boutiques they started in the eighties. They retired, moved out of London to the Dorset countryside three years ago, and my big sister, Jodie, quit secondary school teaching and took on the Camden shop when they moved. I work here four days a week and have done since Russ died, and my best friend, Priya, works five days. And Jodie—well, Jodie just works, with no start, and no end, just one endless cycle. She lives and breathes Tina. Talks about it in her sleep too, according to her husband. I'm not sure she'd ever admit it, but it's as if she's still waiting for the day Mum tells her she doesn't know enough about fashion to run it, and she just can't let that happen. Three years in, though, I can't imagine her doing anything else but this. (I'd never tell her I bet Russ a packet of Twix that Jodie would last six months before quitting in a season-finale level of dramatic showdown with Mum, though.)

Priya nudges my arm now. When I look up, she's grinning at me like she's posing for a photo I'm about to take.

"What?"

"I know that dreamy face like the back of my hand," she says. "This is about Tom, isn't it? Oh my god, it *is*."

"*What*?"

"You're mad daydreaming today. Seriously, Nat, you've been staring like you've been—taxidermized or something. Did you get his number and just not tell me? Have you been *texting*? I swear, I won't tell Lucy. I wish I hadn't told her about the scaffolder, to be honest. She keeps checking in with me, which is sweet and everything, but it's like she thinks she might on the off chance catch me on my knees in the footwell of his van."

I laugh. God, I love Priya. She is one of the only people in the world who can make me laugh without even trying. On the day we met, almost eleven years ago now, she marched right up to me and said, "Settle this debate. Would it be weird for me to write to Jennifer Aniston to tell her I think she handled her divorce with such bravery? Because she did, didn't she? Bless her."

"I mean, I appreciate the discretion," I say, "but . . . who're we talking about? Did I get whose number?"

"Oh, come on." Priya steps aside and puts a hand on her hip. The mannequin judders beside her. "Fit bloke from the bar."

"Oh. *Oh*. Tom." I smile now thinking of Tom, how we both proclaimed to be repulsed by each other, how he happily nominated himself to be the arsehole who stood me up. If every man could be like Tom, I'd never have to grin and bear being set up ever again. "But no. Definitely not thinking of him, Pree. Soz."

"Oh." Priya's grin fades, her large eyes widening, brown and puppy dog. "No?"

"Nope."

She groans, pulls another ribbon at the back of the mannequin's neck with too much gusto, and its stare-y head rattles again. "Seriously."

"What?"

"He was gorgeous. He must've crossed your mind at least once since then. He even had a proper shirt on. And his shoes were shiny. Like he'd polished them himself. Really made the effort, you know?"

"Did he *really*?"

Priya, as usual, misses the sarcasm, like a shuttlecock straight over the head, and nods, wide-eyed.

"Well, in that case," I say, "we'd better track him down. Alert the authorities. Put an ad in the paper. Is Budgens still doing those local ads in the window?"

Priya groans now, huffs through her nostrils.

"Have you seen this man?" I carry on. *"Tom. Whiskey sour drinker. Photographer. Mostly portraits. Nice shirt. Rare ability to polish own shoes."*

"Piss off." Priya laughs.

"Would very much like to date him, marry him, be with him until his perfect teeth rot and decay and fall out of his head. Please write!"

"You're so weird," she sighs, going back to the ribbon.

"My sister? Weird? She's always weird," says Jodie, appearing from the stockroom, an iPad in her hand leaning against her midriff like a clipboard. Hanging from the collar of her jumper is a ribbon bow. "So, what, she's being weirder?"

"Yep," nods Priya, observing me like I'm a washing machine that won't work. "Super weird."

"How am I being weird?"

"Natalie, I could've dressed this mannequin in a hot dog suit today, and you wouldn't have even noticed."

A woman browsing a sale rail of jumpers giggles over at us, and Jodie smiles at her. "I can order anything in that you like the sound of," she jokes in a low, mock-secret voice. "You name it I can get it. Hot dogs. Cheeseburgers. Maybe even a giant prawn."

My sister is such an adult really. One of those people who are completely at ease with who they are—well, unless we're talking high-street fashion. She isn't quite at ease with that yet, but like everything, she's studying it, like it's quantum physics, like sourdough starters. But Jodie—she's a proper grown-up. An adult with a shop and a mortgage and a professor husband and a salad bowl with matching claws. Russ and I felt like we were on our way to that when we moved into Three Sycamore. We *tried* things like that—the salad bowl, making marinades, you know, all the things that adults do, and most of the time it all went wrong. We were chaotic. Eating takeaway at half-past nine at night while Jodie and Carl probably slept soundly, all hand cream and thick novels and fridges full of marinating meat downstairs. We liked to think, back then, that we'd eventually get there. To organized, domestic, adult bliss. But deep down, we knew, cottage or no cottage, salad claws or no salad claws, we just weren't that type of couple. And that was perfect actually. It was us.

"She's been daydreaming," says Priya, as the customer heads out of the warm, vanilla-y scent of the shop to the busy street outside. "Head in the clouds like you would not *believe.*"

"Oh, about hot Tom?" says Jodie, tapping away on the iPad. Her nails are a fresh but short French manicure.

"Wow." I move on to a headless mannequin that's wearing a wrap skirt with flimsy—and quite frankly pathetic—looking ribbon ties. "How do you know about hot Tom?"

"Ah, so you admit he was hot, then."

"Priya, no. Not for me, thank you. And no, I am not *daydreaming* about hot Tom." I'm daydreaming about some more music that was left for me in a piano stool in a busy train station actually, I want to say; about who it could be, about whether it could be—Russ, somehow. Yes! My husband who isn't here anymore, but hear me out, I'm not mad! I swear! But I don't. Instead, I say, "I'm daydreaming about the huge halloumi baguette thing I'm going to order from next door in about fifteen minutes." Which, to be fair, is also true.

Priya laughs and gives an eye roll. "Well, I thought he seemed perfect . . ."

"You would," I say. "A bit of shoe polish, a hoist onto some scaffolding, and you're a goner."

Twenty minutes later, Jodie and I sit in zipped-up jackets and hats, in a slice of spring sunshine out the back of the shop. It's not glamorous at all out here—a dingy, gray island of concrete and bins and delivery entrances—but it's nice to get some air, and we sit at the little metal garden table eating baguettes and bags of crisps we've opened right up to silver squares, like we used to when we were teenagers drinking in our local pub together. It was a shithole little place, but we loved the hot peanuts. (And Jodie fancied one of the barmen. He was blond, called Marc, and wore surfer shorts all year around, which she thought was cool, whereas I worried about his risk of trench foot.) We must've spent a hundred Friday evenings there. Jodie would always stick to her limit—one white wine followed by a spritzer, and I'd get so drunk that I'd end up interpreting strangers' dreams and talking about how I'd always felt spiritually connected to Christian Slater but worried the fickle beast of show business would keep us apart. (Something Jodie counseled me on in our childhood, more than she counseled me on my fear of premature death and chip-pan fires.)

"OK, so—something happened," I say, throwing the words out there, like a lit firework.

Jodie stops chewing, mouth full. "At the bar?"

"No. *No.*" I laugh. *Yes, Jodie, I got off with Tom against the spatchcock chicken embellishment. It was wild.* "No. Something happened at the train station. At St. Pancras."

"Are you still playing there?"

I nod. "Sometimes," I say, and shame prickles up my back. Jodie's the only one who knows about my playing at the station, and although she's only ever supportive, I always find myself playing it down. Maybe I'm worried if I admit it to anyone else, they'll visit—Mum and Dad. Or one of my friends—and watch me. And think a) she's getting better, she's going to go back to work, she'll start playing properly again, at the school she taught at, and oh, maybe she and Edie will make up, start making music again together, oh, how lovely! Or b) poor Natalie. She had everything laid out for her. So much success, so much potential. And now here she is, playing on some germy public piano in front of strangers who ignore her like the scabby pigeons that scavenge for squashed cigarette butts and moldy bits of sausage roll.

"So, anyway," I carry on, as Jodie eats, her eyes hooded and serious, a bright yellow *SMILE, YOU'RE ON CAMERA* CCTV warning on the brickwork behind her head. "The piano stool there—it's a battered old thing, with a lid. Someone donated it, apparently. And I keep things in it, while I play. My hat, scarf. Sometimes my phone. Sometimes a packet of Wotsits."

Jodie smiles, but her eyes narrow, just ever so slightly, as if she's striding ahead, trying to preempt what sort of confession this is.

"And a couple of Thursdays ago, a song was left in it. It wasn't mine, and it was one of the first songs I learned to play—"

" 'Fast Car'?"

"Yes! And I didn't think too much of it, but on Tuesday I went back there, grabbed some coffee, and when I went back for my hat—there was some more music in there."

"So, what, like—sheet music? On paper?"

"Yeah. And this time it was Russ's favorite song."

Jodie stops chewing again, and this time her eyes stay open, wide saucers. "*Really?*"

I nod. "Really."

Neither of us says anything for a moment. A Take That song floats softly outside from the shop its pitch higher, the way it often is on the radio. I hear Priya laugh with a customer inside. "I don't know what it means, Jode. Or what I even feel about it to be honest. Freaked me out a little bit. But—also, I can't stop thinking about it. I know it's stupid, but I can't wait to go back, to check . . ."

Jodie's quiet as she considers what I've said, running the words over in her head, as she always does, calmly, rationally, before react-ing—the mental equivalent of spreading it all out in front of her, on the table, so she can see it all and consider it, clearly. "What do you think it is?"

I lift a shoulder to my ear. "I don't know. I mean—well, it's just weird, isn't it? And I don't think I believe in the afterlife, or spirits or *signs*, but . . . I don't know what to think."

"Right." Jodie nods, and that's what I love about her. She's just so solid, so together. I could stand in front of her and say, "I've murdered someone. It was an accident but it's sort of ruined my life, do help," and she'd take a breath and go, "Right. OK. Well. That's understand-able. Give me an evening and I'll get a plan in place." And although her emotions would probably be waging a war inside her—a tornado of them, a hurricane—on the outside, she would be still. Like some sort of tremor-resistant building in San Francisco. But you know. Prettier. Less stiff. (Most of the time.)

"I mean—it is weird, Nat. And you know me, I'm not one for signs from above either, like—" Jodie drops her hands to her lap, her mouth twitching into a half-smile. "Do you remember when Nan died and Mum kept freaking every time she saw a white feather and wouldn't hear it that there was a whole bloody *colony* of them in her duvet."

I laugh. "Oh my god, I do! And exactly. But that song, it's—I don't know, it's not even well known. Not at all. It was by that band who had like two hits in 2003 that we both loved. Rooster. And—I found the sheet music for it when Russ was in hospital. Had to google for ages. And I learned it properly, in the hospital. I'd always just sort of winged it before and—" I stop, and a sigh heaves its way out of me. "I don't know . . ."

"Are you sure it's not yours?" asks Jodie gently, and I sink then a little, as if the ground beneath me is turning to sand. "Sorry," she says quickly, "I don't mean to make you feel like you're going mad or something."

"No, no, I know. I mean I did print it. But back in the hospital, years ago. Whatever he wanted to hear that I didn't already know off by heart. But I haven't printed anything. Not recently. And none of that music left the hospital. It stayed there."

Jodie stares at me, and I know what she's thinking. That first year after Russ died, I hardly knew what day it was, and then I starved myself, and then I drank too much—still do really—and I didn't even remember people's birthdays. I even forgot my *own* the first year. Maybe I did print it. Could I have printed that piece of music when I started playing at the station and forgotten? It wouldn't be the first time I completely forgot something entirely, like someone came along and surgically removed it, without even a crumb left behind. It happened all the time after Russ died.

"God. It is weird, isn't it? I'm trying to think of some logic, but—"

"I know, Jode," I sigh, balling up the paper bag my sandwich came in. "And all I know is that I can't stop thinking about it, and I feel . . . *excited*. And then I feel ridiculous for feeling excited. Embarrassed. Because what am I even saying?"

Someone two shops down—a Bookmaker's—opens their heavy back door and wanders out into the sunshine, a phone between his shoulder and ear, lighting a small roll-up cigarette between his lips. His faded black T-shirt reads *One tequila, two tequila, three tequila, floor*. He pulls on a jacket, half-arsedly, leaving the front unzipped and flapping open.

"Look—it could be a sign, right?" says Jodie, leaning forward. "What do we know? We don't know do we, what's on the other side, what's out there? We think we know the rules of the universe, but we haven't got a bloody clue."

"But also, it could be nothing," I say, placing the balled paper bag down on the table. It instantly starts to expand like a sponge. "A spooky sort of coincidence."

Jodie nods. "One of those things."

"Yeah. Yeah, you're right," I agree, and with perfect aim, I pick up and throw the paper bag, and it lands, like a ball through a hoop, in the bin.

chapter five

Today I'm later to the station than I think I've ever been in two years. It's close to lunchtime when I arrive. And I had all good intentions last night to be up and out the door on time. I set my alarm, I went to bed early, and I even packed my handbag and put it by the front door, which is a *supremely* Jodie move if ever there was one. I'd wanted so much an early start. Because today is Russ's birthday, and I wanted to be with him longer than I usually am, in the quiet, green grounds of the crematorium. I like to go once a week. It's just a few train stops away, on the bleakest, grayest, busiest road, but the place itself, a pop-up page burst of nature among it all.

But my organized morning went to absolute shit, thanks to nothing more than the antics of Three Sycamore. The frozen external water pipe treated me to its usual winter morning trick, and I'd overslept due to being kept awake until three a.m. by the foxes—"the Sycamore foxes" as Roy next door calls them darkly, like they're a family of criminals terrorizing the town, who, somehow, are always suspiciously able to slip under the police's radar. That's another thing about the countryside, and something I didn't consider once before we moved in: the gaggle of noisy creatures that come out the second the sun sets to collectively conspire to completely mess up your night. "It's country life, Nat. We don't live in a Goosebumps movie," Russ would say as I jumped awake beside him, but I'm sure there's a horror movie pitch in it somewhere: widowed, clueless city-girl stuck in a ramshackle cottage wakes to find foxes shagging outside her window, and her water pipes frozen. *A thrilling caper, says Rotten Tomatoes.*

Eventually, I'd arrived at the crematorium in a tornado of fluster and sweat and rain-soaked hair. But relieved to be there, with him. And I don't think people understand me when I say I *like* to go there, to the crematorium. I get the bewilderment. The only places I used to love to go were gigs in sticky, windowless venues, to the studio with Edie, and to IKEA for candles and seventy-five storage baskets I'd never get around to actually using to completely organize my life. But I do. I enjoy watching the tree we planted for him slowly grow. I enjoy the no expectations. I enjoy being alone, with him, in the quiet, and talking to him like he's still here.

I updated him, as always, on the damp wooden bench from beneath my umbrella, and on everything. From Shauna not dancing with dastardly sounding Don at the wedding ("I really think he might be a shit-bag, Russ."), to the dinner with the girls ("Lucy spoke for seventeen minutes about sinks. Yes, she's still renovating."), and the latest episode of *Line of Duty*. (We used to watch it together on Sundays in bed with peanut M&Ms and slices of toast.) And I also asked him about the music, and I laughed, embarrassed as I did, to nothing but the wet grass and his blossom tree. I also wished him a happy birthday. Thirty-three. That's how old he would've been today. So bloody young, yet the sort of age that is so well established. The sort of age that screams "smack bang in the middle of living my life."

I head straight for Goode's now, and I look like someone who's just been fired out of a cannon. My hair is frizzy with rainwater, and my clothes are damp and stuck to my skin, and my face, I know without looking, is a hangdog special. Eye bags. Mouth, gasping for caffeine. Like someone exhumed from an ancient tomb and shoved into a pair of skinny jeans.

I pass the piano again, on my way to the escalator. There was no music this morning. I looked the second I got into the station. Practically screeched over to it, like a cartoon, clouds of white smoke from the friction at my feet. But it was empty. And if the rain hadn't succeeded, the disappointment of an empty piano stool blew out the meager flame of happiness in my chest with one puff. Ugh. *I know.* I know I shouldn't keep looking for music, *hoping* for it. But I can't help myself. It feels too magical finding it. Too exciting.

The station smells like coffee beans and the earthy smell of rain. God, I want caffeine. *Need it.* I also want enough sugar to take the enamel off a urinal. I want cake for now, cake for later. Medicinal pastries, to fill the huge Russ-shaped hole in my chest and to stop me buying (and consuming) wine. I'm drinking a bit too much at the moment, I know I am, if not only because of the state of the recycling bin—it looks like it used to when we'd have a Saturday barbecue and invite our families and friends (and friends of those friends) and Roy would knock and say, "The bin men won't take those if the lid doesn't shut, you know," which, like most things Roy says, was code for "I wish you didn't live next door."

The escalator carries me upstairs, toward the smell of hot pastries and the damp fug of hundreds of pairs of rain-wet shoes on shiny floor. On the step in front of me, a woman applies a deep-red lipstick using her iPhone camera as a mirror, and I can just about see over the balcony and through the café's open door. Jason is behind the counter, and sitting inside, as usual, is Piercings Girl and Notebook Guy. And today, Mr. Affair and Secretary Girl sit outside. Mr. Affair is a stiff, shiny-faced man who wears slick blue suits and sits hushedly negotiating with his secretary (Secretary Girl, of course), a beautiful woman who wears incredible shoes at least once a week, before they kiss passionately, he leaves, and she cries in the loo. Shauna hates Mr. Affair with snarling passion. (Sure, we don't know that they're *definitely* having an affair, but it seems that way, and Shauna talks about him as if it's fact and as if he deserves fifteen years in some sort of torturous, disgusting love crime prison.)

Oh God.

Fuck.

Is it? It is.

Tom the Target.

Tom from the bar is a stone's throw away from me. Oh, bollocks. He's standing, leaning casually on the rail of the balcony looking down at the phone in his hand, a large brown paper bag with a handle in the other.

I reach the top of the escalator and freeze, like someone's pressed my "pause" button. A man behind me tuts and overtakes me.

He won't remember me. *Of course* he won't. It was a sticky, dark restaurant on any-old Friday night and he was knocking back whiskeys like black currant squash. Plus, Tom the Target seemed to me to be the sort of man who probably chats to random women all the time in bars. My face probably blurred into a crowd of others in his mind. He would've forgotten about me the minute he left for the puking friend at the Burger King. I can whisk past him, if I keep going—keep my head down. Plus, he certainly wouldn't recognize me today. I look like the underside of a foot; like a doll rescued from a fire. Face the color of clay, the bags under my eyes like two saggy, dark prunes. When Tom the Target saw me at the bar, I was perfectly turned out. A thick slodge of makeup on my face, my best dress on, my hair freshly blow-dried and glossy, a night of sleep under my belt, uninterrupted by criminal, ovulating foxes. *Foxes.* Those bloody Sycamore foxes causing me to look like I got caught in a lawnmower. A lawnmower followed by getting trapped in some sort of water *turbine*—

"Hey?"

Shit.

I stop on the rain-damp tiles, twist my face into faux surprise, and grin out a "Oh! Hi! Hello! Bonjour!" and Tom straightens, locks his phone. He pushes his phone into his pocket and smiles. He wants to chat. He wants to catch up. With me, the melted doll. Joy. I bypass Goode's and walk the few paces to meet him.

"*Hi.*" He looks so awake, so clean and together, that I want to put my head into my handbag to hide my own. I know I look dreadful— I caught my reflection in the train window and gave a big shrug. *Who cares*, I'd thought, *it's not like you're going to see anyone besides Shauna and maybe Jason, and they're used to the post-foxes "Are you quite sure you're not ill, Natalie?" face.* Sod's law. That's what this is. Although he did say hello, so I must sort of look like the Me he met in the restaurant.

"Hiya." My eyes drop to the bag in his hand—at the top is a cake box with a window. "And you are—"

"Tom," he says with a smile, putting a large hand to his chest. "From—"

"From the bar. I know. From Avocado Clash. I remember."

"Oh."

"I was going to say—*and you are holding cupcakes.* Bright orange ones, covered in—" I lean to look through the cellophane of the box. "Shoes?"

Tom gives a slow smile. "Yeah. A gift."

"Well, that's very nice of you."

"It's been known to happen," he says, easily. "So, did I *pass the test*?"

"Sorry?"

"With your mates."

"Oh! Yeah. Totally bought it, every last one of them. You're officially a total arsehole in their eyes. Congratulations."

Tom laughs, a flash of white teeth, dark stubble, that lovely angular jaw . . . Jesus, I really do wish I'd at least put on some mascara. I might not fancy him, but I don't really want this face squirreled away in his handsome memory. "Well, if it helps the cause . . ."

"Oh, it does."

"Good."

I give a weak and, I'm sure, rain-stained and ruddy-cheeked smile. "So . . . work. How's it going? Adam Driver stopping by?" I deflect, pull my glasses down from my head and wear them, as if it'll make a difference, as if it's a mask of prosthetics, and not two transparent discs. (I've run out of contacts.)

"Ah. Not today. Doing some corporate headshots. Over in Shepherd's Bush. Friend of a friend. Bloke's a bit of a knob, but the price is right. And what about you?"

"Me?"

"No, that bloke over there with his head buried in a McDonald's breakfast." He smiles. *"Yes you.* Where're you off to?"

"Just . . . everywhere, nowhere. Around."

"Wow." He raises both eyebrows with a laugh. "Aka, mind your own business, Tom."

"I didn't *quite* say that."

"It's OK. I'm a stand-in. I can take it."

And I don't know what it is. But I see him standing there—Tom, in his smart black overcoat, his styled, dark hair, a perfect five-o'clock shadow, and his box of cupcakes destined for a woman somewhere who'll watch him come into the room and feel like her heart might burst into confetti, and I suddenly want to flee. Again. Exactly like the girl he met in Avocado Clash. "I'm off to play piano to nobody,"

I cannot possibly admit, "and eat croissants to stop me drinking too much wine because it's my dead husband's birthday and highly sexed foxes kept me awake, so you know—it's going rather well, you might say. Hashtag blessed."

"I better go," I say instead, doing a pretend glance at the huge gold clock on the wall in the distance. "I've got stuff to uh—somewhere to be."

"Everywhere, nowhere . . ."

"Exactly." I give a weak laugh and turn away, but shoot him a grimace over my shoulder—a quick and wordless "So sorry, can't stop, isn't life just *so mad and busy*!?" and I walk away from him. And from Goode's. I have no idea where I'm going, but I can't now turn back . . .

"See you, then, Natalie," he calls after me.

"Bye," I call back, throwing another quick glance over my shoulder, and he's still looking—kind, nice, together, awake, handsome Tom with the cupcakes and smart jacket, and I don't stop walking until I'm at the other end of the station, at another escalator. I turn around, but Tom's gone now, and for a moment, I stand just staring at the spot we spoke at, my hands gripping the cool rail of the balcony.

"Oh my god, you bumped into the guy from the bar again," says Lucy's voice in my head. "You do realize what that means, don't you, Nat? It's meant to be!"

I roll my eyes at her imaginary voice and lean against the rail. Rain hammers down on the glass ceiling, a thrum of a million raindrops. A whistle echoes from a distant train platform. And there, right in front of me, on the digital kiosk on the tiles, lit up, a bold red rectangle, is Edie's poster. *Oh, Harold! The cult musical.* The musical she's working on now—the path she chose instead of workshopping her own musical. *Our* musical. She plays a teacher in *Oh, Harold!*, apparently. Has a full verse in a song, according to Lucy, belts it out in a skirt suit and spectacles and sounds "totally phenomenal." "Not that I've been to see it, Nat," Lucy had added quickly, "just saw it on Facebook." And I believe her, but Lucy has a short memory. She sometimes acts as if Edie and I no longer speak because she chose a part in an established show over our own project, when of course it isn't just that. It's not even ten percent that. And when I remind Lucy of the ninety percent, of Edie's big, fat, horrible lie and the fact she chose to come clean with it at Russ's *funeral* of all times, there's always an air of "It was a long time ago" and "Everyone makes mistakes." *Mistakes.* Edie did not make a mistake. Edie detonated a gigantic, selfish bomb and left me with it.

Something bubbles up inside me, rumbles, like the rain above my head, like the heavy, metal trains coming in and pulling away. In one whip, I take off my scarf and jump on the escalator, taking two, then three steps down. I'm sweating. My cheeks are on fire.

"You two should see each other," I imagine Lucy saying now, "Edie wants to see you," and I bite back the urge to say aloud, to nobody, to this whole station of people and to the poor teenager in front of me, "Oh, I'm sure you *would* say that, Imaginary Lucy. I'm sure you would with your perfect bloody eyebrows and job and your perfect bloody life. But do tell me, did your friend ever shag the love of your life? Oh? No, didn't think so."

I make my way to the piano, as if it's a life buoy and I'm at sea, lost, meandering through crowds and crowds of people. I look up through the glass ceiling, the sky one big low smoky cloud, and I imagine what we would've been doing today if Russ was still here. Both of us at work, probably, but with plans tonight. That outdoor barbecue restaurant he loved. Or maybe a takeaway at Jodie and Carl's, the four of us, plus my teenage nephew Nick, sitting at their long, oak table, candles flickering, glasses of wine, a game of Cards Against Humanity, laughing so much our cheeks ache. The lie untold, my best friend, Edie, still my best friend. Everything still perfect. It wouldn't have been this, that's for sure. Not storming through a train station feeling like I'm standing in the center of my life that's imploded.

The piano sits empty under the stairs. I'll play. Play it all away, everything I feel. Whatever that is. I don't even know these days. I find it hard to place a feeling, but I know it'll make more sense as I play. I don't always know what I feel until I do. I fancy the high notes, and the all-encompassing chorus full of minor chords that make me feel like they are speaking back to me. The heartache, the pain. I'll play that Foreigner song—one of the first songs I learned by ear on the old, chipped, wooden piano in the cramped hallway when I was nine. Dad's old boss gave it to him when he couldn't afford to give Christmas bonuses. It was thrown out at a school they were refurbishing. Three of the keys were broken. Mum hated it at first. The light, churchy wood messed with her lilac and silver décor. But she learned to love it when I did. It was no Steinway grand, but it was mine.

At the piano, I stand for a moment over the stool. And through the rigid cold of my body, a warm spark shoots through me. Excitement. Hope. I've already checked, I know, but . . . just knowing I could check again. And I promised I wouldn't start this—purposely looking. The hope makes me feel a bit pathetic, like when Russ's mum kept visiting psychic mediums until she found one who told her exactly what she wanted to hear. But as someone chatters loudly on their mobile phone a stride away from me ("No, he's getting veneers, Jonathan," she's saying, "not dentures. Yes. *Veneers*. And honestly, they're as white as the cliffs of sodding Dover.") I bend, lift the lid from the stool.

Like I was expecting, and absolutely not, all at once, my heart . . . it freezes. Falls out of my arse, as Jodie would say. There's a piece of music there. Again. *Again.* It's a clean white sheet, newly printed, like before. Proper, thick, office-y paper. But the song. The song is—*no.* No. It's our wedding song.

I stare at it in my hand, the paper flapping, not in the breeze, but because of my shaking hand. Our song. The song I always played when he was in hospital and his mood was on the floor because it reminded us both of the night we got married. The song we danced to under a canopy of fairy lights, my arms around his neck, our breath hot and sweet from too much cider, eyes scrunched from laughing. We'd eschewed champagne for the wedding. "We are not champagne people," Russ had said. "We are stuffed-crust pizza and cider people and so will our guests be, I'm afraid. Even if it's against their will."

I close the lid and sit slowly down, looking around the station now. People swarm by, all of them busy, with places to go, and it's like the world is on fast forward but I'm on pause. Like something is happening, but I don't understand what.

I look up through the glass ceiling again. A sliver of sunlight, like a repaired tear through the clouds.

I place the music on the stand. I play.

chapter six

When we bought Three Sycamore, so many people made faces—winces, followed by "That'll cost you a bit to sort, eh?" and "But won't you miss the city?" and Russ and I just shrugged. It didn't matter. The money we might have to save to fix things, the upheaval, the change of lifestyle. But about two weeks after moving in, we had a power cut on the same day we found a crumbling beam in the loft, plus the floors and walls bursting with stuff. And not the sort of stuff you dream about finding in the attic of a cottage whose last occupant was a woman who lived to see the forties, fifties, and sixties—it was just *stuff*. Crap. Some of it was cute, but all of it useless, and suddenly *our* problem. I wobbled then. I sat on the closed toilet seat holding a battery-powered candle like a twenty-first-century Dickensian and cried, drying my eyes on a damp hand towel. I missed our tiny, soulless London flat. I missed the bustle and life. I missed Edie dropping in on her way back from kickboxing class. I missed opening a window and hearing a disjointed chorus of strangers' voices and smelling the fug of exhausts and kebab meat. I even missed watching the stupid shirt-tearing fights on a Saturday night. Russ had knocked on the door and I'd let him in.

"Bloody hell, you look like you're conjuring spirits," he'd said, smiling softly at me, perched on the loo seat. "Look, it's just junk, Nat. Stuff. It's . . . *things*. Things can be removed. Things can be fixed. Beams. Electricity . . ." And I told him it all felt weird. That I felt home-sick. Living in the country, half my things still in boxes, a loft bursting with a stranger's past life, candles instead of lights, and not a single Chinese takeaway on Uber Eats. It felt upside down. Like I'd woken up in another world.

"That's because it's change," Russ had said, crouching, placing two gentle hands on my pajamaed knees. "You're a bit rubbish with change, that's all. But change is good. Life doesn't happen without it." Then he'd kissed my forehead and added, "Plus. I'll never change. I mean, our world will, it's meant to. But—I won't. We won't. Right?"

The next day, Russ, so big on being eco-friendly, so big on waste not want not, point-blank refusing to get a huge dumpster (whereas I fantasized about one in the way I used to about hot Hollywood ac-tors having car trouble in front of my house), started photographing everything.

"We can use Freecycle first," he said, opening my laptop, and I re-member watching his big gardener's hands pummeling the keyboard. "We just stick it on here, and then wait for the locals to start scream-ing, 'Fuck yeah, we want a rusty mangle.'"

"You have a week, Russington," I'd said, the phone to my chest as I'd waited on hold to the electric company. "And if that rusty old pile of shit is still sitting there, I'm taking it to the tip myself."

But Russ was right. People practically begged us for a lot of the items, and as Russ lugged old cabinets and metal buckets and reams of mothy, musty material into the lucky winners' boots, I remember thinking how nice it would be to be a little more like him. I was always a bit of a cynic compared to him, and Russ believed in the good in people and taking a chance, even if it meant risking your own time and feelings. I've always just pretended to. I share all the right quotes on Instagram, I read all the right books, but I've never been able to fully cross the threshold, over to it. And now? Well, I'm further from the threshold than I've ever been. The threshold is a spike strip. The threshold is lava. And I am firmly in the room signposted, "It's easier to be a secretly cynical wet weekend, actually, because then you're mostly never disappointed."

But tonight.

Tonight, I knew what was coming. Despite the croissants I bought to try to abate it—used them as sandbags against the flood I knew might come—and despite *smiling* like a creep to myself on the train home, the music, still in my hand, as the day slowly faded, and the croissants slowly eaten, sadness has seeped through the walls, over the course of the afternoon and evening, like damp. Because this is our home. This was our idea, and he isn't here. It's his birthday and I am here alone, and he will never age another day for as long as the world keeps turning. And what happened to us? The Russ and Natalie I could see so clearly in my mind. Saga-holiday-aged. White-haired and happy, and Russ still looking over the boring horticultural magazines he'd read at night on his iPad and say, "You'll leave nothing of them" when I'd be glued to a regency romance on Netflix and absent-mindedly bite my thumbnails to stumps.

And I'm crying again. *Ugh.* Of course I am.

I rub my face, pull my damp, teary hands over my head. I can't keep going on like this, for God's sake. I'm thirty-two. *Thirty-two.* And my enemies are croissants and digital billboards and empty piano stools. A broken record nobody wants to listen to. That's me. No wonder my friends are worried. I can just picture the conversations. "I know this is a bit mean but . . . don't you think she should be over it by now? Do you think she's actually OK?"

There's a sudden knock at the door, and I know from the rhythm of it who it is. I told them not to come, but in this moment, I want them to go away and come inside, fill my little cottage with home and warmth and life, all at once.

I find them—Jodie, my enormously tall brother-in-law Carl, and my seventeen-year-old nephew Nick—bundled up to the neck in scarves and coats on our rickety tiled path. A little glowing family unit. Like something out of a sofa advert.

"The crisis team, reporting," says Carl with a salute. "I'm here to look at the pipe, Nick's going to look at your router, and well, Jodie's going to eat. Aren't you, Jode? She's made something. A . . . what's-it-called. *Cannelloni.*"

"Lasagne." Jodie smiles and proffers a big tray covered in tin foil. "Good time?"

"Never," I say.

Nick smirks. "Hey, Auntie Nat," he says, and he presses a cold-cheeked kiss on mine. He smells like chewing gum and wet grass. Straight from football training, I bet. He used to hate football when he was a toddler. He used to like coloring and Lego and everything that wasn't muddy or outside. "Ick-mun," he used to call mud. I can still hear his little, panicky voice. "Ick-mun! Ick-mun on my trousers. Ick-mun on my huuunds."

"Where's the router?" he says now, and I can hardly believe that husky, teenage voice comes out of him.

"Bedroom."

He nods, blond hair dangling over his eyes. I took the piss out of him last week—asked why he had Nick Carter's haircut and he'd said, quick as a flash, "The nineties are back. Thought you'd heard. What with that super-weird Fresh Prince of Bel-Air jacket of yours you keep wearing."

"And what's the problem with it?" he asks. "The internet."

"It just keeps dropping," I say. "Right in the middle of Netflix.

Freezes. Buffers. Then nothing happens, and sometimes I have to turn it off and then on again, blah blah blah."

"Right. OK to go straight up?"

"Course. Just ignore the bloodied corpse in the corner."

"Pam at number one invited you to Weight Watchers again then? Had it coming." Nick laughs, and I feel a bloom of warmth as I watch him creak up the stairs, smiling to himself, one eye on his phone. Jodie reckons he's "seeing someone." "Texting 'round the bloody clock," she said last week at work. "I'm dying to know who it is."

Carl heads straight out through the kitchen, a spanner in his hand, and Jodie and I follow him through. She sets down the tray on the tiled kitchen counter and whips off the lid. "There's so much cheese in this," she says, "that I feel sure the NHS would ban it. But I know you like extra cheese . . ."

"Jode, you didn't need to come."

"I know." She smiles, her cheeks pink, taut apples from the cold. "But I wanted to. Plus, Nick said he'd missed you, and from a seventeen-year-old boy . . . that's gold dust."

Carl, jangling with the backdoor key, smiles in agreement and ducks outside.

"Carl hasn't got a clue what he's doing, by the way," Jodie whispers, opening the cupboard above her head. "He's going in blind. Clueless. Like a puppeteer performing brain surgery."

"I did wonder how much a psychology professor knows about *plumbing*." I can't help but smile. Carl knows everything there is to know about the human brain, but he once tried to hang a picture on Christmas Eve and blew the electrics. They had to move in with Mum and Dad for Christmas, wait for the electricians of the world to come back from Christmas break.

"He of course knows sod all." Jodie puts a pile of plates on the counter. "He just wants to be useful. But you know, look at it this way—he's qualified to counsel you to a high standard if it all goes wrong and your house falls down. Help you rewire your neural pathways."

"True," I say, taking a seat at the breakfast bar, and Jodie runs a knife along the edge of the orange, ceramic lasagne dish.

"So, are you all right? Has today been . . ." Jodie's words drift off, but she eyes me carefully, her freckles a splatter across her nose. I was in awe of Jodie when I was teenager—and naturally, a tiny bit jealous, but she'd have never known. I was taller than her, despite being three years younger, and I went through a phase of being paranoid my nose was unnaturally big, especially next to hers, with her dainty little cartoon-princess point. Jodie wasn't striking, but she was cute and neat. Sensible, organized, never missing a birthday, or her after-school swim classes. My reputation of after-school activities was like a smoldering graveyard. I tried everything. And gave up on everything. Tap dancing, swimming, karate, circus training (and that was only because I fancied one of the men who taught fire-eating.) It's amazing to me, among uni-cycles and pottery courses, that I never thought to take a piano lesson outside what I taught myself at home on that old eyesore of a piano. It always just felt like breathing, I guess. Something that was part of me, like the color of your eyes, like foods you've always despised.

"It's been OK," I say. "Nobody texted me, though. I thought I might hear from his brothers, but—"

"Did you text them?"

"I did in the end. Teddy didn't reply, and Rob—he just said: hope you're OK. They all seem pretty together. Pretty fine."

"Whereas you—" My sister leans forward and picks a croissant crumb from my jumper. "You just got lost in some pastries, my love."

"*I did.* But I'm glad you're here. I mean it."

"I'm glad you're glad," says Jodie. "And I'm glad I brought you some proper food."

"I eat proper food."

Jodie stops, looks at me, spatula in hand like a fly swatter. "Priya said you ate cold hot dogs out of the tin the other Sunday."

"Yeah, well," I huff, "Priya fancies Clive the scaffolder. What does she know?"

"That cold hot dogs are not a meal," Jodie says, hoisting up a square of lasagne for my plate and sitting opposite me. "Seriously. You're lucky it didn't give you the shits—"

"*Jesus.*" There's a bang from outside, followed by Carl's despairing voice. "Flipping hell! This is . . . Christ on a bike . . ." Jodie looks at me, our forks poised, and we laugh. Jodie starts eating, but I don't feel like I can eat a thing until I've told her.

"Jodie, there was more music."

"What?" She chews, clueless.

"More music was left. Today. In the stool, at the train station."

She swallows, a hand at the chest of her thick, mint-green jumper. "Why must you always tell me these big bombshells while I've got my mouth full?"

"Sorry."

"So did you—see anyone?"

"No. But the song. It was our wedding song. Our first dance?"

"Fuck right off." Jodie puts down her fork with a clatter. "*Seriously*?"

"For real."

"God—are you a hundred percent sure?"

"*Yeah.* Undoubtedly. And I was late there too. Super late. And I wasn't going to look again, because I'd already looked and it was empty—"

"Holy shit—"

"—but I did, and when I lifted the lid, it was just sitting there on the top. Not creased or old or anything. Freshly printed. Look." I get up and grab it from the coffee table in the living room where it sits with the other two pieces, under a heavy, pineapple-shaped candle I've never lit. I slide it across the kitchen counter toward her.

"Jesus," says Jodie finally. "Fuckin' hell. Sorry, I keep swearing. God. I just . . . I dunno."

"I know."

Another clatter from outside in the back garden—a spanner or something similar meeting concrete followed by a pained grunt. It's like a hospital drama's sound effects machine has been left playing on a loop. Jodie calls out to Carl. He calls back, says he's OK.

"So, what—do you think it's him? Russ?" Jodie closes her eyes, winces, like she's just pulled out a splinter. "I mean, I know that's bloody mad and stupid to say, but maybe he . . . I don't know."

"Set it up?" I offer with relief, because I've been feeling like I'm going *mad* thinking this is Russ somehow, but if sensible, grown up Jodie thinks it . . .

"I've got no idea," announces Carl suddenly in the doorway of the kitchen, his hair wet from the rain, droplets dangling on the ends like beads. "Sorry. I'm a classic nincompoop. A fool. I've just got no idea where to begin."

Jodie smiles warmly, pats the space of counter beside her. "Well, you tried, love."

"Thanks, Carl," I say. "Bless your heart, I appreciate it."

"See, I only know how to solve one plumbing problem," he says as Jodie leans, starts serving up his dinner. "And I was hoping it would be that."

"Well, I'm very sorry my pipes and I disappoint you so."

He laughs, wipes his huge rain-wet hands on a tea towel, and drapes it neatly back over the handle of the oven. "So, what're we on about? What's the news in camp today?"

Nick appears then, shrugging, and says, "Sorted. I think. The

Wi-Fi settings were a bit mad. It was all a bit weird and fucked up, so—"

"*Nick.*"

"Sorry, Mum. It was, erm—bollocksed?" he offers, like a salesman presenting a cheaper package. "Buggered? *Screwed.*"

"How about"—Jodie pauses, fork in hand—"*in disrepair*?"

"How about: I'm not a priest." Nick laughs as he takes a seat next to me, folding his long, skinny legs under the counter. "Anyway, what were you all talking about? I heard Mum swearing, the hypocrite. And more than once."

And in that moment, I give a tiny little headshake over the breakfast bar toward Jodie—a wordless "Don't tell them." Because if even sensible, logical Jodie thinks it could be Russ setting it up, it somehow feels like it could be, and that has sparked a little hopeful flame in my stomach. I don't want to risk hearing a skeptic tonight. Especially when the biggest one of all sits at this counter covered in crumbs.

chapter seven

It's there. Another piece of music. It's not even been a week since Russ's birthday, and *there it is*. Bold as brass. Sitting there as if it's always been.

I tear up the escalator toward Goode's like someone racing down a hospital corridor in a soap opera, like a child waking up and storming downstairs on Christmas morning. But when I burst through the heavy wooden door, Shauna isn't there, and Jason looks up at me from buffing a yellow cloth on the counter, like I'm a grenade that's just gone off in front of him. Even Piercings Girl and Notebook Guy look up from their drinks.

"You all right there, Natalie?"

"Is Shauna around?" I ask breathlessly, heat and excitement pounding my cheeks.

"Out back. Inventory duty. And God, has she got the *hump* today." He grins, nibbles at the silver ring at the side of his mouth. "Wanna head out back?"

"Would she mind?"

"Don't see why not," Jason says with a frown, and he gestures with a twist of his head to circle the long, teak counter.

I find Shauna out the back with the door ajar, daylight flooding in, looking down at an iPad like it's a new Egyptian artifact recently exhumed at her very feet. I've never been "out the back" before. Not when I cried after seeing the *Oh, Harold!* poster for the first time. Not when I spilled a whole neon-green kiwi smoothie on myself. Not even when I broke down on my birthday last year when a pigeon shat in my coffee and then on my new cardigan and it was the straw that broke the camel's back. Shauna ushered me into the tiny little toilet then and sponged it out with a faded J-cloth, saying, "Better pigeon shit than any sort of dairy, I say, Natalie. If it were dairy, you'd be kicking up a stink on that train home, and nobody wants to sit next to someone who stinks like the underbelly of a cow."

"Oh, hello, darling," she says casually. "Jason let you through, did he?"

"Broke in." I smile. "Is this OK? I'm not going to get you like . . . fired or something."

"Chance'd be a fine thing." She smiles. "You can break in any time. Rob the food by all means, I won't tell. Just don't rob the till. That'd be a lot of ball-ache admin for me, and I can't be bothered." She rubs her hands down her top, a baggy burgundy blouse covered in biscuit-colored butterflies, and blows out a breath. "I was about to make a tea and sit outside in the sunshine for my break. It's a bloody concrete jungle out there, but the sun has *finally* graced us with its presence. Wanna join? What do you fancy?"

"Oh, the norm, please. White Americano. I'll go and order shall I—"

"Jason?" she calls. "A chamomile and an Americano, white, please, darling. Both large." Shauna turns to me. "Go on, settle down. And tell me where the fire is."

"The fire?"

"You look like you've seen a *ghoul*, Natalie. Like you need some sugar in your veins."

"I *feel* like I've seen a ghoul. A good ghoul, though."

Shauna nods gently, as if she already understands everything I don't even know I feel myself, and with a jangle, the keys still in the lock, she pushes the back door open wider, and I follow her out, onto a concrete courtyard. It's dominated mostly by bins, by chairs and stacked-up crates outside the back ends of shops, but in a window of reluctant sunshine on the tarmac, Shauna gestures for me to sit down at a white plastic garden set. An ashtray sits on the top of it, full of old rainwater.

"So." Shauna smiles, taking a seat opposite me. She looks tired today, her usual pink lipstick and hoop earrings absent, her hair scooped back roughly and pinned into place with a brown crocodile clip. Shauna reminds me of a hamster on a wheel sometimes. Never taking a moment to stop, or take a breath. It's why dancing, I think, makes her so happy. It's for her and only her. Not her boys, not Don, not the shop. Just her. "The fire," she says. "The ghoul. Tell me."

"Someone's been leaving me something," I tell her. "And I think it's Russ."

Shauna hesitates. "Russ? Your Russ?"

"That's right. So, the piano downstairs, the stool, it—"

"Er, Shauna?"

She widens her eyes with irritation, clumps of old mascara on the ends of her lashes. "Sorry, love, hold on a minute—yes, Jason?"

He ducks his round head around the door. "Your spawn's here. For the car keys, or something?"

"Oh, God, I almost forgot. Family bloody admin. A minute. Then I'm all yours."

Shauna disappears inside, and I sit outside below the dome of crystal-clear blue sky, listening to the sound of London bustling below, down on the street. Traffic and trains pulling away, the horns of cars, chatter and distant music, from a restaurant maybe, or even an event. A band, rehearsing possibly. Sound-checking. I wonder if I'd be here, or somewhere close by, if things had been different. Would I be working nearby, with Edie, on *Dotted Line*, our slaved-over cowritten musical? Would she have gotten me in at *Oh, Harold!*, and would that be my poster too? Would I whisk in, and then out again, of Goode's, ordering coffee before jetting off to work, too busy to stop, too busy to get to know strangers, like Shauna and Jason? I can't imagine that—not knowing them.

Shauna's voice drifts through the kitchen and out into the spring sunshine now, followed by the distant, deep voice of who I gather is one of her sons. There's laughter, then I hear her say I love you, and I hear him say it back, and I lean back on my chair, try to catch the back of him. I get the tiniest blur of a glimpse. Tall, broad shoulders. She's right. Her sons aren't total gorgons—well, if going by the back of them is anything to go by, and in my experience, and as Priya says, "You can usually tell hotty from the back."

After a few moments, Shauna appears in the doorway, our drinks on a tray, and a ruddy, flustered look on her face. "Right. That's them sorted. My twins are borrowing the car, getting it MOT'd for me. *Now.* Tell me everything," she says, "and from the top."

♪   ♪   ♪
♪   ♪   ♪

"Well, I say you stake it out," says Shauna opposite me, a chunk of carrot cake sponge between her fingers, like a pincer.

"Stake it out?"

"Exactly that. I can help you," Shauna says with a victorious glint in her eye. I told her excitedly about the music, told her *everything*, and she listened, all peach-cheeked and wide-eyed, and I loved how it felt. In that moment beneath that high, blue sky, on that white, plastic garden chair, I was just the woman with an exciting little story—a *mystery.* I wasn't just Natalie. Natalie Fincher whose husband went and died far too young, poor soul. Natalie Fincher who eats pudding basins of Coco Pops so she doesn't drink pudding bowls of frozen cocktails, and Natalie Fincher who thaws out her rusty old house's pipes with a hair dryer most mornings and usually in nothing but a hoodie and a pair of knickers that have seen better days, while her neighbor Roy likely considers, cordless phone to his ear, reporting her for indecent exposure.

"Do you mean just sit and watch it? The piano? Like a mad spy or something—"

"That's exactly what I mean," replies Shauna. "Why not? I mean, they're obviously coming here often enough, and I know I can't see the piano from the shop, but I could always make a few trips a day, have a little stakeout of my own when the customers allow."

"I could do," I say, tingles peppering my skin. Possibility. Excitement. This feeling—it's like slipping on a warm, cozy jumper after a lifetime of being too cold. "And I know on Wednesdays I'm at work, but I don't have to go home straightaway after we close, do I? I could detour."

"Exactly."

"It isn't far and to be honest, lately I'm never in any rush to get home, so—"

"The house getting you down?" asks Shauna gently, and normally, people asking me about the cottage makes my hackles rise. But Shauna. Shauna means well, she asks for the right reasons—for me. Not to gauge if I'm getting better, if I'm moving on. She just simply wants to know.

"A little bit. A lot actually." I lean forward as if I'm sharing my most hidden secret. And that's because it always feels like I am. "Is it bad I feel guilty? About saying shitty things about it and *moaning* about it and sometimes wishing I didn't live there—"

Shauna's brow wrinkles beneath her wispy, sandy fringe. "Absolutely not. Your home is so important. It's where you go to feel safe, to let your guard down. If it doesn't feel like that for you, then—"

"It doesn't," I admit. "I mean, it did. But it was Russ's dream really, the cottage, and . . . *our* project. Ours."

"And now it's just yours," says Shauna. "And you don't know if you want it to be?"

I look over the table to her, meet her soft, understanding eyes, and I nod, reluctantly, as if, what? As if someone is watching from somewhere, judging, saying, "That beautiful little cottage she's got, in that beautiful place, that her poor husband loved the bones of, and she says it's getting her down! Can you believe the gall of her? The brass neck!"

"Well, look—I told you already, my sons—let them help. They can do it all, and if you need them . . ." She holds up her hands, like someone presenting something.

"I know. Thank you."

"I mean it, Natalie."

We sit and watch a plane bumble low overhead, and Shauna shields her eyes with a hand as she tips her face to the sun to watch it. There's a blue stripe on its tail. I wonder where it's going in the world, what time zone it'll visit, all those pairs of feet resting on the plane carpet, thousands of miles above our heads.

"You know what," she says, glancing at me. "Whoever it is leaving this music, they must be leaving it at a specific time. Did you say you've checked and there's been nothing, and then when you've checked later—"

"It's appeared."

"So, I reckon it's during a specific frame of time. Perhaps when whoever it is, is passing by? If you don't mind, I'll mention it to Jason, and Sasha, too, the barista on a Wednesday. They can both keep an eye out."

I sip my coffee, lukewarm now, cooled by the breeze. "Who could it *actually* be though? It sounds mad, I know, but I feel like it *has* to be someone who knew us. *Knows* us. Of course, there's a chance it's just some giant coincidence. Some other pianist, or something, with the same taste in music. But I don't know. Russ's favorite song—it was by this band that had like, two hits and we saw them live once, and barely anyone knew who they were. It felt like we were the only people in London there. We loved it."

Shauna smiles.

"I just—I feel something. In my chest, in my gut that . . . it means something."

"Well, there you are then," Shauna says gently. "And maybe if it isn't Russ, maybe it's someone meaningful leaving it. Someone who . . . has you in their thoughts. Someone who cares."

"So, what like, maybe one of his friends?"

"Have you contacted any?"

I shake my head. "Not for a while. And honestly—people just don't know what to say." This is one of the things I've noticed. People know exactly what to say when someone first dies—oh I'm so sorry, or life is so cruel, it's so unfair, or he's in a better place and he's watching over you, blah blah. But fast-forward a few months, when they realize you aren't completely back to normal, and they're stumped. They treat every word out of their mouths like a little bomb. *If I say I love my husband, will Natalie think that's insensitive? If I ask her how she is, will she burst into tears? I'm no good with crying, me. I can't cope with it.* And I get it. I do. And while my friends and family were the ones who got me through the first few months after, very soon I started day-dreaming about having a brand-new start, with a brand-new, clean slate of fresh, new people who didn't have anything to measure me against. Nobody who expected me to "get better." How could they, when they had no idea who I used to be?

"I find most people don't know what to say, because they're too busy trying to find the perfect words," Shauna reflects. "They don't realize that you'd rather them say, 'What a pile of shit you've been handed, I'm gutted you're going through it.' "

"*Yes.* That's exactly it."

"It's like me," says Shauna, and for a moment, she looks over her shoulder, as if to check we're still alone. "I had a cry on the phone to my friend after the wedding. After Don wouldn't dance with me and wouldn't let *me.* Then we had the most dreadful argument about it."

"Oh, Shauna. That's rubbish." I knew it. *Dastardly bloody Don.*

"Oh, it's fine." She waves a ringed hand in the air, but her eyes flick to the table, away from mine, and I don't quite believe her. "But I just needed to rant, you know? I just wanted her to listen, but she stuttered and stammered and said, 'Oh, but Don means well. He's a good provider. He's always worked hard.' "

"Well, what's that got to do with dancing?"

Shauna cocks her head to one side and her eyes close, slowly, like an owl's, as if to say, "Exactly."

"It's a pile of shit you've been handed," I say, "and I'm gutted you're going through it."

Shauna smiles. "Same to you, darling." We tap our cups together, in a gentle, knowing cheers. The sheet music, anchored under the saucer on the table, curls at the edge in the breeze, as if itching to take flight.

"I'm glad I've got my dancing, though," Shauna continues. "I went again a couple of nights ago. *Loved it.* I feel like I'm . . . letting go when I'm there. You know? It's like therapy."

I smile. "I'm so glad. It makes me sort of jealous too."

"Come with!"

"Ha." I laugh. "I'm not really a dancer. But I do sort of wish I had a hobby. Something I did out of the house, something else, something new. Everyone has hobbies. Gym. Amateur dramatic groups. Somewhere to let go—"

"Oh my god." Shauna puts a hand in front of her, like a lollipop lady stopping traffic. "I just thought! Hang on." She jumps up and within a minute is back, putting a small, shiny leaflet down in front of me. "Of course, no judgment here whether you do or don't, but we've started allowing some local businesses to stick posters up on the pillar, by the cakes, and a customer of ours put this up . . ."

"A music therapy group," I read.

"Not far from here." Shauna nods eagerly. "It says there, they even welcome volunteers. Trained therapists. *Musicians.* Charity funded, I think."

Something flutters in my chest—something taking flight. Music as therapy. It's always been mine, but—God, could I turn up to something like this? Say if it's a big circle? Say if we all have to get up and share our tragedies? I'd tried bereavement counseling once, but Kai, the counselor, had a policy that he wouldn't under any circumstances speak first, and the first ten minutes would just be us two, in silence, like two idiots in a staring competition. But this . . . maybe I could volunteer. Priya's always saying to help herself, she helps other people. It always sounds a bit like Pinterest-quote-levels of bollocks to me, but then, Priya's always happy, so . . . maybe there's something to it.

"I guess I could look it up. Maybe."

"No obligation," says Shauna warmly. "I just saw it and thought of you. Thought it looked interesting. I mean, how you play—it's enough to heal anyone." She gives a big, round-cheeked smile. "And you know you can always dance with me if all else fails."

"I don't have the rhythm."

"Oh, shush. I didn't either." Shauna sips her tea. "So, will you have a little ask around with Russ's buddies? About the music?"

"I'll send a few texts I think," I say, taking a quick photo on my phone of the leaflet on the table. "I haven't seen Russ's best friend in a while, and he visited the hospital when Russ was in there every single day. So who knows?"

Shauna nods. "No harm in asking him. And meanwhile"—she slides her chair out and stands—"stake it out."

"Do you really think?"

"Sure! Go down there, sit your butt somewhere, take a drink or something with you, and see what happens. You might see something."

"Someone I know . . ."

"That's right. You might rumble them. And—let's not rule this out: maybe you'll meet an admirer. It could be someone you know. Like in *You've Got Mail*? Did you ever see that film?"

I scoff, almost pushing a spray of coffee through my nostrils. "An *admirer*? I highly doubt that, Shauna. And I have seen it. Made me cringe mostly. The ending's cute though. Mostly because of the lovely dog . . ."

Shauna gives a heavy shrug, the bangles on her wrists jingling. "And why wouldn't it be? An admirer, I mean. A nice handsome one, a nice, muscular, softhearted hunk. A lovely Dwayne Johnson. That'd do you."

"Oh, I don't know." I laugh. "I mean, nobody really knows me, do they? You have to sort of be *out there* to have an admirer. And also, not walk around London looking like a cursed waxwork."

"Natalie," Shauna chuckles, "you sit out there on that piano every single week, playing the most glorious music to bloody *herds* of people, and a lovely looking one like you—you reckon people pass by and take no notice?"

"Yes."

She laughs again, throws her head back. "You've a screw loose."

Then she ducks and says, "Our Jason likes you, I think. Said you're *smoking*. Which I think is young lad speak for gorgeous."

"A young lad who fancies everyone with skin, bone, and a beating heart. Aren't I lucky?"

Shauna winks. "*Stake it out.* And meanwhile, I'll keep going to check whenever I can." Then she rubs her hands together and laughs. "Exciting, isn't it? A bit of drama, a bit of a mystery."

Staking out isn't as fun as they make it out to be in films. I don't have a sidekick. There's no funky music. It's just me, in a hoodie with a bottle of sparkling water, staring at an empty piano as sun beats down through the glass ceiling. There's nothing. I mean, this is a London train station, so *of course* it isn't just nothing, but there's nobody suspicious looking, and nobody I know or even vaguely recognize. Tourists play, people stop to bang on the keys, children pose by it, their parents making them sit with their hands poised, and of course there's the odd genius—the ones who are classically trained and fill the station with an absolute symphony, before buggering off to catch a train or grab a burger. But there's nothing. Nobody lifts the lid of the stool. Nobody looks around—nobody has that look on their face that they're doing something and shouldn't be seen. I sit for over an hour, before giving up the ghost, and standing up to head to my platform to go home. But then I see him—just a glimpse. He passes the piano—eyes it, but drifts by. I watch as he ascends the escalator, and heads into Goode's.

Tom.

From the bar. *Tom the Target.*

We barely know each other. I don't even really remember what we talked about back then, in the drunken blur that was that night in Avocado Clash. Did I tell him about Russ? Did I mention the music I'd found the day before? The first piece. No, no, I don't think I did, but then I *had* had a few cocktails. Maybe more than I remember.

On the train home, I open my notes app and type "Suspects" and then "Tom the Target."

chapter eight

The kettle rumbles, and out of the diamond-lined windows, the night is black. *The foxes.* The bloody foxes woke me again. We never had to put up with this in London. Edie and I would stay up all hours writing music in my and Russ's old flat, and I don't remember ever seeing a fox, let alone hear this many screaming like they have fireworks jammed up their arses.

The kettle clicks off, a plume of steam misting up the kitchen window. I glance at the clock above the fridge. Twenty past three. It didn't take much to wake me tonight, to be fair to the foxy little shits. I didn't fall asleep until one, and even then, the sleep was fitful and restless and induced by only one glass of wine and reading that boring Neanderthal book Russ was obsessed with. One glass. And one was all it took really, to help me dim the floodlights of my brain. The piano music is all I've really thought about since Thursday. And I feel almost shame about it, feel myself almost wince when I let the thought step forward, name itself. But it's like something has been lit inside me. This dancing spark. Excitement. Hope. The unknown—the *good* unknown. And who's behind it is all that's on my mind. The way a first crush is, the way that tantalizingly close holiday is. And Maxwell,

Russ's best friend, keeps playing on my mind—I even added him underneath Tom, in my notes app, in my rather dramatically named "Suspects" list. Maxwell works in London, and he and Russ were like brothers. He was the best man at our wedding, and he did not miss a single day of visiting when Russ was in hospital. If Russ was planning something, I feel sure that Maxwell would know. He also knew I played on the hospital piano for him. He was probably there sometimes as I did, listening to those songs float down the corridor. Besides Maxwell, though, and the completely slim chance it's Tom the Target, I'm totally clueless. Out of ideas, full stop.

I make a mug of tea—the berry tea Russ used to drink—and hesitate as I pass through the living room. Our little sofa, tossed with a thick, black throw to hide the old threadbare patches and stains, sits there, like so many things do in this house, an old relic. It was a hand-me-down from Mum and Dad, from their annex, before they started redecorating, and I hated it, longed for a new, fresh, neutral one from IKEA or DFS. Russ loved the oldness of it though. "Nah. It smells of . . . stories." He laughed when I complained it was musty, like my parents' garage, and I'd whinge, show him a ream of plain, modern (soulless, as Russ would say) sofas on my phone screen.

I should call them, my parents. Maybe tomorrow. Maybe next week. I decide against the sofa and head upstairs to our bed.

Under the duvet, I lift my legs and bend them, make a little cubby for my mug. Rain splatters the windows, and the sound of it hammering is all I can hear now. No foxes. No goose-bumps movie screaming. It's stopped. I'm safe. Everything's OK. Peaceful. *Thank God.*

I tip my head to the heavy, splintered beam on the ceiling, and at the watercolor blooms of damp in the corners of the room. We had a Pinterest board, Russ and me, a place where we pinned and bookmarked ideas for the house. Shelves of cool framed prints. Wall colors. Storage ideas. Flower bed hacks (but that was more for Russ of course). It hasn't been opened in almost three years, and the damp hasn't been touched either. None of it has. Life stopped the morning Russ had his accident, really—the morning that with one false move, one turn of a steering wheel, a stranger threw Russ off his bike. Everything we were going to do just ceased to exist. And sometimes I think about that last normal moment before he left the house, his kiss, his wave, the bag of plastic he'd put in the recycling box on his way out, my smile and coffee and bowl of cereal on the coffee table, freeze-framed and floating somewhere in time and space, like those old, abandoned apartments found untouched a hundred years later that are reported in the newspapers every so often.

"You know where they are," Shauna had said about her sons, and maybe it wouldn't hurt if I booked one of them in to help me, they could help me get the place in shape, ready to sell. I have some savings . . .

But sell. Do I really want to sell Three Sycamore? Like—*really*, really?

My heart aches. I do. I think I do. But it's the guilt. The bloody *guilt* that never seems to stop rearing its ugly little head, like a rude guest who won't leave.

I sip my tea, wish the guilt inside me was a ball, dissolving like a lozenge, but of course it stays there, swells to a lump in my throat.

I'll speak to Maxwell first. It's not totally out of left field to suspect him of leaving the music for me, really—he works in the city, and St. Pancras would be where his train comes in. Maybe I can arrange to see him on a workday—he's still in the city, not far from Tina. I think it's best to *see* him too, to ask about the music. If he's lying, I'll know by his face. Even if he's just concealing it to aid in the surprise. Whatever that surprise is, and whose. Maxwell was always a shitty liar.

"He *is* an estate agent after all," I mumble to myself, and I laugh at my own joke in the darkness.

"First sign of madness, that is, Nat," says Russ's voice in my mind.

chapter nine

D o you think this looks like—celebrity dress-down chic?" Jodie stands, her arm around a mannequin as if she's about to intro-duce me to her new fiancé. "You know, imagine a celeb on a Sunday, nipping out, hoodie, teddy coat, holding coffee with sunglasses on. Or do you think it looks like a bag of filthy washing?"

"Um?"

"It's such a hard balance to strike, Nat. Take Sienna Miller. Some-times she dresses like a jumble sale—"

"Mm."

"Layers and layers of scruffy clothing, but somehow it looks cool, it looks—*sexy*."

"Yeah."

"—but it's what they want. *The kids.* You know?"

"Jodie, did you just say the kids?"

"Just checking you were listening," says Jodie, smoothing down the lapels of a woolly teddy coat on a mannequin out here, on the pavement in front of Tina's shop window. "Thought you'd zoned out. I actually meant the opposite to the kids. Older women. Women who have shit to do but want to look nice and cool and *trendy*. I want to make this shop *inclusive.* Not just to younger women, but also older, and older women that don't want to wear bloody curtains and uni-slippers—"

"She looks like Sienna Miller."

Jodie stares at me, hopefully, her eyes, round and bright. "Do you really think? Mum's on her way down and—I want it to be right."

"Definitely," I say. "She looks like . . . like Sienna who's knackered and has just popped to Starbucks and hoped to get there and back in peace but gets papp'd on the way home."

Jodie smiles at me and I breathe a sigh of relief—I've said the right thing. She's always like this when Mum is due to come down to check on things—like someone who's had too much coffee. Like someone who's been told they have an hour to prepare an outfit for the queen, and will be publicly executed if it isn't agreeable. I'm sort of glad I won't be here, and that I'll instead be with Maxwell, having lunch (because Jodie has talked more about Sienna Miller today than *OK* magazine did in the entirety of 2005).

I'd texted Maxwell the morning after the foxes woke me, and he'd texted immediately back, "Sure, Natalie! It'll be great to catch up." And within five minutes, he'd sent me a calendar invite for today, the following Friday, because *of course* he did. Maxwell's life is one long scheduled string of meetings, with breaks to poo and sleep in between. And it's not that I don't want to see Mum. It's just, I always find myself wanting to show her progress when I see her. Like "Look, I've renovated the living room!" or "I'm engaged to be wed, Ma-ma, to a man of fifty thousand a *year.*" But I never really have a thing to report, perhaps except a new ailment, or the discovery of a new brand of frozen chicken goujons I've taken to. I'm lucky really. Mum is a *nice* mum—OK, she's dramatic, but mostly, she's unproblematic. A loving mum, an accepting mum (most of the time). I wouldn't describe her as even ten percent critical. She'd love both Jodie and me even if we sprouted tails, even if we suddenly announced we were handing ourselves over to a science experiment and would, from now on, be heads in jars. She'd carry us around in her handbag. She'd polish the jar, admire our skin through the glass, say, "You're ever so glowy. But then, you both take after me. It was all those grapes I ate when I was pregnant. The doctors marveled at my placentas. Did I ever tell you that? They were *in awe*." But still, I sort of try to avoid her and Dad these days. For classic "I don't want to disappoint my parents" reasons.

"Shit, my phone's dead," I say, looking down at the blank screen in my palm. "What's the time, Jode? Any ideas?"

"It's er—" Jodie stops fiddling with the oversize sunglasses on the mannequin and looks down at her Apple watch. "Is it at one you're meeting him? It's ten to. And—*what*? Well, that is such bollocks. My Apple watch is telling me I have barely moved today."

"I *hate* those watches."

"I haven't stopped today. I never do, but looking at my stats you'd think I was a—packet of lard. A pork scratching with a bank account."

I laugh. "They are nothing but *shaming* watches, my dear sibling. Although Russ loved his. Swore by it."

"It was Russ who convinced me to bloody get one," says Jodie with a smile, leaning to a box at her feet, full of a new range of lemon-yellow and mint-green cardigans.

"He convinced me too."

"Should've been on Apple commission, that bloke," Jodie remarks, and I love, so much, when other people, besides me, talk about Russ as *Russ*, and not in the context of anything else, other than who he was as a person. Not the bike accident. Just him.

"Mine's in the drawer somewhere," I admit, as Jodie hands me a cardigan for my mannequin, who Jodie wants to dress "like Taylor Swift on the school run." "So is Russ's watch actually. Down with all of them, I say. But then I suppose I would say that. I'm not sure what my

Apple watch would say about glasses of wine before bed at one a.m. and three croissants in a row."

Jodie straightens, then rests a hand on her hip. A smile slowly spreads across her face, a perfect arc. "You're different today."

"Am I?"

"I don't know." She leans toward me, pushes hair out of my face, like she used to when we were young. She was always doing it— neatening me up. Before school photos were taken when we'd both been gathered up from our different classes by the school reception- ist, or when I'd pad into her room late at night at fourteen and tell her I liked a boy. Three years older than me, but more like a second mother sometimes. "You do," she says. "You look—different. All sort of . . . glowy and bouncy and sort of—what the—*Natalie*?"

I can barely register her face before my body reacts without my permission. I throw myself down behind the Sienna Miller manne- quin, crouching like someone hiding from a holdup at a bank. And that's because I *am* hiding. At my place of work. At thirty-two years old. In broad daylight. On the streets of Camden Town.

"Natalie, what are you—"

"Shut up," I hiss.

"What?"

"*Shhhhhhh!*"

It's her. I've seen her. Edie. And I haven't seen her in over two and a half years. All this time, frequenting the same city, the same streets, and I've managed to avoid her. Yet here she is, ambling along the street, four shops down, her purse in her hand, her keys in the other. She knows Mum's shop is here. She doesn't know I work here, though. Thank God. *Thank God.*

"What is it?" asks Jodie, bending to speak to me on the floor.

"Nothing. Um. It's . . . cramp."

Jodie's face bunches up in confusion, sunlight catching the perfect sheen of highlighter on her cheeks, which I'm sure she applied at her neat and organized dressing table this morning, in plenty of time, her alarm never once being pressed on to "snooze." An adult. Jodie the perfectly turned-out adult, and me, the ridiculous woman-child crouched on the floor in the street. "Cramp?" she says "What are you actually on about bloody *cramp*—"

"Jodie, I need you to *shush*," I hiss. I sound mad.

My sister looks down at me, her eyes wide. "Is this one of your weird jokes?" she whispers. "I mean, you're funny, but sometimes they're so abstract they're sort of—lost on me . . ."

Then two neat, loafered shoes scrape to a stop on the pavement, and I'm faced with two bare ankles, straight-legged jeans just skimming them, one encircled with a glittering anklet with a horseshoe charm. *Mum.* Ah, fuck. Mum. And she looks down at me like I've just taken a shit in her potpourri.

"Hi," I say.

She doesn't respond, except tips her head, looks up and down the street, because she knows. She *knows* I'm hiding. But then again, you don't have to be a detective inspector to know that. I am quite literally hiding behind a mannequin that looks like it got itself dressed while totally inebriated and/or on fire.

"Natalie," says Mum sweetly. No judgment, but the slightest edge of concern for her youngest daughter.

"Hello, Mum."

Mum nods. "Edie's car, isn't it?"

"What?" Jodie tiptoes to see over the mannequin's bald shiny head.

"The little Peugeot," says Mum. "KOC. The number plate. Don't you remember—cock, I used to say." Mum laughs to herself.

"Is it? I—" Jodie looks down at me. "*Is it?*" she asks me, as if we're the only sane ones in the street.

"She's gone now," says Mum, and I can't work out if she understands or if she is concerned for my mental welfare.

"Is she?" I ask pathetically, looking up from the floor at both Mum and Jodie as Mum nods, her eyes closing, as if she wishes she didn't have to partake in such games. She knows I know Edie was there. She knows why I'm hiding. Of course she does. A baggage scanner in patent shoes.

I stand up slowly and scan the street, like a little mole surveying the land around his silly little hole. Mum's right. Edie has gone. My cheeks rush with warm relief but, like a change of gear, bloom into embarrassment when I see both of their faces. Mum's concerned, the same way she was when I was sixteen and announced I had a date with the twenty-year-old fire-eater from circus training, and Jodie's, the way she used to look at Nick when he was three and cried about going to the toilet because he was frightened the flush would melt his arse off. And I suppose to them, that's what she is. Edie Matthews is nothing but a toilet flush. But to me—seeing her. It's scary. Just like it was for Nick. Because seeing Edie means she might want to talk. And I don't want to hear it. I don't want to hear a word of her groveling, her explaining, her "I just had to clear my conscience, I could not comfort you at his funeral and know that I hadn't told you. But it was so long ago and meant *nothing*. To either of us. You weren't even together yet. I promise, Natalie, It was just sex. Just once. One drunken night . . ."

"Right," I say eventually. "So! Well. We've got lots to show you, Mum, haven't we Jode? Cardigans, things that aren't curtains or uni-slippers—"

"Are you all right?" Mum asks.

"*Me*? Perfect. Fine." I dust off my jeans. "Are you?"

"Course, love," Mum replies.

"*Good*. Erm. Anyway, I have to er—" I check my phone. Its dead, black screen staring back at me again. "I have to go. I'm er—meeting someone for lunch."

Mum's eyes glint then—just a little, like a pebble landing in a pond. "Who're you meeting?"

"An old friend."

"*Oh.*"

"Not like that, Mum."

"I didn't say it was like that."

I lean to kiss her cheek. "You didn't have to. Jodie, I'll be back at two."

Jodie nods and starts wrapping yet another scarf around plastic Sienna Miller who will likely sweat to death before a paparazzo can get to her, and before Mum can say another word, I duck off in the direction of the little Italian restaurant by the canal.

♬   ♬   ♬
♬   ♬   ♬

Maxwell looks exactly like Maxwell always does. Plain but Waspy, and like you're keeping him from something extremely important but he's trying to hide it for the sake of being polite. He looked like this when he worked nights in Sainsbury's as he studied. He looked like this when he was organizing Russ's bachelor party. And he also looked like this—harassed, too busy to stop—when he finally launched his own estate agenting business that now has four chains in the southeast. Maxwell and Russ were opposites. *Completely.* Maxwell is all suits and camel-colored jackets and those weird pointed shiny black shoes that curl at the ends that briefcase holding commuters on the 07:15 fast train on Thursday mornings all seem to wear. But Russ—he was all muddy hands and plaid shirts and torn old jeans he'd wear until they fell apart. But they laughed. That's the one thing I remember so vividly about their friendship—they laughed, and nothing made me feel happier, or more comforted (and admittedly, slightly annoyed at the time) than falling asleep upstairs at our little cottage to the sounds of Maxwell and Russ howling with laughter after too many beers and old episodes of *The Young Ones* downstairs. Materialistic entrepreneur with expensive, ugly shoes and a landscape gardener who took too many photos of the moon, but both still losing themselves over toilet humor and slapstick fights.

Maxwell stands up to greet me, brushing a hand down his crisp white shirt. "Nat, you look lovely. Really well."

"Thank you." I lean to kiss his cheek. It's clammy, and he smells of expensive aftershave and like he might've had a secret cigarette on the walk over here. "Don't really feel it most of the time, but—makeup's a brilliant invention."

"Right." Maxwell chuckles awkwardly and sits down. I sit opposite him, the legs of the chair beneath me screeching as I tuck myself under the table. It's a cute little restaurant, by Camden canal. Round tables with white tablecloths, a little glass of grissini in the center, next to an old, recycled tin as a vase, purple sweet peas propped against the edges.

I take a breadstick and reach for the drinks menu.

"Oh, I ordered us both a drink," Maxwell says.

"Oh. Thanks."

"Some mocktail thing they were pushing. Peaches, I think?"

"A mock and not a cock?" I say. "How tragic," and Maxwell laughs, two blotchy pink clouds puffing onto his cheeks, but I know deep down he wishes I hadn't just said that. (Which is probably why I did.) I always felt I was too much for Maxwell. He would never admit this, but he's the sort of person who prefers women to be all flowers and perfume and pedicures. To giggle at his crap jokes and know nothing about anything he knows too much about. A sexist, probably. But he loved Russ, and when Russ died, he cried just as much as me—and *on me*, apologizing profusely as he did, like he kept finding himself accidentally pissing on my shoes, and not simply showing emotion.

The mocktails arrive and we sip, and we do what you're supposed to do when you haven't seen someone in ages—waffle. We waffle about work, about the weather; we waffle about the holidays we might be planning and what we think of the prime minister and the latest series of *Celebrity MasterChef*. And then—there's silence. Loaded silence where the elephant in the room seems to inflate and inflate, until it's mere centimeters from flipping tables and crushing all the crunchy grissini to crumbs. Maxwell is wondering why he's here with me on a Friday afternoon. He wants to know what I want.

"So, er—" He stabs a straw in the cloudy peach liquid in his glass gently, squashing a mint leaf on the bottom. "What er—what can I do for you? I mean, that's if there is a reason other than just catching up . . ."

"There is," I say. "Got me there."

He smiles, and I search his face for something, because if it is him, or if he knows about Russ's plan to leave me the music, then surely he might be ready for this, somewhere deep down.

"There's something that . . . well, it's been happening, and I sort of want to get to the bottom of it."

He shifts in his seat. "The bottom of what?"

"Well, this is probably going to sound super weird and random and—"

"Mozzarella, tomato, and basil salads?"

A waiter appears at the table, as if he's just popped out of a giant birthday cake, with two large white plates in his hand.

"Um, I don't think that's ours, we haven't—"

"Oh, I—I ordered our lunch too." Maxwell smiles at me—more of a cringe really. "I hope that's OK."

I stare at the plate as the waiter, with his rictus grin, places them in front of us and leaves, two round discs of mozzarella and tomato looking up at me from the table like dead eyes.

"Oh, it's erm—no, it's fine, it's—"

"Sorry, Nat." Maxwell grimaces again, taking a pointless glance at the chunky, expensive watch on his wrist. "I only have until quarter to, so I thought—"

"Oh, no, no, no, no, don't be silly it's fine." It isn't. I hate basil. I think it tastes like chewing on incense. But I have crisps back at the shop, if worse comes to worst. Plus, Jodie always has a Flake in her bag. "It's a good idea. Thinking ahead, planning ahead, and well, this is a classic . . ." Now I'm really lying. If I'm coming to an Italian restaurant, I want carbs. I want pasta and I want butter swirling on the edges of the bowl and I want to walk back to work so bloated, I wish I had a stolen shopping trolley someone could wheel me back in.

"So, what were you saying?"

Maxwell starts to eat but watches me worriedly, like I'm about to ask him out or something, or ask how he feels about impregnating me in Russ's memory and honor. I almost laugh, imagining it. "We could do it through a sheet so you don't have to look at me, Maxwell. Cut a hole in it. Oh, I could get a pedicure. Giggle about flowers as you thrust. Really get you in the mood."

"OK, so—something weird is happening," I say, slicing a tiny sliver of cheese off a mozzarella round.

"Right."

"See, I play at the piano sometimes. In St. Pancras."

"Do you? Like—busking?"

"I guess. Just—well, I don't do it for spare change."

I wish he wouldn't keep looking at me like that—like people do when they find out something about you that surprises them and not in a good way. The "what a shame" face. The "Do you know she's *still* visiting the crematorium every week?" face, the "She was going to workshop a *musical*—an actual show—and now she just busks like a loser to strangers who don't care" face.

"So, well, the other day," I carry on, "there was some music left for me in the stool."

Nothing. Not a glimmer, not even a teeny tiny flinch.

"And at first I thought it was nothing. But then, on Russ's birthday, there was another piece left."

I wait again. For anything, for the slightest micro-emotion flickering over his features, of "Ah, shit, she knows." Of "Ah, that's it, you've got me!" But there's nothing. He actually looks quite bored. A 1950s husband forced to listen to his silly little wife's stories about silly little needlework and silly little trips to the greengrocer.

"Oh yeah?" He munches instead, a whole round of mozzarella just like that, straight in his mouth, like a rat disappearing into a hole.

"And it was . . . it was Russ's favorite song," I add.

"The Rooster tune? The one about the sun?"

"Yes. *Yes.*"

"Wow."

I study his face. Someone a few tables away drops a fork, and it clangs on the ground, like a chime. Our heads turn, as if synchronized.

"And?" he asks.

"And?"

"Yeah, what happened?" he asks, a piece of tomato speared on his fork. It drips two drops of dark, gloopy dressing, one and then two, onto his plate, like blood.

"Oh. W-well." He's just staring at me. He doesn't look like a man who knows more about it than I do. It isn't him. Of course it isn't him. "It's just—the following week, another piece of music was left. And it was our first dance."

He swallows. "Seriously, Nat?"

"*Seriously.*"

Maxwell knocks back a mouthful of mocktail, puffing his cheeks up as if swilling mouthwash around his teeth. He swallows and laughs. "Someone having you on?"

"Well, actually, I did think that, to be honest, at first."

"Anyone would."

"Yeah, but then I thought maybe—maybe . . . it could've been . . ."

Still, he carries on staring at me, munching, his jaw rotating, dicing up another round of beefsteak tomato, and I feel like I want to grab him by the shoulders and make him focus, listen to me, stop bloody *eating*.

"I thought maybe it was something to do with Russ."

He stops everything then. Chewing, blinking, breathing. A mannequin. He'd do well with Sienna, back at the shop. Plus, she never talks, never offers up an opinion, or a fact he might not know. His type, really. "With Russ?"

"Or you. Or one of your friends, maybe?"

He swallows then, as if it's a difficult task, and looks at me like he thinks I'm about to drop a hilarious punch line that hasn't landed yet. "*Me*?"

I laugh awkwardly. "Well—the thing is, they were so specific, the songs. I used to play them at the hospital while he was recovering. Do you remember? They had that donated piano and they said music helped people in recovery and—I mean, his favorite song, left on his birthday, Max. Not many people know that. I just think, how can it not be?"

Maxwell's brow furrows, three deep gouges in the skin, gathering. "How can it not be what?"

"Well. *Him.* In some way."

OK, now Maxwell looks like he might warn me off with a pitchfork. His eyes are wide, his cheeks are tinged with red—the face of a man who's trapped in a building in which the emergency fire lever has been pulled. And I know now that it isn't him, and now I feel ashamed. Small. Ridiculous. The way he's looking at me—it's like those looks my friends always give me. The looks I hate. The pity.

"How can it—" He pauses, leans across the table, and drops the volume of his voice, like he's talking to a tiny, scared child. "How can it be Russ, Natalie, he's—"

"He's dead, yes, *I know*," and my voice is definitely at least four notches louder than his. "Sorry." I push my plate across the table.

"S-sorry?"

"I just—I don't like basil."

"Oh. I'm sorry, I should've waited—"

"No, no, not at all, I just—" I don't know. I feel disappointed. I feel ashamed. Like I've eaten a biscuit in Wonderland and shrunk to a tiny little Natalie on this chair. I'd hoped he'd grin, say, "You've got me," and tell me this beautiful story about how he and Russ orchestrated this in the hospital, making lists, dates, and songs. Idealistic, maybe, but it's what I wanted to happen. And now I just feel stupid. And I'm taking it out on the basil and this frankly disappointing carbless plate of food. "I just wondered if Russ had organized something like this—you know, like they do in films and stuff. Like Shauna said—"

"Shauna?"

"My friend. Her mum. She received flowers on her birthday for the first five years from her husband, Shauna's dad, after he died and he'd organized it with the florist—"

"It isn't me," he says. "And I don't know if Russ would be up for things like that, to be honest." And those words—those words feel like he's just puked up a grenade and it's sitting between us on the table. When Edie first told me about her and Russ, most painful was the feeling like there was an edge to Russ I didn't know. A shadow I was never privy to. This—being told Russ wouldn't be up for doing something like this for me, when he was more quietly romantic, more thoughtful than anyone else I know—feels like that again. A little twist in the gut. A little "You don't know him like you think you do." When I do. I did and I do.

"No?" I say simply.

"I know he was a soppy sod sometimes, Nat—"

"He was."

"But . . . you know. Something like that." He moves his plate across the table and leans, lacing his fingers together on the surface. "What I mean is, I don't think he expected to . . . *leave us.* So I wonder if he'd have even thought to plan anything."

I say nothing, and I nod, just twice. Max is right. The injustice was that weeks after Russ was thrown off his bike, weeks of an induced coma, waiting and waiting for scary test results to point to hope, he was getting *better.* He was recovering. His vision even improved quickly, something doctors said might never happen. He was seeing everything in twos at first, the result of a head trauma—"There's two of you, one Natalie on top of the other," he'd say with a smile, "I can deal with it, but not sure the world could"—and then it migrated into slightly blurred vision. He was recovering fast. Then: an infection. That was fast too, how it took him. It was all too fast. The split second it took for that car to mount the curb, to drive away. The loss of our life as we knew it, the loss of his.

"Look, if it is him, Nat," says Maxwell gently, "he didn't ask me."

"Right," I say, tracing a finger along the stem of the cocktail glass. "OK. Sorry for wasting your time or for sounding . . . *mad*—"

"Don't be silly," Maxwell replies, but his eyes slide to the salad and then he looks at his phone, and I know he's trying to work out in his head how much longer he'll have to stay here. He's uncomfortable. He wishes he wasn't here. But nevertheless, he reaches a nervous hand over the table and puts it on mine. "I'm sorry I didn't have . . . better news."

"Sorry I bit your head off."

"You didn't. And sorry for the basil."

I smile. "You should be," I reply, and Maxwell laughs with relief, retracting his hot, clammy hand.

"So, tell me about work," he says, and I do, just to heal it over, this shared little open wound, and just so the last thing he remembers me saying isn't "I hate basil." And then he wipes his mouth with a crisp, white napkin and tosses it down onto the tablecloth. "Look, I'm sorry, Nat, but I've got to run. I have a massive meeting about this new lettings venture we're launching, and it's—"

"No, no, of course."

"But listen, I dunno what your plans are for the cottage, but your little village—*massively* sought-after at the minute."

"Really?"

"Yup. You know where I am if you want it valued, or if you just want some advice."

He stands, puts down three twenty-pound notes, which I know is far too much for two £8.95 salads.

"Order something you do like. On me."

"Max, don't be stupid—"

"Seriously." He smiles, then he leans to kiss me on the cheek. His aftershave really is too strong, but I'm sure he'll find a woman with a pedicure who'll love it. He's so vanilla. So straightlaced. As if he'd have ever pulled it off—this piano thing. It's far too cool for him. (No offense to him, of course.)

"Take care," he says, and when he leaves, I call over the kind, grinning waiter and order a cocktail (not a mock), plus the largest portion they have of tagliatelle and a side of salty French fries. On the way home, I put a big X on my notes app, under "Suspects," next to Maxwell's name.

chapter ten

They just offered me chips or a jacket potato. To have with our *breakfast*," Lucy says, slotting herself behind the wooden café table.

"So?"

"I ordered scrambled eggs on toast, Priya. You two ordered granola. The woman at the counter acted like it was the most normal thing in the world. I'll be mentioning this in my review."

Priya laughs. "Well, Luce, you do have a habit of choosing weird places. See: Avocado Clash, for example. I pooed for days after that meal. I thought I'd never stop."

People whisk by outside on the narrow streets of Soho, and for a day in May, it's as gloomy as early winter. The sky one big blank sheet of off-white, the rain lazy and mist-like. It's not often I get to see Priya and Lucy together these days—of course I see Priya at work, but it's not like it used to be. Regular lunches and cinema dates and drinks with Edie, Priya, Lucy, and her big sister Roxanne punctuated most weeks. But after Russ, and after Edie, it all changed. Abruptly, really. Plus, Roxanne's and Lucy's schedules are packed out. Lucy's especially. Bullet-journaled to death, with highlighter pens and stickers and motivational quotes from Mother Teresa and Britney Spears. Today, though, despite Roxanne being away with work, and Priya's day off for her second pregnancy scan, Lucy insisted we make it work. "Nonnegotiable," Lucy had said. Because it's my birthday. Age thirty-three. Today, I am thirty-three.

"Instagram said this place was nice," says Lucy with a little shrug, buttoning up her baby-pink vegan leather purse. "'Quirky' was the word they used. That Instagrammer I follow. Sarah-May-Be-Baeby."

"Oh, I like her," coos Priya, stirring her tea.

"Quirky," I say, patting lip balm onto my lips. "Aka weird or shit, and saying it's good only because she's been *paid* to."

Lucy shakes her head, her perfect, sandy, micro-bladed eyebrows knitting together. "No, no, she's not like that. She's honest. Really normal, down-to-earth and . . . Hang on, are these fortune cookies?"

"Yep," says Priya. "I opened mine. It said *Teach a man to fish.* That was it. So I guess I should get to that . . ."

Lucy cracks hers open with one hand. "Mine's . . ." Lucy looks up at us like a wounded puppy. "Empty. Completely hollow," and Priya laughs and says, "A meaner person than I would say *figures.*"

"Piss off." Lucy smirks, then she yelps at her phone and says, "Oh em gee. My architect has *finally* emailed." Lucy is exactly where I always thought she would be in life at twenty-nine. I met her through her big sister, Roxanne, who was my housemate at uni. Lucy went straight to college to study hair design, and she would breeze into our university house parties at age eighteen straight off the train like the polished TV presenter of a reality cleaning show. Immaculately beautiful and obliviously hypnotizing everyone she met, but being more interested in criticizing the state of our bins and "sleep hygiene." Lucy plans. She planned her career trajectory, she planned the age at which she would be engaged. (She met Carlie, her wife, within days of turning that age, on a dating app.) She also planned her home, which they are renovating now, and she's even planning what she wants her *taps* to say about them. She's obsessed with taps at the moment, and has a spreadsheet of front-runners and introduces them, like guests at a party. ("This is the Hanbury X5. It has five settings, an elegant swan neck, and enjoys billiards and sushi at the weekends.") Lucy's life is full. Busy. And she'll say, "I planned it that way." And sometimes it feels cruel. Because I did too. It's just my plan wasn't too keen on following itself through.

"And she's having triplets," Lucy carries on now, pouring a sachet of sweetener into her coffee. "Naturally conceived, too, I believe."

"Who?"

She tuts. "Sarah May-Be-Baeby, Natalie, play bloody attention."

Priya crunches a shard of cookie. "Blimey, this tastes like bunions. Does yours taste like bunions?"

"I was so happy for her." Lucy beams, ignoring us both. She's still on the Insta celeb. She's obsessed with some of them, forgets we don't actually *know them*. "And the way she announced her pregnancy was *so* adorable. So classic. I think we'd do the same."

"I don't even think I'm going to announce ours," says Priya. "Will's mum's the type to offer me a perineum massage and think that's completely normal."

"Did you see it, Nat?"

I stop downing my coffee and meet Lucy's eyes. "Did I see . . ." God, my brain today. I mean, it's always like it's been zapped in the microwave these days, boiled with cloves for Christmas lunch. But even more so today, I can't focus. All I keep thinking about is where I might've been on my birthday, if things had been different. Russ was so good at birthdays. Ignored his own, but mine—he always made me feel like the world's spotlight was on me, for one day. Amazing gifts, surprise holidays, gig tickets, messages from celebrities I used to love in the nineties . . .

"The post," carries on Lucy. "Sarah-May Baeliss, the Instagrammer. I sent it to you this morning. It's her birthday today too."

"Oh, no, sorry, I haven't even checked Instagram yet. I was running so late this morning." In truth, I have quite a strict Instagram habit. A quick scroll of the feed, and then a delicious, escapist check of the #musicians hashtag, all those geniuses, playing and singing like angels in their bedrooms. That's what Instagram is to me really. That, and quick meals I'll never ever try.

"Pipe probs?" asks Priya.

"No, no. Train probs actually. I was coming from the crem, and the usual train was—"

"The crematorium?" asks Lucy, and her eyes stay on me, like they're prized open with matchsticks.

"Yeah." I nod. "The crematorium."

"Oh, right," says Lucy. "I just—I didn't realize you'd been."

"Yep. It'd feel—weird not seeing him today."

"Course it would," says Priya, at the same time Lucy says, "Do you still go a lot then?"

Lucy still watches me, teacup at her perfect, pink mouth, steam wisping in front of her face, as Priya pretends to have seen something very important on the large, laminated menu on the table.

"I do. Every week usually, sometimes every two."

"Gosh," says Lucy. "I mean, I wasn't saying anything, you know . . . just . . ." She clears her throat. "*Anyway.* Shall we—have gifts? I'm *so* excited about my gift."

My heart sinks, like someone dropping a shot in a lake. She thinks I shouldn't still be going. I know she does, and shame wraps itself around me, like a heavy, invisible cloak, and shrinks me, right here on the chair.

"Gifts? I didn't think we did gifts anymore, just cards," says Priya. "God, I've only brought a card with me."

"I *know*, Pree, but Roxanne suggested it and then I couldn't stop thinking about it, and—it isn't much." Lucy wrinkles her nose at me and pushes an envelope across the table. "But I think it's just what you need, Nat."

The envelope is thick and square like a bathroom tile, as a greetings card, and my brain does a lightning-speed roll call of all the things it could be, as I run a finger under the paper seam. A spa voucher? A gift certificate for Lucy's salon? Oh, a gift voucher for a *dumpster*? A plumber? God, that'd be nice, actually—

"*Read it*," squeaks Lucy, as I open a folded piece of A4 paper inside a golden birthday card with bubbling champagne glasses on the front.

Oh. God.

> *Congratulations, NATALIE FINCHER, on signing up for . . .*
> *THE LOUNGE CLUB.*
> *OPEN MIC NIGHT CONTEST.*

Fucking hell.

> *10TH OCTOBER. £200 PRIZE. 8 HEATS. 4 SEMIFINALS.*
> *ONE GRAND PRIZE: £500 PLUS FULL EP RECORDING SESSION.*
> *DOORS OPEN AT 7 P.M.*

"Oh my god." Lucy laughs, butting the table with her midriff, causing it to shake. Coffee brims over the edge of my mug, spilling milky, brown liquid over the envelope. "She's gone *red*."

Priya stares at me, the way someone does waiting for a firework to take off and explode. And it just did. Inside my chest.

"Wow, I—is this—"

"We paid the entry fee," says Lucy. "Roxanne and I. Signed you up. You have to have three songs ready. They have a keyboard there, apparently. And a PA. Whatever that is."

"Oh," I say. "Right. Wow. This is—" I look up at Lucy, her face expectant, oblivious, and I force a smile. "Thank you. I'll, erm. I'll have to see if I can make it—"

"I think this is what you need," says Lucy. "It'll sort you out, work wonders. It's long overdue."

"Is it?" I ask, my voice tiny in the din of the busy café, and Lucy steamrolls over my words.

"As soon as Rox told me about it, I thought, it's a sign. A sign that it was your birthday coming up, a sign that we found out about it when we did—"

"Wow," I say again, like a broken robot. "And—the Lounge Club. Isn't that . . . didn't Edie host events at the Lounge Club?"

Lucy's eyes now slide toward Priya, fingers holding a spoon in her mug, and something lands in my gut. A deep knowing before she's said even a word.

"Oh, erm—I . . . *yes*," says Lucy, the word like a Band-Aid, pulled.

"You saw her? You saw Edie?"

"Well. Bumped into her. It's London, isn't it, small bloody world, and she needed her roots done and we went for coffee after," says Lucy, barely a breath between the words, and I know Lucy. She can't lie. When Lucy lies, when Lucy has to keep a secret, it's like she's got a mouth full of goldfish, and she's waiting waiting for the moment she can spew them out and set them free.

"Oh. Right. I didn't realize—"

"She's still in London, yes. Still living locally. Of course, she has to be, for the show." And I shove down the urge to say, "That wasn't what I was going to say actually, Lucy." I was going to say I didn't realize you were friends again. Behind my back. "We just thought, so much time has passed since—you know. The musical, and the funeral and everything and—well—you have to move forward, don't you? And she really thinks you'll enjoy it," and while words, so many hot, fiery words circle, like a tornado in my mouth, the fortune cookie in my fist shatters.

"Oh!" yelps Priya. "Er . . . so, what does it say?"

I look down at the words in my palm. "A feather in the hand is much better than a bird in the air."

"Er, *what*?" Priya laughs as Lucy squeaks, "See! How much more of a sign do we need?"

♫   ♫   ♫
   ♫   ♫   ♫

I thought this is what I wanted. The ideal, really—another piece of music, and on my birthday, after a soul-destroying brunch with my friends. But it's floored me a little, today. I feel knocked out. Like someone just punched me in the gut, knocked me on my arse. Drained every last bit of energy from me. I was so happy to see it at first, that spark of excitement surging through me like a comet, and the song—it's Nervous Alibi by the Outfield and it was one of my favorites, growing up. I remember hearing it and thinking it was one of the most desperate, saddest songs I'd ever heard, and asking my dad for the name of the song. I'd always add it to mix tapes I'd make for Russ in uni, and I learned it, those beautiful opening notes, and played it for him at the hospital. A kind receptionist had printed it for me. I knew it would make him laugh, hearing it, because he was always so amused at how one of *our songs* was a song about someone who didn't trust their partner to an—in my opinion—unnerving degree. "Not exactly first-dance material is it?" Russ would laugh. How can this not be him? How can Maxwell be in the dark about this? This has to be Russ. I don't understand it, but it *has to be Russ.*

Then I try to play it. I place my fingers on the keys, but my fingers freeze, as if my joints are refusing to take part in this today. I can't. I press the first chord. I stop. Crowds swarm past me, things to do, places to go, lives to lead. And my heart aches, among them all, like a squashed peach in my chest. I think of the brunch this morning. I think of the open mic night. Maybe this isn't Russ. Maybe this isn't someone doing this for *good*. Maybe it's—my friends. Maybe it's Edie. Someone trying to make me do or be something I'm not ready for. I look up, and there's her poster. Of course it is. Bold as brass, glittering— bloody *goading me*.

"Heeeeey," says a voice, "well, if it isn't Natalie from the bar. You gonna serenade us?"

I drop my hands from my head and stare up at him. Tom, from the bar. Tom the Target. Tom the bloody stand-in who always seems to be knocking about wherever I am.

"What?"

The warm smile slides off his face. "Are you—are you OK?"

I glance up at him, and then at the piece of music on the piano stand. My head is full of tangles—like a handful of spaghetti in my skull. I don't know what this is, and now I don't know who to trust. If I can't trust my friends, then *who's left*?

"Why are you always here?" tumbles out of my mouth, and Tom looks blankly at me.

"W-what? Why am I—"

"Here? Why are you always here? I mean, I'm not even here all that often really, myself, not compared to like, a commuter or something, and whenever I am, you seem to be too, and I . . . I'm just asking you, what are you actually doing here? Again?"

Tom looks over his shoulder, as if expecting to see a film crew from a prank show, hiding behind a shop window display, ready to burst out and say, "You've been punked, my man!" and oh, how we'd then *laugh*.

"Natalie, this is—this is London. This is *a train station*—"

"I know what it is," I say, my voice wobbling, "but what I'm asking is why? Do you—is this you?" I grab at the piece of piano music, and he looks at me like I might as well be talking to him in a language understood only on Saturn. I lose my grip on it and it drifts to the floor, like an overgrown feather. "Shit . . ."

Tom slowly bends to the floor and picks it up, before placing it back on the piano, in the stand, but he stays crouched, so he's level with me, here, on the stool.

"I'm here because my studio, where I work, is two tube stops along. I'm working on something for an exhibition at the moment, around here. And my mum—she works here. In the station. And I drop in on her a lot. Keep an eye on her."

I blink. "OK," I sniff. "Work. Family. Good answer." Jesus, this poor bloke. Everything I stuffed down at brunch, after that bloody open mic night, has just been aimed and directed at poor Tom. "I'm sorry," I say.

Tom gives a small smile—a tiny upward curl, just a shadow.

"Your mum works here?"

"Yeah, she works in the coffee place. Upstairs."

"Goode's?" What feels like a brick falls from my heart to my stomach. "*Shauna*?"

His blue eyes narrow, a bristle of dark lashes, then he nods reluctantly. ". . . Yeah?"

"You're—you're her . . . oh my god, are you one of the twins?"

He laughs then, a deep chuckle. "That's me."

"Laurie and *Thomas*."

He laughs again. "Yeah, she's the only human being on earth who calls me *Thomas*. And what, you know her? That's . . . wild . . ."

"I'm a regular customer. She's—I love your mum."

Tom gives a slow, easy smile. "Snap," he says.

A group of teenagers thunder past us on the tiles, roaring with laughter, as another of them trails behind. "Eh, wait, yeah?" he shouts after his friends, and when I look down, he's wearing only one trainer. He hobbles off after them.

"And look," says Tom, gently. "I don't know what this is all about, but I'm not responsible for—whatever this is." His blue eyes flick to the sheet music. "Plus, looks too clever for me. I was just gonna say a big boring hi. Very uncreative. Good tune, though. Retro."

"I'm sorry," I say again, looking at him, crouched down here with me. Handsome, kind eyes. And clearly clueless when it comes to having something to do with this weird, wonderful, batshit charade. "Honestly, I am, I'm just—"

"Tired," he offers.

"God—do I look tired?" I feel relieved, really, that he has at least seen me *once* looking decent and behaving at least half normal. The last time he saw me I was sopping wet and trying to hide my face behind a pair of glasses, and today—today I've presented to him, a madwoman.

He shrugs a shoulder, a cock toward his ear.

"Great. Thanks."

Tom chuckles. "Well, you're allowed to say this stuff to someone who declared they really, really don't fancy you whatsoever in front of a crowd of Avocado Clashers, right? Me. Vince Vaughn. We don't stand a chance."

Despite myself, despite how shit and hollow and like an empty vessel of a human I feel, I laugh. "Plus, I did just speak to you like shit in a train station," I add, "and before you go to work and see *your mum.*"

"Exactly—"

"Who is actual Shauna. Who I talk to every single week. Who I love, and look to like an oracle."

Tom laughs, and now I know, it's so obvious. Tom has Shauna's nose, and the cleft in the chin. The crinkles by the eyes when he smiles—they're hers too.

Tom straightens, adjusts the strap of his rucksack that's tossed over his shoulder. "So, do you wanna . . . walk or something? I've got an hour to kill and—you look like you might need it."

I nod, just once. I know what Shauna has said about her sons, and if she's telling the truth, as oracles often do, he wouldn't be the worst person to talk to. And I need to—to talk to someone who isn't going to look at me like Lucy did, over granola and unsolicited jacket potatoes.

"Sure," I say. Then, "It's my birthday."

Tom's eyebrows shoot up. "Today?"

"Yup."

"Well, that's—*tragic*, Natalie. Seriously."

"Thanks very much, Tom."

"We need to at least get you a cake," he says, holding out a hand. "And a tissue for your eyes, too. You're looking like—I dunno, the *Scream* painting, sitting there. Not a good look." He flashes a smile as I get to my feet. "For you. But especially for me."

♪   ♪   ♪
 ♪   ♪   ♪

Tom leads us out of the station and onto Camley Street. The May sun is out now, high and proud, and the air is a thick mixture of warm, damp pavements, garlic from nearby restaurants, and exhaust fumes.

"You, er—ever been to the nature reserve?" Tom asks, looking up and down the busy road, waiting for a space between traffic to reveal itself.

"There's a nature reserve? In Kings Cross?"

Tom looks to his side at me and smiles, a breeze ruffling his dark hair. "Yep. First time I ever saw a heron was at this place, believe it or not." We cross the road to the opposite pavement, leafier and greener than the other side, as a moped buzzes by, like an overgrown bee. "So, the heron—take a guess at what it had in its mouth."

"Erm, I don't know. What do they even eat?"

"Well, *guess*."

"Um. A fish?"

"Boring."

"OK—a margarita then?" I smile.

He grins. "Surprisingly, way off."

"Guacamole? *Huevos rancheros*?"

"Amazingly, still way off." He laughs. "A rat."

"Oh my *god*."

"I know. So, so grim. I took some photos. I'll have to show you sometime. Heron with massive rat."

"Um. *Sure*."

"Ah, come on, Natalie," he says, nudging an arm to mine, "that's one of my best lines."

Tom slows as we come to a dropped curb—an entranceway—and a pair of tall, wrought-iron gates, like those at the entrance to a zoo in a children's book. An arched metal sign above spells Camley Street Natural Park.

"God," I say, "I had no idea this was here."

"It's a cool little place," he replies. "And maybe we'll see another heron."

"With a *rat*," I say, following Tom down the wide pathway.

"Only if you're lucky."

A few steps on the damp pavement, and the nature reserve swallows us up, envelops us, from the bustle. It's beautiful and messy and wild—one of those places that make you want to say, "You could be anywhere, couldn't you?" And Russ would love this. Russ loved nature, and of course, as comes naturally to gardeners, loved plants and flowers—anything that grows. He loved getting lost somewhere new, too, and not so much heaving cities, or coastal towns, like me, but somewhere like this. Quiet and slow and hidden. And although mud and wet leaves and weird scratchy animal sounds aren't really my thing, today I'm glad to be here, among it all. The air smells like last night's rain and wet soil, and the sun streams through the canopy of trees above our heads, creating lacy shadows at our feet. Already, hidden here, among the trees and leaves and tiny cubbies of reeds and murky water, my head feels clearer, and I feel like a bit of a dick really, for crying on Tom. At a public piano. Like a strange modern art installation. *You see here a woman trapped by her past, being taunted by the only thing she ever trusted in: music.*

"So." Tom slots his hands into his jeans' pockets, beside me on the path. "Your birthday . . ."

"My birthday," I repeat. "Lucky thirty-three. Not sure how that happened to be honest. I feel like one minute I was twenty-one and the next—*poof.* Here I am."

Tom gives a slow smile. "It was lucky thirty-four for me this year," he says. "Not sure how that happened either."

"I was sort of hoping to ignore it, actually."

"And then I bought you a cake," says Tom. "Rubbed your nose in it. Sorry about that."

"And called me tragic."

Tom laughs. "A birthday full house."

"Plus, my friends remembered," I say. "And I had the world's weirdest and shittiest birthday brunch."

"Oh yeah?"

"Yeah," I say as we follow an overgrown path, deeper into the reserve, brushing by nettles, the air thick with the oniony smell of cut grass and wet plants.

"You gonna give me any more than that?" asks Tom.

"Do you *want* any more than that?"

"Um." Tom laughs, says nothing, but holds his hands out in front of him, a gesture to the damp, leafy surroundings, as if to say, "Well, I'm here, in a nature reserve with you on a Thursday morning, aren't I, wise guy?"

"Fine," I say. "Pity party it is."

"Good. Beats a birthday party, in my opinion." Tom shrugs. "You always know what you're getting with a pity party. They're at least nice and reliable."

And as I walk along with Tom beneath the shade of the trees, pebbles and twigs and old leaves crunching beneath our feet, I let all the words spill out of me. I tell him about the piano music. And then I tell him about Russ, and the hospital and the communal piano I'd play as he listened in his bed. And how finding the music has sparked something in me—something new, something unknown and exciting—until brunches, like this morning, that make me feel like I'm living the world's saddest life. I tell him about the present then too—Lucy and Roxanne treating me like a project they just need to get off the ground, and I tell him about falling out with Edie, and how my friends have seen her—had bloody *coffee* with her. And I don't even think I've been talking all that long until I realize I've seen the same class of pond-dipping children, twice.

"The piano music thing is—" Tom blows a long breath through his lips.

"You think I'm mad, right? That I'm losing the plot—"

"No way," he replies, strolling beside me. "I mean—what do people think, you're . . . *miraging* these pieces of music or something?"

"I think maybe some people might think so. That I needed hope and excitement, so I—dreamed it up."

Tom shakes his head. "Seriously—"

"Maxwell thinks it. I think he thinks I've crossed over. That I'm a hop, skip, and a jump away from talking to myself on the bus, dressing my twenty cats in wedding dresses—"

"Who the bloody hell's Maxwell?"

"Oh, Russ's best friend," I say. "I thought it might be him. You know, that maybe Russ had organized it in hospital or something, when things started to deteriorate. In case the worst happened. Like it did."

Tom nods slowly. "And he knew nothing about it?"

"Nothing."

Up ahead, a couple walk slowly, a toddler in a fire-engine-red raincoat between them, their hands paper-chained in a row. "I asked to meet him for lunch, and we went to this Italian place near work, in Camden, and firstly, he ordered us *salad*—"

"Salad?" asks Tom. "What a piece of shit."

I burst out laughing.

I love that Tom is funny, and *actually* funny. Hard to come by, I've always thought, funny guys, but then again, I've not got to know a man since Russ, really. Priya is always saying, "You'll have no idea what's out there if you don't keep your eyes open, Nat," and I always ask her whether she's talking about new life experiences or vintage bargains buried deep in tatty boxes at car boot sales.

"Anyway," I say. "I asked Maxwell outright."

"If it was him leaving the music?"

"Yep. And he said no. Then looked at me like I'd just squatted naked on the table over the breadsticks or something, so that was nice. And I knew for sure then that it wasn't him."

Tom laughs unexpectedly, his chin tipped back. "And what sort of look is that, by the way?" he says. "The squatted-naked-on-a-table-over-breadsticks one. Sorry, but I like to have all the visuals when I'm being told a story. I like an immersive experience."

"It was like—" I look up at him and scrunch my forehead into a scared, confused frown.

"Interesting. I was thinking more—"

Tom stops on the leafy path and pulls his face into a horrified, horror-movie grimace.

"Close." I laugh, and we carry on walking. "Uncanny, actually. That was like looking right at him."

"*Shit*," he says. "So Maxwell thinks you're mad."

"As a hatter. But how else am I supposed to feel? It's music, you know . . . left for me. Or at least it seems that way. Surely, anyone normal would at least wonder. And I've enjoyed it really. The excitement of it. The spark."

"The spark," repeats Tom. "I get it. And plus, this Maxwell dude, he can't judge, right? A man who orders salad in an Italian restaurant . . ."

"And he wears really bad curly shoes too."

"Ah." Tom's hand flies up to his chest, and it lands with a thump. "The man is a villain, the devil himself."

"Shoes and salad," I say. "Says a lot about someone."

"All you need to know."

We come to a gap in the overgrowth, and slow. A bench shaped like a giant concrete staple sits on the mulchy ground, overlooking the murky canal, trees arching above it like reaching hands.

"Shall we sit?" asks Tom.

♫   ♫   ♫
    ♫   ♫   ♫

Narrow boats sit moored up opposite us, and a little chimney of one of them, painted burgundy and blue, plumes a haze of smoke into the air. They're cooking inside, I think. I can smell bacon and burnt toast. Memories flood my head, like a thumb removed from the opening of a hose. Out of nowhere. Clear and as vivid as a movie.

"We used to go on a narrow boat holiday every year," I say.

"You and Russ?" asks Tom. He's holding an old, amber-colored leaf, ironing it out between his fingers.

"Yep. Every October, without fail. I booked one when he was in hospital. A sort of—message to the universe that we *would* be going and he *would* be getting out of that bed and out of that hospital. We didn't end up going of course, but . . . I have nice memories of them, narrow boats."

Tom nods slowly. "What happened to him? The accident. I mean, you don't have to say of course, just . . ."

"No, it's fine." There's something freeing in talking about the accident itself. Almost as if the more I talk about it, the realer it becomes. Like the lines of the drawing getting darker and darker the more it's gone over and over. And the realer it becomes, the easier, slowly but surely, it gets to look it in the eye. Accept it. "He was cycling to work. I was taking the car, and he said he'd take his bike. Said he'd go the scenic route—the A roads. And—we'll never know everything that happened, but someone, from what they could tell, veered into him, mounted this tiny curb, and he was thrown off his bike. Then they drove away."

"Shit," says Tom. "God, I'm so sorry, Natalie, that's . . . awful."

I nod. Because it is. It's not the accident so much as that someone drove away. I comfort myself sometimes, imagining them frightened, *terrified*, crying just as much as I was. Driving off like it was nothing is what I can't stand the thought of. Because he was everything.

"He was put into an induced coma for a while. That was awful. Like some sort of hellish limbo, you know? I had no idea if I was going to lose him or not, and if I didn't, when he came around, would he still even be Russ? Would he remember me? What state would he be in? Not just then, but—forever. It was . . . it was like being trapped in purgatory. Time didn't exist, seasons, other people, life. Just—him."

"And did he wake up?" asks Tom softly. A bird tweets rhythmically, like a distant alarm, in the tree above us.

"He did. And he was Russ. Tired and confused and in pain, unable to move his legs, but—*him*. I will never forget the smile when he woke up. The relief was . . . I felt like someone had looked down and had mercy on me, or something. I couldn't believe he was there. And that's when I started playing piano for him. They had this donated piano and . . . it's good therapy, you know? Not just for him, but other people in the ward too."

Tom nods.

"And he was doing really well. They started talking about physio and everything and then—he got an infection. And . . . it was so fast. I went home that night, packed him some more clothes, his favorite book, and by the time I got there the next morning, they told me to . . . prepare. And an hour later." I swallow. "Gone."

Tom's chest rises and falls. "I'm so sorry," he says.

"I always felt like he was waiting for me. They say that, don't they? That—they wait, people who are dying. For people to leave, or to arrive, or . . . *anyway*." I dab at my eyes, at tears I had no idea were even coming, and Tom intercepts with a packet of pocket tissues. "Thanks." I laugh. "Happy birthday to me."

Tom smiles softly. "You certainly know how to celebrate."

I laugh through my tears. "Come on. Let's see this cake."

"Right," says Tom, "cake. Of course," and between his feet, on the ground, he unzips his bag and pulls out a small cake box. He'd made me wait outside Paul Express on the way out of the station and strolled in, before coming out, hand at the thick strap of his rucksack over his shoulder, and saying, "An old lady in there just stopped me and told me I had lovely, sturdy legs. She actually said *sturdy*," and I'd laughed when she'd floated out a moment later in a fur stole and smiled at him.

"Here," he says now, placing a white, glossy box on the bench between us. "Birthday cake—well, tarts, apparently. Still counts, though. I checked."

Warmth spreads beneath my skin, like syrup, the tears on my cheeks drying in the sun. *God.* Who'd have ever seen this coming? Me and Tom the Target from the bar, on a bench, either side of two strawberry tarts, in a nature reserve on my birthday. But then it's life, isn't it? Weird and unexpected and unknown. It's all it ever used to be for me, once a time. Even though Russ and I, like most people, lived a relatively routine-y, same-things-on-the-same-day sort of life, and as much as we planned to cram so much into our lives together, sponta-neity still ran through it, like a vein. Random dinners out, in restau-rants, on a Wednesday night after work, an impromptu last-minute weekend away, unplanned nights and other people's pajamas when staying over at a friend's after a barbecue went on for too long. And I've missed it, this feeling. I've missed it a lot.

"Thank you," I say. "For the birthday tarts."

Tom nods, crosses his arms. "No worries."

"Seriously. They're officially my favorite thirty-third-birthday gift."

Tom gives a laugh and looks up, squinting at the sun streaming in through the trees. "Ah, well, I reckon you should raise your standards a bit, Natalie, to be honest." Then he turns to me and says, "But then—you did get an open mic night you didn't want and a big ol' Judas stab in the back, so . . ."

"The tarts win."

"By a landslide." He laughs.

A duck skirts across the water, three tiny chicks lagging behind, and someone on a neighboring narrow boat steps out from inside and hangs a towel on an old-looking wooden airer.

"I actually used to want to live on a narrow boat," says Tom. "I used to sometimes pretend I did. When I was a kid. Used to sit on my bed, like . . ." Tom holds a hand to his face like a visor, a sailor looking to sea, and laughs.

"That's quite adorable."

"Think it was envy. My best mate in school, Ben, used to go on boating holidays with his dad and stuff. They were one of those families, you know? Dad comes home at night with a briefcase, kisses his wife on the head, tells them all he's missed them, waffles about quality time together and means it. Brady Bunch–level shit."

"Nah, those people are too perfect."

"Yeah, you're probably right," says Tom. "But I always wanted to do the same. Though . . . my dad. *Not* a boating holiday, head-kissing sort of guy."

"Don," I say, with a nod.

"Don," repeats Tom.

"I can't actually believe your dad is Don. Actual Shauna's Don . . ."

Tom raises his eyebrows and sighs. "Yup. Me either, some-times."

Behind us, the class of schoolchildren, in high-vis vests and welly boots, trundle past.

"Well, if it makes you feel any better, I used to pretend I lived an apartment, in California," I say, "with floor-to-ceiling windows and this amazing view, and . . . with Christian Slater actually. He used to make linguine and hang the washing out."

"*Christian Slater.*" Tom laughs. "You said you live in—Bournebridge, right?"

"Yep. Life had other plans for me. No Christian Slater or floor-to-ceiling windows as yet. I live in a cottage. But it's a proper project. Totally falling down, needs a new kitchen, new bathroom, new—fucking *everything* really. That was our plan. To fix it up."

Tom stares at me for a second, and like a lightbulb pinged on in his head, he points a finger at me. "You're the girl. With the cottage. And the pipes."

"That's me." I laugh. "Jesus."

"What?" Tom chuckles, stretching his long legs out in front of him on the wet grass, crossing them at the ankles.

"Nothing, just—you're Shauna's Thomas. Thomas the twin. Her *Tommy Button.* Tommy Button Madden. Right here. A meet and greet with the real deal—"

"Oh, shit, she says that? To actual strangers? Tommy Button . . ."

"I'm afraid she does. Jason really ribs her about it. That and the fact she calls Laurie and Mark her *squishes.*"

"Laurie'll die when I tell him that." Tom looks at me side on and smiles. "I can help, by the way. With the house. If you want it. Roofing, tiling—that's what I did before the photos. Like the rest of the . . . *squishes.*"

"Before you started collecting Adam Driver stories to share with women you have to pretend to stand up in bars?"

"Actually," Tom says, as the owner of the narrow boat comes out again and hangs two more towels on the airer. One says, *Sea you later* and has a cartoon of a dolphin on it. "Sort of got a confession. Do you know Si, my mate, who was there that night?"

"The night we met?"

"Yeah. Well, about an hour before you came over, he'd set me up with this girl. For similar reasons to yours. Can't bear me being single."

"*Really?*"

"Yup." He nods. "It was—*bad.* She talked a lot about Justin Timberlake. And then she kept staring down at my crotch like there was a movie screening on it. And I wanted rid of her."

"Bloody hell." I laugh. "*Oh.* Hang on. *I* was also a stand-in?"

"Yep." Tom grins. "I even told them you stood *me* up. That when I got back from the bathroom, you'd gone, and I was gutted."

"So, I was nothing but a poor little pawn."

"Afraid so," says Tom. "Natalie, the poor little unsuspecting pawn . . ."

"With nothing but an open mic night and frozen pipes to her name," I say. "And . . . why don't you just tell your friends to stop?"

Tom laughs. "I'm sorry, are *you* asking me that? The woman who made me talk about my job just to kill time in front of *her* friends?"

After a few moments, we stand from the bench, and Tom bends to pick up his bag.

"And how are your pipes these days, by the way," he says, "if I may ask?"

"Bit personal for a Thursday, Thomas."

And as he passes me my birthday tarts, holding the box for a second longer than needed, he looks me in the eyes and says, "That's Thomas Button. To you."

chapter eleven

I stare down at the text message from Shauna as beside me Priya, her nostrils flared, serves a customer. Her morning sickness has tapered off a great deal, but at lunchtime, when food from nearby stalls and restaurants wafts in, she takes breaks to sniff from a Tupperware full of freshly cut lemons to stop the queasiness it sometimes prompts. It's the only thing that helps. That and Pizza Hut chicken wings.

"Nothing again today, angel," the text says. "I'll look again later, but I say it's one hundred percent something that only happens on the days you're knocking about! WE'RE CIRCLING EVER CLOSER!!!" Disappointment settles in my stomach like a stone. Sometimes it feels unbearable not knowing who it is, and sometimes, so exciting I feel like I might explode, grab passersby, say, "Have you heard about this thing that's happening to me? Yes, me! Me, Natalie Fincher!" Lately, it's all that keeps me awake at night (when the foxes aren't copping off), with berry tea and Russ's old smelly Neanderthal books: who is leaving it for me, and why the stool has been empty for a week, since my birthday. Because I don't want it to stop, this sunbeam in the dark. I avoided for years playing those songs again, thinking it'd be like opening a wound, thinking cynically that revisiting happy times from the past was just for the delusional, for people who don't want to admit how shit life is without them. But instead, playing them—Russ's favorite song, our wedding song, that Outfield tune . . . it really is the opposite. It's healing. It brings back such happy memories I'd forgotten, and so vividly, it's like I'm living them again, eyes closed, fingers on the keys. Whoever is leaving it has given me that, along with so much more. The thought of it stopping makes me want to be sick.

"You all right?" Priya asks, her nose poised over the little, square tub in her hand. "Oh, sweet Jesus, these are losing their smell. It's not that I'm even sick. I just hate that hot food smell at the moment . . ."

I smile. "Yeah, I'm fine. Just a text from Shauna. Are you all right?"

"I shall live," she says, bringing a lemon slice to her nose. "And Shauna? Is she the woman at the coffee shop?"

"Yep. We're staking out the piano."

I told Priya about the piano a few days ago. I couldn't not. I wanted to tell her I'd seen Tom again—Tom who made the effort and polished his own shoes—and I couldn't really tell her until I'd told her about the music. She'd beamed when I'd told her. Not just about Tom, although she screamed at that, despite my insistence that it was absolutely not a date, more a rescue, and told me she would very likely have another sleep-gasm now she knew about him buying me a birthday tart. Polished shoes. Pastry. She's easily bowled over. The bar so low, it's only just skimming the ground. But she beamed mostly about the station piano. "I think it's beautiful, Natalie. The music itself, course, but that you play. I think it's bloody gutsy. Brave. But then you do have balls of steel. Always have."

"Have you got any ideas about who it could be yet?" Priya asks sweetly, a lemon slice between her skinny fingers.

"Nope. The mystery continues."

"It's exciting, isn't it?"

"Totally. But—saying that, there's been nothing the last two times."

"Really? That's disappointing." Priya rubs the tiny bump beneath her orange wrap dress absentmindedly and sits down as the customer flits off, out into the busy, sunny street. She's twenty weeks now. Halfway to being someone who has a baby in their arms. Priya. With a baby. Nothing makes you feel more like "Oh shit, so we are actually adults then" than when your friend has a child. "I was talking to Will about it at the weekend," carries on Priya, "and he was proper invested. I mean, we actually paused *Love Island Australia* so we could discuss who we thought it could be, and I'm so addicted to it, I keep talking in an Aussie accent. It's quite a good one actually . . ."

I laugh. "And what's the verdict?"

"On the recoupling?"

"Er, no I mean, what does Will think? About the piano stuff?"

"*Oh.*" Priya giggles and rolls her round, brown eyes. "Bloody hell, am I OK? My head's firmly up my arse at the moment. Sorry. Yes. So, Will reckons it's someone who likes you. Someone you know, or don't know, but an admirer . . ."

"Really? Shauna said the same." I don't add that the list of suspects on my phone has grown. I've added Edie, although I wish I didn't need to. Ever since last week and that bloody open mic night thing, she suddenly seems quite an obvious choice (but a choice I truly hope comes to nothing). Before Russ had his accident, we were about to start workshopping a musical we'd written together. *Dotted Line*—a funny, satirical show about the music business—and she had badly wanted me to carry on. "It might be good for you, to have a distraction, Nat. Get away from the hospital." And when I didn't, she started auditioning again, all the while telling me I should think about the workshopping again, think about playing somewhere other than in the hospital again. I'd taken it as my best friend trying to help me through an awful time, but after the funeral, and after our falling-out,

I doubted everything about her. Our entire friendship. The years and years of love. And now she's back, apparently telling my friends about open mic nights she's running and recommending that I take part, like an entitled, proprietary know-it-all, it seems like it could very well be her. I don't know who I hope it *is* (besides Russ, in some way), but I know I'd prefer it wasn't anything to do with Edie Matthews. Because it'll all be for her own conscience. So she can assuage her guilt. *See, look, I know I hurt her, but she's fine now—look, she's even performing again! And I helped*!

"And what do you think?" I ask Priya, pulling a tangle of hangers from a bin under the counter. It's Jodie's worst job, sorting the hangers and the different types, but weirdly I enjoy it. It's banal. It's mind-numbing. Something you can do without really thinking.

"I don't know." Priya twists a lock of brown, glossy hair around her finger. "I can't decide. I just know it's so romantic I can't cope."

"Well, that's if it isn't someone totally *unromantic*."

"I'm sort of hoping it's Russ," says Priya. "In some way. You know?"

I smile. "I think the same most of the time."

"And I know some people might think that's mad," adds Priya, rustling through her handbag now, probably for peppermint tea bags, or who knows, a secret stashed-away chicken wing (nothing would surprise me), "but I dunno. I have a nice feeling about it. That it'll lead somewhere. Somewhere good."

And she would. Priya is the world's most eternal optimist. She has the kindest, purest heart, especially if you compare her to the rest of us. Unlike Roxanne (and Lucy, who came in a sort of two-for-one deal with her sister), I didn't meet Priya at university. I met her at my first job out of uni, working behind the bar at a tiny live music venue. I would spend every waking moment trying to avoid pulling pints so I could, instead, watch the music and meet other musicians, other people in the know, for Edie and me (we were determined at that time to get a record deal for an eighties pop sound we were trying), and Priya would spend most of her time counseling drunk girls on why they deserved better than the bass player who hadn't looked at them all night. "You're so pretty and intelligent," she'd say, "and I know you don't believe me, but I spoke to him earlier and he was really boring and smelled awful. Like scalp. Like dirty, sweaty scalp. Do you want a boyfriend who smells like scalp? Course you don't. You deserve better. Trust me." Priya is a girl's girl; a woman's woman.

"Priya?"

"Mm?" She looks up from her sliced lemons.

"Did you know about Edie?" I ask. "The coffee . . ."

Priya hesitates, her brown eyes widening. She slowly shakes her head. "No, Nat," she says sadly. "I mean, Lucy told me about the open mic night thing a couple of days before your birthday, and I was against putting you forward really. I was more—on the fence. I didn't realize they did it as an actual gift. And I know they meant well, but . . . Edie . . ." Priya's sentence fades into silence, until she puts down her little plastic tub again and leans across to me and says, "I'm sorry she saw her. That she had coffee with her. And I wouldn't ever want to throw her under the bus, but . . . I wouldn't have. Not without talking to you first at the very least."

I nod. "I know."

"And not because it's my business, the thing between you and Edie, because it isn't. But . . . because it would've been without you knowing."

And I suppose, that's exactly it. What happened between us, and what happened between Edie and Russ all those years ago, isn't really anyone's business but ours. At the same time, my friends know how much it hurt me—how much Edie hurt me—that Lucy could have at least gently and softly mentioned it. But Lucy likes everything in lines, everything clean. She likes friendships how they've always been, and in her mind, it'll be *best friends, fall out, move on, best friends again.* Clean. A to B. That's why this open mic night is nothing but a project. A "make Natalie better" project. A "make Natalie back to normal" project.

"I've got this list of people it could be, leaving the music," I tell Priya, "and I've added Edie to it."

Priya's eyebrows knit together. "God—really? I mean—why would she—"

"She wants to make amends. To quell her own guilt, or something."

"Then surely she'd just . . . call you?" says Priya. "That's one thing that's bothering me about it all, actually. If it's someone you know, why are they doing it anonymously? It's like Lucy said, if it's someone we know—"

"Does Lucy know?" I cut in. "About the music?"

"Did you not tell her? She—she didn't act like she didn't know, she acted like she'd seen you recently."

"I haven't seen her." She'd wanted to. Lucy had sent a text a few days ago—breakfast, she'd suggested, with her and Roxanne, but I'd lied, said I was busy.

Priya freezes and then looks down at her feet. She wriggles her toes in her white slider sandals and looks sheepishly back up at me. "She did ask me a lot of questions. I didn't think. Ugh. I just assumed she knew because you'd told me and—I sort of just said about it, how exciting it was, and she didn't exactly say, 'What are you on about?' So I just assumed . . ." Of course she didn't. Lucy hates to be the last to know anything, because of what that says about her. She wants to be the A-plus, passed-with-a-first friend. She would've hated to say to Priya, "What? Natalie never told me that. I'm out of the loop" because that's almost admitting out loud that she isn't someone's absolutely perfect first choice. (Lucy once read a book on how to be a good friend and carried it around with a highlighter pen.)

"God, I hope that's OK, Nat."

"No, no, of course it is, sorry, I just . . . what did she say?"

"Oh—nothing really."

"*Priya.*"

Priya's eyes close and she winces, her red-painted lips dimpling at the corners. "She thinks maybe you forgot about them. That they're your pieces of music, and you just forgot you kept them in there."

"So I'm planting them on myself."

"But she didn't say it meanly, honestly, she didn't. I think—I think she just worries about you. She's super happy you're playing again, though—"

"Does she worry? It's just she never actually asks me how I am or if I'm OK, not properly . . . Are you worried about me?"

Priya stares at me for a moment, then steps closer, stretches a hand over to mine, holding the tips of my fingers. She smells like lemon zest. "Nat," she says, every bit that counseling barmaid with the Doc Martens and flowers in her hair. "Am I allowed to say sometimes?"

I soften. "I suppose."

"Then: *sometimes.* Because of course I do, and I love you. But in general—no. Absolutely not."

"Why not?"

Priya smiles at that. "Because you're Natalie Fincher. Like I said. Balls of steel."

♪   ♪   ♪
   ♪   ♪   ♪

WhatsApp from Tom (stand-in): Yo, sad little pawn ☺ I have a few hours Saturday morning. I can come over and look at the damp (and pipes if still an issue?) (What a fetching offer!) Let me know if you're around.

chapter twelve

I had totally forgotten he was coming. It slipped out of my mind, like something greased, and he knows it the second I open the door to him in Russ's old cricket hoodie, a pair of pajama shorts and hair like the BFG used me for a twirl around a candy floss machine, my body the stick.

"Ah, shit," Tom says. "You forgot I was coming."

"I—didn't . . ." The morning sun illuminates me like a spotlight, and I squint. An unsuspecting hamster, with its little house removed. "OK, I confess I did. Sorry."

"Do you want me to go and come back? I can go and find a Starbucks or something—"

"No, no," I croak. "I've just put some coffee on. Come in."

"Are you sure?" Tom raises an eyebrow at me and chuckles. "*Nosferatu.*"

"Sorry?"

He bends to pick up a large, handled black case at his feet—a drill perhaps? Whatever it is builders carry these days. Hammers. *Tools.* The man who came to fit our guttering last year even brought his own espresso machine. "Dracula," says Tom. "You know. The sun, vampires . . ."

"*Oh.* Course."

"Too early for vampire jokes, is it?"

"Isn't it always?"

I step aside and Tom squeezes by. I wish I'd remembered. I'd have cleaned up, cleared away last night's dinner and the explosion of crap on the coffee table. I'd have got dressed in something other than this. Tom looks fresh, like someone who sprung out of bed and into the shower at seven, waving happily to neighbors as he put out his bins to bloody lark song. Whereas me—"Monster Mash" would have suited my wake from sleep this morning. God, and he smells amazing . . .

"Do ignore my outfit," I say, "and the mess. And the . . . house in general. Everything really. Ignore everything."

"You should've said. I'd have arrived blindfolded." Tom laughs, pretends not to see last night's dinner and frozen cocktail sachets still on the table, plus my towel, which my wet hair was in until I went to bed, tossed over the back of the sofa. Instead, he just says, "I'm taken with that fireplace, though, if I'm allowed to look at it . . ."

"I never really use it," I say. "It's highly likely I'd start a house fire if I tried. I like central heating. I like pressing a button to be warm."

"Well. It's a beauty."

He follows me into the kitchen. Sunshine streams in, illuminating the old-fashioned, seventies-style brown tiles to almost a fiery orange. Russ actually *liked* these tiles—used to say they "don't make them like they used to." (And he was right, and there's good reason for that, like the way we don't burn people at the stake anymore, or make children sleep in workhouses.) But Russ was traditional, loved things with history, with a story. I like IKEA. I like bright and white and neutrals that never age and storage baskets in every shape and size. He liked house-clearance sales and furniture that might very well be haunted.

"Coffee?" I press the lit-up espresso button on the coffee machine, and it fills the room with a loud buzz.

"Yeah, great. Thanks." Tom puts down the case at his feet, slips his hands in his pockets. "Love the beams," he says, reaching up to the low ceiling and running a hand along the wood above his head.

"Not so sure on these tiles, though, eh?"

"Yeah." He laughs, dropping his gaze to the breakfast bar. "Bit special, aren't they? You can get paint, you know."

"For tiles?"

"Yup. Cheap and easy fix."

"God, I had no idea."

He smiles over at me. "I've got all the tricks, me."

We take our coffee outside to Three Sycamore's tiny, wild garden—but not before I nip off to do something with my hair and get dressed. I find a top that isn't creased, and some jeans fresh off the radiator, and realize, looking in the mirror, that there are two blobs of old eyeliner under my eyes. *God.*

When I get outside (yesterday's makeup removed and extra concealer reapplied), Tom has cleared the old planters off the rusty, cast-iron bench, and our coffees sit there beside each other on the matching table, among a tower of overturned plastic plant pots and a bag of compost, opened and folded over at the seam. The steam wisps into the warm June air. I'm not sure I've sat out here since Russ died. He loved this garden, and although wild, it was total organized chaos. He knew every wild tuft and bush, planted them on purpose. "These are for the butterflies," he'd say, "and these—the bees love these."

I sit down on the tiny bench beside Tom. It creaks. He shifts but our legs still touch, just a tiny bit, his jeans against mine. "Sorry," I say, "that I forgot. That I'm totally disorganized and half-asleep. That my garden is a jungle and—"

"Ah, pack it in." Tom sips his coffee. "You're apologizing for everything today. Outfits. Flowers. And for—*sleeping*?"

"Apparently so." I gulp down a huge mouthful of coffee. "Although I didn't really sleep, so . . ."

"No?"

"Nope. Couldn't sleep. Then the foxes. Again."

Tom laughs, sits back on the bench, resting his coffee cup on his knee. "Proverbial or actual?"

"*Proverbial?*"

"I dunno, I wondered if maybe the foxes was some sort of nickname for being kept up at night worrying. You know when you lie awake at night thinking about that embarrassing shit you said when you were fifteen and *if only I could go back and not say it!*"

"Oh. No." I laugh. "Well, yes, that, always, and actual real shagging foxes to add to it."

"Seriously?"

"Seriously. They're *so* loud."

"Ah, yeah, foxes are dramatic when sexually frustrated. Cheeky fucks," Tom deadpans. "God forbid they take it out on the gym, or order Chinese food, like the rest of us have to." He smiles at me then, a total schoolboy smile, and I can't help but laugh. That is the thing with Tom. He really makes me laugh. Genuinely. That sort of cheek-aching, belly laughing about everything and nothing all at once. The sort of laughter that leaves you feeling light and warm afterward. Therapized.

In the early morning sunshine, Tom and I chat as we drink our coffee, and it feels so safe and lovely, to be sitting here on a Saturday morning with someone else. We talk about the piano, we talk about the weather, and food, and Tom's job. He's been working with a lot of performers at the moment, taking "a shit ton of cheesy head shots" (his words) for a new agency that places singers and dancers in the entertainment teams on cruise ships and sometimes in Disneyland. I ask him if they're the photos he likes to take the most.

"I like faces. People," he says. "So this is a nice way to work with that and experiment and learn. Plus it pays. But I have my first exhibition in December. Booked it in. Some wanky art space in Shoreditch." He laughs, a hand rubbing at the dark shadow of stubble on his chin.

"An exhibition. Do you mean—people come to look at your work?"

He nods. "Exactly."

"Wow. And is that portraits too?"

"Mostly," he says, a thumb tracing the lip of his mug. "It's sort of—heart-on-sleeve stuff. You know? Which I'm finding . . . daunting."

I nod. "I think all art is heart-on-sleeve stuff. Every song I ever wrote was. Even if I didn't think it was at the time, I'd look back and it was like a story of how I felt, or where I was at the time. Like the music knew how I felt, before I did."

Tom meets my gaze, dark lashes, thoughtful eyes, and nods.

"So I say fuck it," I say. "Do it, daunting or not. And if it all goes wrong, you can just showcase a few of your Adam Drivers, and I promise I'll give a rave review."

"I thought you didn't fancy Adam Driver anymore." Tom smiles slowly, the sun catching in his blue eyes. "Or poor old Vince Vaughn."

"I don't." I laugh, and why are my cheeks ablaze? What else did I drunkenly say to him that night at Avocado Clash? I may have minced my words a bit more if I'd known that tall bloke at the bar would be sticking around in my life for a bit, and would soon be having coffee in my back garden. "Toast, on the other hand. He seems sort of in love."

Toast the cat keeps brushing himself against Tom's legs, squinting up at him, the sun in his round, yellow eyes. "He does," smiles Tom. "Why Toast by the way?"

"Ah. When we first brought him home from the rescue center, Russ walked in to find him with his paw in the toaster, trying to hook out a piece of bread," I tell Tom, as he scratches a finger under Toast's chin. "He's an old man. He knows what he likes, and he likes human food. Shreddies and cheese and pickle sandwiches. His name is Sidney, in real life."

Toast drops down onto the floor and shows Tom his white, fluffy belly. "But only on his birth certificate and to government officials, eh, little Toast?" says Tom.

And I can't remember the last time it happened, having someone here to shoot the breeze with. The weekends here feel almost deserted. Like I'm on my own little desert island—just me (and Toast) and this house, the walls of which seem to look at me sadly, like a parent I keep disappointing. Everyone seems to have so much "on." They're firmly pressed on play, and me on pause. Mum and Dad do more now, in their retirement, than they've ever done, and Jodie and Carl, my friends—they're busy, forging and sculpting and *living* lives. But it's nice being here with Tom, this morning. Really nice.

We walk back into the kitchen and place our empty mugs in the sink, and Tom asks, "So, do you have a plan?"

"For the piano?" I ask. "I dunno. I was thinking on Tuesday I could get there extra early and stake it out a bit more, and hope some is left this time because there hasn't been any."

"I actually meant the house," says Tom with a lopsided smile. "But I think the piano plan is concrete too—for what it's worth."

"*Oh.* Right. The house. Course." My cheeks burn—like two warm pebbles against the skin. I worry that everyone thinks I'm too preoccupied with the piano, that's what it is. Me and my empty life, clinging to tiny things that other people might just share as a cute little anecdote.

"And do you mean the music's stopped?" asks Tom.

"Well, I hope not. But—yeah, there's been none for a couple of days. It's sort of . . . been a bit of a downer really."

Tom's brow furrows. "That's weird. That it would suddenly stop."

"And do you mean plans for fixing the house up?"

Tom ducks his head in a nod. "Yeah, so where're you starting, what're the problems . . ."

"Everything," I say with a sigh. "Literally. Everything. It was a project, but now it's just—I don't know what it is. My home, I suppose. That also doesn't really feel like my home most of the time."

Tom nods understandingly, although I barely understand what I mean myself. It is my home. It is *our* home. But it doesn't feel like it, and if it doesn't, what *is* my plan? To live forever in somewhere groaning under the weight of all the work and love and time it needs given to it? To live somewhere that never feels truly like mine—that doesn't make me happy.

"Well," Tom says, "I can take a look around, talk about maybe what you need to do before putting it on the market—"

"I don't know if I even am, though, that's the thing."

"Putting it up for sale?"

I nod.

"OK, well—"

"I mean, I think I might want to. But . . . it's a big step, and . . ."

Tom nods again calmly, watching me, his hands in his pockets. Sometimes I wonder if Shauna's put him up to this. I don't think she has, not really, but I do wonder sometimes whether he shows up, gives me his time, listens to me, *talks* to me, because she tells him I need it. And he does it. As a favor for his mum, the friend of the poor, young widow. Doesn't he have anything else he'd rather be doing than standing here, in this cramped kitchen, with me?

"Anyway," I say, turning on the tap, squirting in a splodge of Fairy Liquid. "You must have stuff to do, things to—"

"Anyway? No, what were you going to say?"

I look over at Tom from the sink, at his kind, watchful eyes, his lips parted. He has a beautiful mouth. I noticed that, at the nature reserve. A perfect, full bow. I wondered if his twin, Laurie, has the same. If his dad does.

"I don't know," I say. "I can't really explain what I mean because I really don't know what to do about this house. I sometimes struggle to *pinpoint* what I feel at all, about anything. But it's like my brain is scared to actually *say* how I feel, because once it's out there, it's out there, you know? You can't take it back. So, it's easier to be like, shrug, I don't know." I pause. Force a weird, awkward laugh. "OK, I probably don't make any sense—"

"No. No, you do."

The water in the sink rises. When I shut off the tap, it sways, like a bubbly, soapy ocean.

"I don't know what I want to do," I add. "Pure and simple. And I don't know what I feel. About the house, my friends . . . the bloody tiles. My life in general really."

Tom watches me again and I feel . . . uncomfortable. Like I've said too much, like I want to gather all the words back up into a little pile and swallow them back down.

"Anyway. Let me show you around, you came all the way here—"

"Do you have a word?" Tom jumps in.

"Do I have a . . . ?"

"A word." Tom slides his hands into his pockets. "When I was in college, we had this mental well-being day, and one of our teachers said: just try to find a word. And I'm a total classic constipated male—shamefully—so half the time I have no idea what I feel, but it helps even now. Starting with a word. Just one, about how I'm feeling. I dunno, but it works, somehow—it's a good starting point." Tom shrugs. "One word usually brings with it another and another and—you get the picture."

I nod. "Yeah. That makes sense."

"She'd say write them down, then lock them away somewhere. Or tell a mate. Whatever works."

"Not sure about telling a mate. They'd probably send an emergency carrier pigeon to the bongo drumming bereavement counselor."

Tom laughs quietly. "Maybe try one that won't? Or you can text them to yourself, like I used to. It's like reading back some fucked-up experimental poetry, though, I'll warn you."

I laugh. "Wowzer."

"Is that your word?" Tom asks drolly. "*Wowzer.*"

"*No.* Not sure I've got one just yet."

"You'll find one. And then probably a truckload. It's how it works." He pushes off the side of the counter. "Right. So, this cheeky damp in your bathroom . . . can I go and have a look?"

"Be my guest."

♫   ♫   ♫
  ♫   ♫   ♫

Tom stays until one p.m. He fixes the broken coving from the bedroom ceiling, hunched over a small woodworking bench in the garden, a pencil lengthways between his lips, and after, the pair of us paint the damp, together, in the bathroom and bedroom with specialist anti-damp paint. I ask him why he doesn't do it anymore—"building stuff."

"'Building stuff.'" He smiles down at me, where I'm cross-legged, painting the bottom of the wall. "Well, it was just sort of decided, when we were kids, really. It's what Dad does. What his dad did, you get the picture. Dad owns his own construction company now. It's all corporate and shiny and—" He screws his face up. "Anyway, I got bored. I always wanted a creative job, I guess. And the idea of staying in the same job for years and years out of habit . . . sort of scared the shit out of me."

"And what does your dad think of the photography?"

Tom gives a small, ironic laugh. "Not real work. Well. That was until a portrait of mine was in the *Guardian*. Then I was the wunderkind son. The Jesus Christ of photography."

I laugh. "Wow," I say, as if to myself. "Just here, hanging with the Jesus Christ of photography, who's fixing my damp and coving. What an honor."

"It's in the Bible, that," says Tom dryly. "Under home improvements."

When Tom leaves, I thank him, and I'm surprised when he hesitates, then puts his arms around me on the path and hugs me. He's warm and muscular and smells like wood and fresh paint and sunkissed skin. "Tell Toast I'll miss him," he says. "I'll bring him some Shreddies next time I come if he's good."

"What a romantic," I say. "He'd like that."

As I close the door, I'm hit by how bloody *nice* it's been to have seen him. To have had someone here, to talk about everything and nothing and to just—*be*.

Plus the house—the house looks a thousand times better, and did almost instantly. I don't know if it's the lick of paint, but it feels brighter and airier. Like the air's clearer to breathe. Like it's no longer a deserted island, cut off from the rest of the world. *I* feel lighter.

I clean up, wash the paint brushes, vacuum, then make a cup of coffee, and take it outside to the cast-iron bench. Sawdust sits on the petals of purple wildflowers Russ planted, like new fallen snow. I close my eyes. Listen. Silence. Leaves rustling in trees. Birdsong. A distant passing car. I imagine Three Sycamore cleared of all clutter, of all damp, of all shabbiness, and painted clean, plain, calming colors throughout. I imagine living in it. I imagine the For Sale sign. I imagine driving away from it, to somewhere new, my car full of boxes, the cat mewing in his carrier. My eyes are damp when I open them again.

Inside, I find my phone, the text on the screen blurred through tears that just keep coming.

"Guilty," I type and send. "Scared," I send again.

Tom replies quickly. "You found two," he simply types back.

I stare at them, two huge words in two tiny bubbles.

And I *am* feeling guilty. Guilty at the idea of walking away from our home, after all the hard work it took getting it, after all the planning. And I'm scared of what that might mean—what my future might hold if I do sell up. What does it mean, if I walk away from our life? What does the future hold? For just me?

Another reply from Tom comes quickly. A single padlock emoji. My words, safe in here.

chapter thirteen

I don't often get nervous. When Edie and I first started out and we performed at open mic nights and unsigned band events, hell-bent on record deals and impressing slick (and often chauvinistic) A&R scouts, it was Edie who'd be hunkered down in the loo. "I won't be able to go on," she'd say every single time, "honestly, I need to go home, Nat, my stomach has lost the plot. It's balls deep in fear. In *terror*," and I'd pep talk her through the door, like a cut-price Tony Robbins, without the shovel hands. "What the crowd thinks of you is none of your business, Eeds!" I'd say, and "One day you'll be ninety-eight eating Pease pudding and you won't give a shit about what a gang of randoms drunk on flat beer thought of you seventy years ago. You'll just be the cool grandma who played in bands. Think of her. Think of cool granny Edie!" But today, like Edie, *I'm* nervous. Proper churning, stomach-is-in-a-state-of-terror, palms-sweating, heart-thumping nerves, and it's ridiculous that I am. It's a music therapy group. It's a group of people turning to music for therapy, through grief, through depression, through illness. It is not a public execution. And yet, my entire body is acting as though it is.

I'd made the decision to come here first thing this morning. I was awake early, and I sat at the breakfast bar watching the sun come up, bathing Russ's wild garden in golden light, and I kept thinking about those words I sent to Tom. Scared. Guilty. And I mulled and mulled them over in my head, kneaded them like dough. Then I flicked to the photo of the Music Therapy leaflet in my phone, and there was something comforting about the idea of a group of people, probably with words like mine—painful words, too small, too big, to look at in the eye—gathering somewhere together, all a little broken, to feel a little more understood. And with music. I got dressed and pushed myself out of the door before I could talk myself out of it.

Now I follow the directions on Google Maps, the robotic, matter-of-a-fact voice dictating in my ear which way to go, like an emotionless friend. It sends me down multiple quiet streets, nothing but alleyways and occasional backstreet garages, and I wonder for a moment if I've actually gone the wrong way and will end up on murky CCTV on the ten-o'clock news. But then it comes into view. "Kennedy Place." It looks like a brick-built factory. Its entrance is nothing but a heavy metal door, the color of cranberry juice, and the sign on the brickwork next to it reads Red Door Rehearsal Rooms. And just like that, a thrill, like a crackle of electricity, surges through me. *Rehearsal Rooms.* It's like something from another life. Like coming across an old photo, or old song you forgot about. Strange and new and familiar all at once. This is all Edie and I did once upon a time. Rehearsed and wrote and played. I knew every rehearsal space in London. Not this one, though. This must be new.

I knock. Nothing.

I try the door, and it opens easily, into a tiny lobby and a flight of thin-carpeted stairs. It smells like a doctor's surgery in here—that clinical, industrial-strength floor cleaner smell—and I can hear music, from multiple angles. The rumble of a bass guitar from upstairs. A clarinet somewhere behind me. Some laughter from the top of the stairs. On the wall is a silver embossed sign, divided into a list of floors, and next to the heading "Floor Three" is NMT, the therapy group I'm looking for.

My stomach turns over like a barrel as I climb the stairs—oh, God, say if I walk in and everyone is in a circle sharing tragic stories, heaving sobs into tissues. Like Weight Watchers. "I've lost two and a half pounds, and my will to live, ha-ha. How about you?"

"Hi!" A man stands at an open door on the third floor, his back leaning against the slice of safety glass. "Another early one today, I see. Aren't we lucky?"

"Is this the right place for music therapy? I saw a flyer—"

"Yes, yes, that's us. Is this your first time?" This man looks like a bird. Tall, gangly, with pointed, sharp features, but a smile that softens them all instantly. He reminds me of every cool, new English teacher, straight out of teaching college, jolly and as-yet unjaded with the system.

I nod. "First time," I repeat.

"Cool, cool. I'm James. I'm one of the therapists, and there's Devaj, too, my partner in crime. We run the program together. He's inside with a couple of our team if you want to go on in, make yourself at home. We've got a few early birds inside already." He jerks with his head to the entrance. "And sorry, forgive me, I didn't get your name."

"Natalie."

"Natalie. Great. Welcome."

There's a small landing past James—a tiny kitchen, the sort you find in soulless offices—gray countertops and light faux-wood doors, and that hospital-y white lino on the floor, with weird flecks of glitter in it—followed by an open door to a huge open space. One wall is completely exposed brick, like one of those backstreet dance studios or youth clubs, and there are chairs and people and instrument cases scattered about the room. It smells a bit like churches.

"Is that the Vox amp?" someone asks, and something warm fizzes inside me at the buzz of electric guitar meeting the metal of the cord.

"Hello, hello!" A short, smiling man in a burgundy-red button-up shirt greets me. He has a stripe of blond dyed straight down the middle of dark quiff. "I'm Devaj. Is this your first time with us?"

"It is. I'm sort of nervous."

"Ah, that's understandable," says Devaj. "But it's all very relaxed, I promise. Shall I give you a quick show-around?"

Devaj welcomes me, all warmth and smiles and proud hand-wringing, and he takes me around the room, my nerves slowly fizzling. Maybe this *will* be good for me. Maybe it'll even actually help, like these things actually seem to for others.

"I'm a pianist," I tell him, and I love the way the words sound coming out of my mouth. I've felt disconnected from that identity; from Musician Natalie. "I used to write with a friend. We were a duet. Sort of folky, poppy stuff. Then we taught at a small school, over in Marylebone? Me, piano, Edie, my friend, guitar and singing, so—"

He puts his hand to his heart. "Oh, you already *play*," he says. "Oh my. Fantastic. But of course, there's total freedom here, you can play and do whatever you like, whatever feels good. You're not obligated to come, you're not obligated to talk, to volunteer, to even integrate. We're really trying to just offer a place for you to just *be* really . . ."

I nod, relieved. "I was sort of worried I might have to—spill all to the group," I say. "You know, have a big ol' cry in front of people I don't know. Stand up, have everyone clap me."

Devaj laughs, a slice of straight, white teeth. "Oh, not at all. But course, if you want to do that too, we can support you. But, really, it's up to you, Natalie—ah. But if I may—Joe?"

Devaj looks past me and gestures with a hand and a smile. "Joe here keeps talking about learning piano. He plays like a bit of a god on a guitar, though . . ."

Joe joins us smiling a lopsided, shy (and almost slightly mortified) smile, and instantly, I recognize him. Because he's *Notebook Guy*. As in *the* Notebook Guy. A regular. At Goode's. The man who always sits over a notebook in the corner, not speaking to anyone. "Joe, this is Natalie," says Devaj. "Natalie here is a pianist."

Joe nods, holds a hand out to mine and shakes it, firmly. "Nice to meet you. I'm Joe. And I'm *not* a pianist. Not a guitar god either, but"—he gives a tiny grimace, a flick of his head to the side—"thanks for the hype, Devaj."

Devaj laughs.

"Nice to meet you," I say. "And—we also have the same taste in coffee apparently." He smiles knowingly. *Ah.* He recognizes me too. I wonder if he has a secret name for me too. *The Haunted Waxwork. Face-like-a-smacked-arse Woman.* "Goode's," says Joe. "Yeah, I've become a bit of a regular over there."

"Me too."

"You guys know each other?" Devaj gives a warm chuckle. "London, eh? Center of the bloody universe. Anyway. Joe. Natalie. We're just waiting for more to join, and then we'll begin, but—just through there, Joe will tell you, is another room. Soundproof and a bit smelly—and we can't for the life of us find the smell—but there's a piano. And a French horn, if you fancy it. Someone donated it so—feel free." Devaj claps his hands together, a man on a mission, and strides off across the threadbare carpet to a little gathering of people at the entrance, who are shrugging off their bags.

Joe smiles at me awkwardly, his sandy eyebrows raised. I've never been this close to Notebook Guy before. He always tucks himself away, at one of the tables in the tiny upstairs seating area, in the corner. But if I had to guess, being up close, I'd say he's late twenties. Maybe thirty. He looks like the sort of guy my sister would've crushed madly on, before she met Carl. He has that intangible, beachy, lifeguard-y look.

Dirty ash-blond hair in short-ruffled waves, hazel eyes, impossibly perfectly square jaw.

"Well—small world." I laugh.

"Yeah. You can say that again."

And his words are followed by an awkward long beat of silence. Someone strums a guitar, the reverb turned up too high.

"So . . . I think I might just—have a little wander," I say, because I worry that he feels like he's lumped with me now—obligated somehow. I mean, this isn't a night class, is it? Beginner's French or creative writing. This isn't a new job, or a new gym. It's therapy. Notebook Guy—Joe—will be here because he's dealing with something; needs healing in some way, like me.

"It's—weird," he says quietly, giving me a look that's almost secret. *Them and us.* "Or at least, feels it at first. Pissing about on an instrument. In a room with strangers you'd never find yourself knocking about with in real life, but I dunno—after a while, you sort of forget you're here. And you—lean into it."

I nod. "I wasn't going to come to be honest."

"Same." He smiles.

"But I just felt I needed to do *something.* I've sort of . . . waited long enough."

Joe nods slowly. "Yeah," he says. "Easy to sort of hope it goes away on its own. That you suddenly wake up better, but—" He laughs, as if despite himself. "Turns out, it's not that easy."

I smile. "I waited for the same. Hoped it might pass. Like norovirus."

"Yeah," he says. "Grief's a little bitch, isn't it?" He pauses. "Well. It's grief for me—"

"And for me," I say. "My husband Russ died. Two and a half years ago. A road accident." And I have never, in all my life, just laid that information out in front of me, like a picnic blanket, to a stranger. But saying it here, in this churchy, cool room, to this grieving stranger feels safe. Already, I feel safe in the knowledge that Joe will understand how I'm feeling more than everyone in my life. Maybe this is why people recommend these things, like drinking more water, like exercising, like phoneless bedtimes. They actually do work. Who knew?

"I'm sorry," says Joe gently. "Two years for me. My big brother. Tanner."

"Gosh. I'm sorry too. Your brother—that must be really hard."

Joe nods, and silence stretches between us, awkward and thick, like an invisible band, but already, there's something that's lifted. Just in that tiny exchange with Joe. Pressure, released. And a sort of irony. All those times I've been at the station, a rain cloud of grief and emptiness following me around, like a dutiful pet, feeling like everyone else had it together, just a few tables over, there was Joe, beneath an invisible cloud of his own.

I clear my throat. "So, I might go and take a look at the piano. In there did he say?"

"Yup. The famous *smelly room.*" Joe smiles, just a tiny one— a graze of teeth on his lip. "They've tried to find the culprit. I even tried. Found an old moldy apple, felt like king of the world—"

I laugh.

"But it didn't work. It wasn't the apple."

"What a plot twist," I say. "And you're welcome to join. If you're learning piano, maybe it might help? Or not, of course. Whatever the ... *music therapy etiquette* is—"

"Ah, there's no etiquette in places like this, really. I've been to enough of them." He laughs bashfully. "Me. The therapy overachiever. But yeah, it's cool with me if it's cool with you. Plus—you haven't lived until you've heard me *unleashing* on a French horn."

"Oh? Any good?"

He laughs. "We're both about to find out."

♪   ♪   ♪
♪   ♪   ♪

"I am—very bad at French horn."

"If it softens the blow, Joe, I think the screech you got out of it encapsulates grief perfectly," I say, and Joe laughs.

We're in the smelly room, which is a small, windowless square with black, tatty, soundproof foam on the walls, and a weak, warm light that casts our faces in shadows. Joe and I have been in here for twenty minutes, chatting in between bursts of my playing. We've swapped the basics, the way you do when you meet someone new in a confined space. He's twenty-seven, works at an "insufferably trendy" speakeasy bar in Soho, and lives in a house share in Kentish Town with two antisocial, work-obsessed nerds, which Joe loves because it means he gets to "wander around the house alone in peace without feeling pressurized to establish some sort of Chandler, Joey, and Ross dynamic." Joe also asks the nicest questions about Russ. "What did he like doing?" "Was Russ into his music?" and it feels so lovely to just talk about him, without anyone worrying, or thinking, *Oh, shit, she's still grieving. I never know what to say when she talks about him, do you?*

Joe weighs the brass tangle of tubes in his hand. "I always look at these things and think, how hard can it be? Surely you just pick up a French horn and blow, and voilà, you just played Brahms."

"I remember thinking that about piano." I laugh. "Surely you just press a few keys in the right order and out it comes. Easy."

"Well, you play like that is definitely the case," he says. "You make it look easy. Like it's being played from a record playing somewhere."

"Ah. Thank you," I say. "Once you can play, you can play."

Joe gives a small shrug in the dim light. "I dunno. I think you're doing yourself a disservice there."

"Am I?"

"*Yeah.* God, yeah." Joe leans to put the French horn back in its case, the little round stool creaking under him. The faintest sound of music floats from the main room, seeping through the sealed crack in the door. "I just think sometimes people can't play like others," he says, straightening. "Even if they're following the same music, it just doesn't sound the same. It's the same way you know an Oasis song from the first note. You can tell who's playing. And you can't even put your finger on what's different, and what's *them* about it. But it just is. You know." Joe stretches then, pushing his chest out, widening his toned arms, like someone who's just woken up, and laughs. "God, look at that, I've gone and got all philosophical in the smelly room."

I laugh. "Well, I think what you just said was profound," I say. "*AF*, as the internet would say."

Joe grins over at me. "The power of the French horn, I reckon," he adds. "It's what it does to you."

chapter fourteen

I can't believe you actually got asked out!"

"Priya, I did not get *asked out*."

"Sure." Priya grins. "Of course you didn't. Why else would a sexy dude like Notebook Guy give you his number?"

"Because he wants a friend?" I offer. "Because his brother died?"

"And because he fancies you," Priya says musically, with a shrug. "The end, my friend. The end."

Priya, Jodie, and I sit out the back of Tina on the concrete, in the bright summer sunshine. We don't often get to do this, have lunch, us three all together. One of us always has to mind the shop floor, but Mum is visiting again, and she just can't help herself. The second she can, she gets back behind the counter, a (totally pointless of course) tape measure around her neck, and chews the ear off any customer who dares utter a single admiring word about her shop. Someone complimented the new range of anklets twenty minutes ago. That's all Mum needed before she launched into a guided history of how she and Dad—"my Colin"—started the business back in a "better time," when the internet didn't exist and people didn't care for organic meat.

"I think it could be perfection," says Jodie, a squashy triangular half of an egg and cress sandwich in her hand. "Joe and Natalie, under each other's noses all along at the coffee shop, grief bringing them together . . ."

Priya nods deeply, like she's listening to a sermon, her hand in a huge plastic family bucket of ready-to-eat chicken wings that smell so strongly of paprika, I know I'll be smelling it on her until closing.

"You two need to stop."

"Natalie," Jodie says sternly. "He gave you his *phone number.* He asked you for coffee. He's hot."

"And you're also hot. It's done. Signed, sealed, delivered," adds Priya, and Jodie raises her sandwich to the chicken wing in Priya's hand, like two wise wizards clinking goblets.

It's been almost a week since music therapy and meeting Joe. The therapy session had been beautiful in parts. Sort of . . . affirming. Moving. A woman had watched wordlessly as I played, simply said thank you when I finished, and left. Someone sang something she'd written, while Devaj played notes on a guitar to match it. That was moving, and I felt I could've even cried, right there, in front of everyone. Some people didn't play anything at all—just sat, in small groups, listening, talking, and not. But it helped, just being there. And Joe. I like talking to Joe. We'd talked for a lot of the session, and then he'd gone into the main room, sat, watched, listened to others. And it was as I was leaving that he trotted out after me, pulling a hoodie over his head, swiping a hand through his hair, and asked for my number. It was casual. It was very friend-to-friend. It was "If you ever wanna talk. Or, you know—hear French horn like you've never heard it before." And I'd walked away feeling like the sun was glowing brighter in the sky. Lighter. Warmer.

"Seriously," I say to Priya and her gooey smile. "I know it sort of sounds like it, like I've picked up some poor soul at a grief group, but it isn't like that. If you were there, you'd see. He was just friendly. Funny. Sort of—deep and a bit shy."

"Because he fancies you and was gearing up to ask you out," offers Jodie. "Of course he was shy."

"No, it was more"—I quickly chew and swallow the Wotsit in my mouth—"*I see you're as fucked up as me, so maybe we can buddy up?*"

Priya, with a chicken wing between her fingers, pauses with it halfway to her lips. "Oh, stop it," she says. "I doubt he thought that. You're not fucked up."

"Well, whatever he thought, it doesn't matter. We're meeting next week, after the session, for coffee, and he seems really nice. I always thought Notebook Guy seemed weird, but—he's not. Not at all."

"I just thought," says Priya, mouth full of chicken, "what a story. You know, to tell at your wedding. In the speeches . . ."

"Jesus, Priya."

"*What?*"

"Cor, imagine him in a suit," says Jodie, turning to me. "Like, can you imagine? He'll make a gorgeous groom." As predicted, I knew Jodie would crush on him. I'd shown her his photo after she asked yesterday—sent her a screenshot of his WhatsApp photo. A photo of him and two other men, around his age, somewhere with snow in the background, ski goggles on their heads. I wondered if one was his brother, but didn't feel I could ask. I was at Russ's tree in the crematorium when he messaged. He sent me a funny gif of a man puffing his cheeks up around a tuba with the words "lest we forget," and for the first time in probably forever, I felt completely comfortable telling him where I was. "Tanner's over at a natural burial place in Poole," he'd replied. "But his girlfriend visits most weeks. She actually took him a slice of Domino's pizza last month (his fave). Anything that naturally decays can stay. And apparently that includes Texan barbecue pizza with extra sweet corn." We'd talked a little after that. Joe told me that Tanner, his brother, was thirty when he died. He got into trouble in the sea, at work. He was a lifeguard.

"He'd actually suit white, wouldn't he?" carries on Priya, as if she's one of Gok Wan's advisors. "He has the face for it. Not everyone has the face for a white suit."

"Totally."

"OK, I'm afraid you're both deluded and I must depart." I screw up the empty bag of Wotsits in my fist and stand up, stride over to the big black barrel of a bin by the shop's back entrance, and drop it in. "I've got to go out in ten minutes, and I do not want to hear another word about how hot poor Joe would look in a tux, white, black, bloody mustard yellow with spots on."

Priya laughs, reaches over, and holds on to my hand. "You're our only source of excitement, Nat. We live boring lives. Go easy on us."

"Raise the bar, my fine friend," I say, leaning and planting a kiss on her head. Her hair smells like strawberry shampoo. "Raise the bar."

"I'm serious," says Priya. "The piano music was enough, and now this."

"Yeah, well, did I tell you there was none of *that* left yesterday? Again. Not very exciting now is it?" There's still been no music left for me since my birthday, and I can't help but think it's over. That whatever it was, has come to an end, and I feel ashamed that it actually makes me feel a bit lost. Like a friend has suddenly stopped texting me back, or something. Ghosted me without explanation.

"God, really?" Priya sags in her chair, and I admit I sort of want to do the same. I loved the spark of finding it. I loved the spark of wondering. And I'm just hoping there's a little lag—an interval—before it starts again.

"Tom checked yesterday, too," I say, "on his way back from work, and nothing. He texted. He's checking today too, so we'll find out soon. He'll be here in a bit."

"Interesting," says Jodie. "Does he text you a lot then? Tom."

Priya looks over at Jodie, yet another chicken wing in her grip, and bites her lip to supress a smile that spreads into her cheeks anyway (beside a heart-shaped blob of barbecue sauce).

"Now what?"

"Nothing," says Jodie.

"No, why were you both looking at each other like that?"

Priya giggles, but stops when she slaps Jodie's hovering hand away from her beloved bucket of chicken wings. "Nothing really, just—well, Tom. You're seeing a bit of him, aren't you?"

"Right?"

"He sorted out your dampness," Jodie says. "*And* he fixed your house." Jodie stares at me, widens her eyes, then bursts out laughing.

"You need help, Jodie," I say, a laugh bursting out of me, despite myself. "That wasn't even a *good* double entendre. It was rubbish. Terrible. Didn't even make sense."

"I thought it was genius."

"And I'm sorry to be a big ol' disappointment, but I have no interest in seeing Joe in a white bloody tux and having Tom sort out my—" I grimace. "*Dampness.* God, Jodie, you are actually quite gross, aren't you?"

Priya laughs loudly. "She's got a point, though. You're drowning in hot men." She pats her stomach. "I'm jealous. Sorry, but I am."

"*Drowning in them.*" I laugh, look down at my watch, but my cheeks are taut with how much I'm smiling. It's nice to have stuff going on. It's nice to have met new people, have actual things to report when people ask how I am, what I've been up to. Even if I don't, much to Priya and Jodie's dismay, want to shag either of them. "Tom and I are going tile shopping because my house is falling down," I say. "Not exactly an aphrodisiac. So, maybe reel your expectations in."

"That *is* romantic, though," says Priya, looking up at the sky, like a philosopher looking for the answer to life itself. "Isn't it, Jode? It's like a glimpse into a future you could have. You and Tom, Nat. Married. Kids. DIY at the weekends—"

"Joe, crying on the other side of the window," says Jodie, "rain pouring down, wishing *so much* it was him, because 'Goddamn it, Natalie, I'll never love anyone like I love you.' "

"You had Joe in a bloody white tuxedo thirty seconds ago." I laugh. "You were writing your *speech* about him. Now he's lonely and heart-broken gazing through my window. Make your mind up."

Jodie slumps, drops her hand to her lap, just half a crust of her sandwich left. "But do you really not, though? Fancy them? Fancy Tom?"

"She doesn't fancy *anyone*," says Priya sadly. "Nobody. Not even Christian Slater anymore, and that's saying something. She always loved him."

I pull the cardigan off the back of my chair. "*Goodbye*," I say.

"And I don't believe her," Priya says to Jodie, as if I'm not even in the vicinity. "There's got to be something there with one of them. A bit of lust."

"Well, Priya, you would say that." I say, smiling. "You're the woman who keeps having orgasms in her sleep. Over the scaffolder with the beady eyes. Over that bloke. The one from *MasterChef.* With the head—"

Jodie bursts out laughing, a spray of lemonade misting the air. "You're having sleep-gasms? Lucky bitch. I miss those. I had so many when I was pregnant with Nick. Poor Carl thought I was possessed. Almost called in the priest."

"Nat, I told you that in *confidence*," says Priya, as Mum appears and says, "A sleep-gasm? What's a sleep-gasm?"

♫   ♫   ♫
♫   ♫   ♫

I meet Tom in a quiet residential street, just next to the World's End pub. The car windows are down, and Tom is in the driver's seat, fiddling with the radio, a finger and thumb at the round volume button. A sparkly shoe air freshener hangs from the rearview mirror, and I lean to the open window. "Nice shoe there, Thomas. Very fetching."

Tom's head swoops up then, and he grins. "Ah, it's my curbside pickup. Car's in for a service," he says. "So I've got the Shauna-Madden-mobile. Does it suit me?" He's wearing sunglasses and a fitted, navy-blue T-shirt, a glimpse of tanned collarbone peeking above the neckline. I can understand why Jodie and Priya are keen for this to be *something*. Tom is hot. Plain and simple. The sort of hot that's hard not to acknowledge sometimes, not to let out, like a held-in breath, "Oof. What a sexy mouth," and "Nice jaw you're gracing us with today. Bet it's good to run a finger along . . ."

"It looks good on you," I say, "especially the pink sparkly shoe. Shall I get in?"

"That's generally how this works, Natalie, yes, get in."

We wind through streets in slow traffic, circling Regent's Park, and the beautiful, three-story Victorian houses of Primrose Hill. Everything is starting to come out in celebration of summer. The leaves are lush and the color of ripe limes, hanging baskets overflow with waterfalls of color, gone are the heavy dark jackets of winter, and returned are the flowing dresses and sandals, in yellow and florals. Everything feels fresh and new. And OK, it's a small thing, but it's nice not to have to worry about the pipe freezing over as I sleep now the weather's warm too, and hopefully, the sun is here to stay for a bit.

"So, I'm in *the* Shauna Madden's car, am I?" I say. "What a treat."

"You are indeed. She's the only person I know who loves driving in London."

"Really?"

"*Loves it.* Loves the bustle of it. Loves the sights . . ."

"And you don't?"

Tom's brow furrows, and he looks at me, one hand holding the steering wheel. "Fuck no. Bunch of lunatics out there. But I need a car for work, especially this morning—had to take some photos over in Richmond. Promo shots for some emo band, actually. They're trying to bring the noughties back, God fuckin' help us. They even invited me to their next gig." He laughs to himself. "But I'll take a car ride. Especially when I've got a decent passenger."

"Are we off to find one, then?"

"Bloody hell," says Tom. "And she brings the dad jokes. What did I do to deserve this?"

It takes ten minutes to get to the tile place, and we park behind the warehouse, which is more of an aircraft hangar. The walls are corrugated iron, and a stark white square of a sign above the entrance has the tile shop's name, along with a cartoon of a man with a trowel—something straight from nineties clip art. Yes, Priya. How romantic. Me, Tom, and a building that's a big, hot, metal coffin on a stretch of gray, potholed concrete.

We make our way across the hot car park, heat shimmering in airwaves above the ground.

"Beautiful, eh?" Tom throws the car keys in the air and catches them, grins at me. "Don't say I don't take you anywhere."

"Wouldn't dare," I reply as a juddering, blue-framed automatic door swallows us up.

The warehouse is exactly what you would expect. Windowless with high ceilings and caged pallets full of boxes and too-bright fluorescent lights. The air smells of something nostalgic too—glue, maybe. A sort of varnish. It reminds me of the construction block in secondary school where we'd make letter holders, and boys would glue-gun their fingers together before getting sent to the headmaster with hands like lobster claws.

"So, what I'm thinking is," says Tom, strolling easily beside me, "tile paint in the kitchen, and for the bathroom, you want something plain. White, or maybe even a gray . . ."

"Oh, good plan."

"Because plain and modern sells. Buyers prefer it."

"Makes sense."

"Not that you've decided yet," Tom carries on, "but . . . well, you said you like neutral too, so, win-win, right?"

Tom points out plain, white, brick-like tiles with beveled edges, white square tiles, and ones in a bluish gray, like fish scales. There's a couple in front of us, picking up samples, holding them against a bookmark-shaped piece of card—a paint color, I suppose. "I think that would go so nice with the yellow," I hear one of them say, "especially if we get white towels, white accessories . . ." And I feel something that practically stops me in my tracks. Right there, in the glue-y warehouse. It's . . . *possibility*. That's the word, if I had to find one. Possibility that maybe, like others do, like these two in front of me, I *can* sell the cottage. I can move. And maybe I can find somewhere new, pick tiles out for that, like these people in front of me—a fresh slate, with no history, no blueprint.

God, imagine not living next to Roy and his disapproving tutting . . .

But then, there it is. Of course it is.

One of the couple reaches for the other's hand and one of them says something, and they laugh. And like clockwork, there's that hot pang that rises like a slow tide. *Guilt.* Russ. Russ loved Three Sycamore. We put everything on the line to buy Three Sycamore. Being here feels like betrayal.

"These are cool, too, no?" says Tom obliviously. "I have something similar at my flat. Flatmate hates them, but I like to think he is a styleless animal, so—"

"Yeah. Let's get them."

"Yeah?" He raises his eyebrows. "I mean, you can look at some more, there's about a *billion*—"

"No, let's just grab them. And go."

Tom crosses his arms across his broad chest. "We don't have to do this if you don't want to," he says softly. "We can—wait? Or you can order some samples online or—"

"No, I do. I do want to do it. I just—I feel like if I don't get them now, I'll talk myself out of it. I'm really good at that. Con-artist levels of persuasion. But if I just buy them, it means . . . it's done."

Tom hesitates, then nods.

"But I want to. To buy the tiles."

"OK," he says. "Well, I reckon three boxes should do it. We're only doing the splashbacks, so . . . these ones?"

"These ones."

We buy the tiles, silently standing side by side at the till, and on the way back, neither of us really speaks. The radio plays, and a warm breeze thick with the smell of cut grass and hot charcoals blows through the car, and I people watch out of the window. I think of Joe, wonder if he felt this when he left Dorset for London, where he lived with his brother until he died. I think of the tiles in boxes at my feet. I think of Three Sycamore. I think of Russ's face at the bedroom window of the cottage the day we viewed it; him in the hospital bed; the car mounting that curb, him being left there in the road, like a hit squirrel, like a bird. This is what happens. This is what happens every single time I try to move forward. It's like treacle. Like vines wrapping around my ankles, dragging me back. The guilt and the grief and the stop signs that seem to appear the second I hold my head up high and choose a path.

"Hey," says Tom, and I've hardly noticed that we've pulled over into a small, quiet residential street. The sort with perfect redbrick Victorian houses and neat hedges and pastel-painted doors. "Do you fancy a drink somewhere? Cool pub round the corner."

♫   ♫   ♫
♫   ♫   ♫

Within minutes, Tom and I are upstairs at a tiny, tucked-away pub, at an even tinier roof terrace which is mostly shaded by a wooden pergola and flowers, which tumble down and along the wooden trellis edges. There are so many. Big, beautiful puffs of pansies and begonias, in reds, corals, and lemon-curd yellows, bees constantly arriving and taking off from their middles, like flights on an airport runway.

Tom and I sit at one of only two tables squashed up here, cold shandies in straight, curveless glasses in front of us. At the other table, a woman sits alone, rolling cigarettes, long blond hair trailing down her back, steam from a small chimney behind her puffing out the smell of the kitchen downstairs. Yeasty batter and hot vegetable oil.

"So come on, is it the tiles?" says Tom, sitting back in the wooden chair opposite me, shaded, except from a beam of sun that hits his tanned arm. "You're quiet. Do you think I've got terrible taste and you're trying to think of a way to break it to me?"

"Nah, your taste is all right, Thomas," I say with a smile. "And I'm OK. Probably just tired, that's all. Didn't sleep well." And of course, it's not that. It's the house. It's moving. Or not moving. It's every decision I have to make and wish I didn't have to.

Tom gives a nod. A warm breeze ruffles his hair.

"Nice place, this, anyway," I say. "Super quiet and tucked away. It's like . . . an old man pub having a midlife crisis."

Tom laughs. "Yeah, I like it. Especially up here. I like that it feels like an afterthought. Like we could just suddenly fall through the roof and land in some old codger's lap because it's not *quite* a terrace, is it? More a . . . decorated roof. This is my old street actually."

"Really? I thought you were a Finsbury Park man."

"Not always," Tom sips. "You see . . ." He points over the trellis, to a squat block of flats, old brick, square sixties windows, wide, brick-built balconies. "That building there. The flat roof. First flat I ever lived in. With my fiancée."

He says those last words, like he already knows it'll make my ears prick up.

"You had a *fiancée*," I repeat.

He gives a deep nod. "Oh, yeah, Natalie Fincher. Eight years ago now. I even got down on one knee. Very basic. Very conventional and institutionalized."

I laugh. "Did you have it written on a dessert in chocolate sauce? *Marry me*?"

"No, but there may have been rose petals. *Argh.* I know. I sicken myself." He laughs, nibbles his lip, embarrassedly. "Anyway. We moved in. Got engaged. And that flat—it felt like the start of my life. Or something. Everything I was gonna have that was . . . nothing like what I'd known. My parents, mainly."

"What's—what's wrong with your parents?"

Tom wrinkles his nose, taps a finger on the wooden table. "My mum's amazing, but she's spent the last twenty or so years of her life being slowly whittled down by my dad."

"Don," I say. "I mean, she never says much, but the things she *does say* about him sometimes—"

"Mm. I really don't know why she stays, Natalie."

"*Really*? That bad?"

Tom raises his dark eyebrows and sighs. "Yup. I think they're together through habit, or . . . stagnation? He's had—Jesus, I don't know, four affairs? That we know of . . ."

"Oh my god. Are you serious?"

Tom nods, gives a sad, lazy shrug. "It's just how it's always been. Since I was about—I don't know. Eight, maybe?"

"Fuck. And Shauna, she's so . . ."

"I know." Tom shifts closer, rests a tanned, muscular forearm on the table. "Anyway. I moved out of there, couldn't wait to be honest, to be away from it, and me and Lou, my fiancée, we found this place. And . . . I was *pumped*. And for about six months, we played out this perfect little scene, you know? We set a date, we decorated, we did the whole straight-off-the-shelf, grown-up-couple thing, and then—she just broke it off."

"Out of nowhere?" I realize, sitting here with him, that we've never spoken about Tom's love life, in any way. (Besides the fact he's single and his friends set him up with someone at Avocado Clash who kept gazing lovingly at his crotch.) And someone leaving him, having an engagement broken off? It isn't quite what I would've guessed for Tom.

"*Ah.*" He gives a sardonic smile. "For me it was out of nowhere, yeah. But three weeks later, she was moved in with some guy she worked with, and it turned out it'd started while we were together, so."

"Ouch," I say.

"*Yup.* I was . . ." He blows out a long sigh, his dark hair bristling in its breeze. "Wrecked. Like . . . blindsided."

"God. I bet. That's . . . hard."

Tom nods. "Yeah, it was. I mean, it was a long time ago now. Plus, we'd have never worked in reality. She was prickly. Once ignored me for a week because I took the piss out of Cliff Richard."

"*To his face?*"

Tom laughs. "I'm not that rock 'n' roll, Natalie. No, it was on TV. And she was obsessed with him."

"Was she an old age pensioner?"

Tom laughs again, surprised, and so do I, and I love the sound it makes, our laughter together, up here on this weird, decorated roof in this weird old man pub. "No, strangely," he says. "Two years younger than me, actually . . ."

"Fucking hell."

"I know." Tom grins. "Bit of a red flag, eh? Anyway. The reason I'm banging on about this is . . . months later, I was still rattling about in the flat, and I didn't know at the time why I found it so hard to move out. But I think that flat sort of represented something that I wasn't ready to let go of. I knew once I moved out, that'd be it. Definitely over. Definitely cheated on. Definitely a jilted knob with rose petals." He meets my eyes and smiles slowly. "But the truth is, flat or no flat—you can't go back. Ever."

"At all?"

A gust of smoke appears behind Tom as the woman at the next table lights up a cigarette.

"I mean, what do I know?" he says. "I just think—I'm not the man who moved into that flat. And I wasn't the day Lou left. And that's—that's how it's supposed to be. We learn, we change, we adapt, we build walls . . ."

"I guess," I say.

Tom sips slowly, and the woman next to us smokes, watching the vapor blown from her lips intently, lingering in the summer air, as if she's proud of it.

"I guess I'm not the woman who moved into that house," I say quietly, as if I'm frightened to say the words too loudly. A car on the road below screeches by, the bass of its sound system rattling through the streets. "I'm not even close."

Tom says nothing, then, "Who is she now?"

"She's—I don't know." I can't get the words out. Nothing comes, and I feel rigid, stuck to this chair. Like my bones are concrete, like the blood has left my body. Tom watches me, then leans forward gently across the table.

"Look, I haven't been where you are," he says warmly. "And . . . I know you feel like you don't need anyone, that it's easier just to not say anything for fear of—well, *bad brunches*. Open mic nights and therapists with steel drums—"

"Bongo drums."

"*Bongo drums.*" He smiles softly. "But—I just wanted you to know I'm here. If you want me to be."

My whole body floods with warmth. Cheeks, ears, legs, chest—like there's a temperature gauge attached to me, like one of those toys with the giant heads. A joke. A joke is usually what I'd always reach for, in serious moments like this, to break the ice, show whoever it is, "I'm okay! Honest!" But it feels genuine with Tom. Real. Like he really, actually means it. And so, I nod, and say nothing else, and just let his words sink into me, absorb, like sunlight.

"Even if you just want to sit and talk," says Tom. "Or sit and *not* talk. I'll even listen to your boring bullshit takes if you like—you know, or those rants about your knob-head friend who doesn't stop talking about all the bread she makes, for example . . ."

I laugh. "How do you know about Roxanne?"

"Everyone has a bread friend, I find." Tom smilingly sips his drink. "And I'd never tell you what to do. And in a minute, we'll go home, and you can choose to only ever chat to me when you bump into me at Mum's shop—but also, if you want to, we can be . . . I dunno, we don't even have to be friends. Maybe I can be—just Tom?"

"Just Tom," I say, my wobbly voice giving me away now. I feel emotional. I feel touched. "Damp-fixing. Walks in nature reserves . . ."

"Tart and tile shopper." He nods, with a smile. "Whatever you need. No judgment."

"Padlocked," I say.

"Padlocked," Tom agrees.

My insides feel gooey. Like I'm made of ice cream, standing in a giant sun ray that's melting me to mush.

"Thank you," I say. "Seriously, Tom."

"Course," is all he says back.

We both lift our glasses to our lips in unison, as the woman at the next table receives an order of cheesy chips. The cheese slurry melted on top of them is the color of French mustard.

"And I am scared." I say, "That's my evergreen word." And it feels like a confession. Like a weight I'm slowly sliding, like a bag, from my shoulders.

"What are you scared of?" asks Tom.

"Everything. Of never feeling like myself again. Or feeling *too much* like myself again. Scared of moving. Of *not*. Of talking about him. Of not talking about him. And I'm scared people don't tell me the truth because they think I'm too fragile for it. And maybe I am. But it's like—sometimes I just want someone to tell me when I'm being a dickhead. You know?"

"We're all scared of something," says Tom. "That's *normal—*"

"Are you? Scared?"

He laughs, gives his usual goofy, class-clown smile, but there's something in his eyes. "God, yeah. Loads of things."

"Like . . ."

"Turning out like my dad. Turning out like my mum. One worse than the other, but both—" He clamps his teeth together. "Yeah, no thank you. Would rather avoid altogether."

"So, what, you don't do relationships?"

Tom hesitates and gives a childlike smile. "Not really. And with good reason, I reckon."

My being an unsuspecting stand-in at the bar sort of makes sense now. A puzzle piece slotting into place, and I stop myself from leaning over and putting a hand on his, although in this moment I really want to. Because it's sort of sad to think of Tom holding himself back from love. He is nothing like his dad. I know that about him already.

"And crocodiles too," says Tom, reaching for a bag of crisps he'd tossed in the middle of the table when we first arrived. He opens them. "I'm definitely shit scared of crocodiles. It's the eyes, it's the lumpy, weird skin . . ."

"Love and crocodiles," I say. "An understandable combo, to be honest."

Tom gives a crooked, guarded smile, eyebrows raised, but says nothing, just jiggles the bag of crisps in his palm as if weighing it up. A wordless "But that's for another time."

"It's koalas for me," I say. "They look like they're dreaming up something. Something bad."

Tom nods earnestly. "Armed robbery," he says. "Eucalyptus trafficking. Wouldn't put it past them."

♪ ♪ ♪
♪ ♪ ♪

Walking back to the car later with Tom, I feel floaty. Like weights have been removed from my shoes. That specific feeling you get after sharing an afternoon with someone. Like you've been in a vacuum, just you two, and an endless conversation you swear could go on for several years if you let it. And just having Tom say that—*I'm here. Padlocked.* It meant something. Shifted something.

"Your mission is to find out what's in Joe's notebooks," says Tom. "I'm guessing bad poetry. Beachy Joe who writes in notebooks in cafés? Screams bad angsty poetry to me, Foxes, sorry, hate to break it to you." A smile breaks out on my face at the sound of him calling me Foxes.

"OK, *Sherlock*."

"*Speaking* of Sherlock," replies Tom. "I did manage to check the piano. But no luck, I'm afraid."

"I assumed," I say flatly. "Ugh, is it bad that sort of breaks my heart a bit? It was getting me up in the morning. That spark, that excitement of it."

"The spark."

"*Yes.* The spark. Exactly. God, that makes me sound like a right saddo, doesn't it? My name's Natalie and mystery paper is what excites me, how about you? *Very normal.*"

"Ah, stop, you could never be a saddo." Tom slows by the car, swings the car key around his finger. "Although I do have a theory. About your music."

"Do you?"

I circle to the passenger-seat door. Someone holding a bunch of flowers waits at the door of a house behind me.

"Maybe it stopped because Maxwell got caught and he's secretly in love with you. Felt bad when you approached him. Didn't want to torture you any longer."

"*What?*"

Tom laughs. "What? I thought it was a good one."

"It isn't."

"I just feel like I might leave music for someone if I was in love with them—"

The person with the flowers is greeted with a whoop and an "Oh, hello!" and the door closes behind them, the knocker jingling as it slams.

"I'm afraid you should stick to photos, Thomas Button. Your fan theories are not welcome here."

Tom opens the car door and rolls his eyes. "Just get in."

chapter fifteen

WhatsApp from Jodie: Good luck today, love! Where's he taking you? (And that is not a bad euphemism, I genuinely am asking where lol.)

WhatsApp from Priya: HAPPY WHITE TUX DAYYYY! Hope you have the best time! I want you to inject details into my eventless, bloated life asap btw. I'm living for it!!!

♫ ♫ ♫
♫ ♫ ♫

Today is one of those classic, airless summer days that turn London into a raging furnace and morph every resident into a grumpy expert on historical architecture. *These buildings were just not built for these temperatures. No tiles, no air-con! British houses keep heat in, they don't let it out!* The rehearsal rooms at music therapy as expected were unbearable this morning, and I lasted all of seven minutes in The

Smelly Room, which smelled like passing a landfill on a motorway. Joe had arrived in the final minute, poking his head around the door. "Sort of ironic that this is therapy," he said, "today it's more like a Bear Grylls challenge."

After the session, we decided that instead of grabbing coffee, we needed something cold, so we ordered iced teas to take away from an empty, just-opened juice bar. A lone photographer from a local paper stood snapping the balloon-arched entranceway on the street, and to mark the opening day, a woman behind the counter had flirtily leaned and slid novelty straw spectacles onto Joe's expressionless face.

"Um. Thanks?" Joe had said as she giggled, and outside, he'd stared at me in the glasses, deadpan, then dipped the straw into the iced tea and sipped. "Not sure if this invention is a win for the species," he'd said, "but anything's a life experience, I suppose," then he'd walked along in them for a while, pale green liquid traveling around his eyes, as I laughed, before he threw them into his backpack, grinning, saying, "That's enough airtime for those, what do we reckon?"

We arrive at the canal now, in Granary Square, the ice in our drinks already melted to thin shards. For a Thursday, it's busy, but the summer holidays mean there are families everywhere there usually aren't. Parents push strollers, children squeal through the water fountains that spurt from holes in the pavement, commuters in their lunch breaks perch on square pallet benches eating takeaway sandwiches, their shirt-sleeves rolled up, collars loosened and unbuttoned.

"So, how are you finding music therapy?" asks Joe. "So far. I know you're only two in . . ."

"Yeah, it's . . . good, I think?" I say. "Plus, I've never really done anything like this before, so I feel like I should persevere—give it some time. It helps Devaj is so *unbelievably* nice—"

"*So* bloody nice," says Joe. "So-nice-you-worry-he-might-suddenly-crack-and-lose-it nice." Joe flashes me a sideways smile, and

I almost wish I could take a photo of him with my eyes, like some sort of Terminator, so I could send it to Jodie. He looks good today. Sort of—boy-band-member good. The tousled dirty-blond hair, the wide hazel eyes, the beige chino shorts and Converse.

"And how about you?"

"Music therapy?" Joe shrugs. "I enjoy it, yeah. I try a lot of things, try and keep busy, but the people are sound at NMT. James and Dev are decent blokes. And music is something I've always sort of gravitated toward. Especially when shit hits the fan. It helped me when Tanner was in hospital. It was music over people. Well. It's always *something* over people for me." He gives a playful smile. Joe's an introvert, and I've wondered, as we've been talking over the last couple of weeks, if that was something that happened after losing his brother, or if he's always been this way. Grief made me withdraw, retract, like a tortoise, disappearing into its shell.

"How long was Tanner in hospital?" I ask.

"About three months after the injury," he says. "He was—basically thrown against a rock, in the sea? He was a surfer. Red-flagged beach. He broke bones, but—it was the head injury he struggled with. The doctors used to say he was lucky really, but—yeah, he'd have never ever agreed with that. *Lucky.*" He laughs sadly.

"God. That's awful."

Joe nods sadly. "He was in an induced coma for a bit—"

"So was Russ. Over at Melrose. In North London?"

Joe pauses, like he thinks I might say more, but then nods, pushing his hands into his pockets. "Nothing much worked, though," he says, as if he's told this story, to himself and to others, so many times that the words have lost all meaning. "They tried, but progress was so slow it was practically nonexistent. And it was like he just gave up." Joe runs a hand through his hair and sighs. "But yeah, the music therapy helps. A lot of it does, if you let it."

I stroll beside him, the hot sun beating down on my bare arms. "I hope so. Music's always been a bit of anchor for me. It's why I was actually tempted by the NMT ad."

"You saw my flyer." Joe smiles. "I'm glad. I didn't think anyone would take any notice. People hate flyers. People are *suspicious* of flyers."

I laugh. "I didn't realize it was yours."

"*Yeah.* Put it up. Waited for Devaj to be prank-called by the pervs of London town," he chuckles.

We wander along, and people trickle by us, cones balancing with mounds of pistachio-colored ice cream in their hands, sheens of sweat glistening on their foreheads. Last year there was a three-day heatwave, and I stayed inside the cottage for the entirety of it. I'd pretended to Jodie that I was simply following the guidance on ITV news, because "they said closed blinds kept the heat out and the cool in, Jode. I'm doing the clever thing by staying holed up! The *wise* thing! Heatstroke causes death, you know, and I do not wish to die." But really, I just wanted to avoid the pressure of it—to mark it with barbecues and pub gardens and photogenic happiness like I used to.

"And what other things do you try?" I ask Joe. "Anything I've simply *got* to do? A cure-all?"

"A cure-all? Besides a lobotomy," Joe replies dryly, removing a hand from his pocket and swiping it through his hair. "Mm, I'm not sure. I volunteer a bit. Visit people over at the hospital every week, people who don't have visitors, which is sometimes supremely depressing, but mostly it's pretty cool. Humbling. I saw a bereavement counselor for a while, too, but she sobbed once after I shared something with her and I felt guilty for *making* her cry, so, yeah, that sort of ended. Abruptly. Got enough guilt without her giving me an extra dose." He laughs. "Oh, but past-life regression. Jesus. Do *not* try do past-life regression."

"Oh my god, did you get put under? Actually hypnotized?"

"Yes, ma'am." Joe looks sideways at me and grimaces. "She basically told me I was some small Tudor boy who was rejected by his father, which I might have been able to get on board with, but then she told me my father was Cardinal Wolsey."

I burst out laughing. "Wow. So, I'm in the presence of an illegitimate Tudor child."

"Apparently, yeah." Joe laughs. "Gonna add it to my dating profile. What do you reckon?"

"Do it. A mention of Cardinal Wolsey and you'll have dates coming out of your ears. You're basically famous. A Tudor Brooklyn Beckham."

Joe and I slow by the railings overlooking the canal, the water thick and gravy-like, and come to a stop, look out. On the verge by the water, there are grassy steps for seating, almost like stands at a stadium, and people lounge back on them, shrugged-off cardigans as makeshift blankets, bottles of water warming in the sun.

"Who'd have thought it, eh?" I say, leaning against the railing. "Two Goode's customers, meeting like this . . ."

"I know," Joe says, smiling thoughtfully. "I see you all the time. Out the front. With the manager. Shauna, is it?"

"That's right. God, I dread to think the *awful* states you've seen me in over the last few months."

"Awful states?" asks Joe, then he shakes his head, presses his pink lips together into a straight line. "Nope. Can't say you've ever looked to be in an *awful state* to me."

I smile. "Well. That's because you're always staring at your notebook, Joe. You haven't taken enough notice."

"Ugh." Joe bows his head, two hands gripping the metal railing, a silver ring on his thumb. "You've seen me and the notebook. Me and my *sad* notebook."

"Course. You're Notebook Guy. Well, you were. That's what I named you."

"Shit, really? Notebook Guy, that's . . ." Joe laughs bashfully. No wonder Priya and Jodie want to see him in a white suit. He has that conventionally pretty face. Troubled eyes, full lips. Like a young Brendan Fraser. "I'm a writer. Poet, actually. Or—I used to be." *Poetry.* A jolt of excitement surges through me at the idea of texting Tom to tell him he's right. He'll be insufferable. He'll be so full of "I told you so's" that I'll have to block him. "But I haven't been able to write a single thing for over—two years now?"

"Since your brother?" I ask.

Joe nods. "Sounds crazy, right? But seriously, nothing comes out. Well, besides *drivel.* And I try. I even do what all the books say, set by all this time for it, try and encourage it to come. Every week, I volunteer a few streets over, I go for coffee, I sit there, just me and the page and—yeah. Nada."

"So—ye olde creative block . . ."

"Ye olde guilt, I think," says Joe quietly. "Everything is guilt for me." And he says those words like they're a question, like he's used to people, like I am too, exclaiming '*Guilt? Why guilt? But you've done nothing wrong!*'"

"For me too," I say. "The guilt is the thing. I'm . . . basically pickled in it."

Joe meets my eyes and nods, a soft, understanding smile at one corner of his mouth. "Same. Joe Jacobs. Marinaded in guilt. Seasoned heavily with it . . ."

"Battered in it."

"Deep-fried in it."

We both laugh, and God, I feel like my blood is warm syrup all of a sudden. He gets it. Joe gets it—gets *me.* And I feel like I could cry, like I could jump over the sodding moon like the cow in the nursery rhyme, break out into a mad barn dance out here on the street, powered by the pure relief of having someone who understands.

A narrow boat chugs down the canal, and a couple below take photos of it on their phones. I think of Tom as it drifts by. Him on his bed, as a child, doing his little sailor look.

He's coming over next Saturday to tile, Just Tom, and I already can't wait to tell him about today. "*Nice one, Foxes*," I imagine him saying, "*you and Notebook Joe swapping guilt and stories by the canal, eh?*"

"If it helps you feel any better," I say, "I get it. The creative block."

"Yeah?"

"Totally. I haven't played or written properly in almost three years."

"You mean—piano?"

"Yep."

Joe's lips part then, the muscles on his face sort of drooping in unison. "Seriously? I saw you a few weeks ago. At the piano at the station."

"That's the only place I do play these days," I say, and hearing the words out loud, here in the summer sun, real and true, makes my heart sag a little, as if it's let out a little sigh. "I used to teach. I wrote a musical with my friend Edie. It was called *Dotted Line*. I wrote and played every single day. It was my happiness, really, playing music."

Joe stares at me. "Is it since Russ? That you've stopped."

A breeze blows along the canal. Warm and sudden and smelling of seaside sugary donuts.

"Yeah," I say. "I played for him every day in hospital. For recovery, you know? And I was so sure he was going to get better that all the pain and worry and my life being on hold—it felt temporary. But he didn't get better. The music didn't work, and then Edie and I fell out, and playing piano for a reason just became this thing I *used* to do. In fact, everything feels like something I used to do."

Joe doesn't say anything, but his eyes stare down at the canal, in deep thought. Eventually he says, "And what did you used to do?"

"God, everything. I sometimes think that's maybe the key: doing everything I used to do. Some of my friends definitely think that. Go back to how it was—how I was. But—I don't know. It seems like another life, doing all that stuff." I sip my iced tea. It's watery, the peach syrup barely detectable now that the ice has melted. "Russ and I saw a lot of live bands. And he was a proper nature-head, so we went to lots of forests I'd moan my way around because I'd wear stupid sandals and get stung by nettles." I laugh, the hot metal railing like a radiator under my forearm. "And we'd find parks and festivals in the summer and stuff, and we shopped for records, tried to find the weirdest, cringiest covers—sat around, made plans for our little cottage . . ."

Joe smiles. "You have a cottage?"

"Yep. Although it sounds much cuter than it actually is. It's—a hovel, really. Needs loads of work. We were going to renovate it. But—well, I don't know what I'm doing."

"I decorated a beach hut for Tanner," says Joe, sliding his phone out of his pocket. "I went all *DIY SOS*. We bought it before he died. Parents said I should sell it, but—ah, I dunno. We bought it together, and Tanner worked on that beach, life-guarding. I couldn't bring myself to do it." Joe swipes through his phone and shows me some photos. A bright orange beach hut, with graffiti and messages written all over it, sits on the beachfront, an indigo sunset behind it, so perfect you'd think it was a green screen. "So, I kept it. Painted it. For him."

"That's so beautiful," I say. "And do you go back at all? To Dorset? To the hut . . ."

Joe shakes his head, slides his phone back into his pocket. "Yeah, I've gotta confess, I've not been for ages," he says. "I don't really like going back. But—you should think about it."

"About what?"

"Getting a touch of the *DIY SOS*es." He smiles. "Doing something Russ wanted. Like the hut. It could help."

"Maybe," I nod, and I grip the railing, and tip my face a little, toward the sun. Would it help? Say—putting in a greenhouse, or decorating the living room in that shade of green he wanted, going through our Pinterest board trying to ignite that flame of excitement we both had when we bought the cottage . . .

A pigeon lands on the railing beside Joe, the feathers on his head ruffled and scraggy, like he's had a hair wash and hasn't blow-dried it yet.

"Oh," he says. "Hey. Ratbag. I mean, nobody said you could join, but okay . . ."

I laugh. "So, this is what you swapped sandy beaches for is it? London pigeons. Dirty canals. And the smelly room."

"Apparently so." Joe smiles. "And the smelly room isn't so bad," he says, touching an arm to mine, "not now you play in it. Ain't that right, Ratbag?"

♪ ♪ ♪
♪ ♪ ♪

It's almost four by the time Joe and I leave the canal and walk back to the train station together, hot-skinned and exhausted and sun-sapped. I wait outside the tiny supermarket for him as he ducks in for a pint of milk for home, and enjoy the wisps of icy air-con of the shop's entranceway. The piano sits there, a few meters away, silent, empty, commuters whisking by it. I peer behind me, through the glass of the shop window. Joe is in a chaotic-looking queue with at least two people left to go before him. And—ugh, I can't help myself. Yes, I might feel disappointed, yes, it might deflate the joy that's puffed me up from my afternoon with Joe, like a big ol' giant pin to the human balloon that I am right now, but I can't not. I have to check it. I can't ignore the tingling and sparking beneath my skin when I think about the chance of there being something there again, in that stool.

I flit across the floor, almost tiptoe, like someone unhinged, like I used to when I was a teenager, sneaking into Jodie's room at night to sit on the end of her bed and make her psychoanalyze the texts Daniel Paphitis from biology class had sent me because "this time he said hello not hi!"

I lift the lid. Slowly.

And there it is.

Another piece of music. As usual, freshly printed, but the paper slightly thicker this time, like card. "Strawberry Swing" by Coldplay. Everyone who knows me well knows I cried along to Coldplay CDs throughout secondary school. Russ agreed once, that if I ever, in a mad turn of events, met Chris Martin, and he, in an even madder turn of events, came onto me, I was allowed to kiss him on the lips, just the once . . .

And as I turn, I see Joe crossing the floor toward me, looking at me like he might be regretting this—hanging out with someone who bounds toward him holding a piece of paper in her hand like Charlie Bucket waving a golden ticket. But the excitement shoots through me like a firework at the sight of it. I can't help it.

"What is it?" Joe asks, half smiling. "Seriously, what's going on?"

"So—this is gonna sound so weird, but—someone leaves me music." I'm breathless, smiling ear to ear, as I speak. I definitely must look deranged. "And . . . it stopped."

Joe's eyes are unblinking, a carrier bag in his hand. *Never fear, Notebook Joe, I am quite normal really. In the right circumstances.*

"Anyway. Some has been left. *Today.* After weeks without it."

"Seriously?" Joe still stares, but suddenly, with his free hand, he reaches up, takes the music from my hand. "'Strawberry Swing,'" he utters. "Wow, this is so—"

"I loved Coldplay," I jump in. "When I was a teenager. And the songs that've been left, they're always sort of important to me. Poignant, you know? Like, they have meaning?"

"And this was left—today? While we were at the canal?" He turns over the page in his hand. Joe looks almost spellbound, even throws a glance over his shoulder, as if he might spot the culprit hanging upside down from the ceiling, all in black. "Jeez . . ."

"Yup." I grin, pull out my phone. "Definitely while we were out. I checked this morning. Sorry, I just need to text my friends and tell them. We've been on tenterhooks about this."

"Really?"

"Yeah!" I laugh, and Joe lets out a confused half-chuckle then, of surprise at probably how hysterical I've suddenly turned. I feel high. I sound high. All squeaky, like it's 1995 and Boyzone just crash-landed in my garden. That spark, that excitement, back in full force. I text Jodie, then Priya, then Shauna. I would rush upstairs to tell her, but Jason said this morning she's off sick, which I don't think I have ever known to happen. "We've all been so intrigued, placing bets on who it could be. We even tried to catch them by staking it out."

"Did you see anyone? On your stakeout?"

"No. Nothing. I still hope, somehow, it's Russ."

"Russ . . ."

I look up at poor, confused Joe. "Yeah, maybe something he arranged. Sorry. I just—literally bounded toward you and screamed about music in your face, you must think I've just landed from Mars. Because of course, I'm *acting* like I've just landed from Mars."

Joe laughs, shakes his head. "Not at all. I just—well, it's proper wild, isn't it? The fact someone did this while we were at the canal. Who would . . . who would do that?"

"I know," I say, and it's that I think about on the train home. Joe and me in the sunshine, and just a few miles away, someone leaving music for me, about blue skies and perfect days.

chapter sixteen

I whoosh open the front door. *"Come in, come in!"*

"Er—"

"I've made coffee. *And—*" I angle the wooden spoon in my hand to point at Tom. "I've made breakfast."

A smile spreads across Tom's face. "You have, have you?"

"*Yup.* Eggs. Toast. Actual mashed avocado—thought it could represent our first-ever meeting. I even bought chili flakes to sprinkle over it. Like all those wanky cafés do."

Tom laughs, ducking to come inside through my low-framed rickety little front door. "No sausages?"

"I'm afraid not, Thomas. I hate sausages. This is a sausage-free zone. It's mashed-up meat all jammed into a weird, phallic case. I don't see what there is to like."

"*Phallic case,*" says Tom. "Scathing. Anyway. It's not as nice, but"—he holds up a bucket—"I brought the grout."

"Perfect. Come in. Let me feed you up as payment."

After tile shopping and drinks, Tom and I had arranged that he would come over in two Saturdays to tile the splashback in the bathroom. I'd sent a text three times asking for a price, and he ignored

them, but eventually texted back: "coffee, and perhaps, a biscuit?" followed by "see you at 10?" And of course, as ever, Tom is bang on time.
Ten a.m. exactly. And something that is not so much "as ever," *I'm*
awake, rested, dressed, and have been since eight. I've cleaned, I've
put washing on, I've filled the dishwasher, and even found the time to
dash to the little Londis on the corner, for avocados and fresh sour-
dough. (*And* the wanky chili flakes, of course.) I couldn't wait to see
him. To tell him about Joe, and the endless afternoon we spent by the
canal on the grass verge, with ice cream and drink after drink. And to
tell him that there was more music left. (And how I frightened poor
Joe, when I shoved it in his pretty face.)

Tom follows me through to the kitchen, where before I answered
the door, I was whisking eggs in a big mixing bowl I have used only
once in my life, and that was on Lucy's birthday, when I baked her a
cake (and fucked it up so badly that Russ and I ate the entire thing—in
giant chunks in front of the TV after).

"I hope you're hungry . . ."

Tom puts down his rucksack and the bucket of grout neatly on
the floor. "I'm *always* hungry."

"Good. Because I've whisked like a hundred dozen eggs. I'm like
. . . Gaston or something." I look up at him and smile. "Sit. I'll put the
coffee on."

Tom takes a seat, and while I fuss with the coffee machine, I can
feel him looking at me and it makes me almost too self-conscious to
turn around. Tom looks good today, but then he always does. Clean
and fresh, his muscular arms tanned, a five-o'clock shadow just perfectly so. And his smell . . . it's always the same. Like clean washing
and hot showers.

"So, you're looking . . ."

"*Alive*?" I offer. "Awake?"

Tom leans his forearms to rest on the breakfast bar and laces his fingers together. "I was actually going to say you look extremely—pretty today."

"Really?" And I'm so glad I'm facing the coffee machine, because my face is suddenly so hot, I feel like I have pizza stones for cheeks. I'm actually blushing, for God's sake. I'm actually blushing. "Probably . . . just makeup. And sleep."

"And you seem happy," he says. "I can see it on your face."

"Can you?" I turn, hand him his mug of coffee.

"Thanks," he says. "And yeah, you'll be surprised what you can see when you look. It's always the eyes."

"Right," I reply. "And the photographer in the room is saying my eyes say . . . happy?"

"*Yeah*, happy and maybe even"—he cocks an eyebrow—"excited about something?"

I can't help but smile, and it's one of those smiles that just keep on going, the type that you can't stop, that spread into your cheeks, and screw your whole face up without permission. "Maybe."

He chuckles. "Maybe?"

And before I laugh in his face, give myself away, hand myself to Tom for an afternoon of piss-taking when he finds out I had a giddily good day with Joe, I turn around and put an oiled pan on the heat. Scrambled eggs. One of the only things I can do without setting myself on fire. That, cereal, and also Super Noodles. "Just—things are good, I suppose," I say. "Plus, I slept well last night. And the night before actually. The foxes are all shagged out, it seems. Sexual appetites officially satisfied."

"Well, that's good," Tom says. "Good for you. And definitely them."

"And what about you?" I pour in the eggs, turn down the heat. "You were online *very* late the other night."

Tom raises his eyebrows. "*Was I?*"

"Well, I went to send you this meme about birds—heron-themed, actually—and thought, no, Nat, it's two a.m., nobody is awake at two a.m. But then I saw you were online."

"You should've sent it," he says. "Why didn't you?"

"Didn't want to interrupt anything," I say. "Thought you might have been . . . you know . . ." I give him a big, ludicrous wink, and he laughs.

"Well, regardless of any—" He throws another ridiculous wink back at me. "Herons always welcome."

"Ah, so he's not denying it," I tease. "And I promise, you can tell me, I won't tell your mum."

Tom smiles sheepishly, sips his coffee. "Nothing much to tell," he says.

"And how is your mum, by the way? I texted, but she took ages to read it. Jason said she's not been well."

Tom sighs noisily, and it tapers off into a groan. "Don't ask, Foxes. Seriously. Save yourself."

"Oh shit, what do you mean? Is she all right?"

Tom shrugs, then stretches in the seat. His T-shirt rides up revealing a tiny glimpse of toned stomach. "Who knows? She got a phone call from one of her mates, Angela, and it turns out this Angela could've sworn she saw Dad over near his work, by the river, with another woman. Outside a restaurant. Holding *hands*—"

"Oh my god."

"I know," he says flatly. "Mum was—well, obviously she was gutted. We were over there for my brother's birthday, and then this phone calls comes, like a fucking *bomb*, and Dad was late, said he was caught at work . . . Anyway, long story short, he denied it, said it was Angela being a bit nuts because she can't stand him—and to fair, she can't. Same as most of Mum's friends."

"God," I say. "I'm sorry. That sounds—*awful.*"

Tom takes in a big breath, his broad chest rising beneath the black material of his T-shirt. "Yeah," he says. "But—God. He's such a good fucking liar, and he's always so devastated." He scoffs, a short burst of laughter. "Seriously, Natalie, he's so convincing. But he schmoozes for a living these days, it's all corporate shit, securing all these mega contracts, huge high-rises and stuff, so . . . transferable skills, I guess. Anyway, it's all blown over now and they're even talking about an anniversary party, which—" He winces, a muscle pulsing in his jaw. "Can you imagine? A *party*? Celebrating their bloody marriage. Makes me wanna . . . emigrate or like . . . go into witness protection."

"Don't do that." I smile at him sadly, take the pan off the heat. "And do you believe him? About the woman?"

Tom turns his hands over on the breakfast bar counter, showing his palms, and grimaces. "I just don't know. As I said . . . he's so convincing. Plus, it's where he works and they're forever taking clients out for drinks and meals and all that shit, so who knows? Could've been absolutely nothing. Could've been Angela reading into nothing. Or it could be something. With him, it could go either way. He had a thing with a woman at work before, so . . ." He sips his coffee. "*Anyway.* Where's this breakfast that isn't sausages?"

I slide a plate across the breakfast bar toward him. "Here. And you're sure you're OK? I can't even imagine having to deal with drama from my parents. Isn't it supposed to be the other way around?"

"Ah." Tom gives a heavy shrug, the large, round muscles of his shoulders rising and falling. "And of course I'm fine. Always am. But now—I'm afraid you're going to have to cleanse the palate and tell me all about your hot date with Notebook Joe. I want a dissertation. I want a fuckin'—I don't know. A Wikipedia page. Subheadings. Quotes. All of it."

"Of course," I laugh, sitting opposite him with my own plate. "Of course. But first things first—"

"It wasn't a date," says Tom. "Yeah, yeah, *OK*, sure, whatever you say—"

"Well, yes," I reply, pointing my fork at him. "I was definitely going to say that, but what I was going to say first was that there was music left again. Practically gave him a heart attack, and I'm not a hundred percent sure he didn't alert some sort of authority about me but—it was there. Brand-new piece."

"Really?"

"Yup. I was so excited. Practically yelped in the station."

Tom laughs. "Course you did."

"I need to load up my suspects list," I say. "Get staking out again, maybe."

"Your *suspects list*?"

"I have one on my phone. A list of people it could be."

"Interesting," says Tom. "Who's on it?"

I leave out the fact his name is on it, and I haven't had a chance to mark it off yet.

"God, barely anyone now. Maxwell was on it for a while. Jodie thinks I should add Rob and Teddy, Russ's brothers, which I hadn't considered. I think Edie's the only name on there at the moment. Which feels like shitting in my own cornflakes, because she's who I really don't want it to be."

Tom chews, thinks. The boiler on the wall clicks twice, then rumbles, like something igniting. "Well, maybe stop shitting in your own cornflakes," he says with a smile. "Plus, it probably isn't Edie. It could be anyone. I mean, you play music to thousands of people every week, and if you think about it, you make a difference all the time to people you don't even know. *Strangers—*"

"I wouldn't say I make a difference, Tom." I scoff a laugh, cut a corner from my eggs on toast. The toast is as hard as plaster. I could probably tile the bathroom with it. "Honestly, nobody really listens to me at the station. That's why I think it must be someone I know."

"Natalie, you play to loads of people every day—"

"Who have no idea who I am, who have places to go, jobs to get to, countries to visit—"

"But they listen."

"Well, *yeah*, but—they listen because they have no excuse but to listen. I'm literally playing in the middle of a public place. In a train station, where people a lot of the time have no choice but to be. I'm ramming it down their throats really." I laugh. "*I know you're trying to get to a job you despise grumpy man in a suit, but here, listen to me! Oh, you don't want to? Tough titties!*"

Tom laughs and puts down his fork. "You seriously think nobody likes your playing, that nobody's day is made by hearing you . . ."

I give a shrug. "Nobody's really taking any notice. Honestly."

"*Sure* they're not." Tom shakes his head, a wordless "I give up," and says, "You're wrong by the way," and picks up his fork again. "So come on. How was Notebook Joe?"

"Oh. He was—" And I grin. I can't help it. It overtakes my face like a rash. "He was lovely. Honestly, we had such a nice afternoon. We chatted and laughed and—he gets it. He gets the music and creative *block* and not feeling like who you used to be and—he even helped me. With ideas for the cottage."

"Ideas?"

"Just—at how maybe it might help, if I think about what Russ wanted. For the house. He decorated this amazing beach hut for his brother. Sort of—in his honor. He said it helped."

"I see," says Tom. "And are you going to—do that here?"

"I'm not sure," I reply, "but it's given me something to think about, you know? Anyway, we've arranged to go to some food festival together next week. He booked tickets. *Me,* Thomas. A food festival. When scrambled eggs is right up there as one of my greatest culinary accomplishments. I reckon I'll set fire to a few food tents just being present."

Tom gives a slight smile. "Wow. That's—so an actual date, eh, Foxes?"

"No," I jump in. "No, I don't think it's a date. Well, it doesn't feel date-y anyway, to me. At least not yet. But it's nice, don't get me wrong. Meeting someone new. *A guy.* And having him just totally understand what I'm going through, not expecting me to be a certain way. He totally got the guilt stuff . . ."

"I'm glad," says Tom sincerely. And I'm surprised, because I expected, like always from Tom, the teasing, the ribbing.

"And—did you find out?" he asks now. "What's in the notebook? Please say you know what's in the notebook."

"Oh my god, Tom, I *did.*"

"*Say it.*"

"Poems!"

Tom makes a sound like someone just stabbed him in the heart with a stake. "Poems? Holy shit, I knew it. I would have laid my entire life on it. My kidneys. My *soul.*"

"Yep. You nailed it."

"Please tell me he's not like those men on Instagram though. You know, who try to write poems on toilet paper with their own cigarette ash and remnants of their irritable bowels—"

I burst out laughing. "No! No, no, honestly. I mean, I don't actually know, he's got writer's block, not written in ages, but—no. I would guess not. Thank God. I didn't get any cigarette ash, bowel-y feelings anyway. . ."

"Of *course* he's a poet," says Tom.

"And a surfer. Well, he used to surf. On the beach. With his brother."

Tom meets my gaze across the counter and shakes his head

slowly, like someone disappointed in the news. "You're gonna be toast," he says.

"What?!"

"A risk-taking, surfing poet. Even *I* fancy him."

"Well, that makes one of us."

"I give you a week, Foxes." Tom laughs. "Then you'll be all, 'Oh, I fancy him, Tom. I didn't think I did but I do, Tom, it's the poems, it's the adrenaline, it's the beachy locks and the way he smears cigarette ash across a page . . .'"

I nudge him under the table with my knee. He does it back, grins at me across the countertop, but leaves it there, just touching. "This time next year, you'll be Mrs. Notebook Joe," he says. "Mark my words."

"You can come to the wedding, then. Bring Miss Two A.M."

"She doesn't like weddings," says Tom.

"Oh. So, there *is* a Miss Two A.M."

"Sausages," deflects Tom. "Such a shame there're no sausages."

chapter seventeen

I've imagined for years what it would be like to see Edie again. To come face-to-face with the woman who tore the final thread keeping my heart in one piece. This was never in any of my imagined scenarios, though. Seeing her today, on a regular, hot, summer's Thursday, in a back street in Euston, was never in any of my daydreams.

This morning, I'd spent what felt like an age getting ready. I'd put on a dress I'd bought at work—one I'd really liked when Jodie had me model it for Tina's Instagram stories—and I'd spent longer than ten minutes on my makeup inspired by a YouTube video I'd watched. I even followed a tutorial on TikTok to get "the perfect" half-up, half-down hair-do and then (half) nailed it. I know it isn't a date, and I know I don't even fancy the bloke. But I wanted to make the effort for the food festival Joe and I had planned to go to after music therapy. I wanted to look nice. And there was a tiny part of me thinking, as I applied actual lipstick in my dusty dressing table mirror, that maybe Jodie was right—maybe it is sort of—and I don't think I have *ever* used this word in my whole, entire thirty-three-year-long life—*fated*. To meet someone who has been through what I have, who completely understands me and accepts me, as I am. To have him right under my nose, at Goode's, for all those months, and have no idea we were feeling the same pain. And my steps were more like springs on the way here. I felt buoyant and bouncy and part of the world. Like I was skipping, on the path to bloody Oz.

But now. Now, I'm frozen. Rigid. Because Edie is in front of me. And I can't run like I do in my daydreams, I can't keep walking, pretending she isn't there, or that I haven't seen her. I can't even dash for an imaginary taxi or bus. I'm stuck here, feet on the bottom step of the rehearsal rooms' stairs, Edie on the ground, having just arrived through the heavy, cranberry juice colored door.

"Natalie." Her hands fly to her chest, then to her cheeks. "*Oh my god*. Natalie." Her words are more breaths than sounds. Whereas I feel like all the breath has left my body and I'm just bones, frozen here on the stairs.

"Hi," I say. No other words will come out. Even my "hi" has blunt edges. I can hardly look at her. Edie looks the same. Her long hair scuffed up in a messy bun, a long, floral, sack of a dress drifting down to her feet. Like an effortless FatFace model. She looks kind. Edie has that face. Kind and sympathetic. The sort people spill their life stories to in club toilets, unprompted.

"I'm—oh, I can't believe it's you." Her beautiful, angular pixie face breaks into a smile. "Are you—what are you doing here? This is—"

"I'm meeting a friend," I say. "He's waiting."

"Oh."

Joe. Joe's waiting outside for me, to walk to the festival in Regent's Park. I'd stayed behind after therapy today to talk to Devaj about an idea he and James have for a song writing therapy workshop—a class to encourage people to write and compose their own songs, about their experiences, about their pain—and Joe had told me he'd wait downstairs. Devaj and I had talked for ten minutes, and from the window upstairs, I could see Joe, patiently waiting for me on the hot concrete below, adjusting his hair awkwardly in a car windscreen's reflection, flattening a part of it, then roughing it back up. It made me smile. I just had no idea this was waiting for me downstairs instead. A moment I have dreaded, imagined in detail, with a churning stomach, for almost three years.

"Wow, Nat, I can't . . . wow."

"I've got to go."

"Natalie—"

"*I've got to go*," I say again.

Edie's deep brown eyes are glistening now, like sunshine on water, as I walk past her, and I know Edie Matthews almost as well as I know myself. She wants to cry. Edie always did cry easily. Soap operas, puppies, little old men at bus stops in pressed trousers and brogues. I loved it about her. Would almost tell her things sometimes, little stories, embellished, just to make her cry, then we'd lose ourselves with laughter over it, Edie dabbing at the blobs of mascara under her eyes, saying, "Why do you do this to me, Nat!?"

"I'm rehearsing," Edie says. I stop on the thin carpet. "We use this space sometimes. And other times we use one over in the West. Do you remember the one—gosh, I can't remember the name of the street, it was—"

"I need to go," I say again. My heart is thumping, like it might drum itself free. I feel sick. Physically sick. I place a hand on the heavy, metal exit—then stop.

"Edie," I say, turning. "Can I ask you something?"

"*Of course.*" Edie smiles a watery smile, and I see her eyes take me in. A drift from head to toe. I wonder what she's thinking. Does she think I've changed? That I've aged? That I've let myself go, since Russ, since we stopped talking. Will she text Lucy later, say, "Gosh, Luce, she looked terrible. I can't believe what it's done to her, the grief. So bloody sad. :("

"What is it?" asks Edie. "Is everything OK, Nat?"

And I soften then, because—it's Edie. My best friend. My writing partner. My do-or-die. Those words that have come out of her mouth countless times over our lifetime. Breakups and rejections and toxic jobs and accidents and creative wobbles and self-doubt. I love her, and I always will. That's why it hurts so much, seeing her. I love her. And she lied to me.

"Are you leaving me music?" I ask, and the question feels like it weighs twelve hundred pounds in the air above us.

"Am I . . ."

"Leaving me music. At St. Pancras. At the piano."

"Are you still playing there?" asks Edie, and a smile, just a tiny one, flickers onto her lips. "Lucy said that you do sometimes, and I think that's . . . I don't know—"

"What, tragic?"

"No. God, no, Natalie. I meant the opposite. I think it's beautiful and brave and—*so you*. You were always so fearless. I always wanted to be like you, you know that."

I stare at her, and a lump gathers in my throat, like a hard, hot ball. I miss her. I really miss her, and I wish I didn't. I am equal parts wanting to leg it down the road and throw my arms around her.

"Are you," I swallow, "leaving the music for me or not?"

Edie shakes her head, her brow wrinkling. "No, Nat, I'm not. And do you mean sheet music? Someone is leaving you sheet music—"

"So it isn't you."

"No," says Edie. "No, it isn't me." And I know it isn't. Edie's a good liar. We already know that, but I know it isn't her. She'd have told me. She'd have said yes to keep me here.

"Right. OK," I say, and I whisk outside then, come face-to-face with Joe, who looks up from the phone in his hand, handsome and sun-kissed and smiling. But I know from the way the door doesn't slam behind me, the way Joe's eyes leave mine and look past me, that she's followed me out, her sandaled feet on the concrete.

"Natalie, don't go," she says.

"I have plans," I reply.

"Then—why don't we arrange to go for coffee or something? I'm free a lot, actually, lately . . ." Edie swoops, stepping in front of me, the long, cottony material of her dress grazing my bare legs. "I miss you, Nat. I really miss you, and ever since—"

"Edie, I . . . I really don't want to do this."

"Please just meet me, to talk. Or . . . or you could come down, to the theater? I'm dying to show you. Honestly, I think of you every single time I—"

"Edie. No. Please. I said I don't want to do this. I really don't."

She looks like I've punched her now. Right in the stomach, a full fist. And I've softened again, like I'm bread dunked in a pond, as I stand here staring at her on the street. My friend. My best friend in the whole world. But when I look at her, I just see . . . *it* happening, in my mind, like a movie scene. Edie. Russ. Together. And I just can't. I *can't.*

"I don't want to be friends," I say. "Sorry. But I don't."

And before she can say another word, I walk away, and then jog, and then run, like in my daydreams, shoes scuffing on the hot, wonky pavement, poor Joe sprinting behind, to catch me up.

"Natalie?" he calls. "Hey, Natalie?"

As I round the corner, out of sight of the rehearsal rooms, I stop abruptly on the street. Two people at a bus stop a few paces away look up from their phones at me.

"Natalie?" Joe appears, and his face falls at the sight of me. "Who was that? Was that—God, are you all right?"

And it's then that I realize I'm crying.

Joe comes toward me somehow, holding two drinks and two square, cardboard containers balancing in his hands. "This is some Jenga shit." He laughs as I take a drink and food box from him. The flimsy plastic cup bows in my hand, liquid running a little down its side.

"Thanks," I say thickly, and Joe lowers himself next to me, on a matching deck chair, the stripes on the material in pastel green and pink, like old penny sweets.

"No worries. I got you cider, is that OK?"

"More than OK."

"Figured you could use a drink," he says with a smile, "and pasta. Pasta's medicinal in my experience. Comforts me better than anyone ever has. Plus, it was the only tent that wasn't packed, and I couldn't be arsed to queue with all the cattle."

"Thanks. And pasta always works." I lift the lid. Inside is a tangle of white, creamy spaghetti . . . and on top, a big purple flower. "Hm. Do you think pasta is still comforting with wanky edible flowers on top?"

"For God's sake." Joe grimaces. "Who decided we'd just start eating flowers? They were probably pissing about, and then we all went along with it, and they felt they couldn't say it was a joke. Mugs. All of us."

I laugh. "Maybe we can eat around it," I say, and my voice croaks. I've cried a lot in the last twenty minutes. Something I did not expect when I copied a pretty Australian YouTuber's eyeliner flicks this morning.

After Joe had sprinted after me, for a moment, I considered just keeping going—to forever be known as that weird girl he met at music therapy who jogged away from him sobbing when they were meant to attend a food festival. I didn't want him seeing me cry. Mainly because we haven't known each other all that long, and also because I didn't want to turn myself into a mess and have that memory of me filed away in his mind forevermore. But I'm glad I didn't jog away from him. Joe was kind and calm. I tried to speak, I tried to pretend I was fine, that they weren't actually tears, but allergies due to "er, lump weed and . . . exhaust fumes?" But then Joe had said, "Let's just walk, yeah?"

We'd walked silently for a while, the streets welcomingly shaded by the tall, imposing buildings of flat blocks, of a dated Thistle hotel, then Joe had talked, easily and interestingly—he's a good storyteller—about work, about his new manager, about his housemate who's recently got a girlfriend who keeps standing talking to him when he's reading at night in the garden, and he's wondering if wearing fake headphones might stop her. Then he'd led us to Regent's Park, shown the tickets to a grumpy man on the gate, and the whole time I hadn't really said a word—just followed behind him, like a dutiful dog, trying to slow my heart, to clear my head. We'd then found a row of three deck chairs among the warm, sweet bustle of the festival, and Joe had told me to take a seat. "I'll grab us some food and some drinks," he'd said, and as he disappeared off into a white, crowded marquee, I'd stared at the high, blue sky, at the rooftops in the distance, and imagined Edie back at the rehearsal rooms—crying, probably, into a colleague's shoulder, saying, "Wow, she's so different, she's so fucked up."

"Are you all right?" asks Joe gently, beside me. He looks gorgeous today. He's wearing a crisp white T-shirt, pressed beige chino shorts, a pair of navy-blue Converse on his feet. And I do wonder what Past Me would think now if she could see this, like a TV season preview—me crying, a gorgeous man who isn't Russ beside me at a food festival—somewhere we'd have definitely visited, on a whim—with a lap of pasta and too-sweet cider. "I mean, tell me to piss off if I'm prying, but—"

"No. You're not prying. I mean, I did just run away from you in the street whilst sobbing in a bright orange summer dress, like a big tangerine."

"Yeah, well, we've all been there," Joe says, and in unison, at his joke, we both smile. Two poke marks dimple his cheeks as he does.

"That was Edie," I say. "She was once my best friend, believe it or not."

"Is that the one you wrote music with?"

"Yeah. I haven't seen her since Russ's funeral. And—I knew it might be painful to see her but . . . that was next-level."

Joe nods calmly. A warm breeze, garlicky, smoky, swirls the deck chairs, ruffles our hair.

"It was a disaster. Because she really wanted to talk, to catch up, to—make it right. And I realized I'm not ready."

"To make up?"

"Yeah. To make up. Move on. Let it go." A couple drifts by us, holding hands, their knuckles holding so tightly they're almost white, and a man with a lanyard around his neck, carrying a huge silver keg, trots behind them. "Tony!" he shouts. "Hey, Tony! Over here, mate."

Joe sips his drink, slowly.

"Edie slept with Russ," I say into the quiet between us. "Before we were together. But they didn't tell me. And then I found out."

"Jeez," says Joe, his face screwing up, like his beer is suddenly mud. "Shit, I'm sorry, Natalie, that's—that's really awful."

And I realize it's the first time I've said that out loud since the day I found out. At Russ's funeral. My best friend had sex with the love of my life before I did. And I never knew.

"Russ and I met in the final year of uni," I tell Joe. "Two of his mates were dating people in our house share, and that's how we met. He was the third wheel. And it took him ages to ask me out. I didn't think he was interested, and yet he said he could never read me, which I found *mad* because I flirted so brazenly with him, it was embarrassing. Like

I was—I dunno, a hop, skip, and a jump away from spraying him like a pole cat."

Joe chuckles, and reaches a thumb to dab a bubble of beer-foam from his mouth.

"I asked him about it, once we were together. 'How did you not know?' And he just said he thought I was like that with everyone. Loud and jokey, you know. But I was hook, line, and sinker the moment I met him. I loved him instantly, if you can believe such a thing even happens in real life and not in those saccharine movies. I loved him for longer. I always used to say that to him—throw it in his face as a joke. 'You say you've loved me for ten years, but let me tell you, I loved you a whole three months before that.'" I smile and feel like tears might explode from me again, like a burst pipe. "And I mean everyone knew. He was all I thought about, all I talked about. Anyway. Before he finally asked me out, he and Edie, apparently—they got drunk and . . . I was in the house too. Asleep upstairs. Oblivious."

Joe's eyes narrow, his forehead creasing. "Shit, Natalie. I mean— What do you even do with your head when you find that out?"

I shrug. "And you know, I really honestly would've forgiven it, if I'd have just known. I'd have been pissed off if she had just told me, you know. If she said, I've been a stupid idiot and I've had sex with that guy you really like, and I regret it. That would have *hurt me*, of course, because she knew how much I liked him. But it'd have been the truth."

"Yeah. Course," says Joe softly.

"And yet, I didn't find out until he died. That's when she decided to tell me. To—to rid herself of her bad conscience or something, I don't know, but—that. That for me was just soul destroying." I start crying again, and Joe pulls a pile of black, restaurant-branded napkins from his pocket and passes them to me. "Ugh. Sorry, Joe."

"Don't be." Joe's hand lands on mine, warm and smooth, and he wraps his fingers around my hand, tucks them under my palm. "You don't have to be sorry."

A crowd of friends—six of them—drift by us. One of them points at the starfish of free deck chairs a few paces from us. "Here?" shouts another. "Grace, shall we sit here?" and Joe and I watch quietly as they arrange themselves on the deck chairs, all drinks and laughter and yelps as they underestimate the drop to the seat.

"I feel like one day I woke up," I continue, "and my life was taken away from me. I was happy. I had Russ. I had Edie. I had—*that*." I gesture to the friends, all giggles, all chat and inside jokes, all freedom. "I had my *life*. I had it all to come. And then it was—gone. All of it. And so was I."

"And now you feel like you're trying to get back to it," says Joe softly.

"Yes," I say, wiping away more tears. "And I can't go back. Because he's gone. But I'm also petrified of moving forward, so what do I do? And nobody really understands that part. They're all about moving on—God, every inspirational quote is about *moving on* and forging a new life and . . . I just want to say: I liked my old one actually. Because I was really happy there, so what do you say to that? And people—they don't know what to say when I say that, and I get it, because I don't know either. That's why I understand them wanting me to get better, move on, put myself back together. Like a weird project they want to fix. Get me playing live again, get me *dating*. A spring clean, a repair and refurbish. How much easier would that be?"

I melt into tears then, surprising floods of tears, and bury my face into a tissue. God, I can't stop. I'm in the middle of Regent's Park on a summer's afternoon *sobbing*. On a deck chair. An edible flower and a pile of spaghetti in my lap. When I come up for air, through blurred eyes, I see a woman at a nearby stand nudge her friend and gesture at me.

"God, now everyone's looking at me," I whisper, hiding my face with one of my hands. Black lines from my eyeliner mark my palms, like pen marks. "I'm such a mess."

"So what?" says Joe. "Screw them. Do you want me to get up and break-dance or something? Start protesting about eating meat? Pretend to propose? People lose their heads over proposals."

I laugh, which makes me cry even more.

Joe squeezes my hand. "I understand, Natalie. I do." And bringing a hand to the side of my face, he runs a finger down my cheek, tucks my hair behind my ear. I peer out from behind my hand. "I'm there with you," he says. "Stuck in the middle. Between back and forward. Stuck in the fuckin' *mud*."

"I think you're further forward than me."

Joe shakes his head. "Empty notebooks say otherwise." Somewhere deep in the festival, an amp is switched on, filling the air with the buzz of feedback. Someone strums a guitar. "And you're not a mess, Natalie. You're—pretty incredible if you ask me."

"I'm not."

"You are," he says quietly. "I wish you knew how much."

A song strikes up in the distance, tinny, slightly out of tune, and someone in the gang of friends on the deck chairs in front of us whoops, raises a hand in the air, shouts, "Woohoo!"

"*Ugh.* Let's rescue this bloody day," I say, drying my eyes, straightening in the chair. "It was meant to be our nice little outing with pasta and cider and sunshine and . . . instead, I'm just snotting all over you."

"At least it's here and not in the smelly room," Joe comments. "I don't think it gets worse than tears in the smelly room."

I laugh. "I'm so determined to find the culprit of the smelly room."

"Everyone always is."

"I'm telling you, Joe," I say, fishing out the flower from my pasta, holding it between my fingers, "I make a *promise* that I will find the cause. I will leave no stone unturned."

"Fine. Make a vow."

"Deal," I say, "I swear it. On this pointless flower. Which I am absolutely not eating, by the way."

Joe leans over and takes it from my fingertips with his mouth, a brush of soft lips. "On this pointless flower." He chews.

Me: A word for you Thomas Button. Understood.

Tom (stand-in): Noted.

Me: And hungry. Note that down too. I've eaten nothing today except someone else's massive edible pansy.

Tom (stand-in): . . . is this a cry for help?

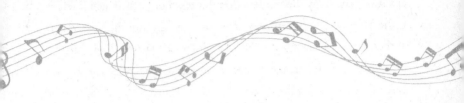

chapter eighteen

A warm hand lands on my shoulder and squeezes.

"Oh, good, my love," says Shauna, looking down at me, "you're *alive*."

"*Hi*." I smile. "I am. Alive and kicking. Just—slightly drowned today."

"Aren't we all? It's unbearable. This country, I swear to God. Can't make its mind up. I'm tempted to fly to bloody Lanzarote and leave all this gloom behind."

London is a moody, humid mess of summer rain today, and the train station's floors are shiny with wet footprints. I didn't come here, to Goode's, last week—the first week I've missed, I think, since I started coming here to the station to play—but of course I stopped by to check the piano. I'd hoped the Coldplay song would be the start of it again, practically bounded up to the stool like an excited Labrador, expecting more music, but there was nothing, and a rock of disappointment had settled in the pit of my stomach.

But my days have been busy in the last week—too busy, really, to feel too deflated, to think too much about it. After the food festival on Tuesday and the totally disastrous standoff with Edie, Joe and I met again on Thursday. Record shopping in Camden (Joe's idea), which turned into lunch, which may have even turned into dinner at his (a barbecue his housemate and his new girlfriend were hosting, much to Joe's horror) if I hadn't had to get back to feed Toast. And there was a part of me that was glad to have the cat as an excuse. I sort of wanted to be alone, to go home when I did, to process it. Joe. Joe exploding into my life. And record shopping. Until Thursday, I hadn't stepped foot in a record shop since Russ. It was nice. Different, of course, with Joe, without that . . . zing, without that *feeling* I'd have when I flicked through vinyls with Russ, but the smell was the same, and comforting. Like old, sun-bleached paper and furniture polish. Russ would even sniff the records. The older, the tattier, the better for him.

"I came in an hour ago," I tell Shauna. "I've been waiting to see you. Jason said you had a thing?"

Shauna takes a seat at the table opposite me, chair legs scraping on the damp tiles. "He said I had a what?"

"An—appointment I think he said?"

"Oh." Shauna nods, almost defeatedly. "Yes, I did. I told him not to tell anyone, though, the little swine."

"Is everything OK?" I've wanted to ask Shauna about Don and everything Tom told me—about Angela and the woman she saw with him—but Tom asked me gently not to, so I keep waiting for Shauna to tell me herself. But she hasn't. Even when she called on Thursday to tell me she too had checked for music. She just does what Shauna always does. She gives the same, cheery, strong version of herself she always does, like she's a one-woman show and believes her audience deserves perfection and consistency at all times, despite how she might be feeling.

"I'm OK, love." Shauna gives a tight shrug. She smells like freshly baked pastry and jasmine. "Fine, as normal. But I've been having this chest pain . . ."

"Oh, shit, are you OK?"

"Ah, fine, fine." Shauna waves me away, the bangles on her wrist jangling. "I had the full works, the doctor was a dream but—he says it's *stress*." Shauna lowers her voice as she says "stress" like she's embarrassed, like it's a dirty word, like it's heresy just to say it out loud in public. And of course, I know why. Don. I bet it's bloody Don. How could you possibly not be stressed when the man you married, the man you had five children with, has had countless affairs? I keep thinking about this. It was bad enough when Edie told me about her and Russ. I questioned everything. My self-esteem shriveled, like an old forgotten lime in a fruit bowl. And that wasn't even an affair, and Russ wasn't even *here*. So, what do you do if you're Shauna? What do you do with your self-esteem then? What do you do with your mind that wants so desperately to look for signs—the tiny things that could be evidence, but could also be absolutely nothing? Because everything is suspicious, is *something*, under the right gaze.

"Is it work," I ask Shauna, "or other stuff?"

"Well, I wonder if it could be my anniversary. Did Tom tell you?"

"No, I don't think he did," I lie. "What's happening on your anniversary?"

Shauna smiles then, a proper smile, that makes her eyes screw up and cheeks glow like shiny apples. "Don and I. It's our thirtieth wedding anniversary soon and we're organizing a party. And of course, you're invited. It's in six weeks. I'll send you the email."

"Oh, wow. And make sure you do," I say, with as much faux surprise as I can muster. "That's so exciting."

"You're telling me," she replies. "I've never really had a party before. But it's stressful. Oh my gosh, so stressful. We've found a venue. Someone Don knows. A client. A hotel they've got a contract with. They have a function-room free—a what do you call it? A *cancelation*. So, he's called in a favor. But all the organizing, Natalie. Honestly. It's keeping me up at night, hot sweats, bad dreams, the lot. Plus, Don's so busy with work, so much of it falls to me . . ."

"Well, if you need a hand with anything—"

"You have enough to do, my darling." Shauna smiles. Behind her, in the coffee shop's doorway, Mr. Affair emerges, putting a phone to his ear. He whisks off in the direction of the escalator. Shauna sees him, looks at me. "He's an arse, that man," she says. "The times that young girl cries over him . . ."

"I wish she'd cut him off."

Shauna nods sadly. "Takes strength, I suppose," she says and she cranes her neck, to see in the shop, to look for her. "*Anyway*. Don't think you're getting away with it, Natalie Fincher."

"With what?" I laugh.

"I need to know everything. *Where* were you and, might I ask, that pretty-faced lad with the notebook, both Tuesday *and* Thursday?"

I laugh even more now—my cheeks immediately bursting into flames. God, am I really this transparent? I'm like a giddy child. "We've been . . . hanging out."

"Oh my god, I love it. Tell me *all*."

"Well, last week we went to a food festival all day, that was the Tuesday, and we didn't say goodbye until, like, ten at night."

"So lovely."

"And then we met up on Thursday, went shopping for records, which is something I used to do all the time with Russ, and . . . I don't know."

Shauna stares at me, her tired eyes coming to life, glittering. A sparkle. "You don't know what?"

"I don't know," I say again, and we both laugh, a burst of warm giggles. "God, I don't even know why I'm giggling and being weird. I am *never* like this. It's embarrassing . . ."

"You like him."

I hesitate, my hands wrapped around my mug. "That's what I don't know, I think," I say quietly.

"Well, look, that's okay. You don't need to know anything right now . . ."

"But I like *being with* him, which is a start right? And I feel like he understands. And it's nice sort of . . . being out in the world?"

Shauna nods again, the two hoops in her ears swaying in time, like they agree and understand too. "Well, I agree that it sounds like a good start. And it's nice seeing you with a little spring in your step, love. It really is. You can see it in your face. The eyes . . ."

"Tom said similar the other day. About my eyes. Got all artsy on me."

"*Did he now?*" Shauna smiles to herself, straightens in her chair— a proud and puffed-up parent. "Well. He's right. He spotted it. Happiness is something you wear, you know. Lights up every part of you. Inside and out."

Shauna pushes her chair out, the legs screeching on the tiles again. A man at the next table, on his phone, looks over his suited shoulder and winces, putting a finger to his ear.

"I'm glad you've found each other," says Shauna obliviously, "there's safety in numbers with this stuff, when you've been through the same thing. It's equal ground. Plus, it's nice to have someone who understands looking out for you."

"Ah, she doesn't need that," says a deep, familiar voice. "She's got me for that, right?" Tom stands beside Shauna, tall and broad, a bag tossed casually over his shoulder. "*Saved* her the other week."

"Oh, hello, my Thomas! And . . . did you? Did he, Natalie?" Shauna stretches her short, chubby arm around Tom's back, and he puts his arm around her. Shauna looks *tiny* next to Tom.

"*Did you?*" I ask.

"*Uh, yeah*? Treated the damp. Saved you from acute asthma. And probably other deadly stuff."

"Wow, OK. Now I understand men," I say. "The *exaggerating*. It really is a thing, isn't it?"

Shauna laughs and pats Tom's flat stomach. "Absolutely it is." She looks up at her son, face bursting with pride, with love, with *I made this tall, strapping man with my own body, thank you.* "Coffee?"

"I'd love a flat white," says Tom. "I've only got about ten minutes, though—"

"I'll be quick," says Shauna, charging off into Goode's.

Tom sets his bag down on the floor and sits in the empty seat opposite me. "So. Natalie," he says. "Light of my life, maker of the wanky scrambled eggs. Long night? Foxes? Pipe status? What's new?"

I can't help but smile. There's something so nice about having someone that knows the dull minutiae of my life, remembers it. All the silly, little, insignificant details. Foxes. Damp. Dodgy pipes. The only meals I can cook without making a crime scene. Plus, Tom always seems to make me smile. He's one of those . . . *infectious* sort of people.

"No foxes. Not lately."

"Proverbial?"

"Neither proverbial nor literal."

"Blimey," says Tom. "You've hit the jackpot."

Tom always looks so well turned out. I said this to him, after breakfast, the other day, that he's a proper grown-up, like Jodie, and he laughed and said, "What exactly does that mean? Besides *Congrats, you're not an oversize man-child*?" and I'd told him. That he's the sort of person who gets up at seven by choice, even when he doesn't need to. The sort of person who says, "Well, why waste the day?" and means it. The sort who's already up when you emerge at ten a.m. with hair like a hedge, with the radio on and a slice of toast and coffee and a well-rounded opinion on the latest headline. He hadn't disagreed, just nodded and said, "Well, for what it's worth, I like your hedge hair. But then, Marge Simpson, in my opinion, is the ultimate woman."

"And how was stuff with little surfing dude?" Tom asks, brushing a smattering of sugar from the tabletop. "You were scant on the ol' detail on WhatsApp."

"*Little* surfing dude?"

Tom laughs at his own joke. "You know what I mean. He's about twelve, isn't he?"

"Twenty-seven, *actually*. And he's fine. We hung out. It was cool."

"Cool?"

"Yup. So, how are you?"

Tom studies my face, then blows a breath out the corner of his mouth. "Fuckin' hell, Natalie."

"What?"

"What do you mean, *what*?" Tom says, laughing. "Honestly, it's like wringing a dry towel with you sometimes. Like . . . talking to some sort of hard-as-nails biker who won't rat on their gang."

"Well, what do you want? His bloody fact file?"

"Sure." Tom folds his arms, the skin taut and muscly against his middle. "Sounds good. Let's have it."

"Fine. His name is Joe, surname Jacobs, aged twenty-seven, he was born in Dorset but currently lives in Kentish Town—"

"Twenty-seven," he says again, as if it's the first time he's heard. "You know what they say. *Young, dumb*—"

"Don't you dare finish that sentence."

"I don't know what you're talking about." Tom grins—straight teeth, that cleft in his chin. My cheeks ache, sitting here. He makes me laugh. Tom always, always makes me laugh.

"OK, so what else?"

"Nothing much," I say. "We went to a food festival, went shopping—"

"And is he—well, you know." Tom winks at me and puts on a ludicrously high-pitched voice. "*Dishy*?"

I laugh. "Nobody says dishy anymore."

"Mum says dishy."

"Your *mum* says a lot of things."

Tom uncrosses his arms and sits back. He smiles. A "Well?" smile. Because he knows. He always seems to know, annoyingly. And before I can activate my poker face, I melt into laughter. I can't help it. My face floods with heat, like my head's in the oven. I cover my face with my hands.

"Oh, shit, don't even *tell me*." Tom laughs. "*Oh*. Oh, you fancy him."

"No."

"You fucking do. *Natalie fancies someone*."

I giggle madly behind my hands, and on the other side of them he laughs, a big burst.

"Holy shit," he says, "you fuckin' do. I knew it. What did I say? Didn't I say you would—Hey, sir, Mister, please, you see here, my friend Natalie Fincher," and when I drop my hands from my face, he is actually gesticulating to someone walking past. A stranger. *An actual stranger*. "She fancies someone," Tom carries on, and thankfully the stranger smiles, amused, but keeps walking. "An actual man," Tom carries on. "An actual person. She hasn't fancied anyone for ages."

"*Tom*. Seriously. Shut the—"

"She hasn't fancied a soul," he calls out as a woman a few paces away looks over her shoulder, laughing. "Nope. Not a soul. Hates all of us. Vince Vaughn. Who's the other one?" Then he talks, as if to a crowd by the table, but only actually to me. "Oh, and sausages. Sausages, too. Sausages really do get her down. Too rubbery. Too *phallic*."

"You're a knob."

He looks over at me and grins. "This is a momentous day, Foxes."

"No, it isn't."

"What is?" Jason arrives at the table with Tom's coffee, an intrigued eyebrow raised.

"She fancies someone."

"Who does? Natalie?"

"God, this is mortifying," I mutter, sipping my tea. "Actually mortifying."

"Guess who," Tom continues.

"Er—you?" Jason says, and Tom bursts out laughing.

"I mean, you'd think it'd come naturally to her, wouldn't you," replies Tom, "but alas, Jason, no. His name is Joe. Twenty-seven. *Twenty-seven*, I ask you," he says, and this time in a voice like his mother's and I am now giggling so much, I feel like my head might explode.

"Good for you, Nat." Jason laughs and he goes back inside the café.

"And this is why I'm *scant on the ol' detail* with you sometimes," I say.

"That's what you *get* for not telling me. So, when you finally do, I wanna call BBC news or, like, Buzzfeed or something—" He sips at his coffee. "Is this why your word was 'hopeful' the other night?"

"Maybe. And also, I'd got this amazing denim jacket in the sale at ASOS, so . . ."

"Seriously, though," says Tom. "It's cool, right? Meeting a guy and—fancying him a bit."

"Is it?"

"Of course it is."

"Says you," I reply. "Using me as your stand-in because *you* don't want to be fixed up on a date."

"I date," he says. "Sort of."

"Just date?"

Tom shrugs. "Anyway. I'm just glad you've got a crush. It's what humans do, right? Fancy people. Imagine for a moment what it might be like to—you know. Get to know them. Spend time with them. Get *close to them*."

"I haven't gone that far yet, thank you. But—I don't know. We're . . . *vibing*?"

"Then of course there's the bit after," Tom continues. "Where they look disappointed. Tell you that you remind them of their uncle Nick a little, and he was always a bit weird at parties and 'Ah, shit, look at the time, gotta go—'"

I laugh. "There is a touch of the weird Uncle Nicks about you, to be fair," I say. "Is that why you don't do anything beyond Just Date?"

"Bit personal for a Tuesday." Tom gives a slight smile "And there's a touch of the weird Uncle Nicks about us all, if you ask me."

Tom drinks his coffee quickly, and before long it's an empty mug, nothing but a puff of foam at the bottom.

"I better get going," he says. "I'm meeting someone over at the exhibition space."

"How's it all going?"

"It's going well, thanks. Not till December, but you'll have to come. Bring a plus-one."

"Course. Will you be bringing Miss Two A.M.?"

Tom pauses, looks at me, and says, "Depends."

"On?"

"I dunno." Tom shrugs. "Will you be bringing little surfer dude?" and before I can answer, he gives a smile, slings his bag over his shoulder, and walks off into the station.

chapter nineteen

Did you see there were ribbons on this lot? *Again?* It's like I'm Pavlov's dog or something. Saw them. Felt like dropping to my knees and screaming." Priya stands opposite me at the entrance of Tina, cradling a bundle of clothes in her arms—some just-in jumpers from the new autumn collection that Jodie is treating like one-of-a-kind preserved vintage gowns discovered in Pompei. It's been two weeks since the day of the humid, moody rain, but the weather has scooped us up and forced us along with its bad attitude—it's like we've been fast-tracked into autumn, a month too early. I've even skipped visiting Russ over the last couple of weeks, not wanting to sit in the pouring rain and squelching mud. I used to hate skipping visits, like he would be up there somewhere, on a chaise longue in the clouds with a clipboard, shaking his head, surrounded by angels, saying, "What a shame. She was such a lovely wife, guys. But now this—not visiting a tree because there's a yellow weather warning. Shameful." But lately that's shifted a little. Russ would understand. He'd be the first one ushering me away, telling me to stay at home, fire up the heating.

"Anyway. The thing is," Priya waffles as I peel a top off the pile in her arms, "some people really do not want a fuss with their thirtieths.

I loved mine. Embraced age thirty. Did not want to stay a day later in my shitty bloody twenties. But I dunno, Luce is—Lucy is—"

"A bit *Death Becomes Her*?" I offer, fishing a hanger through the neck of a jumper (with ribbon sleeve ties, no less). "Would definitely harvest the soul of an infant for everlasting youth?"

"I was going to say private," says Priya. "But yes. Also that. Roxanne says she does *not* want to be thirty, that she's *forbidden* her and the rest of the family to organize anything thirty or special-birthday related, but—I don't know. I know Lucy. She loves a fuss."

"Exactly."

"And Roxanne agrees," says Priya. "She'd actually love it. So, what do you think? Do I trust her sister, go the whole hog? Do I go full-blown balloons and cake and banners, or do we not mention the age and just throw a nice, ageless birthday dinner? The safer option."

"Priya, she's turning *thirty*," I say, hanging the jumper on an empty, shiny silver rail. "She's not going on death row. Although I'm now extremely tempted to buy her some denture glue. Wrap it up in a Tiffany box. Full of thirty confetti that explodes upon opening."

"*Don't.* Can you imagine?" Priya laughs. "And you're right, I say we embrace it. I say we get it all, the lot, even a thirty sparkler for the cake, a bloody sash, and just—go wild."

"Not too wild, though," I say. "We don't want to bring on labor. No offense, but I'm no good with bodily fluids." I look down at Priya's taut, round bump hiding behind the mound of new autumnal blouses I thought looked more like something off the front of a Bee Gees album. (But blouses, even Bee Gees ones, according to Jodie, are "very Insta at the moment.") Priya doesn't have long to go now, and while she keeps referring to herself as "a walking, talking boulder," I've never seen her look so beautiful. Her skin is lineless and glowing, the whites of her eyes bright, her hair thick and shiny, almost like her body is out in celebration for everything it's done, and what it's about to do.

"Just as long as he doesn't arrive before thirty-seven weeks," says Priya, "I'm down with earliness. Plus, it means I could drink—"

"Can you not just have a little one anyway?"

"Ugh, *probably*. But my midwife was a bit weird about it. She basically told me if I did, I'd give birth to Phil Mitchell, and I mean—who wants that? I'd love him regardless, but birthing a little grizzly, ruddy-cheeked Phil with a drink problem? I'd rather not—errr, Natalie?"

"Mm?" I look up from my phone, a bunch of sale tags now tucked between my ear and neck, like my mum used to in the nineties with the cordless landline.

"What on earth are you doing?"

"Me?" I ask pointlessly.

"Yes, bloody you. Is that a picture of Axl Rose on your screen?"

I laugh in her face. "It's from Joe."

"Oh, yeah?"

"Do you remember Russ and I went to that Guns N' Roses concert, years ago? Well, Joe's just texted. Said they're showing some retro Guns N' Roses gig at a little cinema over near him at Christmas. We might go."

"I see," says Priya again, and she seems weird all of a sudden. Like she's thinking something she isn't saying. Priya wears every emotion on her face. She's never been able to hide anything—even the tiniest micro-emotion—even when she tries. (Especially when she tries, actually.) "And it's . . . his idea, is it? To go to the cinema concert thing?"

"Um, yes, it is."

Priya nods again thoughtfully, just a sweet, concerned, oval head poking over the mound of Bee Gees outfits. I put my phone away, take the next top.

"You have a problem with the Guns N' Roses suggestion," I say. "A sentence I'm not sure I ever thought I'd say, but you clearly do . . ."

"No. *No.*" Priya gives a stiff shake of her head, but she stretches her glossy red lips into a grimace. "It's not that, Nat, I don't have a problem with it, but—I don't know. Have you guys ever just sort of— met up and had dinner? Or just plain old-fashioned drinks? I mean, doesn't he work in a bar?"

"We had lunch? After record shopping . . ."

"Yeah, I know, but I mean . . ." Priya's round, brown eyes slide to the ceiling, and she screws her face up, as if she's trying to solve an equation. "I suppose what I mean is, is he trying to actually date you, get to know you, or is he just trying to—I don't know. Do all these things with you. To help you. You know. Like Lucy used to?"

My eyes shoot up to meet hers. "Um—none of those things?" I say. "I think we're friends. New friends who . . . enjoy each other's company?"

"Friends," says Priya.

"Yes. Friends," I reply, as a customer who Priya bundled into the changing room ten minutes ago with an array of outfits pulls open the curtain with a gust. Priya's mouth spreads into a huge smile. "Oh, yes. That color's amazing on you," she calls. "See. That dress was *made* for your skin tone." The customer looks totally made up, like a proud cat, and gives a nod before shutting the curtain again.

Priya turns to me again. "I just want to make sure that you get what you deserve," she says. "Maybe I'm just feeling a bit—maternal. Mama-bear style. Protective. You're my best friend, Nat."

Something sinks a little then inside me. Priya is always happy-go-lucky. Priya thinks most things—except those sexist musicians she'd see off with garlic and crucifixes in our old bar job—are great. She's always optimistic; sunshiny. So, this doubt, this ever-so-slightly neg-ative questioning feels . . . upsetting I suppose. Because *she's* been the one who's been excited about Joe while I've been apprehensive to call it anything at all. And now *I'm* excited about meeting Joe, about this new person in my life who totally understands me, *she's* coming along with the apprehension, plus added suspicion. Irritation prickles up my back, like tiny needles. "You wanted me to meet someone new," I want to say, "and now that I *have*, you're questioning it."

"He's got a surprise for me tomorrow apparently," I say instead, and just like that, I sound like a sulky child.

"Does he?"

"Yep," I say. "See. *Friends.* What *friends* do."

"I just love you," blurts Priya. "You're one of the most important people in my life, and I love you. I just wanted to check in to see that Hot Notebook Joe is as lovely as we thought. That's all. Heart in the right place. You know?"

I stop, ugly blouse half-hooked onto a hanger. "I love you, too, Pree, you know that," I say. "But I'm fine. And—balls of steel, remember? Last time I checked, I still had them. I won't be taken for a ride by anyone."

"Good." Priya smiles softly. "And maybe I was always going to be like this when you liked someone. It's a step, isn't it? A big one."

"I know," I say. "But Priya, I don't even know what it is yet. I'm just happy how it is right now." And maybe it'll move—move from this to butterflies and heat and stomach sizzles and cheek-aching giggly smiles and not being able to take my eyes off him because *God, I want to sink my teeth into his jaw.* But I like *being* with Joe, and maybe that's a start. Right?

"Anyway. So, what do we think? Somewhere like Dishoom for Lucy's birthday? And Christ, will you hurry up with these bloody tops. My arms can't take it. I swear, you'd think Jodie would have a better system. I doubt Zara workers have to deal with this."

"Dishoom?" I say. "Lucy's weird, though, isn't she, with food that has actual flavor. What about the restaurant with the thing? The bandstand in the middle?"

"The Ned. Oh, please don't make me book the Ned. Lucy always puts on a voice when we go to the Ned."

"*Oh, yah, what a fetching tableclawth, darling. We have these back at the estaaaate, but Father thinks they're just wretched.*"

Priya and I giggle, and a sour-faced customer who has been browsing the sale rail for half an hour looks across at us over her glasses.

"And you don't have to book anywhere," I say. "Maybe we can just go to yours. Or mine. Order pizza. Talk about all of Lucy's crushes and exes and our bad haircuts." Priya cackles, like my suggestion is a hilarious joke. But I'm not really joking. It's the pressure that I feel at these things that makes me not want to go. The uniformed, formal thing of couples turning up armed with gifts, in perfect outfits, and ordering three courses, and just the right number of drinks to justify that bill split. I used to enjoy them. Not quite so much anymore. I feel like the sore thumb. I feel like I stand out, alone. Plus, it's been a while since I've seen Lucy and Roxanne. I keep making excuses. That bloody open mic night thing hangs over me like a heavy cartoon cloud, following me around. But just us, blankets and sofas and gossip. It's been so long.

"I think I'm just going to bite the bullet and book Dishoom," says Priya.

I nod, defeated. "Sounds good to me," I say. ("I'll just spend the next few weeks dreading it then, and hoping for a touch of the Norovirus, that'll be fun," I don't say.)

"Talking of Axl Rose, by the way," says Priya, as she passes me another Bee Gees blouse, "the man down the road, at the Bookmaker's. He looks a bit like him. Doesn't he?"

"Does he?"

"Yep." Then she leans to me and whispers, "Had a sleep-gasm about him. Intense-o. I'd even say the best one so far."

chapter twenty

"Now, I refuse to be held responsible when it comes to how *good* they actually are," Joe had said under the stark, bright light of the tube station entrance, "but a girl at work recommended them, *and* you said you used to see everything and everyone in between, so . . . I thought, OK, Char and the Heartt it is."

"Char and the Heartt?"

"I've not heard of them either. But if the worse comes to worse, we can have a good time hating them together? Plus, it's them, plus another band so, if we hate them, maybe we'll like the other one. Straw-clutching here."

Joe's surprise for me is a live gig at the Underworld. We'd arranged to meet at Camden tube station at seven, and the second I saw the queue snaking around the venue, I found myself hoping it wasn't the surprise and hoping that it was, all at once. I haven't been to a live show in years. And I haven't been to one without Russ since before we even met. And the thought of stepping inside, to loud music and dark rooms, both thrills and scares me.

"So, what do you really think?" asks Joe now with a grimace, as we stand on the pavement on the other side of the street, and I realize I've barely said anything since we joined the busy, noisy queue.

"It's—it's great," I say.

"Yeah? It's just you're a little quiet."

"I know. Sorry Joe, it's just . . . been a while since I've done this. That's all. I'm nervous."

"I know," says Joe. "But I thought it might help to remember. And if the worse comes to worse, we can just drink until we forget what a terrible idea of mine this was. Deal?"

I laugh nervously. "Deal."

And he's right in a way. It has helped. I had forgotten how this felt. A late-summer's evening, standing beneath a deep navy blue sky, a paintbrush flick of twinkling stars. The air smelling of perfume and beer and barbecue smoke from a nearby Turkish restaurant, queue a buzzing hum of excitement. Joe stands next to me, and tonight he really looks good—hot, I'm sure Priya and Jodie would say. He's wearing a black shirt, two buttons undone at the neck, and dark blue jeans, and he keeps flashing me this smile—all dimples and knowing eyes, like we're sharing a secret inside joke. I should let go, try to enjoy this. I'm here, at a gig, with him. With "dishy" Joe, someone I'm positive I *do* fancy. A little bit. Maybe this is how I get back to how I used to be: doing all the things I used to do.

"This feels . . . I dunno."

"Claustrophobic?" offers Joe.

"Um, I was going to say like old times? Like I've—stepped into an old photograph or something."

Joe gives an awkward grin. "Oh. Course. Not claustrophobic. Not at all." He leans into me, his arm pressed warmly against mine, and he whispers, "It's just the bloke behind me basically has his lips pressed against my neck. I am deeply disturbed."

"All part of the gig experience, isn't it? Lack of personal space."

"Nah, you should be able to hold your arms out and spin anywhere, anytime, without smacking anyone in the mouth. It'd be a
better world. No life experience should come with a lack of personal
space."

I laugh as Joe straightens, pushes his hands into his pockets, looks
ahead, and then says, "Actually, I can think of one." He looks at me out
of the corner of his eye, then laughs.

"I wondered how long it'd take you to get there."

"A second too long," he smiles.

The venue's doors open and the queue goes down quickly, snaking through to the inside of the venue. My shoes cling a little to the
sticky floor, and although I'm sure it's been cleaned tens of thousands
of times in its lifetime, it still smells of sweat and spilled snakebites
and beer.

We come to a stop, find a small space in the crowds gathering on
the floor before the stage. The platform is empty but lit up, two Les
Pauls resting in stands, a large hot-pink drum kit under the spotlights.

"How're you doing?" asks Joe over the loud music playing through
the speakers. "Feeling good?"

"Yeah!" I shout. "Good!"

"Shall I go and er—get us some drinks?" asks Joe. "Cider, or—"

"Just a Coke please. Diet, no ice."

Joe gives a nod. "Shall I meet you back here, or . . . ?"

"Definitely, I'll wait here. Won't move. Unless you want me to
come—"

"No, no, you stay. Enjoy the . . ." Joe's hazel eyes slide up to a couple in front of us, who have just started kissing—well more like *licking*
each other, their tongues like glistening slugs. ". . . view?"

Joe disappears off toward the bar, a black box in the middle of
the room, the bar staff inside, safely contained like animals from the
crowds. I turn toward the stage. I started counting all the live shows

Russ and I attended, then lost my place. Fifty. One hundred. *Two* hundred, maybe? It was all we did, especially when we first met. From unsigned bands with nothing but a piano and a microphone, to Alanis Morrisette and The Calling, and huge stadium gigs, like George Michael, like Coldplay. *Guns N' Roses.* Everyone and anyone. I filled myself up with it—the music and the energy and the proof; the proof that it could be done. If these people were up there, playing music, their hearts on their sleeves and in their mouths and at their fingertips as they played, then we could do the same, Edie and me. Russ would often squeeze my hand as we'd watch the show. Say, "Be you one day, Nat." God, I miss him so much.

I stand alone, and I watch, scan the room like a spectator, like someone observing an immersive play. Couples, groups of friends, people standing alone. People kissing. People laughing. Hundreds of lives colliding under one low, grimy roof. A sound engineer strolls onto the stage, acts like he can't see us—the hundreds of us standing staring at him—and swoops a guitar over his head, starts playing the notes, the E strings, first and sixth plucked together, A, D, G, B . . .

Joe's been ages. I scan the room for him, but I can't see him. Maybe he's gone to the toilet, maybe he's still waiting at the bar . . .

A second sound engineer enters the stage, take a seat at the drum kit. He hits the cymbal once, chats to someone I can't see—probably someone in his earpiece. He hits it again, then rumbles a beat across the whole kit.

I look behind me again for Joe, and then I see him. He's at the bar, and he's—he's talking nonstop to someone. His mouth moving quickly, smiling. "*Oh man,*" he's saying. "*Yeah! Yeah, that's right!*" It's a girl. She has long blond waves, some of the hair braided, like a band, across her head. She's pretty—super pretty, actually, and she seems beside herself that she's seen Joe. Like he's just got out of prison, like he's been saved from the mouth of bloody shark. God. Am I . . .

jealous? Is that what this is? No, no don't be ridiculous. I'm an adult. A mature adult. Although, God, her lips. They're so pink, so plump. They make mine look like a slit in a sheet . . .

I swoop back to the stage to distract myself. The sound engineers disappear, and I wait. I wonder who she is. Did he just meet her? I feel weird. Ugh. Why do I feel weird?

There's a sudden eruption of screams and cheers as a band walks out onto the stage. Something hot rises in my chest. The lights go down, and all at once Joe appears, brushing against me to get through the crowds. He holds two sloshing drinks in his hand. "One Coke and no ice." He grins.

"Thank you!" I say over the music.

"I just bumped . . ." The rest of his words are lost in the cheers, drowned out.

"*What*?"

"I just bumped into someone."

"Oh! *Wow*."

He nods, then gives a lopsided grin that I can't really read. Half giddiness, half awkwardness. "We used to date."

"*Oh*. Double wow!" *Why* oh why am I talking like a children's TV presenter?

And then the band strikes up, and both the room and my head are so full of music. I turn to the stage, and just as the lights go up again, I'm sure I see him—*Tom*. At the front, but right on the edge, standing away from the crowd, holding a drink to his chest, his eyes fixed on the stage. Then we're plunged into darkness. The leading man sings the first note.

♪ ♪ ♪
♪   ♪   ♪

My brain is scattered. Like someone just drove a box of cartoon TNT into my mind and set it off. I'm—all over the place. That's the expression, isn't it? Like when my nephew Nick was six, and he spent Christmas Day crying under the dining table. "He can't believe the presents he asked for actually exist, and are now his," Jodie had said, "and he's also sad it'll be over by the morning. He's all over the place. He's north, south, east, and west, all at once."

And that's where I am, standing here on the sticky venue's floor.

I may not have known a single song of Char and the Heartt's, but I feel totally exhilarated and overwhelmed. In a good way—blood rushing with lightning bolts. *Alive.* Like something inside ignited.

But I feel sad. And I can't quite put my finger on that bit just yet. Just that I feel it, slowly moving through my body, like syrup.

"I can't hear anything." Joe laughs obliviously beside me. "Seriously, my ears are—totally shot, and I am totally not going to reveal my inner OAP and say anything about it being maybe too loud, but I'm not going to say it either. Did you enjoy it?"

"I did!" I say. "Thank you. Good call on tonight."

"Yeah, I'm very glad there's no need for us to drown ourselves in alcohol to forget." Joe smiles. "And feeling inspired?"

And I force out a "Definitely!" because I'm not sure I can say, "Er, I'm a bit north, south, east, and west actually, mate," to handsome Joe in a packed music venue, surrounded by exhilarated, excited faces.

Joe puts an arm around me then, softly, but squeezing my shoulder gently in his warm hand.

"Glad to hear it," he says, "I hoped you would," and I stand, rigid, like a concrete statue, beside him. I used to be so good at this—and now I feel awkward with it. Like a ten-year-old with a first crush who has no idea what to do with it, where to box it to understand it. Crush. *Is* that what he is? What is it Tom said? That it's nice to like someone, to imagine what it might be like to get to know them, be close to them. I am close to Joe. And I am . . . completely made of stone under his arm, apparently. I doubt that's what Tom meant.

God. *Tom.* I can't believe Tom is actually here somewhere. But it makes sense. Char and the Heartt are the band he must've photographed the other week. Heartt, with two *t*'s, the one who was intent on "bringing back the noughties" inviting him to their show.

"Joey!"

It's her—the girl with the blond waves and lips, and she's squeezing her way through the crowd, a huge glittering smile on her face. She arrives in front of us in a puff of sweet perfume.

"Hey," Joe says, releasing me, and she slides her arms around his neck.

"Thought you'd left without saying goodbye," she says, giggling.

"Not quite," Joe replies, drawing back. "This is my friend Natalie."

"You said! Hi, Natalie!" She's actually beaming, this girl. Like a pumpkin who's swallowed a tealight. "I'm Hollie?"

"Nice to meet you."

"*Same!*" She beams again and turns to Joe, taking his arm. "I seriously can't believe you took my rec. You never trust my recs." Ah. "*The girl at work.*" Apparently also the girl he dated.

Joe laughs. "Yeah, well—"

"How did you find it?" she asks me.

"*Oh.* Yeah. Really good."

"Phew." She laughs. "Thank God. Oh, Sarah's here too. She's—oh, look, there she is. Sarah? Sarah? Sarah's our supervisor, but she's the one who needs the supervising really. Ha-ha. Right, Joe?"

I stand, rictus grin on my face, drink at my lips. God, I wish I could see Tom, get myself out of this. Hollie's nice, but I feel like I'm in a giant vise that's slowly, slowly closing in on me, tighter and tighter. "*How did you find it? He never takes my recs, ha-ha, we have so much fun at work, flirting loads, tossing cocktail shakers into the air in slow motion, our heads tipped back laughing, don't we, Joe?*"

I scan the room again. Tom. Tom, where the bloody hell are you?

Did I dream him up? A mirage, because I wish he was here. I take out my phone.

Me: I'm pretty sure we're in the same room.

Tom (stand-in): Are we?!

Me: The Underworld?

Tom: What!? I'm at the bar.

Me: I'm . . . not.

Tom (stand-in): Ha-ha. So, am I coming to you or are you coming to me?

Me: I'll come to you.

Tom (stand-in): All right!

I see Tom at the bar quickly—easy when he's taller than most of the people in the room, and when he sees me pushing (politely) through the crowds, he holds up his hand in a single wave. Something swims in my stomach at the sight of him. Relief. Relief that he's here, that I've been able to excuse myself from Joe and Hollie and the sexual yearning that kept clouding around her, like some sort of poisonous gas.

"Ah, it's Natalie Fincher," Tom says with a grin. "In front of me, in high definition." I'm surprised when he leans and plants a warm kiss on my cheek, a brush of stubble.

"It's Thomas. Or as his mum sometimes calls him—Tommy Button."

"*Heeey*," he says, ducking, as if sharing a secret. "Keep that nickname under your hat round these here parts. I've got a reputation to uphold." God, he smells nice. "Drink? A margarita? This time I'll get there first." He grins.

"I'm good, thanks." I lift my cup. "Nursing a Coke. So, Heartt with two *t*'s."

Tom laughs. "Indeed. And I take it this was your . . . surprise?"

"Indeed again," I say.

"Interesting," he says, holding his short whiskey glass from above, by the rim. He leans, touches his arm to mine. "And how is he? *Dishy Joe?*"

"Um. He's fine. Yeah, we're having a good time—"

"Where is he?"

Someone squeezes by me, so close their rough, scratchy jacket scrapes along my back, and knocks me off balance (that's what you get for wearing heels for the first time since 2006 because you'd sort of expected to go out for dinner somewhere nice I suppose). Tom takes my arm. "Jesus, man," he says, throwing a narrowed-eyed glance over his shoulder at the culprit. Then he turns to me and says, "Saved your life."

"Again."

"Again." Tom smiles, then looks down at his drink, swirling it in his hand. "But yeah, where's he at? Little surfer dude?"

"Oh er—he bumped into someone he knows. From work. Someone he used to *date* actually."

"Oh. Shit." Tom raises an eyebrow, the corners of his mouth down-turning. "So, what, he's shunned our Foxes, has he? Left her alone? On the night of his *surprise.* Little, wee shit—"

"No, no, it's not like that. I'm fine. *She's* fine."

Tom laughs. "I'm joking, Natalie. And anyway, how did you like the music?"

"Yeah, good."

"Right." Tom sips his beer. "Wringing that dry towel," he says, as if to himself.

"*What?*" I laugh. "What do you want me to do, write a bloody review for *Kerrang*!? Get out a chaise longue? Spew out my innermost fears?"

Tom gives a shrug. "Fuck it. Let's do it."

"And anyway, you're here alone, with neat whiskey, Thomas. Why don't we talk about *that* on the chaise longue?"

Tom swallows his drink and says, "Well—I'm not quite."

"Yeah, OK, *I'm* here but—"

"No, I mean . . . I'm not here alone. I came with someone."

"Oh. Did you?" Embarrassment sweeps over me, like a hot breeze. It makes me swallow. Turns my face into a furnace.

"I did," says Tom.

"Sooo. Miss Two A.M.?" I force a laugh, and it sounds mad—like someone sitting on top of a washing machine on spin.

"If that's what you want to call her," Tom replies, laughing almost as awkwardly, his face practically a wince. And before I can say anything else, someone is sidling up next to him—cat eyes and sleek dark hair and perfect smooth skin.

"They almost didn't let me back in," she says. "This day and age does *not* cater to the social smokers of the world." She wraps her fingers around his bicep, then looks at me and smiles. "Hi."

"Hi," I say. "I'm Natalie. It's nice to—"

"Oh! *Natalie!* You're—you're—the piano girl? Tom told me. He told me all about you."

"Oh. *Oh—*"

"I'm Amy." She holds her hand out, fingernails painted turquoise, and across Tom's stomach, I shake it.

"Amy." I say, "And I'm . . . *piano girl.* Apparently." And I don't know why, but I feel two inches tall. I feel ridiculous. Me. Whittled down to just that—piano girl. The weird girl who plays at the train station and had a weird little mystery. A weird little mystery that'll probably

never be solved because the music seems to have fallen into a man-
hole, never to be seen again, and that's probably good, too. Because
what normal person pins all her hope and excitement in the world on
that. A piece of music. Piano girl. That's me. Not Natalie. Not Tom's
friend. *Piano girl.*

"So what're you two chatting about? Heartt with two *t*'s? Did Tom
tell you he's making an eco-friendly guitar out of bean cans? *Was* it
bean cans? Or chickpeas?" Amy giggles, her hand stroking Tom's arm
now, and I feel—breathless. Like my chest is tightening.

I force a smile. "I better go," I say. "I've chatted for too long really,
and my friend. He'll be wondering where I am." I push off from the bar.
"It was really nice to meet you, Amy. See you around, Tom."

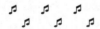

The second band plays beautifully. I prefer them to Heartt with two *t*'s
and his cocky, sweaty gang who Priya would've definitely warned people about in our old job. *"They're up their own arses and they proper
stink. You deserve better, honeys, trust me."* The second band's set is
more melodic, more emotional, and there's a keyboard player who I
can't take my eyes off. It's like she stands playing in an invisible bubble—just her and the keys, her eyes aflame like someone in love. Joe
stands beside me, arm to arm, but Hollie stands with us on the other
side of him, and so does her friend Sarah. Hollie talks a lot throughout the set, like someone bored in a cinema, which irritates me. Joe
listens, though, patiently, as she holds on to his arm and talks into his
ear. By the time the set is over, I'm ready to flee. Of course I am. It's
the live music. It's Joe and Hollie. It's Tom and Amy. It's being here,
like stepping into a past life. It's everything. A tornado, ripping its way
through me. North, south, east, west.

"Are you OK?" asks Joe, the second the lights come up. "You look—
I dunno. A bit pale? Shall I get you something? Some water, or—"

"Actually—are you OK from here?"

"Do you mean, if you go?"

I swallow, tears gathering in my eyes like whirlpools. Thank God for the low lights. Thank God for the black walls and black floors and all the shadows. "Yeah. I mean, if that's OK—"

"No, no, of course it is. But I'm not letting you go without me—"

"Oh my god, Joe, look who's just texted me! He's here too!" Hollie's hanging off Joe's arm but he doesn't move. He's sweet, Joe. Really sweet. And gorgeous. Totally, kneecap-meltingly gorgeous. At the food festival, there was a moment when I actually thought I wanted him to lean in and kiss me. But right now . . . right now, I want to leave.

"You stay." I smile at him and gesture, a tiny head movement, at Hollie and Sarah. Something passes over his face—hesitation. Shame. I recognize it instantly. And I wonder what it's for. Grief and guilt for me are so entwined, and guilt and shame arrive unannounced, often when I'm least expecting it. Is it his shame for being here while his brother can't be? Is it for having fun, moving on? Is it—for me? Does he feel sorry for me?

"Seriously. I'm excited for my bed. You stay, have *fun*. I'm good, I promise."

Joe gives a reluctant smile, and when we hug goodbye, he holds on longer than I expect, and for a second I feel suffocated.

By the time I'm outside, I feel totally sad. Like I'm a deflated balloon of a woman, bobbing along the pavement with a handbag and a nice (but agonizing) pair of shoes. I don't know why. There's too much spinning around in my head, too many things I feel that I don't know how to articulate, to form in an orderly sentence—

"Natalie?"

I stop on the pavement and turn. Tom is jogging across the road to me, in the dark. The Underworld is lit up behind him, buzzing with excited, smiling people, smoking outside, chatting, laughing. It's like being on the other side of the glass, looking into a kingdom I don't quite have the keys to.

"Are you off already?"

My heart jump-starts as Tom steps forward, and a part of me wants to fall into him. To have him put his arms around me, which is ridiculous, because a moment ago, a hug made me feel like I was stuck under water.

"I don't feel very well," I lie.

"Ah, shit, do you want me to—I dunno, we could jump in a cab—"

"Tom, you're on a *date*—"

"So?" Tom shrugs, holds his palms out at his side. "You're my mate. Right?"

Words stay jammed in my mouth, queuing but stuck, like on a broken conveyor belt, and I don't reply. I suddenly feel overwhelmed. The city, the bustle of a Saturday night. Joe inside. Tom, out here, a beautiful date waiting for him on the other side of the street. It's a wave that just crashed over me, on that sticky, sweaty floor. It didn't feel like it used to in there. And then I saw Tom and I felt lifted. Then . . . Amy. Was it Amy? Did Amy make me feel like this? *Oh, God, I'm so confused.*

"Look, why don't we go and grab a cup of coffee or something somewhere."

"I just want to go home, Tom."

"Maybe it was all too much. Maybe we can—"

"I don't need you," I blurt. As soon as I've said it, I regret it. But it shoots out of me like a bullet, and it feels like a release. It feels like protection.

"I wasn't—"

"I don't need you to look after me," I say, and my voice wobbles. "I don't need your advice. On houses. On music. On—on—my life."

Tom says nothing. His broad chest rises with a deep breath, and

228 ♪ Lia Louis

he looks down at his feet. "Natalie, I wasn't trying to . . . I just wanted to know you were OK."

"I don't want it," I say, and as I do, a group of women thunder by us in a gust of perfume and heels, chattering and giggling. They're in *Grease* fancy dress, and one of them has styled their hair like Kenickie's and is wearing a leather jacket with "T-Bird" on the back.

And my heart, right there, sinks. I'm here. I'm here and I'm *stuck* here, and everyone else is out *there*. Joe brought me here tonight. Joe, who I like being with. And yet, here I still am, unable to move my feet from this fucking mud I'm stuck in. And what? I'm jealous of . . . *Amy*?

"Seriously. Please just go."

Tom quietly brings a hand to his chin, rubs it with his thumb and forefinger. "OK," he says. "You want me to go?"

"Yes. I do. Go back to your date."

Tom hesitates, then turns, and I'm surprised in a way, although relieved, when he starts to cross the road back to the club. I watch him walk away, with every beat of my heart thumping and thumping like a slow drum, and turn, head for the tube station. I feel sorry for him. I feel sorry for *me. What am I doing*?

I scan my debit card, enter the hot, gassy tube station, and let the escalator take me down, swallow me up. On the busy platform, I wait. Six minutes for the next tube to Tottenham Hale. I start to shiver then and pull my jacket tighter around me, although it isn't from the temperature. I'm just lost. I'm so lost, and it's freezing me to the bone. Everything I feel.

My ears whoosh from the music, and my head throbs. Maybe you can't go back. Maybe Tom is right.

More and more commuters drift through the entrance, slowly crowding the platform, tight minidresses and suits. People going home, ending their night, people only just starting theirs. Someone in the crowd starts shouting, singing, and someone tells him to be quiet, and they all erupt into laughter. Two people a few paces away kiss, their hands gripping one another's at their thighs. I imagine that's me. I imagine that's Joe with his hands on me. I imagine it's—

"*Tom?*"

Tom appears next to me, on the squashed, crowded platform.

"Had to grab my jacket," he says breathlessly, and I know he must've run here.

"What are you—"

"Anyone ever tell you you're a bit of a dickhead?" he says.

I stare at him. "W-what?"

"You heard. Has anyone ever told you you're a bit of a dickhead?"

A laugh—a strangled scoff falls from my mouth, but tears still film my eyes. "I—well, I—"

"Because you are. I mean, most of the time you're an angel, but— right now, Natalie." He cocks his head to the side. "Bit of a dickhead."

I stare at Tom beside me on the tube platform, more and more people arriving, joining us like lemmings.

The sign above our heads changes to Tottenham Hale: 3 minutes.

"I'm sorry, Tom," I say, and suddenly it rushes through me. This— feeling. The warm, zingy feeling. It rushes through me like a wave. And I stride, close the tiny gap between us, put my arms around him tightly, around his warm neck. He brings his arms around my body, pulling me into him. His body firm, strong. And it feels so nice to be held by him. Proverbially. Literally.

"Thank you," I say into his chest.

Tom draws back, and looks down at me, a tiny smile on his lips. "For telling you you're a dickhead?"

"For coming after me."

"Yeah, well," he says, with a lift of his shoulder. "*Just Tom.* Remember?"

The distant rumble of the tube approaches, and I let go of Tom, step back. A voice on the loudspeaker advises, "Stand clear of the doors" as a rush of wind lifts my hair from my shoulders.

"You OK from here?" he says. "I can ride with you, if you like."

"No, I'm good."

"*Really?*"

"Really."

"OK," he says. "Safe journey, then."

The tube pulls in, people spill out, and I watch him as he walks away. Then I call his name. He stops and turns.

"Sorry," I say, across the platform. Someone eyes me, like I might be about to cause a public scene, as he squeezes by me to get on the train.

"Do you like Dishoom?" I call out.

The corner of his mouth twitches. "Who doesn't?"

"I have this thing. In a few weeks. A thirtieth. I really don't want to go."

"Stand clear of the doors."

Tom smiles and looks momentarily down at his feet. "I'll be there," he calls back, and as I turn away, the tube doors bleeping, Tom shouts my name.

"Mum's anniversary," he says. "I've got to make a toast and—"

"I'll be there," I say.

And as I slide through the closing gap of the doors, a girl with her arms inside her boyfriend's jacket sticks her leg through the gap, causing the doors to stay open for me.

"Thank you," I say, and she smiles.

I watch Tom disappear from the platform through the window, a little spark, there and then gone.

chapter twenty-one

"Electric Light Orchestra,'" Shauna reads, straightening the page on the tabletop with her hand. I found another piece of music this morning, sitting in the stool, waiting for me. "You a fan of them, are you? I've not heard of them, I'm afraid, but then again, I only like ABBA."

"I've not ever listened to them," I say. "But the song's extremely apt. I play in a train station, the song is *about* trains leaving London, so . . ."

Shauna smiles, lifts her tea to her lips. "Well, it's nice to see you smiling, my love," she says. "You seemed sad Tuesday when I called."

It's been almost a week since the gig in Camden, and I'd spent the few days after it holed up at Three Sycamore for the first time in a long time. But I needed it, I think, like medicine. I slept a lot, drank a lot of tea, cuddled the cat, and took a lot of baths. I skipped music therapy, I even skipped the station and crematorium visits. And instead of texting my words to Tom, I wrote them down in a notebook I'd found that I'd got a few Christmases ago and hadn't written in yet. I always kept diaries as a teenager, and it was nice to purge to the page. And so much of it was incoherent really, mad scribblings—emotions mostly, random notes to myself, random feelings, memories. But words flowed when I wrote about the gig with Joe and everything I felt watching those musicians onstage. A total thrill. But mainly nostalgia, the way you feel when you hear an old hymn you used to sing along to at primary school. And no urge, really, to do it again, like Edie and I used to. I sat staring at that sentence for a while on Tuesday morning: *I don't want to play like I used to.* And the question I'd written after it: *And maybe that's OK?* Then Shauna had called to say there'd been no music left, and she'd heard it in my voice, I think. That sort of blindsidedness that knocks the wind from you when you realize something.

"So, how was your weekend?" asks Shauna. "What was your *surprise*? I was thinking about you all Saturday night. Don took me to dinner. After much nagging. I even told him about it, you and Joe."

I laugh. "Did you?"

"I said to Don, I reckon it'll be something like a picnic. Candles, strawberries, stars. He's a poet, they're romantic, aren't they?"

"Ah. Well, I might disappoint you a bit. It was a gig. In Camden."

"A band? Oh. Well, not quite a starlit picnic, I suppose, but how was it?"

"Erm. It was . . . good in parts, but . . ." I hug my mug with my hands, pull it toward me, the warm ceramic against my midriff. "I don't know, it was all a bit overwhelming. I haven't been to a gig for years, and even then, I used to only go with Russ, so . . . it conjured a lot of stuff. Which is good. It's welcome really. But just not really much of a—"

"Surprise," Shauna says.

"Exactly."

She takes a sip of tea, leans back in her chair, and smiles as a family bundles past our table—two tired-looking men, two tiny children, straddling those little pull-along suitcases that double as ride-on toys. They screech with delight as their parents pull them along and sip from takeaway coffees, like they're cups full of the elixir of life.

"Natalie, does it make you happy?" asks Shauna as a fresh, early autumn breeze swirls through the station. "Spending time with Joe. No judgment, just a question. Friend to a friend."

Something sinks in my chest as she says it, even though I know the answer. I even asked myself this as Joe texted on Sunday morning to see how I was, and when Tom called on Sunday night to check in. "You heard from Little Surfer Dude? Tell him I said to go easy on the next surprise. No helicopter trips to the opera in Naples. No 6 a.m. mud runs." He's been texting, checking in every day since the tube platform.

I look over at Shauna. "It does," I reply. "Hanging out with Joe does make me happy. He understands me—the grief—like nobody else does."

"But? Is there a but?"

"I don't know," I say. "Maybe it's just that—it feels a bit—one-sided or something."

"Like he's trying to woo you?"

I wince. "I don't know about wooing me, but—I was sort of hoping the surprise was just—dinner somewhere. I even dressed for it. Wore heels." I smile, almost ashamed, but Shauna doesn't flinch. "Which probably sounds a bit selfish, because the gig was such a nice idea—"

"It's not selfish to *want* something, Natalie," says Shauna. "But what I often forget is that we can't really expect other people to know what we want without saying it out loud. People are barely tuned in to what they want for themselves, let alone what other people want. You know?"

I nod. A muffled announcement comes on the station loud-speaker. A late departure, by the sounds of things, to Nottingham although the person sounds like they're speaking through a sock.

"So, you'd like to have dinner with Joe. Not concerts, not shop-ping, not bumping into ex-friends and eating silly boxes of spaghetti and flowers in fields." Shauna chuckles. "Then why not ask him? You want it. Make it happen."

"So—what invite him out to dinner?"

"Invite him out to dinner." Shauna nods firmly. "I know a perfect place. The place Don and I went to at the weekend. It's by the river, in Kingston. Not too expensive but very cute and quiet, tucked away. Don's always going there for work. He only ever seems to be there when I called the office, and he's a fuss pot. So, I nagged. And he's right to love it. *Sublime.*"

I smile, although what I want to say is that Don should be going out of his way to wine and dine Shauna, after everything he's put her through. What he's done to his son. "*Nagged,*" I say instead. "You mean you asked for what you wanted, what you deserve," I say, and Shauna gives my hand a squeeze.

"She's catching on, this girl," she says.

We drink our teas in comfortable silence and watch, together, wordlessly, as Jason chats up, as he always does, Piercings Girl, and Secretary Girl (of Mr. Affair notoriety) arrives, like clockwork, and waits inside, in the usual corner.

At the end of her break, Shauna stands, picks up her empty cup. "I'll text you the restaurant details," she says. "And if I don't see you, I'll see you at my anniversary Saturday. You're still coming?"

"Wouldn't miss it," I reply. "Can't wait."

"Me either," she says, giving a weak smile, and I watch as she disappears inside Goode's, her eyes not once leaving Secretary Girl, who sits alone.

Tom (Just): I've got two words for you, Foxes.

Tom (Just): Fucking.

Tom (Just): Starving.

Tom (Just): You around tonight? Wondered if you fancied Avocado Clash? They do takeaways now. 😨

Me: Omg, DO THEY? But does the guac still come in the hollowed-out dead cartoon avocados?

Me: And I can't Thomas! I'm off to dinner (no surprises this time) with NJ.

Me: (Notebook Joe, if you hadn't guessed.)

Tom (Just): Wow. He's catching on.

Me: My idea. 😵

Tom (Just): Ah! Well, I'll see you tomorrow, pal. At the anniversary party from hell.

Me: Ha-ha, you'll survive. There will be no crocodiles present. Or declarations of love either.

Tom (Just): Ha. Thank Christ.

Tom (Just): And have a good time tonight.

Tom (Just): With LSD.

Tom (Just): (Little Surfer Dude, if you hadn't guessed.)

chapter twenty-two

Shauna was right. And this is why Shauna, as far I'm concerned, is an oracle in hooped earrings. I'm having the nicest evening with Joe, and we've only just finished eating our starter—a shared meze, with the freshest bread I think I have ever sunk my teeth into. This restaurant by the Thames is exactly like Shauna described. Quiet and tucked away, with low ceilings and wood ovens on show, and it has a perfect view of the river, which sits still and inky beside us, on the outdoor terrace. It's a beautiful evening, autumnal, but not too cold. Glowing heaters nestled under the parasols of every table take the edge off. Shauna didn't quite mention how romantic this place was, though, with its fairy lights and lanterns and moonlit river, and if she had, I might not have booked a table. Might have worried Joe thought I was too keen, too forward. But still, I'm glad I did. Because I can't remember the last time I got dressed up and went out for dinner. It was something I used to do all the time, especially with Priya, Lucy, and Roxanne, but we haven't in a while. Since the brunch, there's something between us, blocking us, prizing us apart. Something that shot through a crack in the ground that morning of my birthday, like a giant beanstalk.

"I'm really glad we did this," I say as Joe pours me another glass of wine from the bottle we're sharing. It's the first alcoholic drink I've had in months. I'm sure even Roy next door has noticed, with his eagle recycling-obsessed eye, just as much as I have. "It's just nice to just—chat. And chill. No edible flowers . . ."

"No smelly rooms . . ."

"No men with lips on your neck in queues."

Joe chuckles, two dimples prodding his cheeks. He looks incredibly gorgeous tonight. No wonder Hollie seemed totally enamored by him at the gig—the full lips, the glinting hazel eyes. He's wearing a pressed white T-shirt, tonight, a black blazer-style jacket over the top, and he's had a haircut—just a little shorter than normal, put perfectly beachy and styled.

"Yeah, it's nice," he says. "Lots of personal space. Where it counts."

He holds up his glass, and I clink mine to it. We drink.

"Natalie," Joe says nervously. "I wanted to say sorry about the gig the other night."

We've texted a bit since the gig, but Joe and I haven't mentioned that night since. I wondered if he could tell I felt weird and sad and confused. That I left early because of it, and not some bizarre, sudden illness.

"You don't need to be sorry, Joe."

"Yeah, I know, but I wondered if maybe it was too soon? I thought it might help. You know, with the not-being-able-to-play stuff, like my writer's block, but . . . it was busy and crowded and fucking *loud*—"

"Joe, honestly—"

"And then . . . Hollie."

Those three words hang there in the air between us, like cigarette smoke.

"She seemed nice," I say. "And you—used to date?"

Joe looks down into his wine, then nods. He knocks back a

mouthful, the Adam's apple in his throat bobbing as he swallows. "Yeah. And we were together. For just over eighteen months."

"*Eighteen months?* That's—blimey, that's quite a long time."

"She sort of got me the job down here," he says. "We were friends, back in Dorset. We were sort of part of a big friendship group, you know? Then she moved down to London for her MA and to work and—I needed a new start after Tanner, so she helped get me set up."

"And you broke up and have to see her all the time? Jesus. That's—hard."

"Mm." Joe cocks his head to one side, gives a wince.

"For her?" I offer.

"Much more than me," he says, nibbling his lip, like he's ashamed of the admission. "We work at different bars a lot of the time, which is good. It's a chain. But yeah. She's still super keen for it to be something. And I'm just—*not*. Which I feel like shit about because she was so good to me after Tanner's accident."

I nod, and I feel a pang of sympathy for Hollie. Loving someone who doesn't love you back is a special sort of agony. Especially when you've held their hand through something unimaginable. It binds you together for life. I think that's what I find so hard about Edie. Edie was my foundation through so much. When my legs were too shaky to hold me, she held me up. And when you've been through something together, when you're still standing because of someone else's love and care, it stays with you both, like a shared tattoo you wear throughout your life until the end.

"I suppose it's nobody's fault if you just don't feel it anymore," I say. "As rough as it is."

"Yeah. And she tries. To sort of—make it okay again? Be friends, be *more*. But—if I'm honest, I find it hard to be with her."

"Why do you find it hard?"

Joe takes a deep breath, his lips a tight, rigid line, and looks across at the river again, the moon reflecting on it like swirls of cream. "She was there when Tanner died," he explains. "We all were. Hollie worked on the beach in the summer, like the rest of us. She worked on the bungee jumpers. With the kids? You know, the trampoline things? Anyway— that day, the beach was red-flagged. It's a warning to people coming on the beach not to swim. But we surfed sometimes when it was like that. Me, Tanner, our friends. We shouldn't have, but we always felt like we knew what we were doing." He gives a small, sad smile, a puff of air through his nostrils. "Anyway, I thought it was fine. It was red-flagged but sort of dying down, and Hollie told me not to, but—I misjudged it."

"You went out in it?"

Joe nods, his body still, like someone stunned, locked in place. "Got into trouble. Tanner was on guard, so he came out. To get me."

Oh my god. Joe's never told me this before. Just that Tanner had an accident. He's never said that he was there. That he was . . . the reason. My heart throbs in my chest, as if bruised.

"Oh, Joe," I whisper. "Joe, I'm so sorry—"

"Yeah." He swallows, knocks back more wine. "He got me to shore. Then this wave came and—there's this rock there and—" He drops his eyes to the table. "Then he was taken to the hospital. But— the last time I saw him, as Tanner, how I've always known him, was in that water. Saving me. And I know this probably isn't true, but when Hollie looks at me, when she's *close* to me, I swear that's all she sees. That it was my fault."

"But . . . Joe—"

"It's all I see," he says, looking up to meet my eyes, "when I look at me."

♫   ♫   ♫
    ♫   ♫   ♫

A group of people a few tables away erupts into laughter, and someone drops a glass on the floor that doesn't smash. It rolls along the concrete.

"Sorry," says Joe, giving a tight laugh.

"God, don't be—"

"Yeah, it's just . . ."

He brings his hands behind his head, like a footballer missing a goal. "I feel like I've just—shat all over the mood."

"You haven't." I reach over, put a hand on Joe's hand. "And I bet she doesn't see it, Joe. I could tell by the way she was looking at you that Hollie doesn't see that. She sees bloody—*sunbeams* or something. I saw her."

Joe smiles sadly. "I know," he says. "But when you know if you'd done things differently, he'd still be here, you see it everywhere. You feel like the world knows you're . . . bad or something. And I see it in everyone's eyes. Even if it isn't really there."

I lean over to pick up the wine bottle, fill up both of our glasses. Wordlessly, we drink, as if it's medicine, as if it's a bottle of calm, but my hand is still on his at the center of the table. He doesn't move his, and I don't move mine.

"I know it isn't the same, but I blamed myself for a while, about Russ," I say quietly. "Why did I have to take the car, why did he have to keep insisting on cycling everywhere? Why didn't I stop him? Why didn't I—I don't know—accidentally poison him with badly cooked chicken the night before so he was too sick to go out? But I try to remember that life is random. And shit just happens and there are no deep meanings to these things, no signs we missed . . . this is not your fault, Joe. None of it is your fault."

Joe smiles, weakly. Then he dips his head, brings my hand up, and puts his lips softly to the skin. He kisses it. My heart quickens.

"Thank you," he says.

"W-what for?"

"For . . . being there," he says. "I don't deserve you."

"Don't be silly." I laugh but he doesn't, and it's like the mood has changed between us. It's thick, loaded . . .

"Natalie, can I . . ."

"Can you?"

"I . . ." Then he clears his throat and says, "Come on. Just. Tell me something interesting. Something lighthearted. And where's this bloody moussaka?"

I laugh and I'm relieved we're back to the lightness of when we first arrived. To surface-deep questions. "Erm—er, well, I successfully made a casserole without setting my house on fire last Monday."

Joe laughs. "Whoa, okay, keep it coming."

"I know. And it was edible. *And*—Oh, I know. There was more music."

"Not in the piano?"

"Yep. Some Electric Light Orchestra tune? Song called 'Last Train to London.' Which is quite uncreative, considering the piano's in a train station, but maybe they're running out of ideas. It's a great song, though, great fun to play."

"Right." Joe smiles, but something passes over his face. It's that look Priya gave me at the shop. It's *almost* like those looks I avoid. The "what a shame" pity faces. Ugh, don't you dare start gracing Joe's face, shitty, concerned, feel-sorry-for-me looks. Those looks are bad enough on Lucy's and Roxanne's.

"Natalie, do you think maybe someone is—I don't know. Fucking with you?"

"What? With the music?" And I'm not surprised at Joe for asking this really. He's a bit—skeptical. Trusts pasta more than people by his own admission. "I don't think so. I mean, I suppose they are in a way, but—it's for a nice reason, so I don't know if that's classed as *fucking with me.*"

"It's just—" Joe nibbles at his thumbnail. "I don't really understand who could be doing it. I mean, who would want to? And the thing is, Natalie—"

"Two moussakas?" A waitress appears from nowhere, our meals on a circular black tray in her hands. Her nails are bright blue, and there's an enamel badge on her chest in the shape of a strawberry milkshake.

"Ooh, yes, that's us," I say. "Thank you."

She sets down the steaming, cinnamony plates in front of us and flits off.

"This looks amazing," I say, and Joe just nods in agreement.

We eat quietly among the sound of low chatter and chinking crockery and occasional click of the heaters, and I'm almost relieved when the waitress returns and seats a couple two tables over. It's a distraction. Somewhere to avert my eyes because the atmosphere has sort of thickened again, between Joe and me, at this table, and I don't know why. They slide themselves onto the bench seating, sitting beside each other instead of opposite. It's an older man and a woman with hair like a fifties beehive, and the older man's hand is cupping the beehive woman's arse, squeezing it, right in my eyeline, like dough.

I raise my eyebrows at Joe, a secret "Bloody hell, look at these two," but he doesn't notice them, he's just looking at me. "Sorry, what were you saying?"

"So, erm, look." He shakes his head, as if waking himself out of a trance. "When I said I wonder if someone is fucking with you . . ."

"No, I get it."

"It just—You said it stopped. The music."

"Yeah."

"Then it started again, and . . ."

"*Yeah.*"

"Do you think maybe someone's playing a trick?"

"A trick?" I still the cutlery in my hands. "But who would play a trick on me? To what end?"

"To take the piss?" offers Joe, as if it's something he's already made his mind up about. The fairy lights flicker in his eyes like tiny fires.

"But then it hasn't worked, has it? Because the music means a lot to me. It's not a trick if it makes me happy, is it?"

"Does it?" asks Joe. "Mean a lot to you, I mean."

"Of course it does."

Joe stares at me, and my heart is sinking. It's that feeling. Like I said to Tom—when I feel someone's thinking I'm too fragile. Like I'm not enough of a full person. That I have an empty life compared to everyone else and *this* is how I choose to get my kicks. I just didn't expect Joe to feel it too, even a tiny bit. I thought he was—an ally, of sorts. Someone that got me and accepted me for exactly who and where I am.

"Oh, God, I'm a rotten cynic." This time, Joe reaches over, closes a hand over mine, and edges forward. "I'm sorry," he says. "Will you forgive my cynical, bitter little mind?"

I smile weakly. "You are a cynic," I say. "You'll make a cantankerous old man one day. A cantankerous old man with one fun memory of novelty straw glasses."

Joe laughs. "I dunno, I just—I care Natalie. That's all."

"I know. And if my hopes are up and dashed, then—I can take that. I'd survive. I'm not a stupid, weak, poor little—"

"Of course you're not. Jesus, you could never be those things." And lightly, and I'm surprised when he does, Joe reaches up and, like on the grass at the food festival, brushes a warm finger down my cheek. I look up. His warm, hazel eyes are already on mine. And they're disarming really. The color of them, the crisscrossing lashes. *Can I?* Can I really let another man kiss me? Like this? In public. Like the beehive woman at the next table, who is now passionately kissing Gropey Man. All tongues, all hunger, all lust. My eyes flick to them. Gropey Man is smiling at her, hungrily, like he can think of only one thing. Because that's where it leads, doesn't it? This is the prelude. And I don't know if I'm ready for that. With Joe—

And then Joe leans, the decision taken out of my hands. He pushes his mouth softly onto mine. His lips are cool and soft, his fingertips in my hair, and lingering there, for just a second, I taste the white wine on him, on the gentle brush of the tip of his tongue.

And I pull away.

I just kissed Joe. Joe just kissed me. The type of perfect, soft, and gorgeous kiss I wondered if I'd ever experience again.

And yet, I felt nothing. Absolutely nothing.

♬   ♬   ♬
♬   ♬   ♬

Priya: OMGGG how was it?! I am dying to hear! Basically SALIVATING with anticipation. Can't bloody concentrate on anything until I hear from you!

Me: Ugh. Don't ask. On my way home.

Me: He kissed me.

Priya: oh my god!!!!

Me: And. . . I didn't feel. . . ANYTHING?????

Priya: ?

Priya: What do you mean?

Me: I felt nothing Priya. Like. . . nothing at all. Sitting on the train feeling like a big broken idiot. 😵

Priya: Oh. I'm so sorry you're sad 🖤

Priya: And Natalie, you are not broken.

Priya: If there is one thing you are not, it's broken.

Priya: Balls of steel. Remember?

chapter twenty-three

I'd hoped Shauna and Don's anniversary party would be a perfect dis-traction from what happened between me and Joe yesterday—just didn't expect this. Total escapism levels of distraction. Stepping into another *world* levels of distraction. Because when Shauna described the party venue for her anniversary party, she failed to mention it was basically a castle—*an estate*. One that wouldn't look out of place on a BBC period drama. I couldn't believe it when my sat-nav led me here, down this sweeping driveway, and the hall appeared, a huge L-shaped building. The way Shauna threw it into casual conversation, I expected a little banquet hall at the most. I did not expect this. This is a lux-ury spa resort. This has a hedge maze and pillars and those suitcase trolleys—the gold ones that are always attached to men in tailcoats. And I admit—I'm very glad I chose to dress up. When I pulled out my trusty little black dress from the back of the wardrobe, I was worried that a) it wouldn't fit me and b) I'd be overdressed. Like someone show-ing up to play in a football match in a ball gown. But I'm glad I took the risk, because not a single fucker in the Madden family—well, Shauna, nor her Tommy Button—told me that they'd be celebrating here: in what might as well be the Bridgerton estate.

I crunch across the gravel, my breath clouding in the air as I walk toward the grand entrance—two large glass and teak-framed doors, with long, gold handles. It's cold tonight, the weather switching into full autumn without a hitch.

"Nah, nah, you've gone wrong, mate." A man in a tuxedo stands at the entrance, a half-full beer in his hand, a phone to his ear. His bow tie hangs untied, either side of his neck. "You need to swing a left there. You're at the golf club. We're at the main house. Yeah, that's it. That's where you're going." A guest, or best man, I suppose, from a wedding party being held in another function room. He steps aside as I approach, and I go inside.

At the quiet reception desk, I open the invite Shauna emailed to me on my phone. "I'm here for Don and Shauna Madden's anniversary party," I say to the man on reception, who has a fixed (and exhausted) grin on his face. He looks like someone who's had quite enough of drunken wedding guests for one lifetime. "In the er—the Coles Suite, is that right?" The man nods and gives me directions. "You can't miss it, madam," he says flatly, "just follow the corridor right around. You'll hear it before you see it."

And he's right. I do hear Shauna and Don's party before I see it, and it's so raucous, I wonder for a moment if it's the *right* party—but when the glossy double white-paneled doors come into view, I instantly see Tom. He's waiting outside, resting easily against the wall, his eyes on his phone, and for a second I almost freeze, there on the carpet. He looks like the Tom I met at Avocado Clash. *Better* than the Tom at Avocado Clash. Tall, totally dashing, as my mum would say, and just—so incredibly handsome. I wonder if Amy thinks this when she sees him. She must. That jaw, those eyes, that perfect mouth . . .

"*Thomas*," I say, "I wondered if your ma-ma would permit you to take a turn of the gardens with me."

Tom glances up, and his face breaks into a smile. "Hey! I was just calling you. You didn't pick up."

"Sorry, my phone's in my bag. But hi. I'm here."

"Yes, you are." He smiles and closes the gap between us, slowly, across the floor. "Well, fuckin' hell, Foxes," he says. "I must say . . . You look good. Better than good."

"Scrub up well, don't I?"

"Putting it lightly." He grins.

"And you—you look positively *dashing*. Very Mr. Darcy. Or maybe—Mr. Darcy's rough and rugged younger brother."

"And have you seen?" He gestures with his hands down to his shoes. "Polished. Bless my little heart. I really tried. Really made the effort."

"Oh, I'm so going to need a photo." I laugh. "To send to Priya."

"Of course. Only reason I bothered to be honest. And—" He raises the camera in his hand. An SLR. Black. A thick, black band attached to it for his neck. "Allow me." He snaps a photo of his feet on the floor, and I do the same on my phone, like his shoes are two celebrities who just arrived at the Met Gala.

"Proper normal behavior this," he says. "And shall we? I'm *positive* dear Ma-ma will be splendiferino'd to see you."

"*Quite*," I reply, linking my arm through his, and something settles in my tummy, like safety, being this close to him. "Lead the way. But no sudden surprises please. I'm sewn into the dress, and slightest bit of pressure and I'm worried I'll be blown out of it."

"Interesting," says Tom. "Sounds like an invitation, to be honest."

He leads us both through the double-paneled doors, and into a room bathed in a haze of blue-purple light. And it is full of people— I mean *full*. It looks more like a wedding reception than a party. Even the dance floor is heaving, all arms and legs and bobbing heads.

Tom looks down at me and widens his blue eyes. A wordless "this is mad, eh?"

"There are a *lot* of people here," I say over the music, and Tom nods.

"*Yup.*"

"And when's your toast?"

"I don't know," he groans deeply. "Soon, I guess? I'm just hoping to die before it's time. A heart attack might be nice. Right over the chocolate fountain, for a little extra drama."

"No, Thomas," I say. "You're not allowed to die."

Tom winces. "Sorry. Bit tasteless of me."

"No, I just mean—well, I need you to finish my damp-proofing first for starters. Then you're free to—go up in beautiful flames."

We meander through groups of people and clouds of perfume and disco smoke until we come to Shauna, who is standing among a crowd of people, surrounded like a queen—and she looks a *adorable*. She's in a dark-blue sequin dress and black tights, with her hair in a beautiful updo. She's glowing.

"My dear heart!" she squeals, throwing her arms around me before I can even hand her the card (and gift voucher inside) in my hand. "Oh, my darling, you're here. And would you look at that—Tom, doesn't she look gorgeous?"

Tom smiles down at me. "Beautiful," he says quietly, and a flicker spontaneously sparks in my lower tummy. Tom thinks I look beautiful. No jokes, no sarcasm. Just: beautiful.

"Right. I want you to meet my gang," Shauna says, as Tom excuses himself to the bar, to get us drinks, and she takes my arm. "This is Jane, and Angela, oh, and this is my beautiful friend Amma." She beams.

"And where's Don?" I ask.

"Oh, he's off sorting a surprise."

"A surprise, eh?"

"For me, apparently." Shauna shrugs but smiles giddily. "I haven't a clue what it could be. And meanwhile—I haven't stopped dancing, have I, Jane? You'll have to dance with me later, Natalie. I can show you my swing team moves . . ."

"I promise I will," I say. "But you get back to your friends, I'm gonna go and track Jason down. Keep him on the straight and narrow."

"Good thinking," says Shauna, and she kisses my cheek. "He was eyeing up the poor barmaid and Christ, the lad needs a muzzle. He was at the bar last time I saw him."

I make my way through the heaving dance floor and head for the bar. I can't see Jason, although it is crowded. And not that I wasn't expecting someone as lovely as Shauna to have droves of adoring friends and family, but I'm shocked at the number of people here, all present and correct, to celebrate the love between two people. Thirty years of life, shared. And I know it isn't a perfect marriage. Far from it. But . . . *thirty years.* Together, in each other's lives. Thirty years of growing up with someone. Jesus. I wonder if we'd have reached that, Russ and I. We thought ten was impressive enough.

"I got you lemonade," says Tom, appearing as if from nowhere, squeezing through the crowd. "I figured because you're driving . . ."

"Perfect. Thank you. And you have—"

"Whiskey. Double," he says. "The behavior of someone who doesn't want to give a fucking toast."

"Just keep it short and sweet," I say above the music. "You know— we're gathered here today . . . yadda . . . thirty years is a murder sentence, bottoms up."

Tom cocks an eyebrow. "Oh, well, *thanks* for the help."

"Tom, you'll boss it," I say. "You know you will. You're good at— words. Better than me. I have to text you mine piecemeal."

An ABBA song strikes up, and the volume increases.

"I just—I feel like it's a lie," Tom says, ducking closer to be heard.

His warm breath tickles my neck. "That I've got to stand there and talk about love and commitment and marriage and . . . it's such a farce, Nat. And I don't want it to be, of course I don't. I just really hope he means it this time."

He looks at me, and there's a dull sadness in his eyes.

"Maybe he does," I say, standing on my toes to get closer to his ear. He smells amazing. Like . . . intoxicatingly good. *What is that?* "Look, you're always telling me that life goes on, and once you've done something, you pass it, and you can't go back, and—maybe he's learned. Maybe he's changed. Maybe he's not that person anymore."

Tom draws in a long breath, and cocks his head to the side. "Maybe."

"Your mum says he's off sorting a surprise for her, and—well, I don't know about you, but I've never been to an anniversary like this before, and this was his idea so, maybe . . ."

"Give him a chance?"

I give a small shrug. "Yeah," I say, touching his arm as a cheer erupts through the room, like a gradual wave. A man takes to the small, squat stage, his back to us, and feedback from the microphone, like nails on a chalkboard, screeches through the speakers.

"Ah, shit. My cue," Tom says. "It's Dad. He's going to make a speech and then he wants *me* to . . . ugh. Shoot me."

"Go get them, Thomas," I say, and he nods, just once, putting a large, warm hand on my waist as he moves past me.

Don turns in the shadows, the microphone too close to his lips.

"Hello, everyone!" he bellows. And he looks exactly how I imagined he would. Handsome, and sharp. Gray and square-jawed, broad shoulders. He looks like Tom, too. They have the same eyes. "Well, would you look at you all?" he carries on.

And—he's familiar. Really familiar. And the realization settles on me, all at once, as he smiles, as he nods knowingly and authoritatively to the DJ.

Oh.

Oh God.

He's the guy I saw in the restaurant with Joe, by the river. Don was the man with his hands all over that woman. That woman who wasn't Shauna.

♪   ♪   ♪
♪   ♪   ♪

Tom's toast went beautifully. At first, he read from his phone, something he'd obviously written up and rehearsed, but then he slipped it into his pocket, said into the mic, "OK, that's enough of that, I feel like I'm giving a bloody sermon," and just chatted—as Tom does. People laughed, of course, Shauna cried, and Don pulled him in for an enormous bear hug, and then Shauna cried even more when one by one, the beautiful Madden brothers—Laurie, Mark, George, and Danny— got up and handed Shauna a gift for every decade of their marriage together. A dress, a bracelet, and dancing shoes for her, plus an extra gift: dancing shoes for Don. That was the surprise. Don and Shauna, to dance together. He'd been practicing, he'd told the room, although it didn't stop him mock-recoiling as he took the shoes from his son, as the room erupted in laughter too. They'd all looked so happy. A stage of smiles, a crowd of whoops and cheers. But I stood feeling like my bones were turning to stone, that my heart was a brick in my chest. Don was with another woman. He was groping another woman, *kissing* another woman. And I saw. I know. I wish I had doubt, but there is none. It was him. It was Don.

After the toast, the Maddens dissolved into the crowd, the dance floor continuing to heave, and I'd found a chair tucked away in the back, and it's there I sit now, sipping my room-temperature lemonade, hoping for once Tom doesn't find me just yet. I need to think about what to do, about whether I should say something. And if not to Shauna, to Tom? God, could I tell Tom? Ugh, I feel sick. I need to talk to someone. Jodie. Jodie will know what to do. She always knows what to do.

I squeeze my way through the crowd and out through an open door tucked at the back of the venue, the heavy drapes lining the wall parted a little. I stumble out into the cold night air. A group, clouded in cigarette smoke and a mist of vapor that smells like blackberries, turn to look at me as I do. I round the corner, as far as I can get from the other guests, and dial Jodie's number. After three rings, she picks up. In the background I can hear the TV—a quiz show, by the sounds of things—and the clink of plates.

"You all right, Nat?" she says. "Sorry, hang on, Carl has this telly on way too loud, anyone would think he was sitting two miles from it with his head in a bucket . . . Nat? Are you still there? Are you OK?"

"I'm fine," I say as the noise of the TV fades. "I'm at that anniversary thing—"

"Oh yeah? What's it like?"

"Yeah, it's—the venue, it's stunning. Like something out of *Pride and Prej* or something . . ."

"Oh, bloody Nora. Very swish. Is Tom there?"

"Yeah, he's inside. Look, Jode, I need to ask you something. I'm having this—actual dilemma."

"Is it about snogging Tom? Because if you're wondering, I think it's well overdue, and my answer would always be *yes. Do i. . . .*"

"No, no," I say. "It's not about Tom. Not really . . . so the other night, Joe and I, we went out to dinner. By the river. And while we were there, we saw this guy—older guy, about Dad's age—all over this woman at the next table. Grabbing her arse and groping her and . . ." A woman walks out onto the grass. She puts a hood up on her shawl-like coat, lights up a cigarette, an orange orb in the dark. "And kissing her," I whisper.

"Right. OK?"

"And—I'm at the party and it was time for Tom's dad to go up onstage and he stood there, with the mic, and I thought—I thought—"

"No. *No!*" says Jodie. The penny has already dropped.

"It was him, Jodie. It was Shauna's bloody husband I saw. Honestly, it was, I'd bet . . . I don't know. My life on it."

"Shit. Oh, God. And you're absolutely sure."

"Yes. A hundred percent. A hundred and *ten.*"

Jodie blows a noisy breath down the line, and hearing myself say these words makes my heart thrum and pound. Fuck. What am I going to do?

"I think you should tell Tom," says Jodie quietly.

"Really? Now?"

"I just—do you think you can carry on being his friend and not say?" says Jodie.

"Oh, God."

"Do you want me to ask Carl?"

"Please," I say breathlessly, the dark air pluming with the steam of my warm, shallow, panicked bloody breaths.

For a moment, I hear Jodie's muffled voice, explaining to Carl everything I just told her, and the wait, listening to their quiet TV in the background, is unbearable. I want to tell Tom. Of course I do. But I don't want to tell him all at once.

I've just told him to give his dad a chance. Mere moments ago. Plus Tom already holds himself back from love because of his parents, doesn't trust it, and I will shatter any tiny bit of hope he still has in it the second I say the words.

"Right," says Carl. "Right, I see," and he talks like a doctor might, if you sat him down and told him you had a tail suddenly growing out of your arse. Unshakable. Years working as an NHS psychologist makes you that way, I suppose.

"Carl says you should probably speak to Tom, as he's your friend," says Jodie calmly. "But not tonight."

"It's a huge family issue," Carl is saying in the background. "Nothing can be gained from causing drama and pain tonight. But ultimately, it's her choice. They do need to know. They're Natalie's friends, and it's what she would want too, if it was the other way around."

A wave of cheers sounds from inside, and I nod, in the darkness, to nobody. I think about myself, and of course, Edie and Russ sleeping together is *nothing* compared to Shauna and Don, but it was the not knowing that hurt the most. The lie.

"Ladies and gentlemen," calls the deep, singsongy voice of the DJ from inside, "please welcome, one of many dances owed, and dances to come: Don and Shauna Madden on their thirtieth anniversary." A happy, upbeat swing song begins and there's an eruption of applause.

"Thank you," I say, down the phone. "I'll take your advice, I think. God, I feel sick, Jodie."

"I bet you do," says Jodie. "What an absolute *shit* that husband is as well."

"The worst."

"Are you going to be OK, Nat?"

"Fine," I say but my voice quavers, and I'm not sure I believe myself. "I'll see you Monday, yeah? At the shop?"

"And Carl says in the end, you should go with what feels right," adds Jodie. "You'll know, when it comes to it. The right thing to do . . ."

♪   ♪   ♪
♪   ♪   ♪

An hour later, I find Tom sitting outside on the steps of the entrance, by the big, sweeping driveway, his phone and camera beside him on the sandstone. The spotlights bordering the gravel drive cast warm glows over the cold ground, and a few paces beyond it, where the estate is and the acres of forest begin, so dark, it's as if someone has put a huge matte-black screen up, cutting us off from the rest of the world.

"I've been looking for you," I say, moving through the entrance carefully, a drink in each hand.

Tom looks around at me from sitting on the steps and smiles widely, and it hurts a little—like a small dagger in my chest. I hate that I know what I know.

"I was looking for you too actually," says Tom. "Then I found you getting talked at by Jason and had to leave you there, sorry. You looked positively *grave*. Didn't want to inflict that on myself."

I laugh, lower myself next to him on the cold steps. "Yeah, he is extremely drunk and talking about how he feels soul mates were invented by the illuminati." I hold out his drink. "Or Jane Austen. One or the other. I wasn't really paying attention."

Tom laughs. "Is this a—"

"Whiskey sour, like at Avocado Clash," I smile. "And I—I have a margarita. Well. A nonalcoholic one. It's *tradish*."

"Thanks." He smiles. "Tradish, indeed."

We sip quietly, nothing but the sound of distant, muffled music from inside. It's silent really, out here in the middle of the countryside. You could hear a pin drop. And it feels almost alien and wrong not to tell him, out in this silence, beneath the starry night sky, with so much space between us waiting to be filled.

"So, come on then. How do you think my toast went?" Tom asks. "Not too bad, was it?"

"I thought it was perfect," I say. "Seriously. Not a foot wrong. And your mum, oh my *gosh*—"

"She loved it, didn't she?"

"*Completely*. I thought she was going to explode with happiness."

Tom nods gently. "Yeah, I'm glad I did it," he says, and he tips his head to the sky. It's one big navy silken sheet tonight, splattered with thousands and thousands of stars, the moon among it, like the center-piece—beautiful and round, maple smudges blurring its edge.

"So," he adds, "any music lately?"

"Yep," I say, "this week. Train-themed, which was funny."

"Interesting."

"And I'd never played it before, so that was also fun. And it sort of reminded me—I haven't learned anything new in a while. It was nice just—getting to know a new song, hesitating over the notes, and then boom, it finally clicks and you feel like—I dunno. The Jesus Christ of piano."

Tom gives a deep chuckle. "Well. That's cool, Foxes," he says softly. "I'm glad to hear it."

Distant headlights light up a strip of the dark, hazy grounds as a car enters the estate. Tom and I watch as it approaches, its wheels crunching on the gravel, and turns the corner, and disappearing again behind the estate, into the car park.

"That moon is something tonight," says Tom, and he slowly reaches for his camera, angles it, and brings it to his face. "I've been so focused on getting ready for this exhibition that I've missed—this. Just—you know. Knee-jerk stuff. Just *ah, shit, what a shot, I've gotta get it*. You know? Those moments that just arise. Perfect, random mo-ments . . ."

I nod, watch him at work, the camera against his face, his lovely pink lips parted, just a little, in concentration. "And are you all set? For the exhibition."

"I hope so," replies Tom. "You're still coming?"

"Of course," I say, as beside me Tom clicks and clicks again, and silence clouds us.

"Russ loved the moon," I say. "He could never resist taking pho-tos of it, and I used to take the piss. Say, 'It'll be there tomorrow, you know, and the next day.' He wasn't a photographer, obviously, but his phone was full of them. It was his last WhatsApp photo actually. His little avatar thing."

Tom smiles gently and brings the camera down away from his face, and leans in close to me. He's so warm, so near, and I—I don't want him to move. I like how it feels, having him this close. I feel safe. I always feel safe with him. "There you go," Tom says, putting the camera between us. Our heads are almost touching. "What do we reckon on that?"

"That's—it's beautiful."

"It's hard to believe it's even real, eh?" and he edges even closer, our arms touching now. His eyes slide up to meet mine, dropping for just a fraction of a second, to my lips. And my heart—why is my heart cha-cha-ing? "And thank you, by the way. For earlier."

"W-What did I do?"

"You got me to practice what I preach," he says. "About how I tell you that you never stay the same, that you aren't the same person you were yesterday . . ."

"I didn't do anything. That's *your* advice."

"No, I know. But . . . you made me feel like maybe I don't need to be scared. That if I can give Dad a chance, that if Dad can change, then maybe I . . ." He smiles, as if to himself. "I don't have to be scared of crocodiles."

And now I want to cry. Because I know what he's saying. He's saying he feels he might, after all, feel he can give himself over to love. And sitting here with Tom, like this, makes me realize how much I care for him. Tom wants to feel less scared to fall in love, less scared to give himself over to trusting someone, to risk being hurt, to risk being the one making mistakes, because I told him to give his dad a chance. Because he thinks his dad has changed. And yet, his dad hasn't. His dad blew the chance the second I spoke it into the room. And I know when he finds out what his dad is doing, he'll retreat again. And the world deserves Tom. Someone out there in the world deserves Tom. And Tom deserves the world. God, how can I tell him? How can I *possibly* tell him now?

I clear my throat, lean away from him.

I shift, just a little away from him on the cold, stone step. "I—erm." I take a gulp of my mock margarita. "I better go soon."

Tom's dark eyebrows knit together at that. "Right. You mean now? It's not late. You've not finished your drink—"

"I've got loads to do."

"Yeah? LSD related? What's he got, another surprise?"

"No, no I'm—" Another gulp of mocktail. And another.

"And how was it? The dinner?"

I can barely look at him. I feel like if I do, I'll tell him, and tonight will forever be known as the night *that* moment happened. Not the toast he did so perfectly, not the beautiful photo of the moon he took. Not this moment, here, with me. But that. I can't. I can't, and I feel like I'm betraying him, every minute I sit there with him, knowing what I know . . .

"It was . . . Fine. It was nice."

Tom stares at me and I feel like . . . does he know? Does he know I'm scrabbling around, trying to end the conversation so I can leave because I'm *keeping* something from him?

"Are you seriously making me wring the dry towel, Natalie?" Tom gives a slow smile. "I won't call Buzzfeed. Cross my heart."

"No, it's just . . ."

Our breath meets in the cold air and mixes into a cloud, and I stare at him. I can't say it. I can't tell him. How could I? No. I need to go home. I need to follow what Carl said. Now is not the time.

"We—we kissed." Oh. *God.* Where did that even come from? Why did I just say that? To Tom? Is it because I can't admit I know about Don and Beehive woman, I'm—what? Confessing to something else? Something I'm ashamed of, too embarrassed to say out loud. . .

Tom's lips part then, and he retracts back, just a little, like someone trying to avoid a ball flying through the air in their direction.

"W-wow. Blimey," he says. "So, you kissed. You and—you and Joe."

"Yes, but it wasn't like that at all, actually, it was—"

"I'm happy for you, Nat." Tom gives a soft, half smile. "Seriously. I can't think of anyone else I'd rather see happy. And I mean that."

And at those words, my eyes fill with tears.

"I didn't feel anything," I blurt. "Nothing."

Tom frowns, his eyes narrowing. "When you kissed?"

"He kissed me. At dinner. And—I felt absolutely nothing. Nothing. *So.* How's that for moving on." I give a tight laugh.

Tom shakes his head. "Natalie, maybe—maybe he's just not for you."

"But I worry," I whisper, tears gathering in my throat. "That there's something wrong with me. That—that I'm like some broken part on the side of a road. Heart, fucked. Heart, empty."

"There is nothing empty about your heart, Natalie."

"But say I don't ever—*get there*—where I do feel something."

Tom looks at me, his eyes darkening. "Maybe . . . maybe it's just not time yet," he says. "And you'll know. When it is."

"Will I?"

"It's unmistakable when you know." He moves his hand until it touches mine and slowly, gently links his little finger around my pinkie. "That's a promise."

A tear slides down my cheek. And I can't speak. Instead, I lean, press a long, slow kiss to his stubbly cheek. I don't want to leave him. I don't want to move from this step. But I do.

Moments later, I leave Tom on the steps, the moon looking over him, and as soon as I get into my car, I burst into tears.

chapter twenty-four

WhatsApp from Joe: I can't make music therapy Tues, Nat, but do you fancy coffee after? I'll meet you there. I think we should talk. Noon?

♪　　♪　　♪
　♪　　♪　　♪

We've hardly spoken, Joe and me. I got home from Shauna and Don's anniversary, and a text came through from him about meeting after music therapy, and I knew, at those words, it would be about us. Our friendship. Joe either likes me and senses I didn't "feel it" when he kissed me, or he felt the same. *Nothing.* Either way, it feels tarnished. Like it'll forever be weird between us: me and my new friend. I didn't reply to him until the morning. Instead, I climbed into bed in my dress, the zip halfway undone down my back, and cried. For Shauna. For Tom. For Joe. For me.

　　And today, I have to face it. Today, I have to meet Joe outside music therapy, and have that awkward conversation with him. And today, I have to pass Goode's, and pass Shauna. All the while knowing what I know. Knowing I need to say something, but having no idea how to arrange the words I need to say into a sentence that'll probably, regardless, totally break a family . . .

I drag myself out of bed and to the bathroom, and catch myself in the mirror. *God.* I look awful. Like someone has sucked the life out of me with a vacuum. Like I need sleep. (And perhaps, a vegetable or two.)

I wash my face, brush my teeth, my eyes fixed on my defeated reflection as I do.

Hopeless. "Hopeless" would be the word I sent to Tom now, if I could. But I don't. He'd call, he'd worry. And I know that next time I talk to him, I'll have to tell him about his dad, and I'm avoiding it. Putting it off, like a tax return or a trip to the post office, even though the magnitude of it is enough to send someone's life spinning off down the toilet. I sometimes think I should tell Shauna first. I always feel so safe with Shauna, but this—this is about *her.* This isn't one of my problems I need her to listen to. This isn't Lucy's attempted project management of my life. This isn't mystery music. This is her life. Her marriage. And how do you even say such a thing over back-hander blondies and coffee? "*So, listen, Shauna, I saw your husband of thirty years kissing another woman, and I have no idea who she is, but she had hair like a Pink Lady and an arse like kneaded sour-dough, so you know, who knows, maybe you could track her down?*"

I sit on the edge of my bed, pull on jeans still warm from the radiator. How did everything go so wrong? In the space of one silly, small weekend?

I'd lain in the dark on this bed all night after the anniversary party, unable to sleep, and scrolled Instagram—nights out, holidays and wines and sunsets and date nights, and I felt pathetic right there in my creaky, old bed. Joe. Gentle, sweet Joe, spilling everything to me, that weight on his shoulders about his brother—it had taken guts. Not only to tell me, but also, to kiss me. And my body reacted like nothing had happened. Like it was a big jellyfish at a dinner table. Nerveless, heartless, and soulless. And it was a lovely kiss. I've had bad kisses, believe me. There was Snake Mark in school and that tall guy I met when Edie and I went to France after our first year at uni. I can't remember his name—not sure I ever learned it—but the spit was so plentiful, Edie heard me yelp and burst into the hostel bedroom like I was in there with someone who just removed their mask to reveal the ghost of Christmas past. Joe was nothing like any bad kiss I've ever had. He was soft and sexy, he was just that perfect rhythm. But I had felt nothing. And combine that with the party—Don entering the bloody stage like a cartoon villain. Tom, on those steps. That finger hooking around mine. "I don't have to be scared of crocodiles." And the way he said "maybe it's just not time"—all of it, gathered and flooded through my bloody eyeballs in endless tears. I fell asleep at four a.m. eventually, the ghost of the Natalie who got dressed for that dinner by the river, buzzing with excitement, lying next to me in the dark, saying,

"Well. What a shitty weekend we've made for ourselves."

And I don't know what to do. There's a small part of me that wants to stay here in my tiny, wonky bedroom, hide my head under the duvet, keep all the curtains closed. But what good will that *actually* do? I've done so much of that over the last three years, and it never helps. It isn't me. *Real* Natalie. Because these things never just disappear, or fade away, I know that. They just get put off. Preserved until you have no choice but to crack open the lid, and finally look at it—deal with it. (And it's always best to do that before it's a big, old, smelly, concentrated, fermented mess.) Rip off the plaster. Step out on stage. Play the first note. *"Facing it is always easier than the moment before you actually do."* I used to say this all the time to Edie before we went on stage. And this hesitation, this feeling, is just that uncertain, nerve-racking moment before.

I turn off the heating and the lights on Three Sycamore, and step out into the cold, menthol morning. I head for the station.

Music therapy goes quickly today. I spend most of it in the smelly room, playing, and I'm grateful, really, that Joe couldn't make it today. There was no pressure to talk or to catch up. Just—what it should be when I come here. Music, and healing. A woman called Marcia wanders in and sits with me for a while too, and asks me, hands kneading a pink and white striped handkerchief in her lap, to play a song by Barbra Streisand. "It reminds me of my mum," she says thickly, "always calms me down. Makes me feel safe."

And as she leaves, she sniffs the air like a police dog, one booted foot out of the room, and says, "That smell . . ."

"Oh, I know," I laugh. "Sorry. We don't know what it is. I've been trying to investigate like some sort of smell detective but—"

"It'll be the electrics," she says. "We had the same back at the house. Thought all sorts—rotten fish hidden somewhere by a narky tenant, sewn into the curtains or something, the lot. But it was something burning. Something overheating. They'll want to sort that if you ask me. Really ruins the mood."

Electrics. I smile to myself, as she closes the door. Joe will freak when I've told him I've solved it. I told him I would. Made a vow, on that deck chair, under the hot summer sun. (On an edible flower, no less.) *Ugh.* I so hope we can still be friends after today. *Please* say he felt the same jellyfish nothingness and we can just chalk it up to— I don't know. Something we can just pretend never, ever happened.

After the session, I stay to help clean up, and to discuss Devaj and James's songwriting therapy class with them again. We stack chairs one on top of the other, in towers, like you find in an unused local theater hall, and wipe the coffee stains from the refreshments table. Rain hammers at the studio's windows, the sky now a heavy blue-gray plume. I'm so glad I came. I'm always so glad I came here, to NMT.

And perhaps that's because therapy works. Who knew? *"Er, I knew,"* says Roxanne's voice in my head. *"I kept bloody telling you, didn't I, Nat? Didn't I?"*

"Right," says Devaj, clapping his hands together. "Natalie, shall we sit?"

He unstacks two red plastic chairs, the sort with a circular hole on the back rest, like in school, and spreads them a few feet apart on the shiny, polished floor, like interviewer and interviewee. Therapist and counselor. From his back pocket, he slides a folded piece of paper. "I've made some notes," he says laughingly. "If I don't make notes, my brain works against me, I'm embarrassed to say," and within seconds, Devaj launches into his pitch—his vision—with so much passion, it's infectious. It rubs off on me, as he speaks, like static electricity. Goose bumps on my skin, the hairs on my arms standing on end.

"I think it would be so useful," he says, "for people to be able to construct a song, words, music, everything they're thinking or feeling . . . and record it. Have it as a memento. A physical milestone to hold in their hand. You know? Something they've achieved, despite whatever they're going through.'"

I smile. Beautiful. Devaj and James's idea is beautiful, and I feel—fired up. I want to help them. And the thought of helping others to write, makes something ignite inside of me. When I stood at that gig with Joe, I knew I missed it. The rawness of live instruments, the loud and quiet beauty of a song, those minor notes that feel as though they're speaking right to your poor, bruised heart. But I knew I didn't want to go back, to stages and sweaty gig circuits, to trying to impress smarmy A and R reps, the second I walked through the door. Though, this—*this*. Helping others through music. And writing. I do want that. And I haven't been more sure of anything in a long time.

"I think it's an amazing idea, Devaj," I say. "Truly. And I know enough about song structure and melody to help. And I'd really love to be a part of it. If you need me."

"Really?" Devaj beams, his dark eyes shining. "Ah, Natalie, that'd be fantastic. Of course we'd welcome you in with open arms. Can we shake on it? Let's shake on it."

"Of course!"

Devaj grins and takes my hand in his tightly, and we shake, across the gap between our chairs. James from the other side of the room, hunched over a box of cables he's slowly been entwining into neat rings, smiles over at us.

"Joe says Dev and I should put a shout-out on Twitter, too," he calls over. "For people who might be able to help, or even contribute toward the studio time? I mean, we're no good at social media, are we, mate? But we need to get our arses into gear with it."

"Totally," I say. "That's a really good idea. Plus, it's good PR for them. Giving away freebies for the greater good. And when they see one studio's doing it, the rest follow, can't help themselves . . ."

"True, true," grins Devaj. "Joe said you're a smart cookie."

"Did he?" I laugh.

"Oh, yeah. He's quite taken with you, I think." Devaj gives a school-boy smile. "*What*, James? I'm allowed to say that, aren't I?"

James holds his hands up, two palms in the air like he's pushing an invisible box. "I didn't say a word . . ."

"It's just, he was so pleased when you turned up here," says Devaj. "The famous station pianist. Course, he tried to hide it behind all his grump." Devaj laughs, as James nods but rolls his eyes, as if despairing of Devaj and his indiscretion. "He's just been helping here for a while now, Joe. You get to know people."

"Joe has?"

"Yeah, he's one of our best really," says Devaj with a shrug. "He's been through a lot, so people relate to him. And that's good for them, good for us. Builds trust and that's what we need. People like you coming here for the help, getting stronger, helping others. It's like a— lovely food chain, if you will." He gives a warm smile, but I freeze, like the air just turned arctic.

"I—I didn't realize Joe volunteered. I thought he came here. Like me. *For* therapy."

"Oh, he used to," says Devaj, casually. "And I suppose still does, technically, we all do. But he mostly just likes to help us out. You know what he's like. Likes to fix people, instead of himself."

"I mean . . . I know he does volunteering at a hospital."

"Yeah, that's right. The place over in North, where his brother was? Yeah, he's a good guy, is Joe. I just kind of wish he gave himself the same amount of attention as he gives to others. But we all have our own stuff to overcome, I suppose." Devaj smiles, then pats two hands on his trousered thighs. "*Right, then*. Shall I print you off a copy of my plan for the workshop? So you can take it home, make some notes of your own . . ."

I nod rigidly, as Devaj bounces off out of the main room to the little office next to the kitchen. And I feel—sick all of a sudden. Like my stomach is on a spin cycle. Joe never told me *he volunteered* at NMT. He never once said *he didn't*, but he talked about how he was a "therapy overachiever," that he'd tried everything, and all those in between too. Why wouldn't he have said he helps here, even just once, in all the conversations we've had? And what Devaj said—"*He tries to fix other people.*" Does he? Is that all he was doing with me? Trying to *fix me*? The festival. The gig. The bloody record shopping.

Rain buckets down outside, the noise drumming louder and louder on the glass, like thousands of tiny fists trying to break through. James twists another cable, slowly and silently behind me, into a large "O."

Blood whooshes in my ears, my heart thumps.

There's something else niggling at me too, teasing apart a tangle in my brain. "*The place over in North.*" That's what Devaj said. Melrose. Melrose hospital was where Russ was. And Melrose hospital is in North London. But surely—

"Bloody printer." Devaj appears then, a piece of paper in his hands. "Got there eventually, though."

"Is it Melrose?" I blurt.

"S-sorry?"

"Where Joe volunteers?" My mouth is so dry, I feel like my throat is coated in tacky glue.

"Oh. Yeah, that's right, yes."

My heart stops in my chest then. I can't speak. Russ was at Melrose. *Tanner* was at Melrose. And Joe never told me—not once. *I* mentioned Melrose, I know I did. So, why wouldn't he tell me? Surely it would be easier to share it, than to not? And if he hasn't—why hasn't he? My hands start to shake in my lap, cold and clammy. God, what is happening? *Why would he not say*? Because if Tanner died not long after Russ, then—they could have very easily been in the hospital together. At the same time.

"Natalie?" Devaj crosses the floor toward me, in two strides, and bends slightly, to catch my eye, here on the chair. "Natalie, are you all right?"

James pauses over the box of cables, and watches me.

"Y-yes," I say. "Um. I'm . . . I'm fine."

"Are you sure—"

"Have you got the . . . the . . . thing, the—"

"Paper? Yes. Yes, sorry, don't know why I'm standing here still holding it." And as I stand as if to attention, my head spinning, swirling, like a thousand jumbled words have just been blown by a hurricane in my mind, and as I take the paper from his hands, run a finger along the glossy, shiny surface—I know. I know why I feel sick. I know why my hands are shaking.

The famous station pianist.

And before I can take another breath, Devaj looks to the doorway and grins. "Ah," he calls out. "Joe! We've just been talking about you."

And I can tell by Joe's colorless face that he knows that I know he's deceived me. And that it's Joe who's been leaving me music.

♫   ♫   ♫
♫   ♫   ♫

Rain falls from the sky, and from under an umbrella, out here in the car park of the rehearsal rooms, I look at Joe across the concrete. His pale skin, his dry mouth. The hood of his coat casting islands of shadows on his face. We'd somehow managed to keep up appearances in front of James and Devaj, and we'd followed them out, watched them drive away, their van jammed with equipment and full-to-the-brim storage tubs. And now it's just us. Just us and a storm that's picking up.

"Melrose," is all I say. "Tanner was at Melrose. You never said."

My chest tightens, like a fist squeezing, because if he isn't withholding things from me, he'd just say, "Er. Yes? He was? *And*?" But instead, Joe looks at his feet and says, simply, "Natalie, I didn't know when to say."

I was right. Not saying was on purpose.

"So, they were in there together. Russ. Your brother. In hospital, together."

"He was moved there," Joe says sadly. "I just didn't know how to tell you."

"You didn't *know*? How about, I don't know, when I said in Granary Square that day, by the canal, and a million times after, that my husband Russ was at Melrose. How about 'Oh yeah, I volunteer there, my *brother* was in there when he was sick, too.' And then we'd have known, said *oh wow, we were there at the same time, how weird.*"

"Natalie—"

"But you already knew, didn't you? You knew Russ was in there at the same time as Tanner, and you didn't say."

Rain hammers down, and a small chimney on the side of the building puffs out white steam into the cold air. I can hear my heartbeat in my ears even over the violent drumming of raindrops, and the sound of distant London traffic.

"I was going to," says Joe. "I promise. The minute you walked into the rehearsal rooms for music therapy, I was going to tell you—that I knew you. That I knew you from the hospital. From playing on that piano next to the ward."

A hand flies to my stomach as he says it. I suspected it—knew it, on a deep level, somewhere within me, just a few moments after Devaj told me it was Melrose that Tanner was treated in. But hearing him say the actual words aloud makes me want to be sick.

"But it felt like—too much, straightaway, you know? To say, okay, yeah, we know each other from the café, but also, I know you from the hospital from two years ago too." Joe talks quickly, panickily. "Then we went for the walk together that afternoon, and after, at the station, someone had left you music."

"*Someone*," I snap. "*You* left me music, Joe. Didn't you? You have been leaving me music."

Joe's hazel eyes close sadly. "Yes," he says, his voice catching in his throat. And I feel like my air is being cut off. I can't seem to take a deep breath in.

"But not all of it," Joe rushes out, his eyes opening again, pleading with me. "I stopped leaving it, but it carried on. And I think it might be your friend. Edie. I've been wanting to say. She said something to me that day and—"

"*What*? This has nothing to do with Edie. This is about you and *me*."

"I know, I know." Joe sounds desperate, like someone pleading for his life, and it makes me want to panic, to run. I hate that he lied—that he's hidden so much. I hate that he's known something all along, all the time I have been opening myself up to him. "Natalie, I'm so sorry. But . . . please listen to me." Joe steps forward, his trainers scuffing on the concrete. I step back, and he doesn't attempt to move any closer. He stays where he is, feet firmly on the flooded ground. "I used to hear you play every day, in the hospital," he says slowly. "I'd see you sometimes. And those songs—those songs you'd play, Natalie, I waited for them every single day. And Tanner waited too. We got to know them. The hospital was so quiet and full of fucking weird bleeping sounds and people breathing and dying and then—then you'd play."

I stare at him, my vision clouding through tears.

"And I'd been volunteering at the hospital, in January. At Melrose, for the first time. And man, it was so rough going back. But I knew it was something I wanted to do. So I went to the station after, for coffee, to gather my thoughts before I went home, and—"

"You saw me play."

Joe smiles sadly, his eyes shining. "Heard you. I knew it was you before I saw you. The way you played. And I wanted to hear those songs again. The ones you played to Tanner and me. Natalie, you have no idea what you gave Tanner and me, in that ward, with your music."

I'm crying now, my face totally slick, rainwater and tears streaking my cheeks. I wipe my eyes on the sleeve of my coat, but it's already soaked, like a heavy sponge.

"You should've spoken to me," I say wobblily.

"I know."

"You should have just *said* something. But, what, instead of just talking to me you—*printed out music*?"

Joe swallows. "It was just meant to be once. One song. I printed it out here, I didn't even know if you'd play it. But then you did, and so I printed another and . . . Nat, if I could go back, if I could speak to you instead, I would. But it just went further and further and then . . . I heard you one day in the café talking to Shauna about it. You mentioned Russ, your husband, and then so did she. She was chatting away to the lad behind the counter after, at how you both hoped it was him leaving it. And I felt like a fuckin' monster, Natalie. How cruel I would be, to admit it was me—just me. Nobody."

"But how could you not tell me? Even if you didn't *then*. We're friends, Joe, you could have so easily—"

"I tried," says Joe. "Which I know sounds so pathetic now, in the cold light of day, but I did. And I just couldn't—and then that music was left after we went to the canal and . . . fuck, I didn't know what to do. I thought—okay, how do I tell her that it was me, but it isn't now? It sounded mad. Like lies. Like it does now. I mean—I sound off my head."

A car drives by, the tires sloshing through the giant pond of the puddle that's gathered in the curb. I feel like the ground is shaky beneath my feet. None of it. None of it makes sense. And like a montage, everything we've ever done together cycles through my brain. The canal. The food festival. Record shopping. That kiss.

"Were you ever my friend?"

"What?" Joe steps toward me, puts a hand to my shoulder. Rain pours from broken guttering behind us, water slapping the ground in great sheets. "Natalie . . ."

"Were you?" I say. "Or were you just trying to fix me? Atone or something? The poor little widow who played songs to sick people, let's help her, get her back to her music, do all the things she used to do with her poor husband, to say thank you, to make her feel better about herself, to make *Joe* feel better about Joe."

Joe looks as though he's been slapped. The color drains from his cheeks. "Natalie, of course you were my friend—you *are* my friend."

"I don't believe you," I reply. "You've kept so much from me, Joe.

And I *told* you. I told you everything. I told you I felt like the world was trying to fix me and all along, there you were, doing exactly that."

"I wasn't—"

"I'm leaving, Joe."

"Natalie, I wanted to say thank you," says Joe, tears in his eyes. He stares at me, his hand holding my arm, pleadingly. "Misguided, perhaps, but . . . that's why I helped you. Because you helped me. You said the music didn't work. But it did for me."

I stare at him, as rainwater fills my shoes. I am soaked to the bone. Every inch of my skin, of my clothes, of my hair . . .

"The kiss was a mistake," I say. "And us being friends was a mistake. This whole thing—it's so messed up . . ."

And I leave him looking wounded, like I've just punched him right in the gut, in the rain.

"I'm so sorry, Natalie," he calls after me. But I don't turn back, and at the station, for the first time in almost a year, I walk straight past the piano and go home.

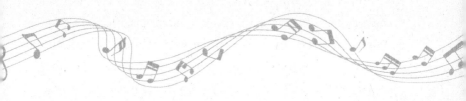

chapter twenty-five

Tom (Just): I dunno about you Foxes, but I'm psyched for Lucy's birthday tonight.

Me: Ugh. Do not go there, I don't want to go.

Tom (Just): Yes you do. I'll be there. And you better listen to Mother Shauna when she says her Tommy Button is an absolute bloody dream on a date.

Me: It's a date, is it?

Tom (Just): Well, a stand-in date. But let me tell you, real or stand-in, I'm a fucking delight on both.

♪ ♪ ♪
♪ ♪ ♪

I don't know how the hell I've managed this. It's a miracle. A modern-day miracle. To be here, at Lucy's thirtieth dinner at Dishoom, looking like a real, fine, and normal person. It's been three days since Joe confessed to me, and I have felt completely upside down ever since.

I'm hardly eating, hardly drinking, hardly sleeping. I was so close to canceling tonight that I even wrote out an "I can't make it" text I didn't end up sending. Because how can I sit with Tom and not tell him about his dad? How can I confide in him about Joe, like I do about everything, when I'm lying to him, keeping things from him, just like Joe did to me?

But then Tom texted, excited about the evening, and I'd deleted my draft cancelation and texted him as normal. I showered. I forced a drink down my throat. And I slathered on so much makeup, I'm sure I'm probably quite flammable. And I decided I'll tell him tomorrow. Tomorrow he's at home all day, he said so himself, and tomorrow I'll call him and tell him everything. I'll invite him over after for wine, after, and I'll even cook sausages, and we will talk. Properly talk. But tonight—tonight, I can pretend. Tonight I can pretend my emotions aren't waging a war inside of me, turning my insides to hot acid. Tonight I can be free and easy and without any bombshells to drop or to share, with my handsome date Tom. Who, true to his word, absolutely *is* a delight. We've only been seated for about twenty minutes at the restaurant table among so many of Lucy's friends and family, and already, he's had many of them in stitches with laughter. He's as charming and as funny as ever. It's like I said, the world deserves Tom. The man even made Roxanne smile.

"Oh, it's Tom from the bar!" she'd shrieked when we arrived. She looks different today. Thinner, tired. Like someone with the heavy weight of the world on her shoulders.

"That's me," he'd announced. "From arse to hero."

"Love it." Roxanne laughed. "I'm Roxanne. Natalie's friend." Then she'd turned to me and said, "And speaking of, where have you been, Mrs. Fincher? Avoiding us?" and before I could reply, she'd clopped off.

Luckily, we've been seated away from them at the other end of the table, and I'd be lying if I didn't say I'm relieved. It's not that I haven't missed my friends. But I know Roxanne, and I know that look she gave me. She wanted to provoke something. She wanted excuses as to why I haven't been in touch, and I am not in the mood tonight to watch her listen to my excuses, looking for holes in them like they're alibis and she's an ex-cop.

"How did you explain, by the way?" says Tom now. "Our little arrangement in Avocado Clash."

"Oh, I didn't. I just said we bumped into each other again and you apologized for standing me up. Think I told them you had a bad stomach bug."

"Great," he says. "What a glowing review."

"Well, if I tell them my ways, they'll never believe me when they set me up again, and then what'll I do?"

"You'll have to start an apocalypse, I suppose, ensure all the men die," says Tom. "Or marry Joe. A marriage of convenience, you know? I think they'd lay off you then."

I force a smile, but I feel cold at the mention of Joe. And it's not just his lies. It's the fact I fell for them—went along with his little "fixer" ideas and was bounding around, grinning from ear to ear, saying to Priya, "Oh, he's my *friend*, Priya. Stop being such a worrier. Look! He bought me pasta! He sent me a photo of an aging rock star! He has nothing but a heart of gold." I should've listened to her, and I'm sure once I do tell her, she'll say she knew that day in the shop, that something wasn't quite right.

We all wait for Lucy now, chatting among ourselves, and Tom and I move effortlessly into easy conversation. I was worried that it might feel different today, because of what I'm keeping from him, that he'd see it on my face like he always does, despite how hard I'm working tonight at portraying the act of "*Natalie is Fine.*" But it's like it normally is. Easy. Safe. Fun. I always get on so well with Tom.

Every time I'm going to see him, I wonder what it is that we'll talk about because it's like there aren't enough minutes in an hour for us. We're strangers who met in a bar. We met by accident. And yet, we talk like we've been perfectly wired to, just for each other. And of course, as usual, he looks good tonight. Impeccably turned out and classically handsome. "Like something out of an M&S billboard," I'd said when I met him at the train station and he'd said, "Colin the Caterpillar, you mean?"

Lucy soon arrives and gives the best faux look of surprise I've ever seen. Of course, she knew about this. Lucy always knows everything. She probably even called ahead, oversaw the table settings. Nevertheless, she beams at us like we've just solved world hunger in her name. "You guys are *amazing*. And you—" She smiles at me, bringing her hands together at her chest. "I'm so happy *you're* here."

"Of course I am."

"No, I mean it. Anchor her to that chair, Tom. *Don't* let her out of it."

And although everyone laughs, I know she means it. There's a barbed tone to her voice. A barbed tone that says, "I mean it. I'll have my eye on you. Don't let me down in front of everyone."

We order food and drinks, and after a couple of drinks, I lean into the evening. And . . . maybe it's going to be okay. Things might feel hard and uncertain right this second, but it *will* be okay. That's one thing I'm learning. All the times I thought I wouldn't be okay, I was. I'm still here. I'm at this table. Time has passed and I'm still here. And so will Tom be, so will Shauna, regardless of how hard times might get, for a little while. Then a hand lands on Tom's arm from beside him.

"Excuse me," she says. She's beautiful, the woman sitting next to him, and I recognize her instantly. She's Lucy's work colleague—I've seen her on Instagram and Facebook posts. Gigi, I think her name is.

She looks like the nanny from any movie (besides, perhaps, McPhee). The sort of nanny you'd fear for your marriage at the arrival of.

"This might sound a bit weird, especially if I'm wrong, but did you do the Sanderson wedding? You know—the big over-the-top do at—"

"The British Library?"

"Yes!"

"That was me, indeed." Tom smiles, and Gigi gasps, presses a delicate hand to her heart. "Oh my god, I was there. You took the most amazing photo of me and my girlfriends."

Girlfriends. I hate people who say *girlfriends*.

"Oh, wow, well—pleased to help. That wedding was—" Tom looks into his glass as if he needs something stiff just to cope with the memory.

"A *joke*?" offers Gigi, and I can see by Tom's face that he's slightly titillated. He likes this sort of thing. The sharp, out-of-nowhereness.

"I was going to say full on, but I reckon I'm safe enough out of contract now to say I don't *agree* with you but I also don't disagree." He laughs. Holds his hand out, just like he did to me at the bar, when we first met. "I'm Tom."

"Tom." She takes his hand and looks up at him all glittery eyed. "I'm Georgina. But people call me Gigi."

"Of course they fuckin' do," I say under my breath, and Lucy's auntie beside me says, "What's that, love?" and I say, "The potatoes. The potatoes here are *lovely*."

♪　　♪　　♪
　♪　　♪　　♪

Lucy's auntie Val is wonderful, don't get me wrong. She's a dream. She's kind and sweet but she has talked endlessly about *Coronation Street* for the last half an hour, and to the side of me, Tom and Gigi have not taken a single breath from the longest conversation ever recorded. Looking at them, it's clear to see why it's called chin-wagging—their mouths haven't stopped. It's a mile a minute, and just when I think the conversation is coming to a close, they start *again*. And they've discussed everything. Food, hairdressers, France, sodding micropigs, and all of it sounding so boring. I wonder if Tom's feeling the same, if he's thinking the same as me, as Gigi tells him about every single accommodation she lived in when working in France, from address to initial deposit amount. Meanwhile, I—well, I've eaten about fifty-six tons of food just for something to do. The waiter keeps looking at me with admiration, like I'm someone who has just broken the world record. I'm expecting a trophy soon, shaped like a giant chicken skewer.

Gigi stands, brushing a hand down the stomach of her tiny cream-colored dress. "Need the loo." She smiles at Tom. "Don't go anywhere."

She slinks off into the bustle of the restaurant, and Tom turns to me.

I make a face, a huge cartoonish grimace, but he grins.

"Yo, Foxes," he says.

"Yo." I laugh. "So . . . French estate agents, eh?"

"What?"

"You two discussing—what was it? Deposits and locations in Bordeaux and—"

"*Oh.* Yeah." Tom laughs, brings a bottle to his lips. "So, what do you reckon?"

"On?"

Tom's eyes widen, as if stumped. "*Gigi.*"

"Oh, is that her name? Erm—well, what about Miss Two A.M.?"

"Dead in the water," he says.

"Oh yeah?"

"We haven't seen each other since Heartt with two *t*'s." Tom grins, downs his drink. "But Gigi and me. We're uh, what is it you said about Joe at first—*vibing.*"

"And look how that turned out." I laugh, but Tom just smiles, gives a shrug. So, is that it then? Has he crossed over into Gigi waters? "So, what, you—like her? You want to . . . ask her out or something?"

Tom stares at me.

"What?"

"Well . . . do you think I should?" And Tom's eyes, on mine, feel like they are totally locked in place.

"Do I think you should what?"

"Shall I ask her out?" he asks, but his silly grin has faded now, and it's like it's just me in the room. Is he actually asking me if I should? Or—God. Is he asking me whether I want him to?

I open my mouth. And I'm shocked by how much I want to say no. How much I want to say mean things about her, make fun of the things she was saying. I'm thirty-three. That behavior—I don't even think I'd have acted so petulantly at twelve.

"Erm—"

Tom looks at me. His beautiful pink lips, that perfect, sharp jaw, that shadow of stubble . . . and I think of Don. I think of calling Tom tomorrow, detonating a bomb under his family.

"I say go for it."

"Yeah?"

There's a long pause between us. "Natalie?"

"I said yes," I say. Then I put my hand on his arm and say, "You deserve it, Tommy Button."

Tom gives a tiny, confused smile, although there's a flicker of his eyebrow, and he leans back in his seat, as if he isn't quite sure I'm not a bit mad, as Gigi returns and says, "I love posh toilets. Do you love posh toilets?"

♪   ♪   ♪
♪   ♪   ♪

The hour passes like gravy through a sieve, and after yet another dish, I can hardly wait to leave. The hope that glimmered earlier has dimmed, like a flickering lightbulb. I'm confused. A bit sad. And Tom has pushed Gigi's hair out of her face twice, and she has had her hand on his leg for approximately six and a half minutes. They're on a date while everyone else swaps seats to swap stories about total bollocks, like job moves and house moves and divorces and *Strictly Come Dancing*. And I think it's time I left.

I squeeze my way to Priya, who sits rubbing her huge baby bump next to Will, her husband, who says hi from behind thick-rimmed black spectacles and a beard he's just started to grow as if especially for fatherhood. "I'm going to go," I say.

"Oh, no, really?" says Priya. "Are you OK, Nat? I've hardly seen you. I was about to come over, I'm dying to talk to Tom. I'll have to introduce myself. Is he OK? And you?"

"Yes, fine. I've just had enough. Tired. Got work first thing, haven't I, and we can't all bunk off in the name of growing an actual *person.*"

Will chuckles warmly beside her, lifts a chicken skewer to his mouth, clamps it between his teeth.

"Course." Priya smiles. "Do you want us to come with you? Will'll come with you."

"No, don't be silly. Both of you, stay on those chairs."

I leave money with Priya for when the bill arrives, and I know I've given too much, but it's like I'm buying my exit or something—buying my peace.

"Where's Luce?" I ask Priya.

"Oh, she's gone to meet someone at the station, they're lost. That Australian. That friend of hers who's just back from traveling."

I look around at the buzzing, busy table. She won't mind if I leave without saying goodbye. There're so many people here. So many people I know she hasn't seen for years, people she can't tear herself away from, catching up, swapping news and life stories.

I make my way over to Tom and Gigi. I place my hand on his arm. "So sorry to interrupt. But—I'm going to leave."

"You're going?"

"Yeah, I figure I've eaten too much and it's getting late and I have work first thing—"

"Let me—shall I—"

"No. No, no!" God, I sound like the TV presenters Nick used to watch when he was a toddler. High-pitched. Slightly unhinged. *Are we having fun, guuuuys*?

"Stay." I force a big adult "I'm fine" smile. "I'll text you later," I say. "Gigi, so lovely to meet you." And when Tom stands to hug me and I loop my arms around his neck, and when he draws back and smiles down at me, handsome, warm, and safe, I feel like I might burst into tears.

Out on the pavement, I feel it swelling in my belly, like a storm gathering. What is this? What is this I'm feeling? It's . . . Tom. It is. I like him. I do. *I. Like. Tom.* Oh, God. I do. I really do.

"Natalie?"

I turn on the damp concrete. Roxanne stands there, her ruby-red dress flapping open in the wind. She grabs at the split.

"Hey." I wait for her to tell me I've forgotten something, that I've left my purse behind, left my phone, but I can tell by her face: she's furious. She's angry. She's angry with me.

"Are you seriously going home? Now?"

There's a beat as I step away for someone to pass me on the pavement. "Sorry?"

"Are you honestly going to leave this party and go home?"

"Rox, I've been here for three hours—"

Roxanne laughs bitterly, shakes her head. "You haven't stayed for the cake. You haven't even seen her open the present we got her. Or any of her presents for that matter."

"Roxanne—"

"Tom is still in there," she says, her words short. "Your bloody *date* is still in there!"

"He isn't my date, he's—and he doesn't mind, he wanted to stay—"

"What are you doing?" Roxanne shrugs, her arms out at her sides, dropping against her sides heavily. A bracelet on her wrist jangles. "I know you're hurting. I know you are. But you are so far up your own arse that you can't for a minute see that other people matter."

I feel like someone has choked the life out of me. I can't speak.

"Roxanne, what are you talking about? I left a party slightly *early*—"

"And you lie."

"Lie?"

Roxanne's face crumples and—oh, God, are those tears in her eyes? Roxanne never cries, and I feel an instant wave of shame that *I've* made it happen. "We invite you places, and you make excuses. You're busy, you're ill—or you just don't text at all. You avoid us. You think we're out to get you, that we're your enemies . . ."

I stare at her and I search my head for an excuse, but actually, I don't have one and I don't want to make one up either.

"Look, I sometimes don't want to come," I say. "I have bad days and sometimes—"

"We all have bad days. And Jesus, Natalie, I love you. But—you're a flake. You're a total flake and you lie to your friends and you throw everything into this bloody Joe, who doesn't even know you, and here we are, desperate for you, and trying to be there for you—"

"Oh, well, I'm *sorry*," I say and now, my back is up, my defenses, like invisible shields, rising. "I'm sorry I make you uncomfortable because I don't let you do for me what you feel you should. To make yourself feel better. So your conscience is clear."

"What?"

"You have absolutely no idea what I have to deal with—*battle with*—every single day."

"Are you—you have no idea either. I lost my job, Natalie. Yeah. Weeks ago."

"*What*? Your job? When? What happened—"

"Your husband died," Roxanne cuts in. "And I know this. I really do. And it breaks my heart, so I don't know what the hell it does to yours. But you have to stop—"

"Stop? Stop what?"

Roxanne stares at me across the cobbles. "What did we get for Lucy?"

"What?"

"What did we buy her? For her birthday?"

I stare at her. "I don't—I sent the money, but I don't—"

"And Edie. Edie's so desperate to talk to you, to be there for you . . ." She shakes her head sadly. "I feel like I don't know you anymore. You cut people off. You cut people out. Because you're hurting and the less of us looking in, the better."

The Uber app buzzes on my phone, and shaking with rage, with upset, with heartache, I walk away to meet the car, leave Roxanne there on the pavement.

"Natalie," Roxanne shouts. "*Natalie!*"

I ignore her.

"Station, yeah?" the driver asks as I shut the car door behind me.

"No," I say through tears. "No, take me to Drayton Road. Number eighty-nine. Hoddesdon."

"Right. That's quite a bit farther, love, so—"

"Just take me there. *Please.* Thank you."

By the time the taxi pulls up outside Jodie's, I'm a wreck. I feel like I'm not even in my body anymore. That I'm a hologram, or that I'm in a projection of a film. I'm walking through water. I can't hear or think or see straight. I stumble up the path.

Nick opens the door, a baggy hoodie skimming his knees, a pair of shorts peeping from the hem. He's smiling, rosy-cheeked, but it fades slowly, like a flame going out. "Auntie Nat?"

"Hi. Um . . ."

Then Jodie appears from the living room in her dressing gown, a glass of wine in her hand, the glasses she wears to watch TV on the end of her nose.

"Oh! Nat! This is a nice surprise!"

And before I've even opened my mouth, I'm melting into tears into my sister's shoulder, Nick is saying "Ah, shit," and Carl is appearing out of the kitchen drying a wok with a tea towel and saying, "Stop just standing there, son, and get the bloody kettle on."

♪   ♪   ♪
♪   ♪   ♪

"Blimey O'Reilly," says Carl. "I would have never seen it coming. I'm usually good with the mysteries, aren't I, Jode? I guess every twist in ITV dramas. But I wouldn't have seen that—that it was Joe. All along."

"That's dark," adds Nick, sprawled on the sofa. "Like, proper dark."

"I think it's beautiful," says Jodie softly, "in a way."

"I don't know what it is." I shrug, cradling a cup of tea to my lap. I'd sobbed into Jodie's shoulder when I arrived, and Carl had quickly made tea, arranged biscuits on a plate, while Nick rolled his eyes and said, "Since when do we eat biscuits off a plate? This ain't a vicarage, Dad." Then I'd got under Jodie's thick, gray blanket with her, and I'd told her everything. About Roxanne and the argument outside the restaurant. About Don, and how I still haven't told Tom. And Joe. They'd listened, my family, these soft, calm, loving faces who accept me for everything I am, and I'd felt held. Supported. Able to fall apart, knowing none of the pieces would be judged or scrutinized as I crumbled before them.

"I don't know what to do," I say. "Honestly, I don't know where to start."

"Well, you should always start with you," says Carl, reaching to the table for a custard cream. "And you haven't done that for a long time, Nat."

"A very long time," adds Jodie, putting her dressing-gowned arm around me. She smells like vanilla body wash and shampoo. "And you know that's what Russ would want for you. He'd want you to be happy. Nothing else other than that."

"You're right." I blow my nose into a tissue. It's streaked with makeup. I must look a mess—a total mess. A walking crime scene.

"If you were a patient," says Carl calmly, munching a custard cream, "my question would be, what is it you want?"

I stare at them blankly, six pairs of kind eyes, waiting on me to speak, the TV turned so low, it's an inaudible mumble.

"It's like I said, I don't know where to start—"

Carl puts his hands together in a single clap. "First thing that comes into your head—"

"Tom," falls out of my mouth.

Jodie smiles, her hands shooting up to her mouth, like a proud mother of the bride catching a glimpse of the wedding gown for the first time.

"Fuck yeah, Auntie Nat," says Nick. "*What*? You do realize I'm eighteen now, don't you?"

"And I think I want to move," I add. "Back to London. *Oh my god. Do I? Gosh, I do.*"

"Fuck yeah, Auntie Nat," says Jodie this time, and we all laugh.

chapter twenty-six

Will Webster has added you to: It's a boy!

Will Webster: Delighted to announce the birth of our beautiful boy, Noah Alex Webster. 8lb 2oz. Priya is a superstar and both Mum and baby are doing well. Dad's a bit of a mess tho!

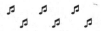

"OK, and you'll be fine on your own?"

"Jodie, I've been on my own in the shop loads before."

"I know, but—"

"But I'm weird at the minute," I don't say. "Because your younger sister is positively off her head and keeps crying all of the time." But they're good tears, that's what I keep telling her. They feel like a thousand unsaid, locked-away emotions, slowly but surely trickling out of me. A slow release. "So, like, you've been constipated for years," Nick had said, "and finally, you're able to—go?"

"You can leave now." I smile at my sister. "I'll be fine. I'm quite looking forward to it. I can be in charge of the playlist, I can eat loads of sweets, and you won't start harping on about substantial meals and stuff."

Jodie cocks her head to one side and smiles, then she leans across the counter and kisses my cheek. She's warm and perfumey. "Call me," she says, "if you need me or if it gets too busy."

"I will. But it won't, and I'll be *fine*. And I'm still OK to close at five? I'm seeing Tom and then to see Priya and the baby."

"Course."

I'm dying to see Priya and baby Noah, who looks exactly like Will minus the glasses, squished down into a little white Babygro. A bit of normality—a bit of grounding, during what's been a really weird couple of days, since Lucy's birthday meal. I stayed over at Jodie's that night, and as the sun began to rise the next morning, I felt like a part of myself had been unlocked. And the tears haven't stopped since. It's like I suddenly want to tear the roof off every shelter I've built myself; the plaster from every wound. Let the air get to them, let them heal. Let *everything* heal. Joe and the music, the thought that he and Tanner were listening to me, all along. About the music left after that—from Coldplay onward. And I still don't know if Joe's right. If it was Edie leaving it. But sometimes she seems the only person who makes sense. And of course, I've cried about Tom. I'm meeting him later, to tell him about Don, face-to-face, after we close. And if it feels right, I want to tell him how I feel. I'll be shitting it of course, completely and utterly, but I'm so sure I want to do it. To tell him I like him. That he's right—that when you feel it, you know. Because I do know. I know it's him. Oh, God, I'm going to cry again. My face is going to be a big swollen blob by the time I see him if I carry this on. Should declarations of "like" be done with a balloon for a face?

The bell above the shop door rings. And there he stands, in the doorway. And he's early. Really bloody early actually. Shit, I haven't even practiced what I'm going to say yet, especially the bit about how there's no pressure on him, to say he feels the same, because—well, I have no idea what he'll even say. We're friends. Tom is . . . Tom is just Tom. Scared of love and crocodiles. Planning a date with Gigi last time I checked. But saying it, feeling it, *knowing it,* is almost enough, without him saying a word back to me . . .

Because I'm not broken, like a part on the side of the road. I can like—and maybe even love again.

"Erm, well, you are about three hours early, Thomas," I say. He's unsmiling, and he looks—*grave.* Pale.

"Hey," is all he says.

"Are you—are you OK? You look like you've seen—a *ghost.* A—oh shit, you haven't seen any koalas out there on the loose, have you?" I laugh. He doesn't.

"Natalie, I need to ask you something," he says, and instantly my entire body flashes hot. From my head, to my toes.

"OK." I swallow, coming out from the behind the counter. "What is it?" He doesn't move. The atmosphere in the shop, despite the heating, is icy. An upbeat pop song thumps quietly away from the shop's speakers. No. No, he can't know, surely.

"Did you—did you see my dad with someone else?"

It feels like someone has just placed a bomb between us on the floor.

"Priya mentioned something at Lucy's birthday, and I just—sort of swept it under carpet. Put it down to crossed wires. But—last night, Mum's friend Amma said she was outside at the anniversary having a cigarette, and she heard someone on the phone. She thought it was you, and you were saying . . ."

"Oh my god, Tom, honestly—"

"Did you know?" he asks calmly. "Just—answer me that, Natalie.

Did you know and tell everybody else, everybody else who's business it *isn't*, before me? Before *Mum*?"

My heart stills and my body rushes with so much adrenaline like someone just stuck a needle of it in my neck.

"Tom, I didn't know. Not until I saw him at the anniversary, and then—then I didn't know what to do."

"What about after it?" asks Tom.

"I'm so sorry," I plead, stepping toward him. "Is Shauna OK?"

Tom shrugs heavily. "She's—fucking heartbroken. It's a mess, Natalie. The whole thing is a mess. But I just—I can't process the fact you knew. I mean, we talk about *everything*—"

"But I didn't know what to do."

"You—you sat with me on those steps. We went out for your friend's birthday, for God's sake—"

"You said you didn't want to be scared anymore, that you wanted to trust and—"

"Trust," says Tom. "Honestly, Nat, at the moment, I just feel the world is full of liars. I don't know who to trust, to be honest. I'm exhausted."

"But I never lied, I just . . ." God. I suddenly understand Joe. What he kept from me, and why. "I didn't want to hurt you. But I was going to tell you tonight. I *was*."

"But you told everyone else."

"I only told Jodie, purely because I didn't know what to do. She must've told Priya and—I can't imagine how shit it must've been to hear that from someone else, but—Tom, please."

Tom shakes his head, runs a large hand through his dark hair, and God, his gorgeous face—he looks gutted. "I need some space, Natalie," he says. Then he reaches forward, and on the counter, he places a brown envelope. My heart feels like it's stopped. Like it's split, right down the middle. "I was going to give you this tonight, so . . ."

And he turns, moves toward the shop door.

"Tom, please," I say.

"And I do trust you," he says. "*Did.* More than anyone."

And he walks away, the little, joyful bell dinging as he does.

I swoop to the counter, my heart banging, my head whooshing. On the front of the envelope, the handwriting reads *for the spark*. I tear it open. Inside are three photos and three pieces of sheet music. A photo of the strawberry tarts attached to a piece of music for "Strawberry Swing," by Coldplay. A photo of Camden Town tube station and the piece of music for Electric Light Orchestra's "Last Train to London." And—now of course it all makes perfect sense. The last photo is one of the moon he took the night with me on the steps, and the last piece of music: "Moonlight Drive" by the Doors.

Tom carried it on. For the spark.

I feel them bubbling up—a fountain of tears. And at the exact moment they spill over the edge, they arrive through the doors—Roxanne and Lucy.

"Nat?" says Lucy, and at the sight of them, yet again I cry.

♫ ♫ ♫
♫ ♫ ♫

Roxanne hands me a cup of tea and says, "Seriously, who doesn't keep vodka in the back of their shop? Have you not seen *Eastenders*? It's like a law. It's like—*shop law*."

I sniff a laugh and sip. Cups of tea. Always better when someone else has made it, and especially when that tea is medicinal. Roxanne sits next to me on the bench in the kitchen and scoots closer to me. "I'm so sorry, Natalie, about our row."

"No, Rox—"

"No, honestly. I am. I was out of order—and the thing is. It's just because I miss you. I'm selfish, Natalie. I'm a selfish cow."

"You are not selfish, Rox."

"I just miss you. That's what it is. I miss you so much." Roxanne sniffs into a balled-up tissue. Her nails are painted black, the thumbnail with a tiny skull. "I really do. And I know what it feels like to want to withdraw, to pull away, and I shouldn't have said what I said to you, Nat . . ."

I shake my head, hair sticking to the damp puddles on my face. "No, I know I've been difficult—"

"We shouldn't try to fix you up." Lucy jumps in now. We've locked the shop. "*Family emergency*" Lucy had scrawled on a piece of paper without missing a beat, before sticking it to the window. *Jodie won't mind for ten minutes. Will she?* "Tom said something to me at the party," she says. "About us. Fixing you up."

"Oh, God, Lucy, I wish he wouldn't have."

"He said about Avocado Clash. About how you brace for it, every time you're out with us." Roxanne puts her arm around me. "Why didn't you just say?"

"Because I don't want you to worry," I say. "I don't want you to look at me like I'm broken or think I need help if I don't want to date, or do the things you think I should."

"But if you need help," says Lucy, "then you should tell us. It's what we're here for. It's actually a very important part of friendship. Studies have shown that true lasting friendships that are built on the foundation of feeling comfortable enough to ask one another for help, last longer than those friendships you feel you have to transact in. You know? I'll do this for her, but only so she might do that for me. It's true. I read it in a book."

Roxanne smiles proudly. "Studies have bloody shown," she repeats, and we all laugh. It feels so lovely to have them here, in one room. I've missed them. And maybe they're right. Maybe I should've leaned on them. Been *honest* with them. What is it Shauna said? We expect people to somehow know what we want, without actually voicing it out loud.

"You all have stuff going on," I say. "Some really good stuff. And I didn't want to rain on that with my negative, grumpy, stuck, cynical bullshit—"

"So fucking what?" says Roxanne. "I know I'm not very gooey and sentimental, but—I'd give a kidney for you. Both if you asked nicely." Roxanne puts her arms around me, rubs the top of my arm gently.

"And what was Tom doing here?" asks Lucy, patting lip balm onto her lips. "He's really lovely by the way. And OK, I'm not fixing you up, but also—I think it's OK to say I think he really, really likes you."

"Oh, I don't think so—"

"He *does*," Roxanne says, touching her head to mine. "It was so fucking obvious at Lucy's birthday. The sexual tension was—"

"He is currently not speaking to me." I look at Lucy. "And last I checked, he had a date with Gigi," I say thickly. "That girl from your salon."

"*Oh my god.*" Lucy stares into the middle distance like a detective who's missed a giant clue, her eyes round saucers. "She said she had a date with some guy. She seems obsessed with him—"

"Tom," I say.

"But—" Lucy stares at me. "I thought he liked you."

"He *does*," adds Roxanne. "I told you, I could sense the tension over my chicken ruby, and it was *palpable*."

"But then," Lucy says, "I guess he knows you're not keen, so . . ."

They look at me then, and they come out—words tumbling in front of us, like a Jenga pile. A mini confession.

"I do," I say. "I am . . . keen."

They stare at me, the air still.

"What?" says Lucy, her mouth stretching into a wide smile.

"I like him. Tom. Really like him. Like—think-I-might-be-falling levels of like."

Roxanne pulls away from me, as if to get a good look at me, and her eyes widen. "Oh my god. Like—properly? Like—don't want him to date anyone else properly?"

"Yes."

"Like you wanna shag his brains out properly?"

I pause. "God, *yes*."

"Oh my *god*," Lucy squeals, bouncing on her heels that clop on the hard kitchen floor. "I said to Carlie, I said, 'That Tom idolizes our Natalie.' I could just see it. The way he was with you at my dinner."

I scoff. "Idolizes."

"He couldn't take his eyes off you." Lucy beams. "I think he loves you."

"He's been leaving me music. I don't know if Priya updated you—"

They both nod, a wordless "duh, of course she did."

"Well, you know it stopped?" From the kitchen counter behind me, I pick up the envelope. "Well, long story short, it was Joe. The guy I met at therapy. Then he stopped. But then it was Tom—Tom carried it on. Because he knew how happy it made me."

"For the spark," reads Roxanne. "Holy moly."

I cover my face with my hands and to my surprise, tears fall, like a dam breaking, as both of my friends gather around the envelope, holding the papers and photos in their hands, as if they're gold bars.

"Oh, Nat," Lucy says. "It really is the most romantic thing I've ever seen in my whole entire life," says Lucy.

"Shit me," adds Roxanne, "and now I'm going to cry. *Me*."

And I feel, one by one, their arms envelop me, tightly, like we're one knitted ball.

"I really like him," I say, my mouth pressed against a mystery shoulder. "And there's a part of me that feels like shit about it."

They pull away.

"Because of—" starts Lucy, and then Roxanne says, "Russ."

"No. No, you mustn't," says Lucy, and then she strides back, standing like that same detective again who's now cracked the case and is about to announce it in front of the whole town. "And you know what I'm going to say."

"What?"

"A feather in the hand is much better than a bird in the air," she says, and she says it as if to a packed audience at the Harold Pinter Theatre.

"The—the fortune cookie." I laugh. "*Really?*"

"I knew it would come good," says Lucy earnestly. "And I reckon Tom is the feather."

Me: Four words.

Me: I am so sorry.

chapter twenty-seven

Today when I play, people crowd me. And it's like they know. They know it's the last time. And of course, never say never. But it feels like the right time. I think I'm finally ready not to be here every Thursday and Tuesday. I'm ready for something new. A new start.

The girls stayed with me in the shop for an hour, on Saturday. Roxanne went to get us some lunch, and Lucy took over at the counter for a while, every now and then, on the best way to smile at a customer, that is "equal parts friendly, equal parts boundaried."

"Tell him," she'd also said about Tom, although Roxanne said, "Errr, maybe make him wait a bit," which, I could tell, really meant "absolutely tell him, and do it with fireworks." And the truth is, I don't know what I'll do. Because Tom wanted space, and that's what I'm giving him. But I miss him. I miss him so much that sometimes, it physically hurts.

The song I'm playing today is Tom's. The final song he printed for me: "Moonlight Drive." And I play for him, and hope, by some small chance, that he's here somewhere. Grabbing coffee. Jogging for a train to his studio. Waiting for me outside Goode's, all lopsided smiles and "Yo, Foxes." But I also play for everyone else—the station, these people, these shops—and when I finish today, there is applause. I stand, and beneath the glass ceiling, I allow myself the smallest of bows. *Thank you*, I say silently, as I do. *Thank you for saving me.*

Upstairs, I find everything as normal in Goode's. Mr. Affair and Secretary Girl are there, as is Piercings Girl. No Notebook Joe. I've been so preoccupied with Tom, and with airing all my wounds, that we haven't been in touch. But I will. Soon. Because despite everything, Joe was, and is, important to me. And knowing he was there, on the other side of the wall, as I lost the first man I ever loved, is a weird comfort. When I had nobody, he was listening, he was there all along.

"Howdy." Shauna smiles as I enter the sweet warmth of Goode's, and I'm relieved. I was so worried that she, too, would want space from me. I've not known what to do, whether to text, to call, just show up here. "What're we having today?" she asks, as she has a thousand times before, and I search her face. She seems calm. She seems— thank God, happy to see me.

A new worker is behind the counter today, her name tag says *Lydia*, and Jason is helping her work the coffee machine. He's styled his hair. He fancies her, no doubt. But then he does fancy everyone with functioning veins and a beating heart.

"The usual, please, Shauna," I say with a smile, "and will you join me? Please?"

"Course," she says softly. "Of course I will, Natalie."

And I wonder when the next time I'll do this will be. I'll be back to see Shauna, definitely. But we've been doing this for almost three years. Tuesdays and Thursdays, coffee and chats and going-off cake. And I'll miss the routine. I'll miss her. But new routines await, and so do new habits. And I'm excited to see them form, all these things that haven't happened yet.

Shauna places down a brownie and a coffee. "The brownie's on me." She smiles, like everything is how it's always been, as if nothing's changed.

"No, you don't need to—"

"Yes, I do."

"Shauna," I say. "I'm so sorry."

"No, darling—"

"No, really, I am." My voice wobbles. "I should've—I should've said . . ."

"It's not your cross to bear, Natalie." Shauna sits down calmly and holds my hand, clammy, tight in hers. "And the reason you didn't is because you care. You didn't want to hurt people. You were in a hard and horrible situation . . ."

"Not as hard as the one you're in," I say. "Shauna, are you OK? You must be—God, I don't know. Don's a—a prick. Don is a massive, massive *arse* and prick and does not deserve you—"

"*Natalie.*"

Shauna throws a glance over her shoulder, the sort of glance someone does to check that they're alone. She turns back to me and slowly clasps her hands together. "We're separating. And darling, I've—" She sniffs, and I see now she's just like me—tears waiting in the wings—because they fall from her eyes with ease. "I'm hurting. I'd be lying if I said I wasn't hurting. But I have never felt freer."

"Really?"

Shauna nods.

"I'm proud of you," I say, and she smiles and says, "You're proud of *me*? Then what on earth does that make me of you?"

I move closer to her, rounding the tiny table in my chair and wrap my arms around her. She's warm and smells like cinnamon and clean washing. And we stay like that, sniveling, laughing, talking muffled, almost inaudible words into each other's shoulders until Jason comes out and says, "Er—never mind. I just wanted to know if you'd shown the new girl how to do the tampons," and Shauna laughs and says, "Oh, Jason, my love, you are full of such romance."

Shauna disappears inside to indeed show the new girl how to install the tampons in the machine in the bathroom, and I sit and watch, how I have so many times from this table, the world go by. This train station. This table, and this coffee, and these trains—all witnesses of the journey from *that Natalie* to this Natalie, to the Natalie I'm becoming. From caterpillar to chrysalis to butterfly.

Shauna reappears and takes a seat again. "All done." She smiles. "And that Lydia—a winner already if you ask me. She's already suggested a new system. For the muffins."

"Jason has a crush on her, doesn't he?"

"On Lydia? *No!* You'll never bloody guess." Shauna edges forward, like she's about to share a secret. "He asked her out. The girl with the piercings. They've had two dates and last week they *kissed.* Right here, in front of the shop."

"Oh my god."

"Yup. I swear, this coffee shop. Something in the brownies." She gives a tired, but genuine smile. "I mean, just look at you. You're— you look different. Even in the few weeks I haven't seen you, you've changed."

"I—I feel different," I admit. "And not to sound cringe and like an Instagram quote, but I do feel like I'm . . . slowly emerging or something."

"That isn't cringe, you big wally, behave."

"Ah, come on, it is a bit." I laugh. "But I think I'm going to take a little break too."

"From here?"

"From Tuesdays and Thursdays. I think I'm going to start writing again. With a class. A music therapy class. Teaching, and writing, and . . . helping people. With music."

Shauna claps her hands together. "Oh, love. Oh, *love*. I'm so happy to hear it. I'm so—oh, come here." She puts her hands out to me and takes mine, holds them across the table. "Oh, I'm so happy for you."

"I'm so nervous, Shauna. I haven't taught anyone anything in a bloody *age* but—"

"Oh, you'll be perfect." Shauna puts her hands to my shoulders, then gives them a gentle squeeze. "You deserve it. You deserve to be happy. Have you told my Thomas?"

"Um." And my heart aches a little, at the mention of him. She searches my face for something, and I feel like she already knows. About how I feel about him. "No, I haven't."

"You haven't seen him?"

"No," I say. "We—I don't know. He wasn't very pleased with me after everything, and . . . I feel like I might've blown it."

"Never."

"He was so upset with me, though. About the party and Don and—"

"Sweetheart, it's not you he's angry with, it's his dad. It's us," Shauna says shamefully, her mottled cheeks darkening to two pink clouds. "He thinks you're out of this world."

"Well, I think he is too."

Shauna smiles proudly. "Go on," she says. "This is the part where you say you've both finally realized you're bloody perfect for each other. I'm waiting."

"I—I don't think." I look at her, her head cocked to one side. "OK. Yes. I have. I have realized that. Oh my god. I've just said that out loud. To his bloody *mum*."

"Oh, *yes*." Shauna closes her eyes and brings both hands to her chest. "Please tell him," she says, eyes opening, a dreamy smile overtaking her face. "Tell him as soon as humanly possible. I'm on top of the *moon*."

God, I wish I could. I wish it were that easy, to just march up to him, right now, right this second, right here, at the top of that escalator, exactly where I saw him after the bar. So tall and handsome and kind . . .

"It's not that easy," I sigh. "He's upset I lied to him. Plus he's dating someone else. Someone called bloody Gigi, and she's obsessed with France and micropigs."

"Oh, well, if he is it isn't serious. Micropigs or not."

"No?"

"Nope. Never mentioned her to me, not even a crumb, so, park that one in the back and beyond." Shauna smiles. "But he does talk about you."

"Does he?"

"*Nonstop.* Doesn't think I've noticed of course, but . . . I notice everything." She chuckles. "Even Jason said it. Said his face drops when he comes in and you're not here."

"Right." My heart flutters, like a bird behind my ribs.

"Look, there's no pressure here. Regardless of him being my son, I'd say do what feels right. Tell him. Don't. But just make sure you're not betraying yourself, Natalie. You deserve to be happy. As I've learned—life is far too short to stay in any situation that doesn't light you up from the inside out. Don't make the mistake I did. Listen to yourself. To this." She holds a hand to her heart.

I kiss Shauna's cheek goodbye, and even Jason, who introduces me to Dolcie—Piercings Girl—and as I'm leaving, for the first time Secretary Girl stands, leaving Mr. Affair with his head in his hands at the table alone. As Secretary Girl passes me, she smiles. A "time to move on" smile. An "I deserve better" smile.

I walk through the station. I don't know when I'll be back. Not long, I'm sure, but I take it all in as if it might be my last. Because it might. My last as this version of myself.

The station is alive, as it always is. Countless people, one after the other, rushing and whisking with places to go. People in love and out of love, in joy and in pain, on their way home and running away.

I stand by the piano, skim a hand across the keys. And for old times' sake, I check the piano stool. Empty.

chapter twenty-eight

The rectangular windows of the little club are steamed up around the edges, when I arrive. The ground outside in Hackney is hard and frozen and even though it's only six p.m., the evening is so dark, the air so cold, it may as well be the middle of the night.

Inside, thick, woody heat thaws my cheeks and thighs instantly, and I see Joe sitting, hunched on a chair, a notebook in his nervous hands. I sit beside him, and it takes him a second before he looks up. At the sight of me, his face explodes into a smile. I know he didn't expect me to come. He'd sent a text last week inviting me to a poetry slam night. He'd finally written something. "You probably never want to see me again and I totally understand. I'm a dick," the text had said, "But I'm writing again, and I'm performing a poem, next Thursday evening at a poetry slam. Here's the address. I'd love you to hear it." And I knew, the second I read it, that I'd go.

"Natalie," he says, standing. "Ah, Nat, you're here."

"Just promise me there're no balls metaphors. Last time I went to a poetry slam it was all about balls. And death."

Joe laughs, two dimples punctuating his cheeks. "I promise," he says, "although I can't really promise the same for anyone else.

Nothing's off the table in this gaff." In front of me, he stands, nervously, as if he doesn't know what to do with his arms. I step forward, put my arms around him.

"Thank you for inviting me," I say, and Joe's rigid frame softens against me. "Thank *you* for coming," he says. "Seriously. Thank you."

We take a seat on two plastic chairs with metal legs. Mine wobbles, uneven on the ground, the little rubber stopper on its end missing.

"And how are you feeling?" I ask. "Nervous? Do you need me to play bodyguard? Make sure everyone keeps a healthy one-meter-personal-space distance away?"

"Er, yes, please," he says, dropping his voice to a mumble. "To both. A man chatted to me earlier at the urinal, then described his work as the Steven Spielberg of poetry so now I'm nervous on—every single level."

"Wow." I laugh. "And you'll smash it, Joe, you know you will. And even if you choke, just—pretend it's part of the art. You know, pretend cry for a bit. Everyone will be like, "Oh my god, your work is raw. People fancy troubled poets. Especially ones who cry."

Joe laughs. "God, I've missed you, Nat. I really didn't think you'd come . . ."

"I just needed some space," I say. "But after this, you are taking me to the pub, and I want you to tell me all of it. Tanner, in hospital, what bay, what bed . . ."

"Of course."

"I probably saw you."

"Yeah," Joe nods. "You probably did."

"Both of us under the same roof."

"Nothing but a wall between us." Joe smiles. "You—you look . . . so happy."

Someone on stage speaks into the mic. He's wearing—oh my god, he's wearing *actual antlers.* Joe is right. Anything *does* go in this place.

"One-two. One-two-test," the man says. "Is that—is that not too loud? It's just—I'll be croaking, sometimes cawing . . ."

Joe and I look at each other and giggle silently.

"Thank you. About the happy thing," I whisper. "And I'm glad you're writing again."

"I am," he replies. "Who knew, I just had to totally fuck up and upset my mate to unblock the creative channels."

"Should've done it sooner," I say.

Joe laughs, and looking at him now, compared to that sallow, scared person on the rainy concrete at the rehearsal rooms, it's like looking at someone who's finally let the sunshine in.

I go to the bar and buy us some drinks—me, lemonade, Joe, something a little stronger, and he nervously sips as the first poet goes onstage.

"So, erm, I'm moving back home," whispers Joe as the poet starts speaking. (It's a poem called "Macaroni Cheese" that opened with the line, "If cheese was the war . . .")

"Home? Like . . . Dorset home?"

He nods. "To Dorset. With Mum and Dad for a bit. I think I need to be with them. Face it. Not avoid it. And I'm thinking you don't ever feel ready for this shit do you? So you have to—do it anyway. So that's what I'm doing. Plus my housemate's getting married and it's insufferable."

"That's amazing, Joe."

"No, it isn't. His fiancée was crying over canapés last night. Some issue with crab seasons and Uncle Gabe's allergy? I wanted to throw myself off the balcony . . ."

"I meant Dorset."

"*Oh.*" Joe laughs, and behind us, someone hisses "shhhhh."

Joe smiles at me bashfully and nibbles his lip. "You'll have to come and visit," he whispers. "Stay a night or two. Hang out."

"Course," I say, "but just so you know, I don't stay anywhere without pansy garnishes. It's a new rule of mine."

Joe barks a laugh, and behind us, someone tuts and says, "Rude."

Two poets go on, one after the other, and one talks so beautifully about love that I'm moved to tears. After she bows and the room explodes into applause, Joe leans and nudges his arm to mine.

"You going a bit soft in your old age?"

"Sort of. I think I might be falling in love." I turn to Joe in the dim light of the club. "Am I fucked?"

Joe raises his eyebrows and laughs. "With Tom. With Tom, right?"

I stare at him. "Um—*yes*?"

"Sorry." He shrugs. "Was a bit obvious."

"And it was him. The music. Tom carried it on."

"Ah, of *course* it was." Joe puts his arm around me then. "And I'm gassed for you. Seriously, I am. And yes. You are fucked. Sorry. In love. Fucked. Same difference if you ask me."

I laugh, and as I look to the side, at his gorgeous, sweet face, I realize how glad I am to have met him, and to have been mere meters from each other, even if we didn't know, as the pair of our hearts broke, almost in unison. And now we're here. Now they're healing.

"I'm glad I found you," I say to Joe, and he nods and says, "Same. Might even go as far as to say you're better than pasta."

And then it's Joe's turn. He's called up onto the stage, and I watch him meander through the crowd, his notebook, bursting with words, in his hand. He stands under the hazy spotlight and puffing out a long breath, he taps the mic twice and says, "My name is Joe Jacobs. And this is a poem called 'The Hospital Piano.'"

chapter twenty-nine

Dear Russ,

I've never been very good at talking to the air when I visit you, so I thought I'd try this. Something I can write and slip in an envelope. Something I can leave by your tree, and hope, somehow, you're able to read or know or feel these words.

Visiting you used to be one of my favorite things to do. Filling the thermos flask you used to take to work, eating lunch from the same Tupperware boxes we'd take on long journeys. Do you remember the first car journey we took? To try to look for your drunk friend on New Year's Eve. Mike was his name? Mick? I can't remember. I just remember that as we waited in traffic, you said, "What's your favorite tree?" and I said who even has a favorite tree and you said, "Me." I'd known then, after those words, after that shy smile, I'd love you forever, and if you'd let me, for a very long time. I did. And I do. I listed the reasons once, to help you fall asleep in hospital. Do you remember that Christmas morning? There were Christmas lights and the

*nurses had put up a little tree, and I felt somehow like
you knew what was coming. The infection, the sudden
deterioration. You woke me up at three a.m. and you
told me not to be alone if you died. And I hated you for
saying it. I hated for you saying the word 'die,' and for even
thinking for a moment there would ever be a time we'd
be apart like that. And I told you off. I told you to fuck
off actually. I remember that part very clearly. Then you
held my hand, and I remember analyzing every part of
your hand, the skin, the nails, everything, because I never
wanted to forget how that felt. Having you there.
Holding on.*

*But I feel I have to let go a little now, Russ. I can't just
drop your hand, though, not right away, but I wondered if
I could loosen my grip—just a little at first. For me. If not
for anyone else. I need to slowly let you go.*

But know I will always love you.

Your Natalie

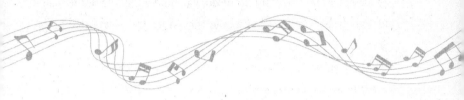

chapter thirty

Me: Three words

Me: I miss you

♪ ♪ ♪
♪ ♪ ♪

Maxwell steps inside Three Sycamore and looks up and around it, in a way that could only be described as "like an estate agent." Looking for flaws, looking for period features, and looking for things he could *just* about leave out in photos for Rightmove to hook in buyers. And it's like it's showing off today, done a deal with the weather gods, knows it's got to put its best foot forward, because despite it being shivering December temperatures outside, the sun is out, and the cottage is lit up from the inside out, sun streaming through the windows, bathing itself in golden light.

"It's nice to be back," says Maxwell, lifting a brown paper bag up in the air beside him. "And I brought some coffee. And pastries. No basil, this time. Not a crumb."

"Yeah, I'm sorry about that, Max—"

"Nah, you're all right," he says with a stiff shrug. "I was rattled that day. Probably wasn't the greatest company in the world."

"Were you?" I shut the front door behind us. It lets out its usual sad little wail. (Couldn't quite hold that in for the nice estate agent, could you, little door?)

Maxwell nods, rocks back on those shiny curly shoes' heels. "A little. I'd just been dumped, so . . ."

"Oh, shit."

And there I was thinking it was all about me. What is it Jodie always says? Nobody's really watching. You think they are, but they're too busy watching themselves. "Well, it's her loss," I say, and Maxwell smiles.

"Well, I've met someone else now. We've been together three months."

"That's great, Max. Congratulations."

"Yeah," he says awkwardly, being sure to keep that emotion locked firmly inside. "She works next door to me. She's a nail technician. Does pedicures and stuff. Anyway. Shall we go through?" And I can't help but smile to myself. Pedicures and flowers. Just what the doctor ordered for Maxwell Sowerby.

Maxwell follows me through to the kitchen, and I get some plates down from the cupboard.

He takes a seat at the breakfast bar, runs a hand along the tiles on the surface. "Did you do this?"

"The tiles?"

He nods, impressed, checking the pads of his fingers, as if he might find pen marks, from where I've simply colored them in with felt tip.

"Well, a friend of mine did. Tom. It's paint. I wasn't sure I believed it would do the job, but—" I hold out my hands. "He did good, right?"

"Definitely." Maxwell grins, lifting two cups of takeaway coffee from the brown paper bag. "He did. It's completely brightened the room. Transformed it."

And I feel a tug in my chest then. It's been a week since I saw Shauna and said goodbye, and I'd hoped, in some way, that she might mention me, prompt him to call me. But there's been nothing. And I miss him. I miss him terribly. But—space. He wanted space. And I know what it's like to need that, want that, as if it's medicinal.

"I've treated the damp too," I say. "And tried my best to clear as much as possible."

Maxwell nods, munches into a chocolate chip croissant. I slide a plate across to him, catch the last couple of feathery crumbs. "Well, look, a cottage like this, Nat—totally sought-after, regardless, really, of how it is inside. I mean, of course, the more neutral the better, but— with access to the trains . . ." He stops then, chews and swallows. "Did you want to sell? Sorry, Nat, I just assumed—"

"I do," I say. "I didn't think that I did, but I do."

Maxwell nods, places the croissant down on the brown paper bag, crumbs skidding across the counter. "Why did you think you didn't want to?"

I slide out a stool and sit down opposite him, and it means a lot, I realize now, as much as it shouldn't, having Maxwell's approval. "Russ," I say. "I felt guilty, selling it. I mean, you know how much he loved this place, Max. He loved this house so much. And he had so many plans for it. We both did. So I stayed. For a lot longer than I probably should have."

Maxwell scratches his head, as if considering whether to do or say something. Then he just comes out with it. "Natalie. Russ . . . he loved you. More than any house. And I was here when you moved in. I know how excited he was. He loved it. And you loved this house because . . . well, because he loved it. But that's what this is, you know. It's just a house. It's just bricks. And tiles."

"Tile *paint*," I add, and he laughs.

"Exactly. These are ten a penny, really. As much as they're lovely, houses are just—houses. But your life—not so much. So, I say live in the way that you want to. That's all he would have wanted." And hearing this from Maxwell, who not only apologizes for simply having an emotion that isn't hunger or pure indifference, but who knew Russ almost as well as I did, feels momentous.

"Thank you, Max," I say. "I really needed to hear that."

Maxwell walks around the cottage, and I don't follow him, just listen to his footsteps creaking on the floor above. I don't know if he wants to, but in case he does, I thought I'd let him say goodbye alone. He emerges at the bottom of the stairs after a good ten minutes.

"His cricket hoodie." He smiles weakly. "I'd forgotten it until I saw it. Hanging on the door."

"Do you want it? Of course if you don't want it, that's fine. I get it can be a bit weird. Dead man's clothes—"

"No," says Maxwell, "no, I'd love it. If you don't want it that is."

"Hate cricket." I smile. "But I know you and Russ loved it. Bored me to tears all those matches you'd watch . . ."

Maxwell tells me what the house is worth, he tells me he can put it on the market for me through his agency, and to "shoot him an email," and with the cricket hoodie over his arm, he leaves, before taking one final photo of the outside with a small smile.

chapter thirty-one

I want you to remember, there are no rules here. You can start with whatever comes naturally. The words and lyrics, the melody—and by melody, I mean just a little tune, plucked out of nowhere, something catchy, something simple. Something you can even hum. Or you can . . . take the guitar, play a few notes on the keyboard, see if anything jumps out. But there are no rules. We want you to feel comfortable enough to just feel and express and play and create, without judgment, and without resistance. Just let whatever wants to come out of you, come out of you. You'll be surprised what's there when you just let go. When you learn to trust yourself."

"Thank you, Natalie," says Devaj. "And a massive thank-you to everyone who's been brave enough to walk through that red door. It's one of the bravest things you'll ever do. And it might just help change your life . . ."

♪ ♪ ♪
♪ ♪ ♪

Edie is waiting in the lobby after the first songwriting workshop ends. And I'm buzzing—*beaming*. My skin, flushed, my heart, bouncing. It had gone so well, and *fifty* people had shown up despite Devaj worrying nobody would, and songs and melodies and lyrics that didn't exist moments before, sprung into life up there, in the studio, before our eyes and ears, like brand-new Spring buds. I feel like the opposite of that Natalie who stood here, opposite Edie, all those months ago, in the summer. Today, I feel like a different person. Steady. Strong. Ready.

"Hi, Nat," she says, and her eyes are shining before I've even got to the bottom step. She's wearing a huge faux-fur coat, her long hair flowing from the edges of a bright purple beanie hat. And I know she's been waiting for me.

"Hi, Edie," I say.

"I'm sorry for just standing here like this. But I could hear you," she says feebly as if she's already prepared herself to be shot down. "I was on my way out, but I heard you. I heard you playing. I heard your voice. And—well, forgive me, but it's been such a long time that I just had to stand and listen."

I feel my own eyes shimmer with tears. "I just wrote a song," I say.

"Oh." Edie smiles, her hands moving up to her chest one on top of the other. Her fingers, still covered, as they always were, in rings. "Oh, Nat, that's amazing."

"My first one. Since . . ."

Edie stares at me across the carpeted lobby, silence, except for a rumble of tires out in the car park. "I'm so sorry," she says breathlessly. "Gosh, Natalie, I am so, so, so sorry."

"I know," I say, and my voice cracks then, at the same time hers does.

"And I know you might never forgive me, and I understand that. I really do." Edie swipes at her eyes, the ends of her gloves staining with tears. "But—please. Please let me talk to you. Just—ten minutes of your time. *Five.* I'll—I'll take anything."

And without saying a word, I wrap my arms around Edie, as in the distance someone starts to play piano, and a woman starts to sing.

♪   ♪   ♪
♪   ♪   ♪

Tom: Hi Natalie. My exhibition is on Friday. Here's the invite. Show it on the door. I really hope to see you there. x

chapter thirty-two

Tom's exhibition is being held in a gallery in Shoreditch, in a place called Zetland House, and I'm late. Super late actually. And not because I wanted to be—to make a sweeping, statement entrance. It's because I could *not* get my ancient laptop to work, to transfer over Tom's gift to a USB stick. I'd called Nick in the end, who came over on his moped and did it in approximately two seconds.

"Not being able to do this, Auntie Nat," he'd said, "has proper Boomer vibes. But you look nice. Saved yourself there."

And I've seen Tom countless times in the last year, but tonight feels different. Because it's the first time I'm going to see Tom, while knowing, without any doubt, how I feel about him. That I'm—well, about to be fucked, the minute I stop falling and hit the floor apparently. (According to Joe.)

In a small white-lit booth, a security guard sits. He has gelled, ginger spikes and is wearing a pair of wire-rimmed glasses. "Good evening," he says cheerily. "How can I help?"

"Oh. Tom Madden's exhibition."

"Do you have the invite?"

"Oh. Yes. On my phone—hang on."

I riffle through my handbag—a black hole, that's what my Russ used to call my handbag. Things go in, they never come out. My keys and makeup bag hit the floor. Well. *Something* always comes out, just not the thing you want.

"Sorry," I say. "Sorry, I just—I can't find my phone—oh! Oh, I've got it. Hang on."

The security guard nods patiently as I scoop up the fallen items.

"I'm a bit nervous," I tell him. "Sweating actually. I'm about to tell a guy I really like him."

"I see," says the security guard, and he eyes my screen, just once, as I shove it in his face. "Well, good to know," he adds with a laugh. "And I suppose—good luck?"

The walls are bare brick here, and the windows like those from an old factory. It's trendy. *Painfully* trendy, as Joe would probably say, and I can hear the hubbub of the exhibition the closer I get. Voices, and glasses chinking, muffled laughter. When I get to the top of the stairs, I'm shocked at how many people are here. There are tons of them, two hundred perhaps, and I feel so happy for him. Already, I could burst with pride, all over the wine and canapés. I just wish I could see a single photo—there are so many people, I can barely see the edge of one. But I see Shauna almost instantly in the crowds. She looks amazing. She's wearing a chiffon blue dress and earrings that are like stained-glass kites, and she is *beaming*. Like if you were to pierce her with a pin, the room would be flooded with light.

"Oh, my doll," she says when she sees me, her arms outstretched. "What a sight you are. Here, come here. Have some wine. Have some posh dough balls. These ones—they're filled with something red but it's *delicious*."

Shauna hugs me, then leaves an arm around me, pulls me into the little crowd she's in.

"These are my boys," she says, and I'm faced with the same four huge strapping lads I saw on the stage, at the anniversary party. They all look like Tom and Shauna mashed together. Handsome, tall, two with a beard, two without. (And of course, there's a smattering of Don to be seen in them too, but we don't talk about him. Except when discussing the "dirty shites" of the globe.)

"So." I grin. "The brotherhood, eh?"

Tom's brothers laugh, a big deep chorus of manly laughter, and Shauna introduces them to me, one by one. Laurie, Tom's (unidentical) twin, keeps looking at me, and it's like he knows. He knows what gift I've got in my handbag. He knows I like his brother. Does twin-tuition still count if it's not actually the twin, but the person who would very much like to bury her face into the sexy neck of the twin?

We stand and chat for a bit, and all the while I'm subtly looking for Tom, who must be lost at sea in this tsunami of people. How must he feel, knowing everyone is here especially for him? Then the crowd parts, and I see a photo—a breathtaking, beautiful, black-and-white portrait of a little girl, smiling.

"Shauna, I'm going to look at the photos," I say. "If you see Tom, tell him I'm here. Somewhere."

Shauna smiles warmly. "You go. But make sure you see every single one. You must."

I squash my way through the crowd and join an unofficial queue of people who stand staring, enrapt, at a photo on the wall. They're numbered, and this is number one.

"Exceptional," says someone behind me, and I want to turn around, say Tom did these. Tom Madden. Yep. Isn't he clever? Isn't he a genius? The Jesus Christ of photography, don't you know?

And as the crowd moves on, it's just me and the first photograph. It's a black-and-white shot of an old man's face, deep-lined, smiling, tears at the edges of his eyes. I feel like I could cry looking at it. He's beautiful. He looks so beautiful and happy and moved. And so am I:

moved. I walk slowly along, two, three, and they are all so beautiful. Their faces, all frozen in time. Smiling, crying, grinning, angling their phones, taking pictures. There's one of two people dancing, holding on for dear life, their heads tipped right back in frozen laughter. I'm smiling. From ear to ear, I'm smiling. I feel everything looking at these photos. Like the people in these stunning portraits show everything on their faces. Joy, pain, awe . . . Tom did this. *Tom did this.*

Then I see him. Tom. My Tom. My Thomas Button.

And God, he looks beautiful. So beautiful that if this were a cartoon, my jaw would be on the floor and I'd be trying to gather it up like a busted-open handbag before everyone noticed.

I'm so relieved when he sees me, and his gorgeous face smiles, slowly. I've missed him. I've hated thinking he was disappointed in me, angry with me. But here he is. Smiling at me. I had no idea what to expect tonight, whether it would be all friendly, civil hiya, Natalie's or normal, cocky Tom, with his "Yo, Foxes, this is Gigi, yeah, we're shagging 'round the clock, thought we may as well." But the way he smiles at me—it's like he's as relieved as I feel. Like he has waited all night just to see me, like I have him.

Tom doesn't say hello. Just addresses me, "Foxes," as he closes the gap in the room between us.

"Thomas," I say, and that gorgeous smell of his practically knocks me off my feet.

Tom takes my arm gently. "Shall we—it's a bit busy."

"Busy?" I say, as we meander through the crowds to a free space, right by the entrance, in front of two teal-blue double doors. "This isn't just busy, Tom, this is—*wild.* All these people are here for you. This place is practically bursting at the seams with them. And all for you."

"I know. What's wrong with them?" He laughs. "They need to get a life."

I laugh, and for a second, we just look at each other. Then

wordlessly, I wrap my arms around him. Tom says nothing, but slides his warm, muscular arms around my waist and holds me to him. A silent understanding between us both. A "sorry" from me. An "I forgive you" from Tom. And being so close to him, his warm, strong body, pressed into mine, turns my legs to jelly. I meant what I said to Joe. I'm falling. I am definitely, without doubt, falling. And fast.

"Do you like them?" he asks softly in my ear, and the hairs on the back of my neck prick up.

"The photos?" I look up at him. "Tom, they're—God, I'm going to cry."

Tom smiles slowly. "Don't do that," he says.

"Seriously. They're—they're incredible. Beyond. I don't even have the words. But . . . I felt everything looking at them. Literally, everything. The one of the old man. I've never seen something so—so beautiful."

Tom releases me slowly, his dark eyes darkening. "I think I have," he says softly and butterflies break free in my stomach.

"And I'm sorry," I say. "I'm so sorry."

Tom shakes his head. "I'm sorry too," he says. "I shouldn't have said the things I said, but—"

"I understand," I say. "And I should have told you, but I was scared and . . . it was—"

"Love and crocodiles. I get it." Tom smiles down at me gently. "God, have I mentioned how beautiful you look?"

I shake my head. "Don't think so." I grin. "But I'm listening . . ."

Tom laughs and says, "Well, you do. Like—*fuck*. Off the scale."

Goose bumps tingle across my skin. "And so do you," I say. "Total M&S billboard levels."

"Ah, well, you know me. Colin the Caterpillar," he says, and I burst out laughing.

"Tom? Tom, sorry, could I just—" A woman in a beautiful tuxedo dress takes his arm. She's holding an iPad, its screen lit with what looks like a spreadsheet. "Sorry. There's someone here from a journal? Said you're expecting them?"

"Oh, erm—Nat, do you want to—"

"No, no, go! Go on. I've not finished looking at the photos, or catching up with Shauna yet, so . . ."

He smiles then, a graze of those lovely white teeth on his bottom lip. "I'll come steal you away soon," he says.

I move through the crowd, toward the photos I haven't seen, and I feel on fire. Does he feel it too? That was—that was heavy, right? That intangible, thick, loaded atmosphere between us. It's never been like that before. Maybe he knows. Maybe he already knows how I feel. A woman cuts in front of me with a giant, gray-wrapped gift. She rests it upon a table in the corner, against the exposed brick wall, nestles it in among a sea of other gifts.

My gift. I can't wait to give him my gift. I reach into my bag and grab the sealed congratulations card (one with an avocado on the front, of course) in my hand, and—oh shit. No way. No, no, no. It's not there. I had it. I had it. *Argh.* Black hole. It'll be this bloody black hole bag.

I skid over to the gift table, rest my handbag on top and sift through it desperately, like I'm Mary Poppins searching for a table lamp.

No. No, it's not here.

I bet I dropped it. I bet I bloody dropped it and the security guard has found it, thrown it away, chucked it in a lost property bucket, pulled the shutters down for the night. I put the card on the table full of gift bags and cards and bottles of champagne, and I slink out in the freezing-cold December night.

♪ ♪ ♪
♪ ♪ ♪

"It's a USB stick," I say to the security guard. "It's red and it's got a little rounded edge, a little silver band around it."

"I'm afraid I've not seen it."

"But it's not in my bag and I know I had it."

"Yeah, it's strange," says the security guard. He's using a torch on his phone to look on the concrete ground. "But it definitely isn't here. What about the street?"

"Oh! The street! The *street,* yes. Good thinking!"

The security guard unlocks the gate and watches me, almost sadly, as I crouch, phone torch to the ground, like he's watching animals scavenge in a bin.

"The thing is, you've only got to get a road sweeper—" starts the security guard.

"No, no," I say. "I mean, what are the odds, that the second I arrive, in the tiny little slot of time that I've been up there, at the exhibition, that a road sweeper would have come along and swept this *exact—*"

"*Natalie?*"

I turn on the pavement, still crouched, my shoes crunching on the concrete. It's Tom, sprinting across the courtyard to the street outside, where I'm squatting on the floor with a phone, a security guard watching me the way someone watches, waiting for their dog to take a shit. "Hi." I smile. "Er, I'm just—I'm just out here."

"I can see that. You're not going already?" Tom gives a nod to the security guy as he joins us. "I am *not* letting you walk out of here after two bloody seconds."

I look at the security guard and widen my eyes, just a little. He gets it. "Ah," he says. And there is so much in that sound. There's "Good luck, love," there's "So this is the bloke you like, is it, who has you scrabbling about on an East London pavement? I see. I see indeed." And he walks off, leaving the gate ajar, just a crack.

"I'm not going anywhere," I say, standing up.

"Then what are you doing out here? On the street?" He laughs. "I didn't get to steal you away yet." Music emanates from a distant bar across the road, and a taxi pulls up. Someone in jogging gear gets out of it.

"You can steal me away now," I say, "or any time"—and saying that feels a little daring. That little flirtation. But I'm sure I see it in his eyes too. That things have changed between us—shifted. From friends to . . . something else. And even if I'm wrong, if it's just banter with Tom, just him being Tom, Tom with the cheek, Tom with the charm, I don't care. Because I'm falling in love with him. And even if that ends tonight, when he knows everything, as much as it'll hurt, it's enough. To feel this. For my heart to be beating this beat again after so long of it being broken.

"They're all for you," he says, his words clouding in the air.

I freeze on the pavement. "What?"

"The photos. Every single one of those photos is for you. Every photo is someone watching you play. At the station." Breath leaves my body, in one gust. A reverse gasp. My hands fly to my chest, as if to keep my heart in place.

"I wanted to walk with you, show you each one. Because I wanted you to see the effect your music has on people—that *you* have on people."

A rush of memories. Of all the times he was at the station, of all the times he said he was there for "work," he was working on his exhibition. For me. *For me.*

"Tom, I . . . I don't know what to say." Tears, as usual lately, already fall from my eyes, and Tom steps forward, stands in front of me, so close I can feel his warmth.

"Say nothing," he whispers. "Just come back inside and see them again, now you know that." Tom reaches into his jacket then, brings the card up between us. "And what's this?"

He lifts his free hand to my face and skims away tears on my cheeks with his thumb.

"You dropped it and left. Like a Deliveroo driver."

I laugh—laughing and crying, all at once, on the pavement in front of the man I'm falling in love with. The man who never gave up on me, not once, not even when I pushed him away. "It's a card," I say. "And it was also meant to be a USB, of a song I wrote. Last week. About you."

Tom looks stunned for a moment, then a gorgeous smile spreads across his cheeks, reaches his eyes, those lovely crinkles by them, those lovely straight teeth Lucy sold to me like a saleswoman almost a year ago in that sticky bar. "About me?"

"Yes. But—I dropped it or something, because I definitely had it, and I wanted you to hear it, because . . . I can say things better with music. But I can't find it. And I had it. Right here."

Tom slowly loops his arms around my waist.

"A song. About me," he repeats. "Wow, it's—shit, it's not a diss track, is it?"

I laugh, shake my head. "No. It's a love song. Because—it's you Tom. It's totally you."

"Natalie—"

"You don't have to say anything," I rush out. "There's no pressure, no expectation or anything at all. You don't have to say anything back to me, because I know I've been giving really mad signals, saying that I'm mossy at the bottom of the sea, and making you talk to me to fend off my friends, and plus, I know how you feel about love and . . . God, I even told you I don't fancy you, over and over and—"

"*Natalie*," Tom says, gazing into my eyes. "It's you, for me too. Of course it's you."

I close my eyes, tears filming them. "I knew it was you under the moon," I tell him. "I knew it on the steps."

"And I knew in the bar—after that margarita you didn't let me pay for." He laughs to himself, moonlight reflecting in his eyes. "And I knew again and again . . . and again, after that."

A cheer sounds from a nearby pub, and music kicks in. "Last Christmas" by Wham!

"And to be honest—" Tom smiles. "I think pretty much *everyone* knows it's you. That exhibition. I might as well be on top of a building dressed like bloody Spider-Man with a banner on a bedsheet. That exhibition might as well be my declaration. To the whole bloody world."

Tom leans then, and gently brushes hair from my face. Then he pushes his gorgeous, warm lips to mine.

I close my eyes, and right there, under that same moon, under the December sky, I feel everything, I feel life, rushing back into my veins.

And just like the night we met, tonight, three words: I choose Tom.

chapter thirty-three

EIGHTEEN MONTHS LATER

Edie knocks on the dressing room door. She peeps her head around it. "How are you holding up, pal?"

"*Edie.* Thank God you're here. And put it this way," I say. "I finally understand all your mad dashes to the toilet before our gigs."

Edie laughs and comes into the room. She smells like floral perfume and red wine, and she squeezes her arms around me. "Relax, Nat," she says. "It's going to be amazing. Better than amazing."

It's the first night—a trial night, Devaj and I are calling it—of the first-ever NMT songwriting showcase. Twenty of our students have written songs, recorded them, practiced them, and tonight they're going to perform them. Their heartbreak and healing in notes and chords and quavers. Their family, their friends, the local papers, members of the public—their truths, for everyone to see.

"They're saying fifteen minutes to curtains," says Edie. "Devaj wanted me to tell you. But I wanted to say good luck, and how proud I am of you." Edie kisses my cheek. "And that if you're ever in doubt, just think of ninety-eight-year-old Granny Natalie. She's not nervous. She doesn't care. She'll just be sitting there with her pease pudding really glad that you did."

♫ ♫ ♫
♫ ♫ ♫

A few minutes before curtains go up, I go and find my seat. And Tom. I can't see him, but I see his empty seat beside mine, next to Mum and Dad, who have come prepared with what appears to be a miniature portable meze. Dad is halfway through a mini roll, and Mum is trying to find the flap on a box of miniature Cornish pasties.

"Where's Tom?" I ask.

"Gone to get you a drink. And how are you, Natty, darling?" says Mum, reaching over, giving my arm a kind rub. "How are you feeling? Good? Bad? Runny tummy?"

"Fine, Mum. Shh. Can you not with the—you know. Not here."

Nick chuckles beside Dad. "Runny tummy," he repeats. "This family are seriously obsessed with bowels. It's *mental.*"

"Oi, you," says Mum. "But I suppose you're not wrong really, Nick. Your grandad's even got a chart, haven't you, Colin? He'll have to show you it one day. It's in a scroll and everything."

Dad nods sagely. "Oh, yes," he says. "A scroll."

Behind me, a hand lands on my shoulder. "My dear heart." And I'd recognize that voice anywhere in a crowd of a thousand others. The voice that comforted me every single week. Soothed me, over coffee and defect cake. I turn to see her lovely smiling, pink face.

"Shauna," I say as she squashes two kisses on my cheek. "Thank you so much for coming."

"Oh, we're ever so excited. Aren't we?" Shauna has arrived with her dancing partner tonight. Kenny. Shy, chuckling, gold-chain-wearing Kenny. Someone she swears is just that, a dance partner, but he seems to us, and everyone else, totally infatuated by her. Tom keeps secretly referring to him as "Step-papa," which makes us both laugh every single time he says it.

People file in, every row filling up. Strangers. Students. And the people I love most in the world.

Jodie and Carl making their way down the aisle to us with drinks, Priya, Lucy, and Roxanne in row six, all losing themselves laughing at something on Priya's phone. And up in the circle—there's Joe. I wonder how he found the busy lobby, the proximity of the queueing. *Lips to necks.* He sits next to Hollie, his arm slung around her, as she talks as she did all that time ago at the gig. Excitedly and quickly and with no spaces in between the words. Joe moved back to London in the summer, after a year at home with his parents by the beach. He and Hollie have been together ever since. There's just one person missing, and I think it'll always feel they are, in some way—Russ. But over the last eighteen months, I've been able to gradually let him go. Small steps, that have slowly led to bigger and bigger ones. The biggest one recently, being Tom and me moving in together, and after viewing what felt like a billion tiny flats, we settled on something even smaller, but perfect for us. A narrow boat. I can't quite believe it's ours, this cozy, blue and beige home on the canal, right in the heart of London. The Heron, Tom wants to name it, whereas I want to call it The Fox and the Button. We're currently running a poll, between our friends and family. (I'm winning by two points so far.)

A warm hand slides around my waist now.

"Hey, baby." Tom smiles into my ear—and he still makes my knees go to jelly. Every. Single. Time.

"*Hi.*" I turn, plant a slow kiss on his lips.

"Got you a drink," he says, handing me a flimsy plastic cup. "How are you doing?"

"Shitting it," I whisper as we take our seats. "Two words for you there, Thomas. Shitting. And *it.*"

Tom smiles. "It's going to be great," he says. "I swear it. I promise it."

"Do you?" And as I reach over, find his hand, hook my finger around his pinkie, he takes my whole hand in his.

"Three words," he says, bringing my hand to his lips, kissing my knuckles. "I love you."

"And I love you," I whisper.

The lights go down. The curtains go up.

The show begins.

THE END

acknowledgments

A nd here we are again: My favorite, favorite part! Thanking all the people who have made this possible, and this time, for my fourth book. *My fourth. OMG.* Honestly. There are some things in life that have you wishing you could step into a time machine, travel backward, to find your past self, age eight, age fifteen, age twenty-one, and tell them something. This is one of them. Past Lia would be in tears of happiness and absolute disbelief at one book, let alone *four.* (But then fifteen-year-old Lia might also be wondering if anything ever came of that 100,000 word fan fic she wrote and worked very hard on, on her mum's old PC in the early 00s.) And as much as it's me, sitting here, most days, tapping away on the keyboard, banging my head against a brick wall trying to fill in plot holes and whys and what ifs, wrestling my twin five-year-olds off my lap who "really just want to tap a few buttons to see what happens," it really does "take a village" to get a book from the spark of an idea, to something you can hold in your hand.

Firstly, I owe so much to my incredible agent Juliet Mushens at Mushens Entertainment. Juliet, you are a wonder. The woman-in-white to my stuck-in-a-fire koala. Thank you for your championing, your time, your passion, your patience, and your honesty. I'm so lucky to have you.

Thank you to the AMAZING Mushens Entertainment dream team, and coagents, and to the totally and utterly brilliant Jenny Bent at The Bent Agency, New York.

To my US editor, the amazing Emily Bestler at Emily Bestler Books. Thank you so much for your cheerleading, your vision, and your total belief in me and the books I write. (And also, for your editing notes which must be my favorite things about edits, haha.) To lovely Lara Jones, thank you for your passion and hard work. It is an absolute *dream come true* to work with you both, as well, of course, as the whole incredible team at Atria/Simon & Schuster.

To my UK editor, Charlotte Mursell at Orion Books, thank you so much for your hard work and passion, and for always "getting" what I'm trying to do. Thank you to Alex Layt and Lucy Cameron, and the whole hardworking team at Orion.

Thank you to the brilliant musical minds that let me pick their brains before writing this. Thank you to my hilarious and talented god-sibling Lewis Brown for answering my musical theater questions and for putting me in touch with Michaela Betts. Michaela, thank you so much for sharing your time, your story, and your talent. Thank you to Lucy Spraggan for being so warm and honest, and answering my musical questions. To Adam Hunter and Sam Hunter of the band Hyyts, thank you for giving me your time and for being so open about your music and your inspiration.

To Ben Shevlin, thank you so much for sharing your inspirational story with me.

Thank you to Professor Alex Easton for sharing your time and expertise.

To the many talented writer-friends I am fortunate enough to know. You are the best faraway work colleagues I could ever ask for.

Thank you to Gillian McAllister, Lindsey Kelk, Lynsey James, Laura Pearson, Stephie Chapman, Rebecca Williams, Lia Middleton, Zoë Folbigg, Nikki Smith, Holly Seddon, Hina Malik, Anstey Harris, Drew Davies, and so, so many more of you who make this solitary job feel less so and more like a community.

To Amanda, thank you for helping me press send, all those years ago, and for helping me get closer to the center of the onion.

To my beautiful friends who accept and love me for the old-before-my-time, Friday-nights-in-my-pajamas hermit that I am. You know who you are. It's so nice to finally have people I can be my whole, true self with. Thank you.

Mum and Steve, Dad and Sue, Bubs, Vicky, Alex, little Lottie and Max, Nan, Grandad, Alan, Marl and Libby, and Patricia. The only reason I can write funny, loving families is because I have one of my own.

To my beautiful babies, and to my Ben: thank you for loving me. As long as I have the bubble of us five (plus, the cat, of course), I have everything I need. I love you. (And to my Tyler, thank you for helping me fix my plot holes. I know I'll be doing the same for your own books one day. Mark my words.)

And to you, the readers. To everyone who has read my books, reviewed, reached out to me, spread the word, made beautiful posts. Thank you. You are so important. Without you, I wouldn't be able to do this.